watermind

watermind

M. M. BUCKNER

TOR®

A TOM DOHERTY ASSOCIATES BOOK

NEW YORK

WATERMIND

Copyright © 2008 by M. M. Buckner

A Tor Book
Published by Tom Doherty Associates, LLC
175 Fifth Avenue
New York, NY 10010

www.tor-forge.com

Tor® is a registered trademark of Tom Doherty Associates, LLC.

Library of Congress Cataloging-in-Publication Data

Buckner, M. M.
    Watermind / by M. M. Buckner.—1st ed.
        p.   cm.
    "A Tom Doherty Associates book."
    ISBN-13: 978-0-7653-2024-7
    ISBN-10: 0-7653-2024-X
    I. Title.
    PS3602.U29W38   2008
    813'.6—dc22

                                                        2008034262

First Edition: November 2008

Printed in the United States of America

0   9   8   7   6   5   4   3   2   1

For Jack, always

and

For Bonnie and Larry

Acknowledgments

In researching the unusual events described in this book, I have drawn on numerous books, articles, websites, and eyewitness accounts. However, most names in this story, some dates, and a few locations have been changed to protect individual privacy.

Loving thanks go to my spouse and soul mate, Jack Lyle, for constantly believing in me. I also owe tremendous gratitude to many friends and colleagues whose patient advice and kind support made this book possible. In alpha order, some of these many friends include: Mary Helen Clarke, Lionel Currier, Joe DeGross, Mary Bess Dunn, Susan Eady, Steve Edwards, Joel Hinman, Skip Jacobs, Rob Karwedsky, Jan Keeling, Cindy Kershner, Thomas Longo, Bonnie Parker, Nathan Parker, Wil Parker, Martha Rider, Robert J. Sawyer, Bobbie Scull, Jason Sizemore, Carole Stice, and Ava Weiner.

Earnest thanks go to my editor, David G. Hartwell, for his keen insights and guidance. And deepest appreciation goes to my agent, Richard Curtis, whose wisdom and unflagging confidence in this project have kept me buoyant through crashing waves.

He maketh the deep to boil like a pot;
he maketh the sea like a seething mixture.

Job 41:31

Prologue

As the twenty-first century dawned over western Canada, three grad students saw their weather experiment ruined when their expensive "mote" computers washed away in a storm. The students were devastated. Their elegant motes! Each tiny device represented an epiphany of microengineering—with waterproof sensors, memory, processors, and radio transceiver—a complete weather station no larger than a diamond chip.

Linked in a wireless network and powered by a mere fractional watt of sunlight, the 144 miniscule units could have lasted a hundred years, parsing climate data in Alberta's old-growth forest. Instead, the costly pinheads washed out of the trees, sluiced over the mossy ground, dribbled into the rain-swollen Milk River, and dashed away South.

For miles, they swam in sync through lambent Canadian waters, then whooshed over the US border in a tight little pack. After surging into the jade-green Missouri, they recirculated for nine weeks at the confluence of the Yellowstone, accosted by fertilizer, engine oil, and genetically modified wheat germ. Eventually, 139 washed free and siphoned through the intake of the Garrison Hydroelectric Plant, where they blasted down a power tunnel, whirled manically through a turbine, then drooled out to the tailwaters below. Their circuits crackled with new information.

For a month, they quizzed a crate of tractor diagnostic chips dumped in Lake Oahe. Near Sioux City, they passed a landfill spewing rotted fragments of eggshells, coffee grounds, old desktop computers, and human estrogen. One full week, they rumbled with a broken Game Boy. From there, the Missouri cut straight and deep through the heartland, till they plunged into the rust-red Mississippi, the fifth largest river in the world.

The Father of Waters bedazzled them. Within its fluent grip streamed nearly 400,000 tons of refuse from half the continental US and part of Canada. The motes waltzed along with pacemakers, depth-finders, baby monitors, and electronic car keys. They relayed signals from lost hearing aids and sunken memory cards. GPS channel buoys lent them guidance. As they snapped up data, their shared memory burgeoned.

South of St. Louis, three motes got trapped in a plastic grocery bag, but the survivors whisked onward, quizzing sputum, jism, and Pentium chips. Where the Ohio River boiled in, they conferred with a roaming cell phone, tossed by its desolate owner from a bridge in Ithaca, New York. The Arkansas brought them methamphetamine and strontium-90.

Yet despite their speed and curiosity, their willingness to seek out strange new worlds, only one mote made it all the way to the Gulf of Mexico— where, cut off from its network, it quickly overloaded and fried. As for the remaining 117 pinheads, the river marooned them at Baton Rouge.

Almost one year from the day their journey began in Canada, less than two hundred river miles from the sea, the motes landed in a foul riverside marsh of petrochemicals, burned-out cars, trashed appliances, and mud. Within this addled broth, frogs grew humps and appendages, bacteria colonized battery cells, and active chips migrated from their motherboards to populate clouds of algae. The water stirred with signals and ring tones. And the motes formed new bonds.

The place was called Devil's Swamp.

1 Emergence

Slosh

Wednesday, March 9
10:55 AM

"Ooh. Sexy rhythm." CJ Reilly stood knee-deep in orange mud, gyrating her slender hips to the music pulsing through her iPod. "You wrote this song?"

"*Eh oui.*" Max Pottevents slapped a mosquito and shifted his shovel to his other hand.

"Tell me everything about zydeco," she said, twirling and swinging her bucket.

Around them, the broiling marsh stank of dead fish, and black rainbows marbled the oil-slick pools. Chemical waste sizzled among the reeds. Flush against the river, Devil's Swamp foamed like a wet sponge.

Max squinted through his goggles at a distant field where their coworkers were cleaning up a spill of hazardous toluene. "Zydeco? It come from *la musique Creole.* Little bit French, Spanish, African. Throw in some hip-hop, reggae. Pinch of blues. Zydeco mix up like gumbo."

As they pushed deeper into the swamp, the ground heaved and sucked beneath their feet, and the insides of their coveralls dripped with sweat. Both of them wore heavy hip boots, goggles, and gloves, and both—for separate reasons—were finding the conversation difficult.

CJ turned up her iPod. "I hear accordions, right? What else?"

"Eh la. Accordión." Max suspected his pretty coworker was patronizing him. "Guitar, bass, drum. I play *frottior.* That the corrugated rubboard. Make the sweet sound."

CJ liked his accent, almost French but not quite. He wore a red bandana tied over his curly black hair like a pirate. He called it a *paryaka*.

"Ooh look." She stooped to touch a water moccasin.

"Stop." Max gripped her arm.

"Scared of a little snake? You taught me how to pick them up."

"Not that one. Back away slow."

She kicked the deadly snake with her boot, then danced off through the cattails, laughing. Max frowned and followed.

Humps of debris had washed in from the river, and CJ noticed a rusting white box wedged against a cypress stump. "God, it's an old Apple computer." She kicked at the gutted computer and the stump, then fished in her pocket for her crumpled marijuana spliff. "We can sit here."

Again, Max sighted the distant crew. She knew what he was going to say.

"Not far enough, *lamie*. They can see us."

"You're paranoid. They don't care what we do." She lit up and inhaled.

"I rather we smoke after the end of the day," Max said for the second time that morning.

When she lifted her goggles to wipe sweat, he saw the damp rings denting her milky cheeks, and he bit his lip. She looked so fragile. Her eyes mingled all the colors a pair of eyes could be—gray green blue brown black. And like her, they changed with the passing clouds.

CJ stubbed out the spliff. She felt grumpy and restless—premenstrual. This time of month made her want to kick her own shadow. "Your music is good. You should do something with it."

Max lowered his head. "Sa just a home recording. For studio time, we need the *largan*—money." He knew she had no experience with music, but the kindness in her voice warmed him. For Max, CJ's presence in this *puant* swamp was like a snowdrop in spring—something that couldn't last. They'd met on this job two months ago. They'd been lovers for six weeks.

As he crashed a path for her through soggy, chest-high brambles, she asked about his lyrics, his melody, his syncopated beat. The girl had a gift for questions. He tried to speak well and to make himself clear, but the day was hot, and her attention wandered. She fanned her face with her gloves. "I hate this suit."

Max shook his head. "Ceegie, it's the rule. We gotta wear 'em."

"Mm." CJ enjoyed the way he pronounced her initials to rhyme with squeegee, but she detested his reverence for rules. She stuffed her gloves and goggles in her pocket, and unzipped her coverall to the waist.

Max worried his lips between his teeth. "Child, you gonna get splash in the eye. Get eye cancer."

"Don't call me a child." She was twenty-two, and Max was only three years older. She wriggled out of the upper half of her coverall and knotted the sleeves to keep them from dangling. Damp patches dotted the front of her thin cotton undershirt, and she saw him watching her nipples harden. Through his goggles, his light brown eyes looked golden.

They slogged on through quivery black mire. Knife-sharp palmettos sawed at their coveralls, and soon, dense thickets walled them in. The last thing Max wanted was to get lost in two hundred acres of toxic quicksand. He checked his Ranger Joe wrist compass. The needle jittered wildly from East to North. He'd never seen it do that before.

"What's wrong?" The marijuana made CJ giggly. She grabbed his wrist to see the compass needle dance. "Must be magnetic interference. Power lines or something."

When they reached a grove of tupelo gum, Max listened for the sound of the river to get his bearings. Then he hacked at a mesh of catbriar with his shovel. He was thrashing so powerfully at the thorny vines that when he broke through, he almost bolted out the other side.

"Ho!" He staggered to a halt and gawked at what lay ahead.

CJ came up beside him and dropped her bucket. "What *is* that?"

They stood close together on a muddy slope, staring down at a long comma-shaped pond that was fringed with rancid grasses and covered in a sheet of—*ice*. They glanced at each other, then faced the frozen pond. White, pearly, gleaming like sequins, the ice cooled the surrounding air. A skim of meltwater coated its surface, and a fine layer of mist shimmered just above.

CJ knelt and touched the ice with her fingertip. "How could ice form in this weather?"

"Put your gloves on, *lamie*." Max pried up a large stone with his shovel and heaved it onto the frozen pond. When it skidded several yards, he listened to the echoes. "It don' sound like ice."

Before he could stop her, CJ crawled onto the pond.

"Come back, girl." Max reached for her hand and missed. He swore under his breath, while she giggled and kept crawling.

"See. It holds my weight. I bet this pond is frozen solid."

Max stood on the bank, wishing she would come back and knowing she wouldn't. He couldn't put into words what he sensed about her, that she had a raging wind trapped in her chest.

He poked the ice with his shovel, and it rang like a steel drum. F sharp, he noted. When he struck it again, the shovel sank three inches down and stuck fast. "Huh," he said.

The shovel wouldn't come out. He planted his feet, took the handle in both hands and heaved backward, then slipped on the muddy bank and fell.

CJ burst out laughing. "Good work, King Arthur."

Max's face darkened, and she realized he might not get the sword-in-the-stone reference. He hadn't finished high school. It was one of the many little divisions between them. She hid her smile and crawled closer.

The shovel stood like a flagpole in the ice, and her touch set it swaying back and forth. When it slipped sideways and fell with a clatter, she jumped.

"*Mauvais,*" Max whispered.

CJ touched the smooth ice. "It didn't leave a mark. The ice just sealed over."

She stood up and curled a strand of auburn hair around her finger. Harry would know what this is, she thought, yanking her hair till it hurt. Harry, her father. Celebrated winner of the Cope Award in chemistry. When he died a year ago, she quit MIT without finishing her doctorate.

Still, as she walked to the center of the pond, she remembered reading how ice could form at room temperature. "Some catalytic reaction must be absorbing heat," she said.

"Come back, *lam.*" Max paced the bank, trampling weeds.

"Could the toluene spill be reacting with other pollutants?" She stomped the ice to check its tensile strength and nearly lost her footing. "Wow, it's slick."

Then Max saw her nose wrinkle, and he knew she was plotting monkeyshines.

"Hey Max, we can skate."

"Naw, girl."

She put on her headset, got a running start and slid across the pond in her rubber boots. Shadows moved across the surface, altering its texture from glass to white sand. Her marijuana buzz made everything radiant. She zigged and zagged, dancing to Max's zydeco. "This is fantastic," she said, gliding farther and farther away.

But when she noticed Max's hangdog look, she returned to the bank, hiding her disappointment. The first time Max took her dancing in West Baton Rouge, she loved the way his body moved, wild and free, shining wet in the dripping heat of the dance floor. But lately, he'd gone tame.

No, that wasn't fair. He had money problems—she didn't know the details, but she knew he couldn't afford to lose his job. As for her, she'd taken this gig on a whim, like all her choices lately.

She removed her headset and sat cross-legged on the ice, facing him. Waves of cold penetrated through the seat of her coverall. "Your music's really good," she said again, smoothing and straightening her spliff. "Got a light?"

"Hoo, check it. My compass playin' 4/4 time." He held out his wrist to show her. The compass needle swung much stronger than before, back and forth in a steady rhythm. "Accent on the third beat. Same as my zydeco tune."

"Max," she whispered, "I think the magnetic interference is coming from this pond."

"You spookin' me, girl. Magnetic?"

He tried to pull her off the ice, but she laughed and scooted away. "Lots of things produce magnetic fields. Even our blood is magnetic. It's no big deal." She dug her lighter from her thigh pocket and relit her marijuana joint.

"Ceegie, don't. This petrified octane might catch fire." Max listened for cracks.

CJ took a drag, then offered the joint to Max, but he waved it away. While he glanced nervously from his compass to the pond, she tried again to decide if he was handsome. The goggles covered his best feature, his honey-brown eyes.

She had often speculated about his race. Except for his light eyes, he looked Native American. He had the straight nose and high cheekbones of the Seminole people. But he was very swarthy. At different times, his skin reflected tones of olive, ebony, and loam. Surely some of his forebears had crossed the ocean in chains.

"Who you mad at?" he said abruptly. "You mad at the whole world?"

"Who says I'm mad at anyone?" She inhaled deeply from her spliff.

"This pond might blow up, kill us both. You don' mind. They fire us for smoking weed. You don' mind." Max sucked his teeth.

"I do mind. I do."

When she gave him the spliff, he held it between his fingers, watching it burn. The paper made a soft crinkling noise. "Your *popa*'s spirit need to travel over, *lam*. You got to let him go."

CJ swiveled away, and a brief ache clapped through her temple. "I was drunk when I told you about him. Forget it."

Six weeks was the longest she'd stayed with one guy in months. Maybe this was the day to end it. She batted a swarm of gnats.

"Let the dead bury their dead," he quoted from the Book of Matthew, though he knew she had no faith in spirits. He gazed at the delicate nape of her neck, sunburned satin pink. He tried to imagine something to say that would hold her. But there was nothing. She couldn't be held.

"My God. Look at this." She stared into the glassy depths of the pond. Max craned from the bank. Ten inches down, her iPod lay embedded in the ice. She'd forgotten setting it down on the pond. She lay flat on the ice and listened. "Your music's still playing."

"Get off that ice now," Max said.

From the corner of her eye, CJ saw a blue-green light shimmering in the ice like a liquid crystal display viewed on edge. "Bi*zarre,*" she said, drawing out the last syllable.

She was going to say more, but the next instant, the ice opened and swallowed her. Faster than the possibility of thought, the pond sealed over. Cold waves needled through her chest. She couldn't move or breathe. Two feet under, she lay curled on her side like a frozen fetus. Her wide-open eyes stared up through clear solid layers at Max, who gawked down at her. Inches above her head, his muddy soles made skid marks as he knelt and clawed at the ice.

Zydeco rumbled in loud maddening waves, and her lungs burned with a useless muscular effort to suck breath. She saw Max lift his shovel and stab at the surface, and the ringing blows hurt her head. Then something frigid and waxy pushed into her mouth.

She tried to scream, but she couldn't. The pliable ice slid down her throat and gagged her. Freezing wet jelly fingers probed her ears, her nostrils. The ice oozed through her thin shirt and slid under her clothes. She felt it penetrating her esophagus, her vagina, her urethra and rectum. Her heart walloped. Ice slivered under her fingernails and pressed her corneas. Everything squeezed.

Then, as fast as it had trapped her, the ice liquefied and buoyed her up. She thrashed, and Max caught her wrist. "Ceegie!" He hauled her out and pulled her to the bank, where she lay dripping and gasping in his arms. Water leaked from her eyes and nose, from every orifice. She couldn't tell if she was crying and pissing herself—or if the very saliva in her mouth was that . . . that freakish ice.

With a violent shudder, she turned and stared at the pond. Coughing spasms raked her lungs. Again and again, she hawked and spat phlegm. What lethal chemicals had she swallowed? Her mind floundered. Even now, deadly toxins might be sluicing through her arteries, corroding her brain, annihilating her cells. Could this be the final judgment on her life?

But there was no mark on the pond. The ice had solidified again. It looked exactly as they had found it, blank, frosty white, immaculate.

Drip

Wednesday, March 9
12:20 PM

CJ Reilly had always known there was something wrong with her, something insidious and concealed, not noticed by strangers. She kept a catalog of her faults—impatience, lying, egotism, disrespect, snap decisions, reckless driving—yet she could never find the one word that defined her wrongness. If only she could blame it on a chemical imbalance, treatable with meds. But no, she wasn't like her father. Her personal evil loomed under the surface, churning her shallows and troubling her depths.

Her father Harry shot himself in March, a year ago, when the winds blew sleet that nicked her face like shattered window glass. Boston floated in a sea of icy brown slush, and her MIT friends were too slammed with lab work to notice her withdrawal. After the funeral, she bought a four-wheel-drive Range Rover and fled South, moving every couple of months and taking random jobs. She covered a hotel night desk in Atlantic City, analyzed cat stool for a veterinarian in Norfolk, taught aerobics in Myrtle Beach.

Myrtle Beach was the best. She lived in a shoreline motel, and every day she walked the wet sand. The ocean's immense blue swell saturated her dreams. Skipping along its foamy fringe was the only time she forgot to think about Harry. When rain kept her from the shore, she grew despondent and wanted to chuck it all. Face the final judgment. Take her punishment. Pay her debt. Then oblivion. Just knowing that course existed gave her a prop to lean on. Plenty of other people had done it before. She wouldn't be the first.

She kept moving. Money was not an issue—her father left her a trust (locked up in a bank that doled out interest. Even dead, Harry contrived to regulate her life.)

Thinking about Harry gave her a rancorous stomach pain, as if she'd swallowed raw aspirin. She told herself she was overreacting—her family issues were trivial. True, her mother walked out when she was two, but lots of mothers dumped their kids. And Harry kept strict rules: no carbonated drinks, no TV, no boyfriends. But plenty of fathers pushed their daughters to excel. Starting MIT at age fourteen, that was supposed to be a good thing.

When she saw Quimicron's ad, the words "Hazardous Waste" tantalized her. She ripped the ad from the newspaper and fled South again. One year later, she found herself choking on her own vomit beside a pond in Devil's Swamp.

"Don't call anyone!" She knocked the cell phone from Max's hand.

"Girl, we gotta get you to the hospital."

He cradled her in his arms, but she twisted away. "We smoked pot, remember? One look at my bloodshot eyes, they'll give us urine tests, then they'll fire us."

Max grasped her shoulders in his large powerful hands. "It's your life, Ceegie. You been *exposed*."

"I didn't swallow anything," she lied.

Nausea almost gagged her again, but she fought it down. Her hands were trembling, and an ugly taste dried her mouth. Could this be her oblivion? But she had put Max at risk, too. Quimicron had zero tolerance for drugs, and Max would never find wages like this again. She smashed her fist against her knee.

"Okay," she said after a moment, "I'll drive myself to the hospital. You go back and pretend nothing happened. Tell Rory I got stomach flu."

Max crushed her to his chest. "I'm not leavin' you."

For a while, they argued and kissed, and finally, she resorted to more lies. She told him she was wanted on drug charges in another state. After that, he agreed to go back and cover for her. But as soon as he was out of sight, she vomited a gut-load of water.

Shaky and anxious, she found her Rover and drove out the rutted dirt access road to Highway 61. But instead of turning South toward the hospital, at the last minute she changed her mind and veered North toward the Roach. There was something about hospitals, the astringent smells, the sense of entrapment. She remembered the night with Harry. No, she wasn't going to any hospital.

Behind the Hardee's drive-thru, a quarter mile north of Devil's Swamp, she swerved into the driveway of the Ascension Motel, fondly called the Roach Motel by the Quimicron crew who lived there. The Roach crouched like a blue cinderblock bunker, with concrete balconies, a despondent cactus garden, and a sign offering rooms by the day, week, or month. Quimicron negotiated a discount for its hazardous waste workers. The high wages drew migrants from all over the region, and Quimicron wanted them housed close to the work site. CJ's room faced the back, overlooking the blacktop parking lot, three Dumpsters, and a wild verdant grove of pin oaks.

Her room felt stifling. She opened the window, but closed the drapes, then shed her dripping clothes. Wiggling out of her underwear, she replayed the morning's events in her mind as pond liquid sluiced down her neck and chilled her.

The motel room held the minimalist contents of her vagabond existence, a few good clothes draped over the backs of chairs, some books, her laptop, her phone charger. She found a clean plastic cup in the bathroom and wrung several clear driblets from her hair. Under the bright fluorescent light, she swirled and sniffed the brew as if judging wine. But it showed no odor or color. No obvious particles.

Liquid sloshed in her hip boots and coverall pockets, so she collected all she could find until the cup held about a hundred cubic centimeters, enough for a lab analysis. She covered the cup tightly with a plastic ashtray and found the yellow pages in the nightstand drawer next to a Bible. Only a few commercial laboratories were listed in Baton Rouge, none available to the public. Some New Orleans labs had rebuilt after the latest hurricane, but New Orleans was seventy-five miles South, too far to drive before the close of business—and she couldn't wait a whole day. CJ slid her thumb down the page and scowled.

Then she dutifully called and reported her sick time to Elaine Guidry, the

Quimicron personnel officer. She told Elaine that she'd contracted *ciguatera* fish poisoning from eating spicy deep-fried red snapper at the Shrimp Hut on Lafayette Street.

"Laws, Carolyn. What next? Leprosy?" Elaine had lost sympathy for CJ's elaborate excuses.

In the shower, CJ poured antibacterial liquid soap over the plastic bristles of her hairbrush and visualized leprosy. Hansen's disease was the kinder name for it. People in Louisiana still contracted that ancient malady. There was even a local colony, a "leprosarium," in Carville. CJ scrubbed herself from scalp to toenails with the plastic hairbrush till a scum of skin cells and hair clogged her drain. She didn't know the official wash-down procedure for toxic exposure, but she assumed it had to be torturous. The scene at the pond kept rushing back at her. The congealed taste. The obscene fingers. She inhaled shower water and almost choked.

Then she held her eyes open under the punishing spray and forced herself to stand still and take the sting. She let the water scour her ears, nostrils, and the back of her throat. She swallowed and induced herself to vomit again. She leaned over the tub drain and heaved.

The hairbrush left her skin raw and tingly, so after rinsing, she took a quick tub soak with moisturizer gel. As she sank into the sudsy warmth, Max's tune kept echoing in her mind. He sang her the lyrics in Creole, in his sweet sonorous baritone. But when she asked for a translation, the English words didn't sound as cheerful as she'd expected.

> Woman, you are my weather.
> You mark off my time.
> Raise me in spring, love me in summer,
> Bury me in the fall.
> Come winter's end, will you raise me again?
> You blow the rain through my soul.

The tub rim was giving her a neck cramp, so she got out and toweled off. The cup of liquid still waited on the counter, and she'd known all along there was only one lab nearby that stocked the specialized equipment she needed.

"Quimicron," she said aloud. Then she wrinkled her nose and scrutinized her wardrobe.

Maybe she'd been wrong to ask Max about the lyrics. She'd intended to make an opening, to share some mutual understanding with him. "What does that mean," she had asked, "to blow rain through the soul?"

Simple man, he only smiled and shrugged. "Music ain't supposed to be translated."

She jerked a blouse off a hanger.

Trickle

Wednesday, March 9
3:17 PM

As CJ wove through a stream of trucks down Highway 61, she lowered her window and tossed out a Ziploc of prickly green marijuana buds—the last of her stash. From now on, she wanted a clear head. She stepped on the accelerator and visualized her destination. The Quimicron lab was on the top floor of Building No. 2. She'd passed it once, on her way to pick up the crew's paychecks. She'd even peeped through the glass door to check out the equipment. The room had been vacant and dark. What she couldn't know was that the staff chemist had just started chemotherapy for lymphoma.

Highway traffic grew thicker, and so much hot dust spewed through her open window that she closed it and flipped on the AC. Two days ago, she'd scraped frost off her windshield. Louisiana's restive climate exasperated her.

A wave of red lights on the road ahead made her jam her brakes, and the truck behind her skidded. She eased onto the shoulder and craned to see around a big silver Peterbilt. Pipeline construction ahead. Fifty yards down, she could see cars trickling past orange-and-white pylons that clogged the right lane. She veered onto the gravel median, and as she zoomed past the Peterbilt, the driver made a rude gesture. She pressed her accelerator and sprayed gravel. Everyone should drive on the median, she thought. It was the smartest way to clear a traffic jam.

As more drivers honked, she fought a rising irritation. Why did these citizen vigilantes try to enforce stupid traffic rules? She wasn't hurting them. Traffic should flow like the Internet, with every data packet finding its own quickest path. Cars should come equipped with artificial intelligence—to make up for all the brainless drivers. When her right turn came, she had to cut off a red Honda and swerve through a hail of horn blasts.

Quimicron's main plant lay within a private ring levee, a thirty-foot-high earthen fortress designed to hold off the Mississippi floods. Only Building No. 2 protruded above the ring levee. Fronting the canal, its upper windows kept watch over the comings and goings at the Quimicron barge dock. Quimicron's property encircled the blunt northern end of the canal and took in much of the swamp where CJ had been working. A gated entrance, motion sensors, and electrified chain-link fences kept intruders away from the plant, and video cameras monitored every building and parking lot. But CJ carried an employee badge, and she'd made friends with the gatehouse guard, a sweet pimply kid named Johnny Poydras.

At the Quimicron entrance on Highway 61, she pulled to the shoulder, checked her mirror, and wiped a red line of lipstick off her teeth. She was wearing serious slacks, a linen blazer, and a white button-down blouse. She was trying for an "authorized" look, as in "authorized entrance."

Johnny Poydras grinned and waved her through the gate with the *Godzilla* comic book he was reading. She drove up over the ring levee, passed through the chain-link fence gate, and dropped into the gritty brown basin of the Quimicron plant. On the front steps of Building No. 2, she adjusted the badge clipped to her lapel and whistled a saucy tune to buck up her confidence—Max's tune again. He was out there in the swamp, shoveling poisoned mud and worrying about her. "Oh Max, I don't deserve you," she whispered.

The new plastic cooler she'd bought at Wal-Mart resembled the type chemists used to transport field samples. It contained one clear plastic Baggie of liquid, labeled with a set of official-looking made-up numbers in black felt-tip. She gripped the cooler handle, stuck out her chin, and ran up the steps to the front door.

Several people milled in the beige lobby, but no one took notice of CJ and her cooler. The guard in the booth glanced at her badge, then wordlessly buzzed her through the turnstile. Quimicron SA employed several thousand people at its Baton Rouge plant, and many, like her, wore the blue badges of temporary contract workers. She paused at the drinking fountain to calm down, then hurried upstairs to the fifth floor. Sure enough, the lab was empty and dark. But the door was locked.

CJ waved her badge across the card-reader mounted beside the door, but its light-emitting diode stayed red. She should have known her temporary badge wouldn't grant access. Several people passed up and down the hall, so she couldn't stand there shaking the door lever. She picked out an attractive well-dressed man who looked like a manager.

"Excuse me, this lab is locked, and I've got a horrendous deadline. Will your badge open it?"

The man glanced at her, then at the lab door. She must have interrupted him deep in thought, because he seemed a bit unfocused. He was middle-aged, slim, and fit-looking, with a nut-brown tan and fine dark Mediterranean eyes. His chin was a smidge too long, but she liked his full head of blue-black hair, just silvering at the temples. He wore it longish, combed back behind his ears like a poet.

"This door was supposed to be open," she lied. "There's an EPA guy waiting on the phone for my data. He's threatening to fine us."

The man read her badge aloud. "Carolyn Joan Reilly."

She hated that name and had to bite her lip to keep from saying so. It was her mother's name. The personnel office had made a mistake printing the whole revolting thing on her badge. She nodded. "That's me. Staff chemist."

The man wore casual clothes, expensive but not showy. A Montblanc pen bulged in his shirt pocket, and CJ thought he might be a lawyer. Late forties, she guessed, close to her father's age. His features were gaunt, as if he'd been fasting, and one of his eyebrows arched higher than the other, giving him an aristocratic expression. Yes, this guy definitely qualified as handsome. She could tell he was deciding the same thing about her.

"You're a temp," he said.

"I'm a consultant," she bluffed. "I'm trying to bail your company out of a major jam with the EPA, and they're waiting for my analysis. Can you help me or not?"

The man wore his badge clipped to his belt, so she couldn't read his name. "What are you analyzing?" He spoke with a trace of accent, as if he'd learned English as a second language.

"Toxic waste." She popped her cooler lid. "Wanna see?"

He stepped back and shook his head, then pulled his badge out on its retractable cord and waved it across the reader. The LED changed from red to green.

He said, "Be my guest, Carolyn Reilly."

Inside the quiet lab, CJ locked the glass door and waited till the man disappeared down the hall. A small surveillance camera dangled from the ceiling, so she drew deep breaths and stood straighter, trying to appear official. She hoped the guy behind that camera was reading a comic book.

But he wasn't. Security officer Gene Becnel monitored his screens with the vigilance of a cotton rat. As soon as he noticed her presence in the lab, he checked his personnel schedule, then slotted a DVD to make a high-resolution recording. Next he took a bite of his Kit Kat bar and poised one finger over the alarm button. His great doughy buttocks inched forward in his chair, and with rapt concentration, he watched her take a Baggie of liquid from a white plastic cooler.

Spread

Wednesday, March 9
4:01 PM

Devil's Swamp glistened under the white-hot sun, and a vaporous stench saturated the air. A line of workers in goggles and respirators shoveled gelatinous orange sludge into barrels, then banged the lids shut with rubber mallets and loaded them on flatbed trucks. It was slow, heavy work. The toluene spill had spread over five flooded acres.

When Rory Godchaux signaled the mid-afternoon break, everyone dropped their shovels and retreated to the shade, where Rory hosed them down from a tank on his pickup truck. Then they ripped off their gloves and goggles and headed for the water coolers.

First thing, Max tried to call CJ. Squatting beneath a water maple, he listened to a recorded voice say the subscriber he was seeking could not be found. She had turned off her cell phone. Max chewed his lips. The girl didn't go to any hospital. He should have dragged her there by the scruff of her neck. Crazy child. He keyed her number again.

Overhead, the maple branches rustled faintly in the breeze, while blank cellular static whistled in his right ear. She must not want him to find her. He clicked the phone shut and jammed it in his pocket. He knew she was grieving for her *popa*. Her flighty turns were not always her fault, he wanted to believe that. But sometimes she drove him *gen vètij*—dizzy.

He sighted out across the swamp and located the tupelo gums, beyond which lay the frozen pond. His muscles tightened, remembering. Everything about that ice felt wrong. He should never have given his word not to tell. He glanced at the crew chief's white pickup. Rory was sitting inside, talking on the radio. Max worked his lips in and out. The sound of crickets sizzled through the air like hot popping grease.

Sometimes it was right to break a promise. He had half a mind to go find the crazy child, haul her to the doctor, and get her detoxified. Yeah, and if he tried that, he could already hear Ceegie's answer. He looked at his broad rough hands. What was the good of having such strong hands?

Wind sawed the trees back and forth, and sun glittered across the jellied orange mud. Max swallowed a mouthful of ice water and felt its coolness spread down his gullet. He thought about how everything in the world tended to spread. Chemicals through the mud. Sounds through the air. Smells. Words. Someday, maybe everything in creation would spread through everything else, and there would be no difference between anything.

Right now, for instance, the wind was mixing sounds. He listened to the sawing branches, the cricket noise, the beeps from Rory's radio. Mixed together, they made the whole swamp sound menacing. Max dropped his head. He couldn't go on feeling this way about Ceegie.

"Look sharp. We got a bossman from Miami in town," Rory announced to the crew.

The lethargic workers eyed him. They lay sprawled in the grassy shade, slurping ice water from plastic cups. "Look sharp, ha ha. We do that."

Rory spat tobacco juice into the grass at his feet. "Clock's tickin', *mes amis*. Back to work. And suit up good, case we get inspected."

With one last look at the tupelo gums, Max drew on his gloves.

Swirl

"Water." CJ spoke aloud in the empty Quimicron lab.

Gene Becnel cocked his ear. Gene had long since alerted his security staff and placed a respectful call to the plant manager's office. Two guards stood outside the lab door, waiting for Gene's order to arrest the intruder, but Gene couldn't give it. He patted sweat from his cheeks and covertly scratched the poison-ivy rash on his forearm. Mr. Dan Meir, the plant manager, leaned on the back of Gene's chair, watching the screen over his shoulder. Mr. Meir said hold off, see what she's up to. Worse, Mr. Meir had brought another man, a stranger from the Miami office. Gene didn't like people coming into his control room, breathing his air. At least Mr. Meir was a bonafide ex-US Marine. The Miami stranger looked foreign.

On the surveillance monitor, the female intruder was running one of her tests again. Gene didn't like the way she kept talking aloud, as if somebody was with her, someone his cameras couldn't see.

"Bizarre," CJ said, completely unaware that she had an audience. She'd run all the quick tests twice, but they only confirmed what her eyes and nose told her. The sample she'd taken from the poisonous effluvium of Devil's Swamp was pure water, pure enough to drink.

She rested her chin in her hand and stared at the spectrophotometer display. Her analyte of H_2O contained nothing more than a trace of skin particles, probably her own, and mud, probably from inside her boot, plus a fleck of waterproofing material from her coverall pocket. "Okay, Harry, what next?"

Questions swirled in her head. What kind of chemical reaction could form ice in hot weather? And purify toxic slops into clean water? And generate a magnetic field that pulsed in time to zydeco? Why had she fallen through the ice but not Max? And when the ice formed, what happened to all the heat?

She sat in one position, doing and saying nothing, for long enough to make Gene Becnel's thigh twitch. He wanted to stand up and stretch. He wanted to gulp another Kit Kat bar. He wanted the big brass to get the hell out of his booth and let him do his job.

Gene already knew who she was—a college girl, probably a flag-burner, she came from up *North*—a word that, in Gene's lexicon, rhymed with *Goth*. His state-of-the-art Texas Instruments security system, one of the great joys of his life, had already read the Radio Frequency ID tag in her badge. The RFID contained her employee number, which linked to her personnel file in the central server. Carolyn Joan Reilly, female, twenty-two, short-term grunt on Rory Godchaux's cleanup gang. Perfect cover for a terrorist.

"That's weird."

Her agitated voice tripped Gene's internal alarms. Even Mr. Meir bent closer to watch. Mr. Meir had a good sense about people. Gene acknowledged that much.

The female suspect poured some of the clear liquid into her cupped hand and let out a giggle. Gene used his camera zoom so they could see the little glassy blob rolling around her palm like a bead of mercury. "Amazing surface tension," she said. When she poked it with her fingernail, it glued itself to her finger.

She played with it for a while, shaking and blowing at it, making it wobble on her fingertip like a ball of clear Jell-O. With her free hand, she pecked a few notes into her laptop. But when she used the beaker's rim to scrape the little glob off, it smeared all over her finger. A second later, she started shaking her hand really hard and squealing, "Ow, ow, ow!" She rushed to the sink and held her fingers under the gushing tap. Then she dried her hand on a paper towel and examined her skin.

Gene couldn't see anything wrong with her hand. Her finger wasn't even red. After that, she drifted off into lala land, as Gene would later tell his mother. She peered down the sink drain for ten solid minutes.

When she started gathering her things to leave, Gene swiveled in his chair to face the higher-ups. "Want us to apprehend her, Mr. Meir?"

Dan Meir rolled an unlit cigar around in his mouth. He was a short, compact gray-headed man of sixty-two with kind green eyes and a permanent squint from decades in the sun. He wore a military buzz cut that he religiously trimmed and sprayed each morning so it glittered like tin foil. Everybody liked Dan Meir, even Gene, who was hard to please.

Meir spoke to the Miami stranger. "Do you think she's dangerous?"

The brown-skinned foreigner glanced up from something he was reading on his Palm. He needed a haircut, Gene thought. His hair hung down over his collar.

"I know who she is," the foreigner said. Sure enough, he had an un-American accent. "Let her go, but keep tabs on her. Meir, we're due at a meeting."

After they left, Gene chomped a savage bite of chocolate. "Stand down. Let her pass," he commanded his men over the radio. Yankee leftist. Sure, let her go. "Moselle, hang back and follow, but don't let her see you. Report to me every five minutes."

"Roger that," said Ron Moselle.

Rill

Wednesday, March 9
4:49 PM

CJ didn't see the red Toyota pickup follow her out of the Quimicron parking lot. One idea fixed her attention as she drove over the ring levee and waved good-bye to Johnny Poydras at the gate: she had to get a chunk of that ice. After darting into the traffic on Highway 61, she raced the short distance to the Devil's Swamp access road and veered into its rutted lane, trying again to imagine what chemical interactions could have formed that astonishing substance.

Mentally she ticked off its properties: powerful surface tension; rapid phase shift from solid to liquid; a magnetic field that responded to sound; possibly a flashing light; and it could *purify water.*

Questions rilled through her mind. Could the chemical-freezing reaction have fused all the pond's impurities, leaving behind the pristine meltwater that saturated her clothing and hair? And what could explain its strong surface tension? Or the peculiar prickling sensation in her finger, as if the substance had suddenly dropped sub zero? The way her finger still tingled, she wasn't positive she'd washed it all off.

She studied her fingertip. The skin appeared smooth and healthy—though she'd chewed the nail to the quick. The ice's riddle fascinated her. All her instruments showed the substance was chemically pure H_2O. Was there something her instruments couldn't see?

"Pure water," she chirped, bouncing in the driver's seat. If she could figure how the freezing-purifying process worked—well, the potential applications made her giddy. As Harry often said, the greatest discoveries came by accident.

A hundred yards in, she pulled off the muddy road into a patch of willow, shut off her engine, and climbed out. She didn't see Ron Moselle watching through the brush as she stripped down to her underwear and stepped into her coverall. She tugged on the hip boots, still damp with what she now knew was clean, drinkable water. Down the road, the mainline levee rose like a linear green mountain, walling off the riverside wasteland called the *batture*. The Devil's Swamp access road wound over the top of the levee like a brown water snake.

She walked along the road to the patch of bare mud where the cleanup crew usually parked. But all their cars were gone. Only one green van waited by the fence gate. She checked her watch. Still over an hour before quitting time. So where was the crew? As she walked closer, a Quimicron security guard stepped out of the van to meet her. He wore a side-arm, and he was drinking 7UP.

"I work on the crew," she said, showing her badge. "Where is everybody?"

"Swamp closed, sweetheart. You got the rest of this week off."

"But I was here this morning. What happened?"

"Take it easy, honey. They don' tell me nothing. Now head on home and enjoy you' vacation. Chief be callin' you next week."

They found the ice, she thought. And they're concealing it. She hurried back to her car, shoved her gearshift into reverse and roared away, swerving around a red Toyota pickup, and pounding the steering wheel with her fist. "Dammit! They're going to steal my ice!"

Simmer

Wednesday, March 9
10:40 PM

CJ shut down her laptop and rubbed her aching temples. All evening, she'd been holed up in her motel room, reading about Devil's Swamp. One thing Harry had drilled into her: When in doubt, gather information—all kinds, through every channel, using every tool available. CJ's online research had turned up plenty.

Before 1950, Devil's Swamp had been a fertile marshy woodland centering around a hamlet called Alsen. Settled by freed slaves, the families had peacefully farmed their land for a hundred years—until 1964. That was the year local officials built the first hazardous waste dump in the swamp. By 1970, against the protests of its mostly poor, mostly black residents, the lush wooded marsh held over a hundred toxic lagoons, incinerators, and landfills, and Alsen faded to a ghost town. At latest count, thousands of tons of unnamed waste simmered in the swamp's two hundred trackless acres.

In 1986, the EPA found PCBs ranging up to 13,200 micrograms per kilogram in its waterlogged soil. They also found arsenic, lead, mercury, volatile organics—and the first of the mutated frogs. So they issued fishing advisories and posted warning signs, and environmental organizations filed lawsuits. The defendant list read like a government advisory board of Big Oil, Big Agriculture, and Big Biotech. In 2004, Devil's Swamp was proposed for the Superfund National Priority List.

Bleary-eyed, CJ wandered out to her concrete balcony and leaned on the rail. The breeze had grown sharp and chilly. "I hate corporations," she muttered. Then a premenstrual cramp made her clench her ab muscles. On the western horizon, a fat half-moon hovered. Gibbous, she thought, like her belly.

Max waited below in the parking lot, gazing up at her like a swarthy Romeo. She watched him pace along the line of muddy pickups and SUVs, grateful that he had come at her call—again, and even more grateful that he'd forgiven her—again.

Max smiled and waved. Then he stalked to the dark end of the building, pressed against the cinderblock wall, and peered around the corner. The stranger was still there, sitting in his red Toyota truck, talking on his cell phone. He'd parked in the shadow of the Dumpster, not a favorable sign. Max hoped he was waiting for something innocent like a drug buy, something that didn't require his involvement. Max had never liked the Ascension Motel. With an uneasy foreboding, he rolled down the sleeves of his work shirt and buttoned his cuffs. The night was growing cooler. He walked back toward the front of the building.

And there under the light stood CJ. Slim and straight, pale as fresh milk, defenseless in the harsh motel light, she looked more like a budding child than the world-weary adult she tried to impersonate. A hank of her auburn hair had come loose from her ponytail and fanned across her cheek. She stared off in the distance, chewing her thumbnail, oblivious to her surroundings, lost in her usual interior tide.

"The moon's down," he said. "We can go. But I don' like it."

Neither did CJ like it. Alsen's story incensed her. As she stumbled through her motel room getting ready, she fumed and kicked furniture. She crushed her Quimicron pay stub in her fist. She despised the chemical industry. Unlocking the secrets of molecules, forcing artificial unions, synthesizing compounds with effects no one could foresee. "To make a killing," that's how Harry put it. To make a quick buck.

Yes, Harry had sided with the corporations. When he wasn't lecturing at MIT, he was off consulting with CEOs to "maximize shareholder value." She accused Harry and his corporations of playing creator, only without omniscience or compassion. But Harry never listened. When she raged about eco-disasters, he answered with his trademark sarcasm: "Carolyn, don't be naïve."

CJ pulled her shoelace so hard, it broke in her hand. "We are not the end!" Harry used to rant when she accused him of soaking their planet in poison. She pictured him crouching at his desk, a tweedy graying scholar, slicing the air with his hands. His mad eyes seemed to glow.

"Poisons are our medicines. They grow our food. They kill the germs and weeds and vermin we don't want to live with," he stormed. "And yes, they're killing us, too. But life doesn't end because we die."

"What'll survive us?" CJ had shouted. "Black mold? Viruses? That's hideous."

"Human judgment does not apply!" he wailed. "Carolyn, you're a bleed-ing heart. Like your mother."

CJ remembered knocking over a wineglass. "And you're already dead."

How viciously they had fought. On the last night she saw her father alive, they had raged.

From her balcony at the Roach, she hurled her coverall and hip boots down the concrete stairs to the parking lot. Max noticed her mood and kept quiet. He loaded her gear in the Rover, along with the portable magnetic field finder he had "borrowed" from the company shop at her request. She took her usual place in the driver's seat, and when she slammed the Rover's door, he said, "Settle down, child."

"You settle down," she snapped.

Max opened his window and leaned out. Ceegie's tone pained him. Sometimes her voice went so sharp and thin, it hurt his ears. He whistled softly through his teeth. This night was starting off badly, and more than once, he'd considered walking away. But he couldn't let her go alone into Devil's Swamp. It wasn't in him to abandon her. So he leaned out the window and let the night air cool his face.

Later, as they lurched onto a rutted back road, CJ touched his hand. He was slouching against the passenger door, hanging his elbow out the win-dow. Neither of them had noticed the red Toyota following with its head-lights turned off.

"Max, I've been a total bitch. How can you stand me?" she said.

He squeezed her knee and hummed a line of melody, not the song from that morning but something older and more languid, a bolero. The glowing dashboard lit his features, and CJ felt a sudden rush of fondness.

For an instant, she wanted to throw on the brakes, nuzzle into his arms, and make love right there on the leather seat. The thought of traipsing through Devil's Swamp in the dark terrified her. Especially after reading the EPA report. But if she hesitated, Max would try to talk her out of going—and he might succeed. She was already second-guessing the whole venture.

After all, the ice didn't belong to her. Quimicron employed dozens of scientists—real ones, not college dropouts. Probably, they'd already analyzed the ice and filed for a patent on the chemical reaction. That's what she hated most, that they would keep the process a secret and claim they'd invented it.

"Sell it for money," she muttered.

Her fingernails sank into the leather steering wheel. If the ice could transform poisonous swill into safe drinking water, that could benefit millions of people around the world. Quimicron didn't have a right to profit from that. She shoved hair out of her eyes. But who was she to stop them? The whole system was bogus. She had half a mind to turn her car around and get on a plane to Mexico.

A raccoon scurried through her high beams, and she swerved and splashed through a pothole to miss it. Somewhere in the darkness ahead lay the pond. She could almost see the blue-green light again, ranging just beyond her periphery. What chemical effect could produce luminous ice that pulsed in time to music? Deep in her brain, nerve endings prickled with curiosity. She kept driving.

Squish

Wednesday, March 9
11:33 PM

A cold front moved through the swamp, and the warm sloughs respired a malodorous fog. CJ coasted the last hundred yards and parked against a barricade of palmettos. Max opened his door, and cold mist wetted their faces. When they climbed out, the ground felt spongy underfoot. CJ shimmied into her coverall, and Max shouldered the heavy bag of tools. They trudged through dew-drenched grass up the sloping ring levee.

From the top, they could see Quimicron's mercury floodlights gleaming across the canal water, and far in the distance, boat traffic winked along the river. But the two hundred-acre swamp lay in cold darkness. Max and CJ slid down the levee bank into the pitch-black undergrowth, covering their flashlights with their fingers to damp the light. Not far away, they heard the voices of the guards.

"Ouch!" CJ tripped and fell. Something sharp prodded through her glove. It was a piece of rusting concertina wire. When she tried to pull away, it tangled around her arm.

"Ceegie, you hurt?" Max helped her work loose from the coiling wire, but its razor barbs tore holes in her glove and grazed her palm.

"We should both think about tetanus shots," she said.

After that, she moved more cautiously, creeping on bent knees, holding her muffled light near the ground and vividly recalling the symptoms of tetanus: muscle spasms in the jaw escalating to full body convulsions powerful enough to break bones.

Under the moonless sky, her flashlight caught the glowing red eyes of a baby alligator. Bullfrogs bayed rumbling choruses, and tree frogs crooned. Grasses rustled with movement. An owl screamed. Sawbriars chewed at her boots, and heavy dew soaked her gloves. Max stayed close. Even with his compass, it took them an hour to find the northern end of the canal.

Across the water, mercury lamps brightened Quimicron's dock like a surreal apparition in the black landscape, and loading cranes hovered like giant insectile arms. Three barges bobbed in the ebony water, moored by heavy cables. The chain-link fence glittered with moisture, and behind the fogged upper windows of Building No. 2, people were working late.

They skirted along the canal. Mosquitoes swarmed thicker near the water, but at least the rippling reflections helped them see their way. "It's through here." Max pointed into the dark swamp, then rechecked his compass. "I'm pretty sure."

CJ studied her electromagnetic field finder. Nothing yet. An impulse of affection made her squeeze Max's hand. "Lead on, Ranger Joe."

As he angled through the rasping dewy palmettos, she realized how confidently she trusted him to find the path. She wouldn't have dared this escapade without him. Max didn't want to do this. Yet here he was, loyally guiding her through the dark. She followed close and touched his back for comfort.

Technically, they were breaking the law, but CJ wasn't worried. No one would ever know. Besides, they were employees, weren't they? And she was good at talking her way out of complex situations. She played her flashlight over Max's square shoulders. With another impulse of guilty fondness, she hugged him and made him stumble.

"*Lamie* child, you afraid of the boogie man?"

"Hell, yes." She found his mouth and kissed him. Max was a kind, good man. Life would be so peaceful if she could only decide to love him.

"Who's there?" A white beam spotlighted them, and they froze. "Stop, or I'll shoot," said a gruff male voice.

Branches snapped as the man approached, then something yanked her arm. It was Max. He switched off her flashlight, and they sprinted blindly through the swamp. They blundered over sodden grass clumps, slipped in mire and splashed through puddles of unknown liquid. Lights shafted around them.

"Stop!" the guard yelled. Gunshots exploded.

Max caught CJ's waist and pulled her down hard. They crouched in a foot of cold soupy muck, surrounded by tall dripping grass, and CJ feared her breath was roaring louder than a hurricane. Surely, the guards would hear and fire their guns again. Guns! Of all the scary things in the swamp, she'd never imagined guns.

When her breathing calmed down, she whispered, "Which way is the pond?"

"Ceegie, we gotta lay still."

Behind them, boots trod through sucking mud, and flashlight beams wavered in the glistening grass stems to their left. CJ caught the faint shape of tupelo trees just ahead. She gripped Max's shoulder. "It's that way, isn't it? Behind the trees?"

He touched her lips to make her be quiet.

"Max, we're this close. I have to get that sample."

She heard him inhale. The lights and footsteps were circling farther away to the left. "Wait a little," he said.

After ten minutes, they crept toward the trees, half-squatting so the grasses would screen them. They moved deliberately, trying not to make noise. The frogs and birds had fallen silent, and every time CJ broke a stem or heard the mud belch under her foot, she froze in midstride, expecting an explosion of bullets. When they reached the grove, her muscles ached with cramps. The air felt wintry. And there was no mistaking the silver crescent of frost that glimmered through the tree trunks. They felt their way through slick wet roots to the edge of the pond.

Cupping her flashlight behind her hand, CJ took a quick peek at her field finder. Condensation fogged the screen, so she wiped it with her glove. Yes! A highly energetic field radiated from the pond. It was EM—electromagnetic. Her instrument showed a frequency slightly higher than FM radio. She wanted to laugh out loud. "Look, Max!"

"Shhh." He switched off her light again. "You watch for the guards. I get your sample."

From his tool bag, he brought out an ice pick, a cordless drill, a chisel, and a mallet. CJ lined up three sterile plastic sample jars in the mud and twisted off their lids. Then she crawled up the clammy bank and lay prone at the base of a tupelo sapling. Flashlights twinkled through mist on both sides of the pond. Half a dozen guards were searching in a grid pattern. She lay in the waterlogged brush, wondering about the source of that EM field. The sudden chatter from Max's cordless drill on the ice rang like a Klaxon.

"Over there!" the guards shouted.

Lights converged toward CJ. She half-crawled, half-rolled down the bank to the pond. "They're coming."

Max dropped the drill and got up to run. But CJ seized the first tool she could find, the mallet, and started banging away at the ice. She no longer cared about noise. After coming this far, she didn't intend to leave empty-handed.

Max gripped her wrist. "We gotta *parti vite.*"

"One more minute!" She held the chisel against the ice and tried to drive it into the pond with the mallet. But her hand slipped, the mallet banged her fingers, and the chisel skittered across the pond out of reach.

"Please, child." Max's voice broke. "They gonna shoot us."

"Go then. I'm staying." With aching fingers, she searched in the dark for the chisel. Close to panic, she leaned out over the freezing cold ice and felt blindly along its surface. She didn't want to leave the bank. That ice had swallowed her. As she slid forward a few inches, she remembered the throes of suffocation.

Max's long arm circled her waist. He was kneeling beside her on the ice, holding on to her for safety. "I won' let you go, *lam.*"

At last, her fingers closed on the chisel. Then she felt it sink. Under her warm hand, a small circle of ice softened to slush. She held fast to the chisel, but the cold numbing slush closed around her forearm.

"It's happening," she whispered through a throat constricted with terror. For some reason, only a small circle of ice had thawed to slush, and it was not refreezing as quickly as before. She held her arm rigid, afraid to move. "Max, turn on your flashlight."

Max fumbled in his pocket, and when the light came on, they saw the chisel eighteen inches down and CJ's arm sunk above the elbow in a column of slushy ice. The slush measured only six inches across, but instead of refreezing, it was very slowly widening.

"There they are," shouted one of the guards.

Max clicked off the flashlight. "Can you lift your arm outta that mess?"

"I'm fine. Get my sample jars," she whispered.

"I'm not leaving you, girl."

"Do it!"

Too late, she realized how accurately she had reproduced Harry's caustic tone, the tone she hated—but it worked. Max slid over the ice on his knees and returned with one of the jars. Flashlight beams flickered through the trees, then closed in, drenching the two of them in a pool of light. "Stop whatever you're doing," said the hoarse voice.

"Dip as much as you can. I'm all right," she whispered, trying to hide her stampeding fear. Sunk to the armpit, her skin burned with cold. To the guard, she said, "We're not doing anything wrong. Give us a break."

Max shielded her with his broad back. He reached around her and scooped up half a jar of the milky slush.

"Good. Seal it," she whispered.

"Stand up," said the guard. "Turn around and face me."

CJ said, "We were making love, okay? I have to button my blouse."

Max twisted the jar lid tight and quietly stuffed it down CJ's shirtfront. Then, nervous with concentration, she eased her arm out of the slush. They both let out a tense breath when her dripping hand came free. As the melting circle continued just perceptibly to widen, they eased away from the bank where the unseen guards waited with blinding flashlights.

"Stand up. I'm drawin' a bead on you right this minute."

"When I say go, run like hell," Max whispered.

"I can talk to them," she whispered back, watching the circle of melting ice. "Oh. Oh God, Max!"

The melted area instantly expanded in all directions, and they plummeted into a bath of glacial Jell-O. Under the surface, CJ screamed and choked. When she felt Max's leg lashing out, she grabbed his ankle. Faster than she could comprehend, the slush liquefied completely, and they surfaced together, splashing and gasping for breath. They were yards away from where they'd gone under. Bullets popped like firecrackers.

The frigid temperature caused CJ's chest to contract. She couldn't get her wind. Violently she groped for Max's arm, and when he recognized her hysteria, he dove and came up behind her, then caught her chin in the crook of his elbow. More bullets popped. The guards were firing into the air, but Max didn't know that. With powerful sidestrokes, he hauled the panicked girl to the far edge of the pond, dragged her from the water and shoved her into a willow thicket. He put his hand over her mouth to hush her noise. Only then did he comprehend his own shock.

"Lie still," he whispered, pressing her struggling body into the mud.

Amid a snarl of willow shoots, he lay on top of her and kept her from moving while the guards crashed through the brambles, calling to each other and
cursing. Their flashlight beams roved around the pond, but Max lay still,
crushing CJ beneath him. He could feel her heart thumping, and when he
moved his hand away from her mouth, she kept silent.

Max would have lain in the mud till dawn if necessary. But ten minutes
later, inexplicably, the guards called off their search and withdrew. Their
grumbling voices faded into the distance. Max and CJ listened until they
could no longer hear briars rasping against wet coveralls or heavy boots
squishing through mire.

"We're safe." CJ twisted beneath him, clamped her legs around his body
and drew his face down for a kiss. "You saved my life," she said, trembling in
his arms. She almost said, I love you.

As she nuzzled against him and licked his ear, only then did she see the
faint outline looming against the mist, not two yards away, like a terrible
horned beast transmogrified from a nightmare. Its single eye burned scarlet.
Before she could speak, the monster made a hideous noise, like the sliding
click of metal against metal.

Max rolled over and switched on his flashlight. There stood Ron Moselle,
wearing infrared night-vision headgear and covering them with his Ruger
semiautomatic. He'd been dogging their steps all evening.

"Y'all are under arrest for trespassing," he said. Gene Becnel had finally
given him the go-ahead.

Ripple

Thursday, March 10
9:00 AM

There are places on the globe where currents coalesce. Call them strange
attractors—crossroads, melting pots, deltas of convergence and recombina-
tion. These focal gathering points exert a stronger gravitational pull than ordinary places. You know them. Certain cities, islands, coasts. They collect not
only physical sediments but also tides of history, drifting languages and arts,

the flotsam of our hopes and fears. Their slow pickling eddies stir and coddle until the diverse elements merge into something novel and unforeseen. Something like zydeco.

Dan Meir, Quimicron's plant manager, turned up the radio on his desk. The local station was playing "Paper in My Shoe" by accordionist BooZoo Chavis. Meir needed the music to calm his nerves. He'd just had a call from FOWL—Friends of Wetlands in Louisiana.

"Damned bird lovers wanna send in an inspection team." He shook his head and chuckled. "They must think they're the United Nations."

He rocked back in his chair and squinted out his fifth-floor window at the barge canal. Steady drizzle roughened the gray water and drenched the workers on the dock. His workers, his dock, that's how Meir thought of the plant he'd managed for seventeen years. His gray buzz cut glistened with hairspray. He tugged at his collar, hating the tie. Lately, he'd gotten used to golf shirts. A former marine sergeant, his aging body still rippled with hard muscle, but creases patterned his neck, and wrinkles rayed outward from the corners of his eyes. Although the morning had dawned cool and rainy, Meir felt like steamed beef. Raindrops pooled and slid down his office window, and he thought about the man who had died yesterday.

Across the desk, Gene Becnel rubbed the rash on his forearm. His short blond hairs stood up like sewing pins across the top of his head, and his obese buttocks lolled off both sides of the narrow chair seat. Gene's field of interest did not include bird lovers or employee funerals. He had two terrorist prisoners cooling their heels in a basement locker room—prisoners he'd incarcerated on his own authority. Gene didn't doubt he'd acted in the right. The yankee flag-burner and her pothead boyfriend were dangerous malcontents, but here was Mr. Meir diddling over whether to contact the parish sheriff. If Gene were in charge, he would call Homeland Security.

The third man in the room, the brown-skinned Miami honcho in the three-piece suit, lurked in a corner, and Gene felt his presence like a neck itch. He twisted to see what the guy was doing, and the stranger glanced up briefly from his work. He sat with one thin ankle crossed over his knee, balancing a laptop and gripping a cell phone between his ear and shoulder. Gene noticed his fancy silk socks, the airy-fairy kind that went all the way up his calf. Now and then, the guy mumbled something foreign into the phone.

Gene squared up his stack of collated reports, still warm from the copier. "The girl's from up *Noth,* Mr. Meir. You wanna see her file?"

"I've seen it." Meir chewed his Oliva cigar, and the Miami guy said nothing. Gene found their indifference shocking.

The door opened, and Ron Moselle ushered in the female perpetrator. She still wore her muddy coverall, though she'd unzipped it and knotted the sleeves around her waist. She looked sleep-deprived. Good. Gene had ordered his men to keep both prisoners awake all night—to soften them up for interrogation.

CJ, however, felt anything but soft. Her pelvis blazed with cramps, and her bloated brain wobbled in her skull. She wore the expression of a ballistic missile. She didn't see the stranger in the corner, and she didn't know the obese blond security chief, but she recognized Dan Meir, the plant manager.

She went straight for him. "Meir, you're going to wish you never heard my name."

"Take it easy, Miz Reilly."

"Screw easy. Eight excruciating hours you've kept me sitting on that bench, shining a light in my face and not even a cup of water. I'm going to sue this company all the way to the Supreme Court. I'm going to put your face on CNN. You're going to rue the day you held Max and me at gunpoint. I'll never stop. I'll—"

"You're a consultant, yes?"

CJ whipped around and faced the stranger who had spoken. She hadn't noticed him sitting there in the corner. He was the good-looking manager who'd used his badge to unlocked the lab for her. Caught in a lie already—her face grew hot.

When the man looked her up and down, she became conscious of her mud-streaked face, filthy clothes, and bare feet. In reflex, she crossed her arms and scowled.

"Carolyn Reilly?" Hollows formed under his gaunt cheekbones. He had the same tanned face she remembered, the same longish black hair. His eyebrows were thick, black, and straight, as if someone had painted them on with a ruler. When he stood and offered her his chair, he looked like a Spanish lord. Or a Spanish inquisitor.

She didn't want a chair. She wanted to vent. But he kept waiting, saying nothing, courteously holding the chair and wearing a polite expression that was not quite a smile—till finally she shrugged and plopped down.

Mildly, he said, "We have a complete record of your activities for the past twenty-four hours."

CJ gripped the chair seat. She tried to keep her face blank.

"We also have this." He lifted a sample jar of milky liquid from Meir's desk.

"That's mine." She made a grab for it.

"I believe not." He moved the jar beyond her reach, put a hand on her shoulder and gently forced her back into the chair. "This material was stolen from Quimicron property. But why did you take it, Carolyn?"

She blinked. He was baiting her. Surely they had discovered its properties by now. She could picture the corporate bigwigs popping champagne corks to celebrate their newest patent—a chemical reaction that squeezed pure drinking water from toxic swill.

But who was this Spanish aristocrat, some sexy shark from the legal office? He probably wanted to nail down Quimicron's property rights. The sample swirled in its jar with a tantalizing shimmer. She'd netted something real this time—something she could analyze. She lifted her hand a couple of inches, yearning to hold it.

Meir sat hunched over his desk, examining his cigar as if it were inscribed with runes. CJ wondered why Meir was letting this lawyer lead the meeting. She scrutinized the Spaniard more carefully. His ID badge was tucked in his pocket so she couldn't read it. Maybe he wasn't a lawyer.

The stranger's glance raked across Meir and the blond man as if he were weighing them in a scale. She watched him stroll to the window and hold the cloudy sample jar up to the light. The liquid gleamed like mother of pearl.

"Carolyn, do you know what this is?" His glance sliced toward her like a rapier.

That trace of accent. Like nothing else she'd heard in Louisiana. When she crossed her arms and clamped her jaw, he lost his careful mask, and a gust of animal ferocity twisted his face. CJ pressed back in her chair, startled.

But his mild civility returned at once, and he almost managed to smile when he asked again, "Carolyn, what is this liquid?"

She blurted, "Haven't you analyzed it?"

"We overnighted a sample to our Miami lab." He sat on a corner of Meir's desk, facing her. "Yesterday, one of our employees fell into a pool of this material and—died. I almost said 'drowned,' but in fact, he had a heart attack. Were you aware of the accident?"

The room went white. CJ couldn't see the stranger's face, only the bright window. "At the pond?" she asked weakly.

"Manuel de Silva," Meir said, stubbing his cigar in an ashtray. "Had a wife and three kids in Mexico."

"It appears something frightened him to death," said the Spaniard.

CJ laced and unlaced her fingers. That pond—she should have warned people. Again she remembered her powerless struggle to breathe, and her ragged nails sank into the upholstered chair seat. Max wanted to phone in the accident. She should have let him. The Spaniard stared down at her as if he could see her thoughts.

Meir said, "Please tell us. Didn't you hear a man's dead?"

"Maybe we should lock her in solitary," said the blond man.

"Gentlemen, I'd like to speak with Ms. Reilly alone."

The Spaniard delivered this request quietly, but there was no mistaking the command in his voice. The blond man seemed ready to argue, but when Meir got up and left the office, the blond man followed.

After the door closed behind them, CJ didn't know if she felt relieved or panicked. Once again, the Spaniard gazed into the sample jar as if it might reveal a vision. The pearlescent fluid stirred like the silty white glitter in a child's snow globe. He handed it to CJ, and she took it in both hands like a precious jewel—or a ticking bomb.

Shift

Thursday, March 10
9:35 AM

"Yesterday afternoon, when Manuel de Silva fell into the contaminated pool, witnesses said it froze over. Just like that." The Spaniard snapped his fingers.

CJ flinched. She could feel him watching her reaction. He tilted Meir's desk chair around and sat facing her. Their knees were almost touching. "You know about this," he said.

She placed the jar on the desk and tucked her shaking hands beneath her thighs. Now was the time to confess, before others died. But after all, what did she know? She watched the sifting jar, backlit with sunbeams. In that jar

lay the truth. She longed to test and probe that glittery fluid the way the
pond had probed and tested her.

The man's left eyebrow quirked upward, distracting her. As he leaned
closer, courteous but unsmiling, she noticed again the touches of silver at his
temples. His irises were very black, very hard to read. His manicured hands
rested lightly on his tailored trousers. She noticed his loosened silk tie, his
open collar, his bare throat. Without thinking, she glanced at his mouth.

Immediately, she reddened and shifted away. "Quimicron can't claim this.
It belongs to the world."

"What belongs to the world?"

His black gaze riveted her attention. But she would not let this corporate
mouthpiece bully her. She remained silent.

"You have your father's spirit," he said.

"What?"

"I met your father once. Dr. Reilly lectured in Buenos Aires."

She gawked at him.

When she failed to speak, he said, "You have his eyes."

"Liar." She shot to her feet, knocking the chair backward. "I won't be part
of your lies. If you don't make this discovery public, I will."

The man seemed bewildered. "Carolyn, I promise, there will be no lies."

"And don't call me that. I'm CJ." She pointed to the phone on Meir's desk.
"If you're not lying, phone the newspapers. Let people know about this."

He rose and lifted the desk phone receiver. "What shall I tell them? Shall I
say we've found a lethal material six miles from Baton Rouge, that we don't
know where it came from, or how widespread it is, or how to neutralize it?
Shall I tell them how de Silva died? Maybe we should evacuate the area, do
you think?"

CJ opened her mouth, but his questions confused her. She righted her
chair and sat down.

"Even in Boston, you must have read about the hurricanes." His voice carried an edge. "The first one was called Katrina, remember? The governor ordered an evacuation, but thousands were left behind. They were trapped and
terrified, and that's an ugly combination. It turns decent people into savages."

He circled behind her and grabbed the back of her chair. She sat para-
lyzed, trying to process what he was saying.

"Surely you remember the looting and burning? Everyone in Louisiana remembers, I promise you that." He let go of her chair and began to pace. "People here are teetering on the edge of a maelstrom. Every year, the Mississippi runs higher, and the hurricanes blow harder, and the local citizens are trapped between. Meanwhile, the entire southern edge of this state is sinking into the Gulf. Thousands of acres have gone under, and I'll tell you an open secret, Carolyn. The next public scare may start a bloodbath."

When he paused, CJ bit her thumbnail. He gestured toward the phone. "Do you still want me to call the media?"

She kicked Meir's desk with her bare foot. After a moment, she spat out three words as if they burned her mouth. "I don't know."

"Help us, Carolyn. We have the material contained in an isolated pond. This is our chance to study it and plan a sensible response." He put the sample jar in her hands. Then he clipped his own ID badge to her shoulder strap. When his hand brushed her bare skin, she reddened. He said, "You know where the lab is. Tell me what's in this jar, and I'll give you a job on our science team."

She read the name on his badge, then glanced up. "Roman Sacony?"

He nodded.

She read the badge again. "You're the Quimicron CEO?"

"Correct." His face was unreadable.

She held the jar against her chest, imagining the well equipped lab waiting down the hall. "I'll do it on one condition. Max Pottevents keeps his job."

Ooze

Thursday, March 10
11:15 AM

Roman Sacony glanced at his watch, then squinted up at the sun, a pale white glare behind a film of haze. Cold rain in the morning. Clammy heat at noon. This was spring in Louisiana. The day was getting away from him. He strode quickly through the waist-high weeds, automatically counting strides to measure the distance, a habit he'd developed in youth. He'd ordered the site of the migrant's death to be cordoned off, and he was hiking through the swamp to have a firsthand look at this mysterious quick-freeze pond. Trouble, that's what he expected, and logic told him it might be expensive.

He still didn't know what substance the pond contained. Carolyn Reilly had not yet begun her analysis. After her long night, Dan Meir insisted on driving her home for a shower and rest. Good administrator, Meir, but too sentimental.

Roman jumped over a weed-choked ditch and pondered the bizarre coincidence of the late Dr. Harriman Reilly's daughter working on his cleanup crew. Roman had reviewed her file. He knew about her astonishing IQ, her top grades at MIT, her interrupted studies, and checkered job history. He'd also seen the video of her work in the lab yesterday. The girl knew chemistry. It nettled him that the plant's regular chemist had fallen ill. When Roman needed data, he didn't like to wait.

A white-tailed doe broke through the brush and leaped across his path, heading for the river. He pursed his lips at the pair of spotted fawns that galloped after her. Ahead, machinery droned. This de Silva episode would stir an investigation. Since his company had expanded from Argentina into the US, he could hardly move without exciting some regulatory investigation. Workplace accidents were the worst.

Carolyn Reilly was holding back information. Spoiled white brat. Why couldn't she tell the truth? Still, there was something appealing about her bright hazel eyes. Yes, she was pretty, in a vanilla-crème sort of way. Her short reddish hair reminded him of a feather duster, the way it stuck out from her head. But what was she hiding?

When he mentioned the migrant's death, her cheeks had flushed, and her pupils had dilated, classic signs of deception. Oh yes, she knew something. He counted his steps and analyzed possible scenarios. He had the kind of mind that wouldn't let go of a problem till he'd sliced it a dozen ways and forced a solution.

No one paid him special notice when he approached the trampled area around the pond. In his coverall, breathing mask, and Devil Rays baseball cap, he looked no different from the rank-and-file workers, which was what he preferred. Incognito, he could move about and observe more freely, though the heavy clothing made him sweat.

He watched his field hands. Mexicans, Haitians, dark-skinned Creoles, they were southern people like himself. He squinted across the canal at Building No. 2. Meir's office staff were mostly *Anglos*. That would have to change. He adjusted his breather and resumed pacing.

The crew was just getting started. He counted eighteen rolls of black filter cloth piled up and steaming in the sun. Next to the rolls lay a heap of T-shaped steel posts, too disorganized to quantify. From these materials, and from a load of hay bales that Meir had ordered, his workers were rapidly erecting a silt fence to contain whatever pollutants had coagulated in the pond.

He studied the shallow crescent pool—liquid now, no trace of the alleged ice that had flash-frozen Manuel de Silva. After careful examination and a few measured strides along one bank, he estimated its surface area and guessed at its average depth from the height of protruding tree trunks. Then he did a rough mental calculation of its volume, less than a thousand gallons, maybe four liquid tons. He broke off a willow branch and poked experimentally at the ooze.

Roman knew a lot about manipulating chemical compounds, but only through years of hard study had he learned to maneuver people. That morning, he'd seen the Reilly girl struggling over whether to trust him. He stabbed the mud with his branch and sneered. How predictably these *Anglos* misjudged his accent and his Latin skin. He relished proving them wrong.

To maneuver Reilly, he had used the seductive approach. His wealth and power beguiled women—it was a simple fact that he accepted at face value and used to his advantage. He had calculated its effect on Carolyn Reilly, and already, it was working.

At the pond's edge, he stirred the water with his willow branch and watched brown particles circulate up from the bottom. At heart, he cared more about tasks than people. Yet for all his chilly exterior, Roman didn't see himself as a heartless man. He lived ascetically, ate simple food, rarely drank alcohol. His two vices were dark rich coffee and rough sex. He preferred prostitutes, where the exchange was unambiguous. Only one woman had ever gotten close, and that was long ago.

He adjusted his respirator and thought of Harriman Reilly's daughter. The girl interested him, but she lacked discipline. She splashed her feelings around like heavy perfume, and logic warned him to avoid getting doused.

When his phone vibrated, he unzipped his coverall and reached into his pocket. The Miami office was calling—appointments to be rescheduled, flights to be rearranged. He yearned for a cup of Argentinean espresso, but more than anything, he yearned for the lab report. Waiting irked him.

Strands of green algae caught on his willow branch as he stirred the pond. Certainly, he was eager to learn what pollutants had intersected here in his swamp. If this liquid had indeed formed ice, what extraordinary chemical reaction had absorbed the heat?

The question intrigued him, but pressing business demanded his attention elsewhere, and this pond was not in his schedule. The strands of algae streamed through the water like a dead girl's hair, twisting and writhing in whatever direction he chose to move his branch.

Dr. Harriman Reilly had lectured at the *Universidad de Buenos Aires*. Roman remembered him well. A harsh brilliant man with searing hazel eyes—the kind of eyes Lucifer must have turned on God. Roman hadn't lied when he said the Reilly girl looked like her father. She called him a liar. He tore the algae out by its roots and almost smiled. He had been called worse.

Gulp

Thursday, March 10
5:32 PM

Dan Meir signed the papers for the transfer of de Silva's body back to his family in Oaxaca. Cause of death was given as "accident," nothing more specific. The parish coroner was Dan's old fishing buddy, so between them, they worked out the details.

Elaine Guidry, the personnel officer, sat nearby addressing the manila envelope. Along with the letter of condolence, Meir had written a check for $20,000 to de Silva's wife. He wanted to send more. Contract workers were not covered by life insurance, but Meir had found surplus funds in his supplies budget.

He reached for his box of cigars, then changed his mind. Rich sepia sunlight angled through his window, and gulls wheeled over the canal seeking crawfish. Their squawks sounded peaceful. Halcyon, he thought, a word from one of Elaine's perfume bottles.

"That's about it," Elaine said as she jogged the pages together and stuffed them in the envelope with the check.

When she got up to file the copies, Dan watched her move. Elaine was his second in command at Quimicron. They'd worked hand-in-glove for years, and on days like this, they sometimes talked about retiring. Maybe he could guide fishermen up the bayous. Maybe she could open a day spa. Yeah. Sometimes they liked to dream.

Elaine's full figure gave Dan a comfortable place to rest his attention. She had tanning-bed skin, brassy curls, and eyes as blue as steel. He liked the way her body jiggled like a cluster of plump grapes. He especially favored her derriere. She noticed where he was looking and gave him a better show by bending over the file cabinet. She took out a bottle of Jack Daniels, poured two glasses and handed him one.

"Thank you, doll." He held the glass without drinking.

She said, "Rory's got three shifts working out there. Do we know any more than we did?"

She watched him swirl the brown liquor in his glass, then she moved behind his chair and rubbed his knotted shoulders. With his silver hair and permanent squint, she thought he looked like Clint Eastwood, only shorter. Elaine had been seeing Dan Meir on the sly for sixteen years. Though he had a wife, two grown children, dozens of friends and a new grandbaby, still no one understood as well as Elaine did how he took things to heart.

Usually she tried to make him forget his worries, but today, an uneasy tension pervaded the entire plant. Word was spreading about de Silva's strange death in the unnatural ice. Along the corridors of Building No. 2, people gathered in clumps and whispered. There were no jokes in the break room. Meetings were canceled. Healthy people called in sick. And this morning, one of the computer programmers tried to sneak a handgun past the security station. He claimed it was for self-defense.

So instead of distracting her lover with funny anecdotes and gossip, today Elaine couldn't refrain from asking again, "Dan, do we know any more?"

But the answer he gave didn't settle her mind at all. He gulped half his drink and said, "Not a blessed thing."

Waft

Roman Sacony. CJ had heard stories about Quimicron's chief executive. He was said to own a penthouse bordello in downtown Miami where he entertained cabinet members and admirals. Cunning, that's what she sensed about him. Devious. But that image didn't square with the solemn man working beside her in the lab.

Sheathed in a white smock and latex gloves, he handled the equipment as if the lab were his second home. He'd studied science in school and liked to keep his hand in, that's what he told her. From the way he rushed her along, though, she assumed his real motive was to get the results in a hurry. Roman Sacony came on smooth as glass, but she suspected he was hiding sharper facets.

The unpadded work stool cut off circulation in her bum, and the climate-controlled air felt too still and dry. She straightened and stretched, knocking the rack of tubes at her elbow. Roman glanced up briefly. The pond water in the tubes sifted like pearly milk.

He returned to his task, operating the laser nephelometer to analyze the water's turbidity. His dark profile cast a trim silhouette against the wall as he measured the light scattered through a droplet. She watched him scribble notes on a clipboard.

Slim and wiry-muscled, he must work out, she decided. She didn't realize that she could smell his pheromones and that he could smell hers. Their molecules of sexual scent wafted on air currents too fine for conscious awareness, but in the shadowy subliminal undersides of their brains, both of them recognized the chemical code.

They exchanged sidelong glances. CJ was the first to look away.

Her tight-fitting latex gloves were making her hands sweat. She and Roman had been working for hours, both absorbed by the riddle. She'd been analyzing the sample with a technique called FAIMS—field asymmetric waveform ion mobility spectrometry. But now her test was growing tedious. The electrode probe rested in a small beaker of the pearly colloidal fluid, and as it scanned for ions, the screen painted repetitious, hypnotic line graphs. Her eyelids grew heavy. She toyed with the rack of tubes at her elbow. Some of them had frosted.

Curious, she bent closer. When she took one of the vials in her hand, like magic, the frost reverted to liquid. Had she dreamed the frost? No. Two other vials still glimmered with a white coating. She rested her cheek on the countertop to view the tubes close up. Fanciful arabesques of ice painted the glass with fractal fans and pinwheels, reminding her of winter mornings in Vermont, waking up in her drafty boarding school dorm to find Jack Frost ornamenting her windowpanes. Her breath fogged the glass tubes and turned white.

"Come see this," she called to Roman. But when she looked again, all the frost had melted.

"What?" he asked.

She sat up and rubbed her eyes. "Sorry, thought I saw something. My mistake."

With a slight frown, he returned to his own experiment.

The lab had no external windows, no way to judge time, and CJ had forgotten her watch. Yet she could tell from the way her mouth watered for cheese pizza that the day was far advanced. Overhead, raindrops pelted the metal roof of Building No. 2.

She rubbed her itching nose and watched Roman scribble. It was strange, she thought, how quickly lifelines could change course. Yesterday, she was shoveling toxic muck into barrels. Today, she was rubbing elbows with a sexy CEO in a state-of-the-art chemical lab. But she had no intention of helping him profit from her compound. Whatever this substance was, it emerged spontaneously. It didn't belong to anyone.

She picked up a test tube and shook it till it foamed. Something in this colloidal fluid could freeze-clean water. She marveled at a process no human mind had conceived. A miracle of nature—if you counted the public waste stream as part of nature. By rights, the compound's formula should be treated as open-source shareware, freely available for the common good. That's why she'd accepted this job—to make sure that happened.

Well, among other reasons. CJ's reasons were always a little mixed. Of course, she wanted Max to keep his job. Plus she needed access to Quimicron's lab. Maybe also, at some unacknowledged level, she wanted to spend a little more time with Roman Sacony.

But her main reason, her top number one objective, was to decipher the pond fluid. Simple curiosity—she wanted to know what it was. As she studied the foaming tube, she could almost hear the tiny bubbles hiss and chatter in a secret language. Once she deciphered the formula, she would publish her findings on the Web, and then Harry wouldn't be the only famous chemist in the family.

The problem was, she and Roman had already run the obvious tests, and the results bewildered them. The sample did not generate an EM field or flicker with light. It didn't form a ball that rolled around in her hand. Except for the frost, which she may have imagined, and the foam, which quickly melted, the liquid just sat there at room temperature, clouded and obscure, giving off a faint methane stink as it slowly mixed and stirred with random molecular motion.

Physically, it could be defined as an emulsified "colloid," a fluid in which billions of microscopic particles were dispersed in continuous phase, like star systems in space. Every cubic centimeter held a living zoo—phytoplanktons, diatoms, bacteria, nematodes, amoebas, mold, various types of microinvertebrates. The colloid's largest component by far was ordinary water. And not surprisingly, its second largest component was a clear organic gel called proplastid—a kind of botanical ur-matter found in most plant and algae cells. In other words, swamp ooze.

She remembered studying proplastid in graduate biology. It was an all-purpose gel that could morph into whatever internal "organelles" a plant cell needed to conduct photosynthesis, store sugar, even synthesize chemicals to grow and breed. This particular Devil's Swamp brand of proplastid came from algae. CJ spotted hundreds of free-floating algae organelles in her sample.

Of course, she found the usual laundry list of Devil's Swamp pollutants, too: mercury, lead, cadmium, dioxin, perchlorate, petroleum derivatives—plus an ample load of toluene from the recent spill. Then there were standard river-borne contaminants: detergents, pesticides, dry-cleaning fluids, textile dyes, synthetic sweeteners, birth control hormones, ibuprofen, used motor oil. And the multiplicity of dissolved and particulate solids almost defied count. Among the clays, metals, asphalt, concrete, loam, and glass, CJ found copper ore from the Rockies and metamorphosed rock leached from the Adirondacks.

But more interesting were the infinitesimal crystals that seemed to give the watery gel its shimmer. Each one was sealed in a film of proplastid—like watertight plastic shrink-wrap—and the chips were too fine and lightweight ever to settle out. Plus, there were so many different kinds. At first, she mistook them for extremely fine sand. But when one of the larger crystals passed through her analyzer, she detected a complex alloy.

Fortunately, Quimicron owned a scanning electron microscope, so she isolated a few of the crystal specks for close study. The first one she examined under the SE scope held a layer cake of materials: a sheer metal base, two diaphanous tiers of silicon doped with phosphorous and boron, another metallic film, a coat of plastic, and as a grace note, a whisper-thin sheet of glass.

"It's a microchip," said Roman.

CJ jerked in surprise. "I don't like people peeking over my shoulder."

"Forgive me, but this is fascinating. Those particles on your screen, they're semiconductor chips. That one"—he tapped the layer-cake speck— "if I'm not mistaken, that's a photovoltaic cell."

He moved closer to enlarge the screen image, and when their arms touched, CJ scooted over to give him room.

"Lots of devices use photovoltaic chips like that. Solar-powered radios. Road signs. Outdoor lighting. This probably washed into the river from a landfill." He adjusted the microscope to capture more views of different crystals.

CJ found the variety of microchip designs astonishing. Sealed inside their clear proplastid beads, they were as different from each other as seashells.

"Microchips are used in everything," he went on. "Cell phones, cars, coffeemakers. Landfills are full of them." He pointed to another shape at the edge of the screen that curled like a snippet of transparent tape. "Let's have a look at that."

She centered the glossy shred in the microscope. It, too, carried a shellac of proplastid, and along one edge lay a row of what looked like black piano keys.

Roman smiled. "Three guesses what those are."

CJ wrinkled her nose. "Spider eggs?"

"Bar magnets." He tapped the screen with his pen. "Small deposits of iron, magnetized to store information. I'm guessing that's a bit of magnetic strip off someone's credit card. What else is in your magic jar?"

The SE microscope found plenty more gel-encased particles, and CJ's experience with Internet searches helped identify them. Before another hour had passed, they tagged an alphabet soup of minuscule computer elements: adders, buffers, comparators, decoders, flip-flops, inverters, level translators, monostable multivibrators, parity generators, programmable timers, relays, transceivers.

"Unbelievable." CJ laughed. "We've hit the mother lode of smashed-up computer entrails."

Roman kept count of their inventory. Along with the relatively massive light-emitting diodes and radio frequency identification tags, there were nanochips measuring billionths of a meter, tiny fractions of the width of spider silk. They also found splinters of a shattered Centrino microprocessor, a reset chip from an inkjet printer cartridge, and a quartz crystal from an old wristwatch, not to mention clusters of carbon nanotubes and a scrap of surgical fabric used to reinforce the human abdominal wall.

Their most exciting find, though, was a microarray—a chip dotted with living DNA designed for "biofab"—biological fabrication of living cells for use in organic computer circuits.

"This is too wild." CJ shook her head and laughed.

"Actually, it's the opposite of wild." Roman scrolled through the material safety data sheet they'd found online. "This array was manufactured in 2001 in Cincinnati, Ohio."

"Our colloid is severely miscellaneous," she said.

"What we have here"—Roman tilted the half-empty sample jar—"is an encyclopedia of techno-litter."

His laugh sounded natural for once. She liked the sound of it. She liked his resourcefulness in the lab. The way his black hair waved loose and long around his head, with its glints of silver at the temples, reminded her of Beethoven.

"I suppose we shouldn't be surprised," he went on. "Most landfills leak when it rains, and everything eventually finds its way to the river."

"Yeah, shit runs downhill." She opened her mouth in a wide yawn and leaned back on the lab stool to stretch.

Roman glanced at his watch. "Look at the time. I owe you dinner."

"Pizza," she said without hesitation.

Earlier that day, Meir gave her a ride to the Roach, but she was too keyed up to rest. After a quick shower and change, she gobbled a PowerBar and hitchhiked back to the lab. Since then, she'd had nothing but Coca-Cola. Now she was running on very little sleep. The image of melted cheese on a warm yeasty crust made her rip off the latex gloves and reach for her cell phone. She'd set the Domino's number for speed dial.

"How about a large pepperoni with double cheese?" she said.

"We can do better than that." Roman removed his own gloves and laid them on the counter. "I know an oyster bar with a view of the river. They're open late."

He stood facing her, leaning back on one hip, not quite smiling. Did she imagine a seductive sparkle in his eye? Quickly she glanced away, but the afterimage of his dark Argentinean features lingered. His sexual pheromones had seeped osmotically through her blood and stirred a reaction. She felt tingly. The thought of a one-night fling with her boss made her long to be reckless, and the same impulse that drove her to quit MIT whispered to her now: *Do it.*

But something held her back. Some scruple of loyalty or guilt. In a word, Max.

"I'm not dressed for a restaurant."

"Dressed?" He laughed one short syllable. It sounded less natural than before. "This is Baton Rouge. You look fine."

"We still have work to do," she hedged.

A savage look warped his features as he browsed the instrument displays. Some of the tests were still running, and she sensed his impatience. She felt it, too. So many unanswered questions. After all these hours, they were no closer to learning the colloid's secret.

Roman took a step toward the nephelometer, then came to a halt and stuck his hands in his pockets. "We've made a good start. The team will be here tomorrow."

He meant the science team. Two experts were flying in from Miami. CJ felt ambivalent about meeting them. "I'm tired, Roman."

It was the first time she'd called him by name. Did most people call him Mr. Sacony? She couldn't remember. Anyway, to hell with it. "I spent last night with your guards in the locker room." After saying this, she giggled at how it sounded. Then she slid off the lab stool and swayed. "Whoa. I think I'm dehydrated."

Roman filled a clean test beaker with water from the lab sink, and she drank it. He wiped the dribble from her chin with his handkerchief. "You're exhausted. I forgot about your night of incarceration. Come, I'll drive you home."

She wavered, imagining his car, the contained smell of leather, the intimate privacy. In his car, she might be tempted beyond her scruples. But her Rover was still parked at the end of a dirt road somewhere near the levee. "I have—"

"One condition, right." He arched an eyebrow. "We'll stop for pizza."

Drum

Thursday, March 10
11:45 PM

Later that night, long after CJ had eaten her fill of oily Sicilian crust and gone to bed alone, Max continued to shuffle groggily on a creaking wooden platform, rasping his calloused fingers over his *frottior*. The waterfront bar smelled of urine and smoke, and a cloudburst drummed on the roof. The raindrops kept better time than the *nomm* standing next to him, smacking the congas out of rhythm. Max was playing with a pickup band for fifty dollars, and he needed the money. His five-year-old daughter had to see the doctor again.

Marie kept having earaches. Sonia, his ex-wife, said it was nothing, but Max worried anyway. He agonized over Marie's baby teeth, like satiny seed pearls. He imagined they were growing crooked, or too far apart, or too crowded. He fretted about her lungs. Her chest seemed so thin and delicate.

Yet Marie was a lovely girl. Small for her age but full of sparkling mischief, as quick and lithe as a water sprite. He felt unprepared for such a beautiful daughter. Her fragility made him ache. She'd inherited Sonia's green eyes and brown hair, but she had her father's complexion. And she loved to dance the zydeco.

As Max shambled his heavy limbs in time with the music, Marie's laughter echoed through his head, winsome, merry, like water flowing over round stones. He wanted to write a song like that. Lately, he'd been working out a melody just for her. He pictured her kicking up her little feet to his tune in shiny white patent-leather shoes. He wanted to give her new clothes and a pretty silver necklace. He wanted to send her to a fine school. He wanted so much for Marie, so much more than he'd ever had. Sometimes the volume of what he wished for her crushed him like a wave.

He felt that wave now as his weary fingers scratched the rubboard. He hadn't had a full night's sleep for two days. Almost mechanically, he moved his feet to the rhythm and mouthed the lyrics. Cold spring fog drafted through an open window and soothed him. The rain beat time overhead. Only a little while longer. The bar closed at midnight. Then he could go home.

Drizzle

Friday, March 11
7:45 AM

The sloughs and marshes of Devil's Swamp exhaled a chilly breath of ground fog that hung translucent in the air. Droplets beaded on waxy leaves, and water trickled in rivulets through the spongy biomass of soil and rot. Pools shivered beneath an icy drizzle, and bubbles rose. In the crescent-shaped pond, the dense bottom layer of fluid suddenly inverted to the surface, trapping warmer layers beneath. And the mud sighed with osmotic fullness.

Back at the Roach Motel, CJ found most of the extra-large pizza still waiting on her kitchenette counter when she woke. Barefoot and cold, she stood in her underwear and wolfed down a slice. The two-liter bottle of Coke had warmed to room temperature, but she drank some anyway. She also flipped open her laptop and plugged into the motel's dial-up Internet service.

By the clear morning light, she knew she'd been wise not to invite Roman Sacony into her room. More than once since her father died, she'd awakened to find a stranger occupying her bed. Some brief acquaintance whose unwashed body invaded her sheets. Too many evenings, she had embraced a kind knight—only to find in the morning a troll with sour breath and chin stubble.

Then came Max. Wrong background, wrong job, wrong style, completely unequivocally wrong. Max had remained a knight.

Mist beaded her window and blurred her view of the parking lot. She drummed her fingers on the glass pane. The motel dial-up took an eon to connect. As soon as the browser opened, she Googled Roman Sacony. While the results trickled in, she showered, dressed in serious business clothes and styled her hair for the first time in weeks. She was going to the airport to meet the science team.

The tantalizing enigma of the ice revolved through her stream of consciousness. Roman wanted to know where the heat went, and so did she. Some unprecedented chemical reaction must have absorbed or converted or stored it somehow. And did that same reaction also produce the electromagnetic field? Maybe a downed powerline was trickling current through the water. But there were no power lines in Devil's Swamp.

She browsed her Google results, clicked on *Time* magazine, and read that Roman Sacony held a doctorate in material science from the *Universidad de Buenos Aires*. He hadn't mentioned that. The article described how he'd expanded his family's Argentinean business and established a beachhead in Miami. Under his command, Quimicron SA had swelled into a midsize conglomerate. Roman Sacony was multilingual, a pilot, a marathon runner, never married. He was forty-eight years old—exactly her father's age on the day he died.

She shut the laptop and chewed her fingernail. Something about Roman aggravated her. He was flying back to Miami this morning, and the fact that he would be hundreds of miles away gave her a sense of relief. She dug through the litter on her bed, found her cell phone and called Max.

"Ceegie, what happened? They don' tell me where they took you."

Her conscience wrenched her. She should have called sooner. "I'm fine. Are you up? I'll come over." Max lived across the river in West Baton Rouge, a few miles away.

"I'm workin'," he said. "They got us stakin' out the pond, watchin' to see nobody fall in."

"You're working in the swamp?" Good, she thought. Max still had his job.

"Yeah, and it's raining. Bunch of protestors met us at the gate this morning. They standing in the rain, waving signs, carrying on. Call us 'bird killers.' One *nomm* tried to sneak in."

"Max, is the pond . . . doing anything?"

"Just old sump water. Kind of floury. We got backhoes filling in the little bayou that flows out the bottom. Gonna make sure *djab dile* stay put."

"What did you call it?"

"*Djab dile.* Devil milk. We gonna scoop it up, seal it in barrels. Did you hear about Manuel?"

"Yeah." CJ's attention wandered. Something Max had said triggered a vague alarm.

"Lord, *lamie,* every time I think about what mighta happened to you, I go crazy."

His plaintive baritone weighed on her. "Don't worry about me. I have a new job." She told him about the science team.

"*Sa grand.* That's where you belong." He sounded genuinely pleased.

She cradled the cell phone between her ear and shoulder while she ran a motel shoe-mitt over her black high heels. "Do you know anything about Roman Sacony?"

"Mr. Sacony, he the head man. He live in Miami. Why you asking?"

"He was here in Baton Rouge. We worked together in the lab last night. He's . . . well, not what I expected." She rubbed the soft shoe leather till it gleamed. "He's pretty smart."

"Aw." Max seemed to meditate over this news. He said nothing for a while. She slipped on her shoes. "So what do you think about him?"

"I guess he's rich," Max said softly.

"But can I trust him? Does he mean what he says?"

"Ceegie, I gotta get back to work."

They agreed to meet later, and after she clicked off her phone, she sat on the edge of her bed for several minutes, feeling vexed and not knowing why.

Lather

Friday, March 11
9:52 AM

The general aviation office occupied a new brick building near the south ramp of the Baton Rouge Metropolitan Airport, close to the private hangars. CJ waited alone in the passenger lounge, reading an article about hybrid aircraft. Rain pummeled the metal roof, and water writhed down the window-panes like transparent snakes. She glanced at the clock. Her science team would land soon in the company's Hawker jet, and she was supposed to chauffeur them to the plant and brief them.

She hadn't seen Roman that morning, but she'd met with Elaine Guidry. There were tax documents to complete, nondisclosure forms to sign, policy memos to read and abide by. Now that she'd become a full-fledged employee, the corporation wanted to bind and shackle her in paper.

Waiting in the airport, she remembered how Elaine had rubbed her hands with lotion while they talked, how the lubricious white lather had foamed between Elaine's plump fingers, and how her bracelets had clinked together.

"Mr. Sacony is giving you an extra special raise, sugar." Elaine leaned across the desk, and her powder-blue sweater stretched across her full bosom. "You musta made a real nice impression."

I'm still free, CJ wanted to shout.

Thunder rumbled in the distance. The vinyl airport sofa squeaked every time she moved, and the vase of wilting tulips gave off a fusty reek. She snapped through the magazine as if she meant to rip out the pages.

Through the window, she saw two people crossing the tarmac, leaning into the downpour and trailing identical black zipper bags on rollers. Her colleagues. The magazine slipped to the floor. She felt almost light-headed. This was her first real job working with bonafide scientists on a project of consequence. She hadn't yet acknowledged how much it meant to her. She wiped her sweaty hands on her skirt. Yes, she'd actually worn a skirt.

Her soon-to-be collaborators were pushing through the glass doors, shaking their wet clothes, stamping their feet and looking grim. The first was a tall morose Asian woman, well over fifty, rail thin and boney, with an iron-gray braid coiled at the crown of her head. Even the pouring rain had failed to dislodge her long hairpins. That would be Li Qin Yue, the team leader, a specialist in petrochemical engineering.

Behind her dawdled a lanky young blond man in a dripping black raincoat who squinted through thick fogged glasses. Peter Vaarveen, biochemist.

CJ touched her short pony tail, took a deep breath and went to meet them. In her best Boston manner, she stood ramrod straight, greeted each of them by name, and offered her hand to shake. Quietly, she wondered who she was trying to impersonate.

"I'm CJ Reilly," she said. "So glad we'll be working together."

Peter Vaarveen ignored her and made a beeline for the men's room, while Li Qin Yue glanced briefly at her outstretched hand. "Where's our car?"

CJ stood rock still, holding out her hand, seething. Then she marched out to the rain-lashed parking lot, leaving them to follow as best they could.

"Frankly, I can't understand why Roman hired you," Li Qin Yue said a few minutes later, climbing into CJ's Rover. Soon, they were bowling up Highway 61, clinging to their seat belts as the Rover hydroplaned through standing water. CJ was driving over ninety miles an hour.

"Roman sent me your credentials." Yue had to raise her voice above the din of rain. "You're hardly qualified for this project, despite who your father may have been. But, like all of Roman's young protégées, you're pretty."

CJ glared at the woman, speechless and red. The windshield wipers scraped frantic arcs across the wet glass.

"Lighten up, Yue. We just got here." Peter Vaarveen sprawled in the back seat, using his wet zipper bag for a pillow. He looked about thirty, but his hair was so pale, it gleamed almost white. Even his eyebrows and eyelashes looked bleached. He spoke in the clipped nasally accent of Long Island, New York. "At least Reilly's ABD. That's something."

ABD. All But Dissertation. Yes, that was something. CJ clawed the steering wheel. Those three letters plunged her back into the caustic atmosphere of grad school. The posturing, the backbiting, the corrosive political angling for grant money. Her shoulders knotted, recalling the intense pressure that, every year, drove MIT students to leap from campus towers.

True, she had finished her coursework. All she lacked for the PhD was one groundbreaking experiment and the book-length documentation to explain it—her dissertation—two years' work if she pushed hard. She'd been working on chemical desalinization of ocean water, a cheap new process . . .

But that was her father's world. And Harry died.

She braked hard and skidded onto the turnoff toward the Quimicron plant, spraying the fence with mud.

"Yee-ha." Peter Vaarveen slid across the backseat. "I'm awake now."

Later in the lab, Peter rubbed sleep from his white-lashed eyes and made fresh coffee while Li Qin Yue frowned at CJ's test results. The Chinese woman seemed all skin and bones, and her sallow, age-freckled skin puckered in bags under her eyes. There was nothing soft or lovely about her, yet her ramrod posture spoke dignity. "There's nothing in this analysis but polluted water."

"Right," CJ said.

"This couldn't have created the effects you described."

"Right." CJ clenched her teeth.

"Who collected this sample? None of this has been properly done. We'll have to start at the beginning."

"Right."

"Peter, are you awake? I need new samples. See if you can find your way to the site. You know the control procedures. And take the illustrious Ms. Reilly with you. I can't train a novice today."

"Aren't we in a jolly mood." Peter zipped open his bag and lifted out a rack of empty sample bottles, each labeled and dated. He signaled to CJ. "Lead on, oh illustrious one."

As they left, he winked at CJ and smirked. "The Queen Bitch rules."

CJ's hands balled into fists. "I'll show her who's qualified."

Peter gave CJ a quick sideways perusal, and his thick glasses magnified his eyes like pale blue fish in an aquarium. "Is that how you dress for field work?"

C.J. touched her skirt self-consciously. Under his black raincoat, Peter wore old jeans, a sweatshirt, and sneakers stained with red clay. Why had she donned this ridiculous skirt? "I thought—" She reddened. "Give me ten minutes to change."

"Christ," Peter muttered in his New York twang. "Amateurs."

Seethe

Friday, March 11
11:00 AM

Li Qin Yue worked alone in the lab. Shoulders tight, vertebrae creaking, she reviewed the curious list of techno-trash Carolyn Reilly had recorded in the sample. Some of the notes were in Roman's handwriting. She twisted one foot round and round, making her ankle bones pop. Outside, the rain clouds tore apart in sudden brief bursts of sun, and luminous shafts roved over the sodden earth like spotlights. But Yue didn't notice.

The data did not surprise her. Americans threw everything in their rivers. She pecked scathing notes into her Pocket PC. She herself had been raised in Taipei, an island nation that knew the value of hoarding and husbanding. On her Pocket PC screen, the cross-hatched scars from her aggressive stylus mirrored the crosshatched worry lines on her brow.

While the sample fluid seethed in its jar, her mind lingered four states away in Miami, where she'd been formulating a new composite jet fuel. Hack work, she called it. Demeaning. Slutty. Once upon a time, she had revered the elegance of the Periodic Table. It was the alphabet of the *Tao*, the All That Is, or so she had gushed in an undergraduate essay. But now she whored her knowledge to churn out saleable products. She did it for Roman Sacony.

"Semiconductors, diagnostic chips, benzene rings." She read Reilly's list, and her stylus scratched noisily. Behind her, unseen bubbles formed in the jar and migrated upward. "Bipolar transistors, disintegrated circuits, polysilicon conductors, a working logic gate . . . Working?" She shook her head. "Not likely, Ms. Reilly."

Thinking of the Reilly nymph made her teeth itch. She picked up the jar and shook its milky contents. Her distorted image frowned back from the curved glass.

Li Qin viewed herself as skinny and plain. She didn't try to be charming. Life had gone sour, so she didn't see any benefit in playing sweet. She knew Peter called her the Queen Bitch. The only reason anyone tolerated her, she thought, was for her brains. In her life, three men had loved her, but she hadn't noticed them. The only man Li Qin had ever noticed was Roman Sacony.

She slapped the jar down hard on the counter and turned away, failing to notice its sudden fluorescence of frost.

Smear

Friday, March 11
11:19 AM

As CJ's Rover caromed over the curb and barreled into the Roach's flooded parking lot, she silently railed at herself. Idiot! You always do that. Like you're back in school, turning yourself inside out to please asshole teachers. You don't need the approval of those pretentious geeks. She stomped the

Rover's brake and skidded through a deep puddle of rainwater. When she ground to a stop in wet gravel, she sat clawing the wheel and stewing.

"Harry, get out of my head," she whispered.

Thirty minutes later, dressed in coveralls and waders, she and Peter Vaarveen were picking their way through the muck of Devil's Swamp. The rain had stopped, and as the sun warmed the earth, humidity settled on every stem and leaf like a residue of oil. In addition to the coveralls, goggles, and hip boots, Peter insisted that they both wear respirators. Worse, he had duct-taped their rubber gloves to their sleeves for added protection. Apparently, he viewed the great outdoors as a death zone. His voice rattled through the respirator as he delineated their sampling procedures.

CJ knew the drill. She'd done more than enough fieldwork at MIT, and she hated being lectured by this sarcastic twit. She walked fast through the spongy bog, trying to outdistance him. Peter never got in a hurry over anything. Still, with his long legs and handheld GPS, he had no trouble keeping up.

The area around the pond had been trampled to raw mud by Rory's work crew. Stands of green tupelo and palmetto lay chopped and shredded, stumps uprooted, pepper vines slashed. Even the insects had been sprayed. The long comma-shaped pond lay exposed to full sun.

Sweat trickled under CJ's goggles and ran in her eyes. In her hot coverall, she barely listened at first to Peter's languid instructions. He explained how his sterile collection bottles had been treated with a preservative to maintain sample integrity, and how each bottle had to be kept sealed until the last possible second. Once a bottle was opened, she watched him rinse it with site liquid, then filled it to the top and reseal it so no air was trapped inside. Air might alter the sample's composition, he explained.

Before leaving Miami, he had calculated exactly how much liquid they would need to run all the necessary tests, and he'd studied aerial photographs to identify a grid of sampling sites, both within the pond and in the surrounding sediments. He'd brought measuring devices, stainless steel tools, a list of coordinates, a handheld GPS, and a marker to label each sample by location. He'd also brought a minicassette recorder to dictate field notes.

Grudgingly, CJ began to pay more attention. She felt chagrinned to recall her own sloppy process. No wonder she'd botched the test results. But then, she'd collected her sample at gunpoint. Though she didn't say so, she acknowledged the value of having experts involved, even jerks like Peter Vaarveen and

Queen Bitch Yue. The more accurate their process, the quicker they would learn about the ice—and the sooner she could release the findings. So, like a rank intern, she dogged Peter's steps, carried his tools and followed orders.

"You'll want to check for electromagnetic readings," she suggested, but Peter didn't answer.

Rory Godchaux's crew was just finishing an earthen dam to shut off the small creek that trickled from the pond's lower end. Around the wreckage of steaming mud and stubble, a plastic silt fence sagged under a weight of collected rain, and its drooping black scallops looked like funeral bunting. A few workers were reinforcing the plastic with straw bales.

Rory Godchaux, as dark and knotty as an old walnut tree, sat in his pickup truck supervising. Because the Miami people were watching, he'd ordered the crew to wear full regulation hazmat gear. Everyone looked alike in their coveralls and breathers, but CJ recognized Max's familiar square shoulders and slim hips. He was operating a heavy spiked roller, tamping down the soil around the muddy dam. She waved to get his attention, but he was too busy to see her.

The sample collection took all morning. As the temperature mounted, a greasy haze rose from the wet ground, and the sun turned their waterproof gear to steam suits. Humidity fogged CJ's goggles, and itchy sweat trickled down her legs. Her duct-taped rubber gloves felt like Byzantine torture devices. When Peter wasn't looking, she removed her goggles.

As he was packing to leave, she said it again. "You need to check for an EM field."

A short laugh rattled through his breather. She couldn't see his face. "Reilly, almost everything radiates an EM field. Cars, buildings, power lines. Force fields practically overlap the planet. So leave the thinking to Yue and me, all right?"

"I found an EM field in this pond!"

He snickered. "You probably read the currents around your digital watch."

She threw her tools down in the mud. "Mid-range frequency. Wavelength about one meter."

"Yeah, sure." Peter lifted the rack of bottles and turned to go.

"At least look at your compass. You'll see the needle dancing."

"I use GPS," he said without looking back. "Bring along my tool kit. It's cocktail hour."

"Bastard." She threw a lump of mud at him, but Peter kept walking.

Fifty yards away, Max was standing in the shade with his respirator draped around his neck, drinking water and talking to Rory Godchaux. CJ ran toward him, lumbering sideways through the slurry. When she reached him, she ripped off her sweaty face gear and threw it down. The taped gloves trapped her hands and enraged her. "I need your compass. That jerkwad won't believe I found an EM field." She flailed her arms as if to sling off the gloves.

"Easy. Cool down." Max held her shoulders to quiet her, and he made the mistake of grinning. Rory shook his head. CJ was famous for her rages.

"You think it's funny? Couple of clowns. Just give me the damned compass," she said.

Max tugged off his gloves which, CJ observed, were not duct-taped to his coverall. Neither were Rory's. She scowled at the tape binding her own wrists and found new depths of loathing for Peter Vaarveen. When Max unstrapped his Ranger Joe, she snatched it from his hand and studied the needle, which briefly jiggled back and forth, then settled on one clear direction.

"Tha's true *Noth*, missy, just where it's always been." Rory's chest shook with silent chuckles. "You satisfied the Earth is still round?"

She ignored them both and headed toward the pond.

Seep

Friday, March 11
1:44 PM

Peter had vanished. He must have found someone else to carry his tool kit. CJ buckled the Ranger Joe compass around her wrist, though the heavy band dwarfed her small arm. The needle pointed steadily North. She took her time, scouting around the pond, watching the needle, and whispering, "Where did you go?"

Sheer curtains of heat wavered in the air, refracting the landscape with shining wet mirages. As CJ clambered over the earthen dam, she paused on top to consider the small creek that seeped away below the pond. Its flow was all but arrested. Only a little black water still oozed down its silty bed.

Max would have called the creek a *bayou*, the old Choctaw word for "stream." Yet as CJ shaded her eyes and traced its course across the bog, she saw not a single stream but a tangle of crisscrossing trenches, seeps, and brooks. She gazed toward the horizon where the main channel disappeared. Then she began to follow the water.

Sloshing through warrens of dripping fetterbush and wax myrtle, sinking to her thighs in hyacinth-choked quag, she held the compass out in front like a divining rod and watched its needle for a sign. Fluid welled from the ground like percolating coffee, and the bayou's main channel grew wider and deeper. She hung her breather on a limb and ripped off her duct-taped gloves with her teeth. Everything she touched felt wet and slick. Again and again, she had to wipe moisture from her compass dial.

As she waded along the stream bank, frogs and turtles plopped into hidden pools. A green snake undulated across the water, craning its head at her. Distracted, she stepped into a hole, and the water almost overtopped her hip boots. After that, she took more care, feeling for the bottom with her toe before shifting her weight.

Soon a canopy of hawthorn and deciduous holly closed over her head and transformed the creek into a shady cave. Wild mint lined the banks, and climbing ferns draped in frothy green curtains. CJ didn't know the plant names, but she felt a difference. The cool air smelled fresher. Deep in the shade, a few early white crinum blooms scented the breeze.

The creek grew clear, cool and dark as it gurgled around sunken branches. In the shallows where the water jetted through gravel, a cloud of minnows schooled. She stooped to watch their ceaseless rotation. First one group would take the lead, then the next, each rank moving into the stronger current to feed and breathe, then dropping behind to draft and rest. Like synchronized swimmers, they shifted and kept place, adjusting to minute changes in the stream flow.

She scooped up a handful of water. The liquid pooled in her palm as clear as glass. It looked pure. She sniffed it and found a clean absence of smell. A sudden intense thirst urged her to taste it. She craved its coolness. She held the water to her lips. Then she remembered the EPA report and flung it away. As water trickled through her fingers, the droplets flashed in a chance ray of sunlight, then struck the stream in a cluster of widening rings.

"You've been here," she whispered.

Fifty yards down, the green canopy arched open to reveal a punishing blue sky, and beyond lay the dishwater-gray barge canal. Directly across from Quimicron's loading dock, the creek decanted its pure nectar into the canal's gray swill in a plume of dazzling sparkles. CJ waded to the confluence. She could see the creek's clear plume fanning nearly twenty yards out. And the water looked—unreal.

Reflections emanated from deep inside, from *layers*. Astonished, she stooped till her face hovered inches above the surface. The water glinted like a stack of acetate sheets. She could see the layers with her naked eyes—ultra-thin films with iridescent rainbows sliding between.

She plunged both arms into the water, and the layers shattered. Icy rainbows spiraled through her fingers, and the liquid fan seemed to pixelate. Each tiny sparkle grew linear, hard-edged, like a machine-stamped square of quicksilver. For an instant, the glittering fan trembled with agitation around her arms and legs. Then it dashed away and diffused into the gray canal. And CJ's compass danced.

Stew

Friday, March 11
6:20 PM

Carolyn Joan Reilly knew about pure water. When she was just a brainy little school kid, Harry took her along to the Kyoto World Water Forum. Bright-eyed and susceptible to strong impressions, young Carolyn perched in the front row for a week, taking notes.

She knew that water covered eight-tenths of the planet, but it surprised her to hear that less than 3 percent of it was fresh, and most of that was either frozen or locked underground. She'd never imagined fresh water was scarce. Yet humans had fought over water since their earliest history, and human-built reservoirs had shifted enough weight on the Earth's surface to alter its planetary spin.

When Carolyn learned that people dumped two million tons of filth into the Earth's fresh water every day, she immediately got online and transferred her entire personal savings of $3,255 to the World Water Organization. Young Carolyn was not a believer in moderate deeds.

"One child every eight seconds." That was the phrase that stuck in her mind, that and the graphic photos of babies dying from waterborne illness. Those grainy, black-and-white little faces obsessed her. "Water pollution causes 80 percent of third-world disease," she wrote in her notebook. When her father's lecture promised salvation through chemistry, she wanted to believe him.

Years later, in Max Pottevent's West Baton Rouge apartment, she paced the narrow path between his bed and the TV, remembering. Hot spring air breathed through the open window, and hot perspiration collected in her hair.

"How does it filter out the impurities? Chemical flocculation? Electrolysis? Maybe it gives the pollutants an electrical charge, then repels them away from its EM field."

"Tell me again, what is the EM field?" Max liked to watch her theorize. He liked the way her hazel eyes lit up.

"It's both an electric field and a magnetic field. The electric force makes electrons oscillate back and forth, and the magnetic force makes them spin in circles."

Max laughed gently, trying to picture this craziness. "Sound like cha-cha-chá."

CJ rapped the top of an oversized stereo speaker. "This minute, the colloid may be dissolving in the canal. We may never know what's in it."

Max's apartment was barely larger than her motel room, but he'd wedged in a confused assortment of hand-me-down furniture and mismatched audio equipment. A network of wires spread like veins across the ceiling and streamed down the paint-chipped walls to link his various components. His *frottior*, the corrugated rubboard he wore on his chest and rubbed with his fingers to make zydeco rhythm, hung on his wall like tribal armament. He watched CJ twist and pivot and retrace her steps.

"Those dweebs won't listen to me. They aren't finding a damned thing in the lab samples. If it weren't for that dead worker, they'd say I dreamed the whole episode."

"You'll feel better after you eat." In the kitchen alcove, Max whistled a soft tune and chopped okra on a small wooden board by the sink. He'd already diced a bowlful of celery, peppers, and tasso smoked pork. In a pot on the stove, garlic and filé powder simmered in olive oil, suffusing the air with a savory tang.

She flopped on his bed and kicked at the loose covers. The room felt muggy and close—why couldn't Max install an air conditioner? Her lower back burned with dull pain. She wanted her damn period to start.

"Madam Yue went ecstatic over a few silly nanoparticles," she said, thinking of the sample. "Half-organic, half-synthetic. She thought she'd found a new branch in evolution. But I looked them up on the Net, and they're just a man-made chemotherapy virus that targets a certain kind of tumor. They probably rotted out of the gut of some cancer patient who suicided in the river."

Max winced at the image. CJ was twitching, kicking her heels into the mattress. He tried to distract her. "Girl, help me cook this dinner. Ol' Max teach you a skill. You ever use this tool before?" He held a can opener.

She got up and absentmindedly ran her finger along the cans of tomatoes and sweet corn he'd arranged on the counter. "What if the colloid dissipates, and we never find it again? It can purify water, Max. If we could mass produce that process, think what it could mean."

Max opened the can of tomatoes. "This stew taste better with fresh vegetables, but the season's too early."

"We have to look for it." She reached across the counter and squeezed his arm. "Now, Max. Tonight. We have to borrow your uncle's canoe."

She peered up at him with all that crazy eager shine in her eyes, that shine he could never resist. She witched him, that's the excuse Max wanted. But he knew it wasn't true. Everything he did for her, he did with open eyes. The swamp was dangerous, and she was likely to be rash. He knew better than to yield, but when she said his name that way and beguiled him with those eyes, he suffered.

A few weeks ago, he had taken her fishing in Bayou Grosse Tete using his Uncle Nebulon's pirogue. That was a good day, just the two of them off away from other people. He taught her to bait the hook and watch the current. As a courting gift, he gave her a pair of castanets. She loved them, she said. He showed her how to hold the wooded shells in her palm, hook the cord over her thumb, and clap a zydeco rhythm. They laughed a lot that day, and he never once got the feeling she was sizing him up.

"Please help me find it, Max. I need you."

He dumped the tomatoes into the pot, and the oil spattered. Before he could answer, she said, "I rented a dive suit."

He dropped his spoon. "You rented what?"

"I can't find the EM field anymore. I think it may be lying on the bottom of the canal."

Max turned off the stove and faced her. "You not going in that evil water again."

She set her mouth in the way he'd come to recognize, and he groaned softly. *"Lamie,* it kill once. It'll kill a second time, I promise you."

For an instant, her hazel eyes went dark. She remembered the pond, the panicked suffocation, the fear that moved up her spine like a cold hand. But next, she saw only the pixelating fan of rainbows. Those *layers.* She had to know what made them. Her face flushed with adrenaline. "Are you saying I have to do this alone?"

Dip

Friday, March 11
10:09 PM

The canoe paddle dipped in a steady plash and trickle as Max eased his uncle's pirogue through the barge canal. Fog blanketed the water, and Quimicron's mercury floodlights cast a violet sheen through the mist. After moonset, the night had turned damp and chilly. CJ couldn't get used to how fast the weather changed in Louisiana.

Max sat in the stern, powering them forward with smooth strong jay strokes, while she wrestled into her scuba gear.

"If you see any sign of ice—" he said.

"I promise, Max, I'll surface immediately."

"Immediately," he repeated, giving her a stern look, though she couldn't see him in the dark.

She'd rented the commercial drysuit from a mom-and-pop outfit in Port Allen. When they asked for her scuba certification card, she'd flashed her Quimicron badge, spun a quick tale about a rush project, and promised to fax her credentials later. It was her Quimicron badge that convinced the owners. The hope of getting more work from one of the largest corporations in the parish made them willing to bend the rules.

HAZMAT blazed in orange letters across the dingy black drysuit. Made of vulcanized rubber and nylon layered with chemical-resistant coatings, the suit crackled and squeaked as she tugged it on. Compared to its bulky squeeze, her coverall had been a light summer dress.

The suit's baggy legs ended in watertight drysocks, reminding her of the awful bunny feet in her childhood pajamas. She despised the clammy drysocks, almost as much as she hated the locking ring system that connected her gloves to her sleeves. The drysuit felt like a straightjacket. She squeezed into the neck yoke that would connect her integrated dryhood and breathing mask. Once locked into the suit, no part of her skin would be left exposed. That offered some comfort.

Owls cooed as she yanked the shoulder zipper closed, then examined the dryhood, pretending a confidence she wished was real. The guy at Port Allen had showed her how to rig the complicated regulator, and CJ had a quick memory, but it was hard to do everything in the dark. A cold rain had been spitting off and on, pinging their boat with a sharp pecking sound. When she lifted the air tank, it slipped and crashed against the bottom of the pirogue.

Max whispered, "Go easy, child."

"Don't call me child." She was afraid to tell him she'd never dived before. The closest she'd come was snorkeling in the Bahamas. "It's only forty-five feet deep," she said in a fake casual tone.

She'd already raked the Internet for every available fact about the barge canal. She knew the Corps of Engineers maintained its depth at forty-five feet to accommodate ocean-going freighters. And according to an online scuba manual, she could stay at that depth for up to eighty minutes—if her air lasted. CJ had no idea how long a tank of air would last. Her pressure gauge read three thousand pounds per square inch. Three thousand sounded like a lot.

Always keep breathing, the scuba Web site cautioned, and ascend slowly to avoid decompression sickness. The site offered pages of verbiage about the importance of training and certification, but CJ assumed that was propaganda. After all, people did this for fun.

Cool fog seeped around her ears and made her shiver. *R-r-r-rip!* Max yanked a length of duct tape from the roll. In the distance, a night bird screeched, and nearby, something large plopped into the water. CJ could hear it swimming. She assured herself it was a bullfrog.

Max taped the field finder to her left forearm, wrapping the duct tape around and around. To her thigh, he affixed the submersible electric current sensor. She'd rented the instrument to look for electricity trickling through the water. If she found it, that would explain the EM field. Then she'd simply have to track down the source, maybe a faulty connection at one of the nearby factories, loose cable, ungrounded generator, something like that.

Max clicked her submersible flashlight to check the battery. "Ceegie . . ."

She kissed him. "You're too good to me."

When she drew away, he touched her cheek, and on impulse, she fell toward him again. They kissed longer, and as their salivas merged, his musky scent brought a flush to her skin. He seemed to be radiating waves of attraction like a hot dark lodestone. Without conscious will, their bodies aligned. As she pressed her mouth against the soft thudding artery in his neck, her air tank smacked the gunwale.

He kissed her ear and laughed. "You want to make love in this pirogue?"

Her hazel eyes glittered. "We did it before."

He embraced her, but the clumsy tank and scuba gear got in their way. They grappled and bumped awkwardly. "Let's go back to my room," he whispered.

His words broke the spell, and she drew away. "Later. After we're done."

Where the unnamed creek drained into the canal, Max set their anchor, and CJ fumbled with her flashlight. Fog gathered around them. She sprinkled Listerine over the latex mouthpiece inside the breathing mask. It looked chewed and dented by a hundred sets of teeth. With a grimace, she tugged on the hood and stuck the nasty thing in her mouth. It tasted like an old tire. Max helped her seal the neck yoke.

She found herself panting. The mask obscured her vision, and the circus-clown flippers tripped her up when she tried to move in the pirogue. The tank felt like an anvil strapped to her back. Finally, she swung her flippered feet over the gunwale, sucked a deep breath through the mouthpiece and mentally reviewed the rental guy's instructions. Had she attached everything properly? Was the air turned on? She lashed her sample jar with a lanyard around her wrist, then rolled over the gunwale and fell in.

Burble

Swirling darkness. A roar of bubbles. The cold penetrated her suit.

Her flashlight splintered through turbid green murk, and the mask narrowed her view like side-blinders. Filaments of algae floated in front of her, and through the watery roof above, Quimicron's floodlights wavered like agitated ghosts. She was sinking.

Where was her depth gauge? Her ears began to ache. She batted through the water searching for the long snaking hose that held her console of gauges, but she couldn't find them.

Deeper darkness. She felt tipsy, disoriented. When she kicked her ill-fitting flippers, her left calf cramped, and she had to stop. She kept sinking.

Idiot, don't panic. You can do this.

At last, she remembered the trick of clearing her ears. She squeezed her nose through the latex mask and tried to sneeze. Abruptly the air trapped in her ear canals evacuated with a painful, screeching hiss. Above, the wavering floodlights faded to black.

Weights. The rental guy had stuffed her pockets with lead weights to help her descend. The guy had showed her the quick-release tabs in case she needed to dump the weights. And there was a vest to inflate, to compensate for the weights. The buoyancy compensator, that's right, the BC. She found the BC pull cord and yanked hard. But instead of inflating, the BC released a fountain of air bubbles, and she sank even faster.

A low raspy wail echoed inside her mask, and she realized it was her own shriek muffled by the mouthpiece. She couldn't remember what to do. Then Harry's snide laugh resounded in her memory. "You overestimate your intelligence, Carolyn, as your mother did."

"No," she said aloud, biting the mouthpiece. Slowly and deliberately, she reached behind her hood and located the hoses connected to her tank regulator. As she continued to fall steadily into the murk, her glove slid along the left hose and followed it to the end, where the console of gauges dangled. Illuminated by her flashlight, the depth gauge read thirty-four feet. Not so deep. Relax.

The empty sample jar floated above her arm on its lanyard, exercising a gentle upward tug. She felt along the front of her suit for the release tabs to dump her weights, and her hands closed on a pair of large cylindrical handles. "Yank 'em hard," the guy had told her. Okay.

But not yet. Not until she found the colloid and took a better sample. She directed her flashlight beam onto the field finder. Oh yes. The EM field was pulsing. She bent to read the sensor taped to her thigh. The sensor showed weak electrical current zipping through the cold water.

"I was right," she gurgled aloud through the mouthpiece. "You're down here on the bottom."

As she watched the sensor, the electric current alternated rhythmically to and fro, as steady as surf. Then a strange sensation enveloped her—a premonition—so slight at first that she didn't understand what caused it. But as she continued to fall, its origin became obvious. The water below was glowing.

She sank into a region of a million tiny flashes. Each infinitesimal wink flared almost too swiftly for her eye to register, but together they gave the water a faint milky light. Deeper still, the flashes came thicker and faster, and soon she was surrounded by luminous agitation, like snowy static on a TV screen. Her current sensor went wild, and she laughed. "You!"

The display made her forget how cold the beautiful liquid was growing. She felt like an astronomer sighting a new galaxy. It was just at that moment that her flippers touched down on the bottom and her tank struck a rock.

Metal on stone, the loud *clang* echoed through the water, and at once, the flickers vanished. As she plunged into the silty bottom, her flashlight showed nothing but muddy clouds stirring up from the canal bed. She came to rest sprawled on her side, and she held still, breathing in shallow pants, hoping the flickers would return. When she switched off her flashlight, chilling darkness closed in.

Minutes passed. She began to shudder with cold. The thought of checking her air gauge weighed on her mind, but she didn't dare turn on her light and frighten away the flickers.

Frighten them? CJ, you're an idiot. They don't have feelings.

Yet she couldn't shake the sense of a presence in the water. She felt it sucking the heat from her body. You. What are you? *You killed once.* She took fast shallow breaths.

"Use your logic," Harry's voice punched through the cold. "Every phenomenon has a scientific explanation."

She longed to turn on her flashlight to get a better view of her sensor screen, though the small unit couldn't give her much data. Damn, she needed better equipment.

So, okay, maybe the flashes came from foxfire. Or maybe from light-emitting diodes like the ones she found in the sample. But why had the flashes stopped?

She chewed the old mouthpiece. It happened when her tank struck the stone.

She had no idea how long she'd been underwater, but her teeth were chattering. She couldn't lie in the frigid mud forever. She was on the point of pushing up, but her mind kept circling on the flashes. Somehow, the sound of her metal tank hitting the rock had stopped the flashes. Could this extraordinary liquid *respond to sound?*

Carefully, she switched on her light and unscrewed the sample jar lid. A burble of air rushed from its throat and wobbled upward, rapidly expanding in size. She saw the sphere of air double, then double again as it rushed toward the surface. Then the dark cold water seemed to close around her like a tomb. With a shaky hand, she replaced the lid on the full jar of liquid. Then she checked her air.

"Jesus!" she hissed through the watery mouthpiece. The gauge was verging into the red zone—less than five hundred pounds of pressure left. She had to reach the surface fast.

She grasped the release handles to dump her weights. But she paused. Ascend slowly, the Web site had warned. If she dumped her weights, this clown suit would bob to the surface like a balloon, and her lungs would expand like that air burble from her jar. How was she supposed to ascend slowly? If only she could remember how to inflate the buoyancy compensator.

As an experiment, she pushed off from the muddy bottom and tried to kick her way up in the loose, oversized fins. This merely stirred up more silt and gave her another leg cramp. After a short struggle, she sank back to the canal bed. The rental guy had loaded her down with far too much weight.

She checked her air gauge again. Only three hundred pounds. She was breathing fast, using too much air. She grasped the weight release handles and whimpered.

You're an idiot, CJ.

"Like your mother," Harry's voice resounded. She gnawed the bitter mouthpiece.

Calm down. Think it through. The canal floor slopes up on either side. You can walk out.

She sat in the mud and tried to tug off the flippers, but her gloved hands were numb with cold. Next, she tried to estimate which side of the canal would be nearest. West, she decided, away from the Quimicron plant. She checked the compass in her gauge console, but the needle danced wildly. The EM field was still pulsing. She decided simply to walk in a straight line. But when she tried to move, her flippers caught in the muddy canal bed, and she tripped.

Think, CJ. Turn around. Walk backward.

The gauge read one hundred pounds of pressure. She moved. Lifting one flipper from the mud, setting it down, lifting the other, she hobbled backward through the frigid dark water with no guide but a terrible intuition. Gradually, the canal bed sloped upward. How far was the bank? Which bank? Notions flitted across her mind. Max waiting in the pirogue. Harry scorning her incompetence. Her mother—absent. *Will she care when I die?*

Without warning, the flashes returned. They didn't flicker like random static this time. Instead, they pulsed in unison, making the water blink on and off as steady as a heartbeat. CJ watched, amazed. The blinks were synchronized. Almost unconsciously, she paced her steps and breathed in time with the blinks, gliding backward through a nimbus of illuminated milk.

The water grew warmer. Much warmer. Soon, a foam of tiny bubbles seemed to buoy her up. Walking came easier. She no longer had to fight against the heavy weights. The microbubbles rose around her like champagne carbonation, and the effervescence seemed to lift and carry her along.

When air stopped flowing through her mouthpiece, she panicked only for a second. Then a curious detachment overtook her. Here was death. She could simply relax and let it take her. She had imagined it so many times. Maybe this was the moment.

But the water kept blinking and fizzing, buoying her limbs, almost urging her along. She exhaled her last breath very very slowly, wondering not about death at all, but about the bubbles. What triggered their release? And what kind of gas were they? She would have to find out about those bubbles.

And suddenly there was Max, hauling her to the shore. He had followed her movement by the bubbles. She clawed at her suffocating hood. The rubber was so blistered with acid lesions that Max was able to tear it open with his hands. When air touched her face, she inhaled a loud raking wheeze of swampy freshness. Max hugged her to his chest. They were sitting in two feet of silt near the canal's western bank. She had walked out.

Drool

Saturday, March 12
5:16 AM

Except for an occasional shiver, the canal bordering Devil's Swamp lay quiet. In the morning cold, its warm upper layer vaporized with glacial slowness, spewing lethargic geysers of mist two inches high. Beneath the surface, digesting microbes effervesced methane, and lazy currents swashed against the banks.

Dan Meir stood on the dock of Gulf-Pac Corporation, Quimicron's next-door neighbor, one of the five other factories lining the barge canal. Meir zipped his coat one-handed while, with the other hand, he clutched his phone and replayed his wife's voicemail. She'd left the message sometime yesterday. Their youngest son was getting married.

They'd come to this—he and his wife—exchanging their most intimate messages through voice recordings at AT&T. He would try to remember to call her back. Little Danny was getting married. He gnawed his cold cigar.

Near the end of Gulf-Pac's ruined dock, Hammer Nesbitt and Roman Sacony inspected broken chunks of concrete. A section of the canal bank had caved in, undermining part of Gulf-Pac's dock and nearly drowning their surprised night watchman. Gulf-Pac blamed the accident on Quimicron's recent chemical spill, and Roman had flown back from Miami without stopping to pack.

"This ain't the only cave-in, just the biggest." Hammer Nesbitt dug his little finger in his ear. He looked rheumy-eyed and grizzled from lack of sleep. "There's mud slides all along this section of the canal."

Hammer managed the Gulf-Pac plant, producing soil conditioners and herbicides for American farmers. He was jowly large-bellied Texan, over six-and-a-half feet tall, and when he stood next to Roman, Meir thought they looked like Mutt and Jeff.

Meir felt sympathy for the Texan. Hammer had a mess on his hands, what with his dock out of commission. To Meir, the caved-in bank looked like glazed ceramic. He'd seen that effect at a beach once, where lightning struck the sand. But he didn't mention that point. Hammer was already riled enough.

"I'm drillin' bore holes under my ring levee as we speak. Gotta check and see if it's still sound." Hammer pointed his finger menacingly at Roman. "You know what that costs? I guess you'll find out."

Meir noticed how Roman's nostrils widened. Impatience—or contempt? Meir didn't know his elegant CEO very well. Roman Sacony was too aloof, too focused on business, not a guy you could relax and share a beer with. Meir watched curiously to see how the cool Miami capitalist would mix with his irascible Texas poker buddy. Like matches and gasoline, he expected.

Too bad. Meir believed in getting along with neighbors. A little chitchat, a few favors, a touch of social lubrication went a long way. You just had to know how to communicate.

Crows squawked from the hackberry trees, and a chill wind whipped the men's nylon jackets. A front had moved down from Canada. Meir mouthed his cigar and examined the dark clouds streaming overhead. When that cold moisture met the warm air over the Gulf, there would be hell to pay.

"It ain't natural." Hammer spritzed mud off his tooled leather boots at a water spigot. His Texas drawl rose and fell with the wind. "My people say the canal's pH is way down. And the water's too fuckin' cold for this time of year. You drop a thermometer in there and see."

A Gulf-Pac skiff milled up and down the canal, illuminating the early morning fog with spectral searchlights. Roman measured the size of the cave-in with his eyes. Above the glazed concavity, tufts of burnt crabgrass still clung to the sheer-cut edge. With quick agility, he jumped down from the dock and climbed into the sandy hollow. The walls felt as hard and smooth as porcelain.

He was still wearing the suit he'd worn in Miami the day before, and the wind cut through his light pants. Through most of his weary flight back, he had teleconferenced with Gulf-Pac's executives. Now his eyes hurt, and his right ear felt bruised from hours on the phone. One of the other neighboring plants had lost nothing more than a set of stairs leading down to the waterline, yet the manager insisted on compensation. Roman shoved his hands in his pockets and counted his change by feel. Pure greed drove these northern *bastardos*. They knew his toluene spill couldn't have caused this.

He took a coin from his pocket—a thin US dime—and scratched the glazed sand. The material flaked away like mica. It looked blistered, almost crystallized. He picked up some of the flakes and folded them in a handkerchief. Then he noticed the smug fat Texan eyeing him.

Americans, these pompous white-skins called themselves. As if they owned the entire Western hemisphere. Wasn't he American, too? Didn't his native pampas wave with golden grain? And didn't his Andes Mountains gleam with purple mist? Could any place be more beautiful than Mar del Plata, his childhood home?

He eyed Hammer Nesbitt and thought of his mother's yellow porch by the sea. How many afternoons he had languished there, reading his hoard of *Time* magazines to polish his English. How many hours he had brooded over the slick ads for wristwatches and cars. Didn't his America shine as spacious beneath God's shedding grace? Yet the victories and tribulations of his southern continent hardly ever won a place in *Time.* How he had despised and envied the flashy *Anglos* for ignoring him.

That was the past, he reminded himself, flipping the U.S. dime in his hand. Today, the *Anglos* were his customers and neighbors. He turned his back on Hammer and swallowed hard. Subpoenas were already mounting on his desk. Gulf-Pac had more lawyers than profits these days. Ah, but they would not find this *Latino* easy to bend.

"Hammer's worried about the EPA," Meir explained to Roman, warming his hands with his breath. The wind burned his ears crimson.

Hammer took out a handkerchief and noisily blew his nose. "That's right. I don't like those yappy government dogs snoopin' around. You got to clean up this mess pronto."

"Clean up your own goddamn mess," said Roman.

Meir relit his cigar. While Nesbitt ranted about the toluene spill, Roman stepped over the orange barrier to get a closer look at the water. A reek of chemicals and rotting vegetation rose from the canal, and one whole corner of the concrete dock had broken away, exposing twisted iron rebar.

Roman noticed a curious fungal growth clinging to the piers under the dock. When he stooped to examine it, he saw a globby buildup of what looked like tree sap or glue clustering in transparent layers. With each small splash of ripples, the growth seemed to drool a few millimeters higher up the piers.

The globby masses glistened with wetness. Roman knelt and probed the nearest one with his Montblanc pen. Instantly, all the sap on all the piers splashed back to the water. The growths fell *simultaneously*—as if they were linked. Not a trace of the sap remained. Roman examined the tip of his pen. It was dry.

He kicked a loose lump of concrete into the canal, and its liquid *plunk* echoed. This morning, he was scheduled to negotiate pricing with his Panama shippers. Also, he had to firm up an oil refinery deal in Mobile, Alabama. On top of that, a Brazilian banker was flying to Miami to discuss a new natural gas port in Fortaleza. Roman's thoughts whirled in a mélange of English, Spanish, and Portuguese.

His company was stretching in many directions this year, acquiring new sites, expanding product line, diversifying its business model. For a decade, he had logged eighty-hour weeks, amassing the critical elements for this advance. He'd borrowed a great deal of money, and these three deals would be crucial. He didn't need this Baton Rouge snafu, not now.

Yet here he stood in the reeking Louisiana wind, shivering with cold and sensing instinctively that his overfed, overbearing Texas neighbor was right. The cave-in was not natural. Neither was the colloidal decoction in the pond, and logic assured him the two phenomena were connected. Something had gone very wrong here. To prevent further lawsuits, he should seal off the canal at once.

But that would not be an easy task. The barge canal was a public waterway serving five other companies besides his own. This had to be handled with discretion, and Roman knew that he, personally, would have to persuade the authorities and the other company owners to agree. He scowled at the green canal water, calculating its depth.

When he tossed his shiny US dime in the water, it sank with a fluent kiss. Down it sifted, glinting reflections, till it vanished in the blurry depths.

"Where did it go?" Roman said.

Meir squinted. "Your dime?"

"No. The sand. There should be a hundred cubic yards of sand from the cave-in. Where is it? There's no current to wash it away."

Hammer Nesbitt moved to the dock's edge and said, "Maybe it spread out over the bottom."

"Get divers and lights. Get photographs." Roman scowled. "We'll talk later."

His phone vibrated, and while Meir and Hammer Nesbitt took shelter from the cold, he checked the screen to see who was calling so early. A name he didn't recognize.

Spew

Saturday, March 12
5:44 AM

Across town in a windowless office, Hal Butler swung his hairy feet off his desk and sat bolt upright. "Roman Sacony? Uh. Hello." He hadn't expected to reach Quimicron's chief executive officer.

The nightshift manager must have routed his call straight through to Sacony's cell phone. This was a miracle for which Hal Butler had not prepared. He slapped magazines and books off his desk, searching for a pen. The multimillionaire Quimicron CEO was considered visiting royalty in Baton Rouge. What a coup to get Roman Sacony live on the phone.

Fumbling for blank paper, Hal gave his credentials as publisher and editor of the *Baton Rouge Eye,* the state capitol's only alternative newspaper. His words spewed out, though he neglected to mention that he was the tabloid's sole employee. While Roman complained about the early hour on Saturday morning, Hal fished for the pencil he'd stuck in his wiry copper hair.

Hal practically lived in his cubbyhole office, situated above the quick-print storefront owned by his cousin, where his idiosyncratic journalism surfaced each week on crisp fresh newsprint the same color as his skin. Hal looked about forty years old, but in fact he was thirty-two. Thin of limb and chest, his body fat had localized in his low-slung belly. Hal Butler did not get out much.

Without windows, his reality lost the rhythm of day and night. He experienced the world by phone, Internet, TV, streaming audio, and mail order.

Through the years, his sheltered existence had sharpened his senses. He often got his best interviews in the odd hours. He scribbled Sacony's name on the back of a magazine and said, "What's going on in your swamp?"

Hal hadn't heard about the frozen pond or the cave-in. His timing was a coincidence. He'd gotten a tip about mysterious midnight lights in Devil's Swamp. *The Eye* wasn't above running an occasional ghost story for local color.

"Wonder what the EPA will think about your secret late-night activities?" Hal pressed.

Sacony barked a laugh. "You're on a fishing trip."

"Uh-huh, I plan to bring my fishing boat up your canal." Hal had no idea what his threat would yield, but Sacony's response surprised him.

"You're welcome to visit, Mr. Butler. Drive out to our plant, and my assistant will give you a tour. I hope you'll do an article on our new pipeline construction system. We have a patent pending."

Sacony rattled off so much boring minutiae about pipeline stumps, bearers, and connector pins that Hal's coffee went cold. To shut him up, Hal agreed to take the press kit, mentally crossing the Devil's Swamp ghost story off his list. Looking back later, Hal felt like an ass for letting Sacony bamboozle him. But Hal's time was coming.

Lick

Saturday, March 12
5:55 AM

CJ woke with a shriek.

"Shhh," Max whispered, wrapping her in his arms. "You been dreaming."

She clasped her legs around his waist and pressed into his body heat. A damp draft was trying to seep under the blanket. Max had left his window open. What was the dream? Her cheeks were wet from crying. She felt ill.

Max rubbed between her shoulder blades and kissed her eyebrows. "It's early. Saturday morning. Go back to sleep."

"I'm such an idiot."

"Naw, girl. That's not right. You the most intelligent person I ever met."

"Intelligence is overrated." She pulled the pillow over her head. Mornings were the most difficult, waking up, finding she was still alive. Last night, she'd come close to the judgment, the final escape. But then—

"You just lookin' for your sync is all." Max stroked her hair. "You got the music. Just got to find the down beat."

She turned and kicked the covers, letting in the cold. "I made insane decisions last night. It's like I can't escape my mother's genes."

CJ had told Max about her mother. Feckless, whimsical, weak, Carolyn Joan *mater* had abandoned her husband and tiny daughter, not to save the world, not to rescue the weary or solace the sick. Not even to elope with a lover. She'd gone to California to study glassblowing, that's what Harry said. CJ remembered the sparkly glass animals her mother sent one year for Christmas. CJ had smashed each one with a rock.

"*Lamie,* you got to calm down." Max cupped her round bottom in his hands and moved her closer. "You 'xpect too much. Sometimes you forget the Lord made us all outta mud."

"Is that so?" She nuzzled closer.

"Yes." Max kissed her hair, her neck. "You know what mud is?"

"No, what is mud?" She licked his chest. His nipple tasted of salt.

"Mud is everything in the world all mixed up together." He kissed her mouth, long and thoroughly.

"Mixed up, that's me." She slid her hand down his taut belly and gripped his penis.

He groaned and moved closer and entered her. They rocked in the rumpled sheets of his bed, ignoring the cold, making the wooden headboard creak back and forth. She crawled on top, and when she began to climax, her back arched, her eyes shut, and she screamed through her teeth, letting the spasms wash through her, hoping they would wash her clean.

Drop

"A genuine nutcase." Peter Vaarveen grinned and batted his white eyelashes. He was lounging in the Quimicron lab, drinking Starbucks. A line of crimson sunburn underscored each of his eyes, where his plaster-white skin had been exposed between his goggles and respirator. His thick glasses magnified the humor in his eyes. "Yeah, this is macadamia deluxe."

CJ bit through her thumbnail when he dropped her ten-page report in the wastebasket. She'd spent the last two hours writing up her canal dive, worrying over the adjectives and laying out plans for collecting more data. Peter dismissed her findings in less than two minutes.

She retrieved the crumpled pages. "Go see for yourself if you don't believe me."

"See what? Fairy dust in the water? ET lights? Maybe it's the spirits of drowned river rats."

"Asshole." She squeezed past him and headed for the door.

"Think twice before you show that report to the Queen Bitch." He gave CJ a wink. "She'll kick you off the project. Doesn't matter how much tail you're giving Roman Sacony. When it comes to the science team, the QB rules."

"I am not—" CJ realized she was blushing. Without thinking, she wadded up her report and threw it at Peter's laughing face. Then she stalked out of the lab.

Peter's wisecrack made her skin burn. But however much he infuriated her, she knew he was right about the Queen Bitch—Queen Bones would be a better name. Stomping down the empty echoing hall, CJ realized that without better data, Yue would annihilate her. She halted, retraced her steps, then halted again. Building No. 2 felt hollow and deserted on Saturday morning, like a refrigerated morgue. Despite the cold weather, the AC was pumping hard.

CJ ran down a flight of stairs, paused at the landing, had second thoughts and climbed up again. Instead of knocking on Yue's door, she went to look for the plant manager, Dan Meir. He'd always seemed like a decent, sympathetic type. The receptionist station was dark, so CJ gave a quick rap on Meir's door and poked her head in. There sat Roman Sacony.

He'd taken over Meir's desk. His laptop hummed, and he was talking on his cell phone. He barely glanced up at her intrusion. His nut-brown tan seemed deeper than before, and his thick wavy hair hung down in his eyes. He seemed so distant and cold that she thought he didn't recognize her. Then he beckoned with a single finger and pointed to a chair.

She came in, closed the door and seated herself at the small conference table, where Dan Meir had been temporarily relocated. Meir was also talking on a cell phone and punching a laptop. He gave her a benevolent smile. His kindly expression reminded her of someone's uncle.

Several minutes passed before either of them took a break. From their conversations, she gathered an emergency had transpired in the canal. Meir was authorizing overtime pay, and Roman was asking someone about cofferdam gates. She sat on her hands and listened.

Roman clicked off his phone and met her eye. "What do you have for me?"

His demand startled her, but it was the opening she wanted. Her fingers gripped the chair seat. "I found electric current in the water, and there were synchronized flashing lights."

"Slow down. You're talking gibberish." Roman leaned across the desk. "Did you say synchronized?"

"Last night I dove in the canal and took a sample. I think the electric current—"

"You dove in the canal? What about the pond?"

"It's not in the pond anymore. It slipped down the creek."

Roman closed his eyes and nodded.

"What the hell is it?" Dan Meir's eyes narrowed to creases. "Are you telling me the white stuff that killed Manuel de Silva also caused the cave-ins?"

"What cave-ins?" CJ glanced back and forth between the two men.

Roman leaned back and seemed to peer at some disturbing image in midair. "E-mail me your report. And it better make sense. You can go."

The abruptness of his dismissal stung CJ. She couldn't believe this was the same man who'd offered to buy her dinner. But he wanted her report, that was the main thing. And he didn't call her a nutcase. She got up to go.

As she was passing through the door, he said, "Reilly, don't make another dive without permission. Got that?"

Her first impulse was to blurt something defiant, but Roman's next words softened her anger. He said, "I need you safe."

Cascade

Saturday, March 12
9:07 AM

She walked back to the lab, smiling. Even Peter Vaarveen's wisecrack didn't upset her. Roman took her report seriously. He wanted to keep her safe. *See, Harry? Somebody respects my opinion.*

She turned up her nose at Peter, then linked her laptop into the company WiFi. One more time, she reviewed what she'd written earlier, polished a sentence, changed a verb. She laid out her hypothesis as succinctly as possible and tried to restrain the flights of fancy her father so often ridiculed.

First, she recapped her basic assumptions: The colloid had evolved from a mix of river-borne trash and Devil's Swamp pollutants. It consisted mainly of water emulsified with algae proplastid, and it held suspended microelectronic components, which probably came from obsolete computers and appliances dumped in landfills. The emulsion produced ice at room temperature, and it could purify water.

For a while, she debated editing out the water purification part. Roman might immediately seize on the profit potential of cheap clean water and try to claim it as corporate property. On the other hand, she wanted to impress him with her intellect—so she left it in.

Next, she summarized her new findings: the underwater lights, the gas bubbles, and the electric current that generated the EM field. The flashing lights could be light-emitting diodes. LEDs appeared in everything from kids' toys to car keys, and even a feeble current could make them glow. The gas bubbles could be ordinary methane. And the electric current might flow from a faulty connection in a nearby factory. The current itself may have triggered a reaction that caused the ice. She noted how scientists in South Korea created ice at room temperature using a chemical process that rapidly absorbed heat. Perhaps something like that occurred in Devil's Swamp. She admitted the combination of effects might be simple coincidence.

But CJ didn't believe in coincidence. She felt certain the cascade of diverse phenomena had a common origin. Through the night, she'd been struggling with theories, and the next part of her report launched into the kind of wild speculation that would have made Harry sneer.

The colloid might be generating its own internal energy. They'd found intact photovoltaic cells in the emulsion. The gluey proplastid protected them from water damage, and the Louisiana sunshine could have easily reactivated them. Trash photovoltaic cells may have been trickling electric current through the swamp for years. Over time, the current may have ionized the colloid like an electrolyte and dissociated its various chemical pollutants, thereby releasing pure water. The science team should check for electrolysis.

In her concluding paragraph, CJ's fancy truly left solid ground. What if the current triggered other electronic trash in the water? Switches, thyristors, transceivers, memory chips, they'd found a treasure trove of microcomputer elements in the lab sample, all sheathed in proplastid gel. What if the current prompted some of these components to fire signals to each other?

Each tiny computer element carried a small piece of programming, just a fragment, but who knew how they might interact. Given enough time, even the simplest combinations could yield elaborate complexity. The electrified microchips may have self-assembled into a crude data-sharing web in the water, perhaps the embryo of an entirely new class of water-based computer network.

As she reread this part, she chewed both thumbnails to nubs and retied her short ponytail three times. In the end, she e-mailed the full report.

Waiting for Roman's response, she agonized over the gaps in her reasoning. What about the response to sound? She hadn't even addressed that. So many unknowns.

Twenty minutes later, he replied with one sentence. "Suggest methods to neutralize it."

"No!" She banged her keyboard with both fists.

"Did your boyfriend break his date?" Peter grinned. His magnified eyes loomed monstrously behind a row of test tubes.

CJ got up to pace. That wasn't the answer she'd expected. Shivering in the chilly AC, she found a lab coat hanging behind the door and slipped it on. Then she sat down and keyed rapidly. "The colloid offers a rare opportunity for research. We may find important beneficial qualities. Our goal should be further study. I'll suggest methods for that."

The reply came back almost immediately. "Containment in progress. Short-term study okay. Priority goal is neutralization."

"How can you be so stupid?" she said aloud. She almost keyed it, but Peter's sardonic chuckle stopped her. She glared at Roman's message. Then she punched her laptop keys, letting anger drive her to extremes. "We may be witnessing the spontaneous birth of a sentient liquid neural net."

At first, there was no reply. She knew she'd gone too far. Why did she have to say *sentient*? Stupid theatrics. Finding her thumbnails too short to chew, she gnawed a strand of hair. Peter was fiddling with the SE microscope, studying more samples from the pond. She got up and looked over his shoulder at tumbling droplets of fur.

"Hairy little mutants." Peter snickered. "I think they're synthetic nanowhiskers fused to *Cryptosporidium* microbes. There's a little bit of everything in this freaky water."

CJ heard her laptop chime. Roman had already responded. "Your field data is interesting, but your conclusions are invalid. Sorry, I do not believe in swamp creatures. Goal is neutralization. Go to work."

Swamp creatures! She didn't speak aloud this time because she didn't want Peter to make fun of her. In grim fury, she closed her laptop, shoved it in her bag, and walked out of the lab. Swamp creatures indeed. Conclusions invalid. That's exactly what Harry would have said. How dare he dismiss her like that? She didn't need this damned job. She stomped out the front door, crossed the parking lot, and climbed into her Rover.

The outside air felt marginally warmer compared to the building's icy AC. Yanking off the lab coat, she thought of several incisive remarks she should have e-mailed back to Roman Sacony. She slapped the steering wheel. Then she opened three sticks of cherry-flavored gum, stuffed them in her mouth, and masticated.

Sip

As CJ sat in her car bickering with herself, another young woman sat in an air-conditioned cubicle in Building No. 2 monitoring Quimicron's local servers. Systems administrator Rayette Batiste liked the peace of Saturday mornings. Alone in her cube, without the distracting noise of coworkers, she soaked in the cozy hum of her rack-mounted servers. Four screens glowed on her desk. An update was installing. In the chilly AC, she buttoned her old cardigan to her chin, sipped hot tea, and watched the update's progress. Between times, she kept a weather eye on employee e-mail.

Faithful Rayette had a mission: to defend Quimicron's local area network. She made it her aim to root out and expose every instance of phish, virus, spam, porn, or profanity that might besiege the corporate servers on her watch.

Thin, solitary, with straw-colored hair and sky-blue eyes, Rayette did not think of herself as a prude. She took innocent pleasure in the e-mail gossip that scrolled down her screen. It made her feel connected to the social web of her company. And though she rarely spoke to anyone face to face, she led an active anonymous life in the discussion forum sponsored by her church. Naturally, when her CEO, Roman Sacony, visited her parish, Rayette took special note of the e-mails he passed through her charge.

Rayette knew every detail of the operation unfolding in the swamp. She knew about the special gates Roman had ordered to seal off the canal entrance. She knew about the threatened lawsuits, the media embargo, the science team. She had read every word of CJ Reilly's report—three times. For, unlike Roman Sacony, faithful Rayette did believe in swamp creatures.

As a rule, she kept away from windows facing the unhallowed swamp. She didn't like that view. Since learning about the thing that killed Manuel de Silva, she'd been hiding in her cubicle, frightened and friendless, agonizing over what to do with her terrible knowledge. Imminent doom seemed to hang over her workplace like a monstrous cloud. Did her duty lie in speaking or keeping silent?

She launched a browser and entered the Holy Trinity discussion forum. Perhaps Jeremiah would be online. Rayette always trusted Jeremiah's advice. While the page loaded, she prayed for guidance and opened her dog-eared King James. The pages fell open to the Book of Job.

" 'Behold now Behemoth . . . He lieth in the covert of the reed. The shady trees cover him with their shadows. The willows of the brook surround him. Behold, he drinketh up a river . . . He can draw up Jordan into his mouth.' "

Rayette closed her volume, and her lips began to tremble. The Lord's Word was sometimes harsh but always clear. He was giving her a warning. He wanted her to speak. With shaky fingers, she tapped the keys to retrieve CJ's confidential report about the swamp beast. Hardly breathing, she posted the report online.

Hiss

Saturday, March 12
12:45 PM

Rick Jarmond's voice burbled through the phone, "So how long are we talking about? A couple hours?"

Roman could hear him chewing and swallowing. His voice sounded young. He seemed to be speaking through a mouthful of bread dough.

"More like forty-eight hours," Roman answered. "But this is a slow time of year, so it shouldn't cause a problem." He held the cell phone away from his bruised ear.

He didn't enjoy calling Jarmond at home on Saturday to beg permission to close the canal, but it was necessary. He'd chosen Jarmond because the young man was low on the Corps of Engineers command chain, less experienced, therefore easier to manipulate. As a junior civilian manager in the regulatory office, Jarmond had just enough authority to grant the permit.

Roman looked at his watch, then paced to the window to check the sky.

Thunderheads were gathering. "Only five companies will be affected, Rick. I've spoken to the owners, and they've given the okay."

"Well, that's a plus." Rick Jarmond belched. "Sorry, Rome, you caught me having lunch. Now let me get online to look at my map and my regs. Sounds like you need a Section 10 permit. I'm gonna put you on hold a minute."

Roman shut his eyes. He'd spent half his morning on hold, clutching this *maldito* cell phone. He'd left his Bluetooth ear loop in Miami—an unfortunate lapse. But who knew he'd spend four straight hours in conference calls?

His Styrofoam coffee cup held a dry brown ring at the bottom. It squeaked when he gripped it. His phone ticked static. He was beginning to see this entire *embrollo* as a personal war.

Roman longed for an assistant who could handle these minor emergencies, but to his regret, he had never found a man or woman worthy to be his second. Lawyers, accountants, technicians, administrators—he kept a full complement on staff. But none of them possessed the will to do what he would do. No one thought fast enough or pushed hard enough. Everyone let him down.

"*Cabrón,*" he hissed. The vacant phone kept ticking.

Along this *Anglo* river, regulatory jurisdictions converged and overlapped with all the clarity of mud. To close the canal, he had garnered the consent of five other companies, as well as the Coast Guard, the EPA, the Mississippi River Commission, the sheriffs of both East and West Baton Rouge Parishes, and several departments of the Louisiana state government. On a Saturday.

He counted the seconds till Rick Jarmond came back on the phone.

"This toluene spill, my records show you used genetically modified bacteria to clean it up. *Deinococcus radiodurans.* Is that right?"

Roman ran a hand through his hair. "The EPA approved it."

Another pause. Roman's nerves stretched taut.

"Okay, what's your fax number, Rome? There's a request form you need to fill out."

Roman crushed the Styrofoam cup. Screw your form up the backside.

He didn't say it—in Spanish, English, or any other language. Instead, he laid the phone down and took a breath. The other officials had responded well to his calm reasoning. They'd accepted his apologies for troubling them on the weekend. This would be a temporary canal closure to finish his cleanup. Two days only. Commerce would not be affected, and the canal environment would benefit. Roman was a persuasive talker, despite his personal reserve. And his company paid hefty taxes. Most everyone was falling into line—all but this green kid, this *simplón* Rick Jarmond. Roman picked up the phone again.

"I need this closure today, Rick, within the hour. How can we expedite this?"

He heard the man slurping liquid through a straw. The *simplón* must be dining on takeout. Sneering, Roman opened his laptop to check the Corps organizational chart. He noted the name of Jarmond's superior. Col. Joshua Lima, the New Orleans district engineer.

"Well . . ." The young man took another bite of lunch, and Roman heard his wet grinding mouth sounds. "Tell you what, Rome. You fill out this form and get the Coast Guard's okay, and—"

"I'm holding the Coast Guard permit in my hand," Roman said, only a mild lie.

"Well . . ." More chewing. Roman ground the Styrofoam cup under his heel.

Leach

Saturday, March 12
2:01 PM

Downstream from Baton Rouge, on a mud-red river inlet, stood the white-washed cinderblock headquarters of Belle Chasse Marine. A fly-specked card taped to the front door announced, "Back in a Minute." But CJ waited over an hour before a dark green Eldorado finally pulled up the gravel drive and an elderly man in sweat-stained work clothes shambled out with a ring of keys.

Pewter clouds brooded over the river, and the air hung breathless, waiting for rain. CJ jumped down from her Rover. The plunging barometric pressure made her temples throb. "I need to rent a boat. Small, quiet, and powerful, with plenty of room for equipment. Someone told me this was the place." She had decided Max's pirogue was too slow.

"Ho-ho-hold up, missy. You speakin' too fast. Me, I'm Beauregard Chifferee, but you might as well call me Punch like ever'body else. Now, what was your name? I don' hear too good."

The man's eyes were so glazed with cataracts, CJ wondered how he could drive a car. Rusty stains dribbled down over his shirt buttons, as if he'd just been chewing sugarcane or tobacco or some less licit flora. His skin was the color of bread mold.

"I'm CJ Reilly." As she shook his pawlike hand, she reminded herself to decelerate. In this part of the country, conversations went more smoothly when she respected the local speed. She smiled at the old man. "Do you have anything like a cold drink? I'm parched."

"Sure, Miss CJ. I got a refrigerator full of Diet Mountain Dew. All my doctor lets me drink anymore is that diet mess. Please, after you."

As she passed into the cool shady interior of the concrete shed, she smelled something sweet and musty. Damp dust and cobwebs had mingled to breed a fine gray skim over every surface—engine parts, vinyl chairs, decades-old catalogs, curling multipart forms. Even the lightbulb that dangled from the ceiling was flocked in gray. CJ had a feeling that if she stood still long enough, the gray skim would engulf her.

Punch's chair creaked under his weight. He leaned forward, opened a small refrigerator under the counter and drew out two frosty plastic bottles of green soda. Their Mountain Dew labels were smudged with fingerprints. CJ eyed them.

"This boat you need." The old man winked. "Small, but plenty o' room. Quiet, but powerful. You don' want me thinking you're a drug runner."

CJ opened her mouth. For someone who didn't hear well, he'd caught every word. She studied the mottled old man and wondered how much truth she should tell him. As little as possible, she decided. She perched on a greasy chair.

"I'm a photographer for *Wilderness* magazine, and we're doing a special on Louisiana marsh fowl. You know how skittish these marsh birds are. I have to sneak up on the little darlings to get close-ups."

"Birds? Eh la, you probably looking for the green woodpecker. Ever'body want to see that sucker. Audubon. Sierra. He's a fast little demon. Tha's why you need all that power."

"Exactly, the green woodpecker. I might have to chase him a long way."

"Oh yeah, 'specially since he don' live on this continent. Green woodpecker live in France."

CJ felt herself blushing. The old man swallowed his sugar-free soda, and a very large bug scuttled in the corner. Far away thunder rolled like breaking surf. She drew her knees together. On the shelf beside her, a stack of old batteries drooled ashy globs of corrosion. Punch took another swig and crackled his plastic soda bottle.

"Okay, I'm trying to bust a big polluter in Devil's Swamp," she blurted. It was nearly true.

Punch watched her a few more seconds, then broke out with a howl of laughter. His chair squeaked as he chuckled. "Bust a polluter at Devil Swamp. Missy, tha's like sprinkling perfume in the outhouse. You're not from around here. How much you know about ol' Devil Swamp?"

"I've seen birds nesting there. It's not completely dead."

"Dead, naw. Too much alive is what it is. Critters mixing and fornicating in all that slime. Unholy matrimonies."

CJ felt an involuntary shudder. The approaching storm charged the air. She rubbed her arms.

The old man rocked back and scratched his stomach. "Animals in that place ain't natural. You seen them frogs with six hind legs."

CJ nodded. Unfortunately, yes, she had seen the pitiful creatures kicking around in circles. Malformations were common in Devil's Swamp.

"And I guess you heard o' the skunk ape," Punch went on. "Hairy demon, seven feet tall."

She shifted nervously and tried to smile. "What are we playing, liar's poker?"

"This ain' no lie, missy. Skunk ape been living in that swamp for two hundred years. Lotta folks seen him. Smell like rotten egg and cow shit, pardon my terms."

"Come on, Punch. Give me a break."

"My theory is, he's a descendant of them outlaws that used to hide in there. Got lost in them bayous, got to living wild, crossbreeding with skunk and muskrat. Folks see lights at night, way back in them cypress thickets. Eh la, skunk ape still there."

CJ fingered her sweating Mountain Dew. "I don't scare that easily."

The old man's smile showed more gaps than teeth. "Long history in that place. Slave traders. Lynchin's. Murders. I seen a white woman in there once. Tied to a tree, stabbed all up and down her arms and legs. Hair burned off her head. They say she had man parts and woman parts both."

CJ set the soda down. "Do you have a boat to rent or not?"

He ran a splotchy tongue over his teeth. "What it is, is the juxy-position. Water, mud, and heat. Too much of them three items juxy-posed together, they grow things unnatural. Like that baby they found."

"Baby?" She did not want to hear this story. "Two-headed, I'm sure."

"Don' be smart, missy. I seen the baby myself. Man-child with a extra leg growin' outta its hip. Little bald stump. Toenails all crowded together like kernels on a corncob. Born right there on the edge of Devil Swamp."

CJ felt sweat trickle down her neck. The old man's cloudy eyes gave no hint of teasing. She'd seen the blue-collar houses backing up to the levee behind the swamp, and she'd read about the birth defects. God knew what egregious poisons had accumulated in the soils—and leached into the water—and diffused into the air. She tried to shake off her uneasiness by assuring herself that Beauregard Chifferee was the most accomplished liar she'd ever met.

"So what about that boat?"

Thunder cracked overhead, and she jumped in her chair. Punch grinned.

A week's rental on the Velocity Viper, including a trailer and hitch, cost twice what she'd expected. The old man proved to be a crafty negotiator. But cost wasn't an issue to CJ. Harry had left her with deep pockets.

Punch called the Viper his "drugstore special." For a small boat, the Viper had plenty of cargo space, plus unusual outfitting—behemoth twin engines and four oversized fuel tanks. There was also a beefed-up muffler system Punch had personally designed for hushed moonlight journeys.

He didn't ask a single question as he helped her load the equipment she'd "borrowed" from Rory Godchaux's supply van, a chemistry field kit, goggles, gloves, boots, three rolls of duct tape, a freshly laundered coverall, and some tools. She'd also packed her field finder, electric current sensor, flashlight, PowerBars and a gallon of Coca-Cola. Punch provisioned her with two extra twenty-gallon cans of boat fuel—which she had to pay for in advance.

Once she cast off from Punch's dock, she cut a few turns across the brown inlet, getting the feel of the Viper's controls. The overhead clouds changed from pewter to iron, and a few heavy raindrops fluttered on the wind. She kept circling back to Roman's words: "Sorry, I do not believe in swamp creatures."

That belittling tone. Nothing infuriated her more than sarcasm. It had been Harry's sharpest weapon.

"Darling, your sentiment would be charming in a Peter Rabbit story. . . . No need to apologize for your B+ in calculus. You're a B+ sort of person, dear, like your mother."

CJ opened the throttle and roared across the no-wake zone, churning up eddies of mud. As her bow upended, spray pelted the windshield, and she leaned out to let the wind blow in her face. Why did only the worst moments stick with her? There were many times when Harry had been kind. He'd chosen the best schools for her, the best books. He'd taken her to hear the Boston symphony every month of the season. Why couldn't she remember their long talks about music and art—and chemistry, always that—the fundamental language of the universe.

The problem was, she looked too much like her mother. The color of her hair. The shape of her nose. Even her voice reminded Harry of the other Carolyn Joan. He told her so once, after a particularly long and fiery discussion that left them both out of temper. He said he loathed the sound of her voice.

As she left the inlet and entered the terra-cotta river, the rain came. It plastered her hair and rilled down her face. In seconds, her clothes were drenched. She had to swerve around a fishing skiff. Upstream, two towboats were passing each other, filling the river with their twenty-barge tows, each barge weighing over a thousand tons. And just across from the downtown waterfront, a colossal Singapore freighter was making a wide turn into the Intracoastal Waterway at Port Allen.

The rain fell in curtains, and as CJ watched for an opening in the heavy traffic, her throat ached with words she couldn't express. Harry, you weren't fair. Why did you leave me?

She steered through the narrow slot between the towboats, bucking through the wake and daring the rain, ignoring the furious yells from the deckhands. At that moment, more than anything, she needed speed.

Bead

Saturday, March 12
8:27 PM

Max sat on his front porch, tipped back in a wooden chair with his bare feet on the rail, fingering an old portable Casio keyboard that lay across his lap. The rain was already tapering off, but a remnant of water still dripped off his roof and made a liquid bead curtain around the porch. One block away, the mighty river hummed background bass, accompanied by cymbals of traffic on Interstate 10. Max hadn't bothered to plug in his amp, so the melody from his keyboard existed only in his mind. But that was enough for Max.

The night was good. He felt the sweaty, exalted relief of just having finished a song. The tune had incubated for months in his mind, drifting in and out of focus, growing humps and appendages, verses out of meter, beats out of rhyme, a mixed-up jumble of nonsense. Still, the lyrics kept collecting in his notebook, circling around an idea without a name. And finally, tonight, the song had emerged whole and alive on his page, as if placed there as a gift. He tipped back in his chair and smiled at God.

Above the low-pitched tin roofs of his West Baton Rouge neighborhood, a fat half-moon glimmered through clouds. Its rays barely penetrated the urban nimbus of street lamps. Crickets cheeped in the wet grass, and one whippoorwill cooed its lilting query, "Come, come to me?"

Max played the whippoorwill call on his silent keyboard, then improvised an answering riff. He swallowed beer from a sweating brown bottle, set it down beside his chair and played his new song again, voicelessly whispering his lyrics to the angels. This night was good, but the day had not been.

A barge sank, and no one knew why. Lots of people were mad, but Max was tired of worrying about it, tired through and through. Soon, he would put on his good shirt, drive across the river and play three hours of pop tunes for a high school dance. He would play keyboard tonight, not his *frottior,* and pop music bored him. But his ex-wife Sonia had left a brown envelope at his door, stuffed full of Marie's doctor bills.

He hadn't told Ceegie about his daughter, Marie. Although he believed in speaking the truth, he suspected his family obligations might drive Ceegie away. He glanced around the empty old porch. Drive her away?

Wind shifted across the rooftops and blew the clouds West, and for an instant, the river sang louder. The gusting currents distorted all sound. Max took another sip of beer, and the alcohol esters seeped through his flesh. He wondered what Ceegie was doing tonight. One thing he knew—she wasn't answering her phone.

He tipped back in his chair. The moon's half disk glowed through a forest of pipes and cooling towers in the nearby industrial park, and he ground his teeth against the bottle's glass neck. When the whippoorwill called again, its voice echoed through shifting airy distortions. "Come, come to me?"

Glisten

Sunday, March 13
6:30 AM

Twenty minutes before sunrise, the canal water stirred with a ceaseless restive sloshing. Its waves left a dark waterline along tree trunks, concrete piers, and barge hulls. Higher it rose with each subtle ebb and flow, higher up the piers and hulls, higher up the rocks, oscillating with heat, wind and friction, building up layer upon wet glistening layer of surface cohesion, till it succumbed at last to the pull of gravity and collapsed under its own weight.

CJ didn't see it. She was driving her rented Viper upriver from Baton Rouge. She'd intended to start much earlier, but last night, everything went wrong. First, she couldn't find a place to moor the boat. She had to park the trailer at a strip mall. Next, she drove all over town looking for a satellite phone.

Finally, she located a pawnshop near Interstate 10 that carried some of the things she needed. Not all the merchandise looked new. Some of it may have been stolen. In any case, she found a GPS with electronic compassing, a more sophisticated magnetic field finder, a radio frequency spectrum analyzer, a canteen—she bought everything that looked useful.

By the time she'd finished shopping, fatigue forced her back to the Roach to crash. Too bad, she slept through the night, and this morning, there was already too much light and activity on the water to pass unnoticed. Dodging north of the barge canal entrance, she edged along the lush green shore of Devil's Swamp.

Nothing was natural about this part of the lower Mississippi. For hundreds of miles on either side of the river, manmade earthen levees stretched longer and taller than the Great Wall of China. Engineers first started the twin berms in the early 1700s, but after the infamous flood of 1927, the levees evolved into fortresses.

As the nation's ever-expanding pavements and hardscape constantly increased the volume of drainage runoff, the floods came swifter, higher and more often. And the engineers raised the walls repeatedly. Now the mainline levees towered over forty feet high, like a pair of grassy mountain ridges. Riprap and concrete reinforced them on the river side, and stone dikes winged out at intervals to keep the main current channelized.

But no levee protected Devil's Swamp. It lay exposed in the *batture,* the miry borderland between river and levee, because the engineers had not judged Devil's Swamp worth saving. That fact made it easier for CJ to conceal her landing.

Instead of docking at a treeless riprap wall, her Viper nosed in among overhanging willows and grounded in mud beneath a canopy of green branches. After tying up to a tree trunk, she tugged on her coverall and hip boots, then hiked through the swamp to a high solid knoll and settled in to spy on the activities in the canal.

She lay flat in the grass and studied the ravaged canal banks with her binoculars. The eroded places gleamed like melted glass. Four times she paged Max before he returned her call. Rory had him hustling with a repair crew, shoring up another undermined area near the Quimicron dock. He called her on his cell phone from the men's port-a-let.

"A barge sank yesterday afternoon," he whispered. "Merton, he say the canal stink like sulfur around that barge. He say the water eat through the hull."

"Impossible." CJ batted away mosquitoes and remembered the ruined dive-suit she'd had to pay for with her credit card. "The canal's not acidic enough to dissolve steel."

"I saw the hull," Max said. "Eaten up with little holes. And some of the cargo leak out. It just *disparét.* Divers look all over to find it, but no trace left."

CJ's throat tightened. "What kind of cargo was it?"

"What they call 'moly'," he answered. "Merton say it's the *loa* spirits. They outraged by how bad we disturb the Earth."

She frowned. "You don't believe that voodoo stuff."

"*Voudon*," he said. "Gotta go, *lam*. I see you later."

CJ turned off her phone, rolled on her back and stared at the brightening sky. She thought about the stolen barge cargo. Was the colloid *feeding*?

The clear dry air chapped her lips, and she bit off loose flecks of skin. Moly. Molybdenum. She tried to remember what she knew about this element. Silvery-white, tough as nails, a transition metal used as a catalyst in petroleum refining. It was used for something else, too. Filaments. Ultrafine microscopic wires used in electronic devices.

Her thoughts kept circling the colloid's response to sound. Sound traveled faster underwater, but what *was* sound? Compression waves. Crests and troughs of high and low pressure.

An owl flapped its wings and startled her. When it swooped down from a nearby tree, a small rodent screamed a death cry, and CJ jumped. Then she wrinkled her nose and tried to scratch an itch through her stiff coverall. She'd been working on another theory. Something about field attraction.

She knew an EM field could develop a kind of cohesion or coherence— like the surface tension on a water droplet. And its force could move charged particles. Could that be how the colloid maneuvered? Maybe, through alternating waves of attraction and repulsion, the EM field steered its charged particles through the water like a flock of birds. But what was controlling the EM field? A mix of curiosity or fear turned CJ's skin to gooseflesh.

Reek

Sunday, March 13
6:42 AM

While CJ lay in the swamp grass, pondering riddles and picking at mosquito bites, Roman Sacony paced in the fifth-floor conference room of Building No. 2. The recycled office air smelled of bodily exhalations and cleaning fluid. None of the plate-glass windows would open. Elaine Guidry, Meir's buxom blond assistant, sat watching him while he speed-read her memo. But the typewritten words filtered through to his brain more slowly than usual. He was still thinking about the Gulf-Pac exec who'd just slammed out of the room.

Elaine had written the memo at his request to remind the plant's employees of their nondisclosure agreements and the penalties for leaked information. Elaine's wording was too polite, and he feared it might not have the intended effect, but he had no leisure to edit. "Cut the first sentence, and send it," he said.

Elaine batted her mascara-rimmed eyelashes. Most men paid her more attention. She wore her coral-pink cashmere sweater belted tight at the waist, and last night she'd touched up her highlights. But despite the rumors she'd heard about her lascivious CEO, Roman Sacony was all business. She gathered her notes and bustled out.

A line of people waited to see him, and a stack of message slips indicated the number of calls the switchboard had fielded. He wasn't ready to deal with voicemail yet, but he flipped through the handwritten messages. Insurance people. Lawyers. Worse, Rick Jarmond had faxed another Corps of Engineers form.

Adrenaline flooded his muscles, and blood flushed his brown cheeks. He had never once lost a fight to the *Anglo* bureaucrats, he had never given ground. But this adversary in the water had no face. Why did it have to emerge on his property? Why now, when so many critical issues were converging? Jarmond's fax shredded in his hands.

He needed data. Solid ground beneath his feet. He was tired to death of these fluid situations. He spread the torn paper on his desk and took a calming breath. His priority had to be containment—in every sense. Contain the damage, contain the information, contain himself. He waited for his spate of anger to recede.

This morning, the Corps permit had come through, and he'd ordered a pair of coffer-dam gates to close off the canal. The gates were made from a new nanostructured carbon composite, impermeable, hard as diamonds, the toughest building material ever developed. Horst Corporation used the gates to hold back thousands of tons of water while they constructed bridges. Roman would use them to trap his faceless enemy and put an end to his cash drain. Then he would make the colloid *disappear*. Imagining this end, he almost smiled at Rich Jarmond's form.

Already, the gates were steaming up the Mississippi River on a barge, accompanied by the diesel-powered crane that would lower them into position. He expected them by noon. Until then, he would force himself to remain calm. He flipped his cell phone open and called Yue. "Has it moved?"

"No change in location," she shouted. Roman could hear a lot of background noise. Yue was speaking from Gulf-Pac's loading dock. "It's completely invisible. Some trick of light. I'm tracking its energy field."

"Still expanding?" he asked.

"Correct," she said archly. Li Qin Yue resented anything she couldn't explain.

"E-mail me." He ended the call and marched to the window, willing the watery *picaro* to show itself. But the canal rippled the same sluggish gray as ever. Yue said the colloid simultaneously reflected and refracted light, like a million tiny mirrors and prisms, so all you could see was dappled water.

He paced to his desk, then returned inevitably to the window. Sealing the canal would be time-consuming, but straightforward. More difficult would be the task of sealing people's mouths. Over a hundred Quimicron employees and twice as many Gulf-Pac people knew about the cave-ins. Another twenty workers had witnessed the damaged barge.

The barge was lying dead in the water even now, listing on its side for all to see. Roman leaned against the window and frowned at the lopsided hull. The concurrent timing could not have been worse. Employees were already buzzing that the canal was "hexed." Somebody put a *gris gris* on the water, they said. In an hour, Meir would call them into the warehouse for a stern lecture on confidentiality. But Roman doubted that would be enough. Everyone had smelled the acid reek in the water. His enemy would not be so easily covered up.

He checked e-mail. Damn the science team. Yue and Vaarveen were his best people, yet they had no coherent facts to give him. The water registered temperatures near the freezing point, and they'd confirmed the electromagnetic field, that was how they finally located the colloidal mass. They'd also verified the electric current and the ionization Reilly predicted, and they'd found wide variations in pH. Their other findings were so contradictory and improbable that Roman might have questioned Yue's competence—except he knew his team leader too well.

Li Qin seemed grave when she showed him her scans. She'd found astonishing structure. Complex accretions of microchips and proplastid drifted through the water, invisible to the naked eye, detectable only through the SE microscope. Yue found them always in paired chains, electrically positive and negative, circulating randomly through clouds of ionic fluid, constantly disintegrating and reforming. Yet the structures persisted like a chemical host—a chemical "ghost," Yue said in her weariness.

Further sample analysis turned up more exotic techno-trash: molecule-size electronic switches, radionuclide microbes designed to absorb nuclear waste, tomato DNA laced with goldfish genes, silver nanoparticles created to kill odor in athletic socks.

He checked her data. He trusted her method. He just couldn't absorb how fast the technology of the very *small* had accelerated since the turn of the millennium—or how fast its detritus had spread into the waste stream.

But that wasn't the worst. Yue could not explain why the EM field had increased 12 percent in strength. Nor could she say why the colloid's volume had doubled. The expansion alarmed Roman more than anything. The field now measured forty yards across, and Yue estimated its volume at eight liquid tons.

Vaarveen had a bundle of probes and sensors dangling in the water, and Yue kept drawing new samples, re-running her data. But that flakey brat, Reilly? She'd gone missing. For all her brilliant gifts, she was about as dependable as a brush fire.

At least the EM field allowed Yue and Vaarveen to keep tabs on the—what should he call it—pollution slick? Peter Vaarveen dubbed it the "Quimichimera." Stupid *Anglo*, Vaarveen made everything a joke. Roman would never have hired him if Yue hadn't insisted.

A chair got in Roman's way, so he kicked it aside and resumed pacing. For the time being, he'd convinced the officials to keep this matter out of the press. Petroleum execs understood why this sort of business should remain private, and the agencies managing the river had no wish to stir up public anxiety. But this Corps guy, Rick Jarmond, he was a different animal. Young and green. He took his regulatory job way too seriously. Roman drummed his fingers and scrutinized the phone.

Instead of calling Jarmond, he looked up another number in his Palm—Oceano Mundial, a New Orleans-based company specializing in environmental remediation. Roman always counted on OM to clean up his oil spills at sea. They were expensive, but they got the job done. He regretted not calling them to deal with this toluene. Meir had downplayed the spill, said nobody cared about one more fish-kill in Devil's Swamp. Meir swore he could handle the mop-up with some contract workers and a few loads of a genetically engineered bacteria. Bad decision. Roman flipped open his phone and keyed the number for Oceano Mundial.

Glitter

Sunday, March 13
11:05 AM

The coffer-dam gates arrived early. On a barge pushed by a line-haul tow, they glittered like a stack of colossal sky-blue platters lashed down with gigantic chains. HORST CONSTRUCTION gleamed in fancy script across the towboat pilot house. CJ slapped a mosquito. She often wondered why towboats never towed anything. They always pushed from behind. Max called to tell her about the gates. He'd been calling every chance he got.

Steam rose from the ground where CJ sat. Seeds swelled and sprouted. Insects swarmed, and birds plucked them from the air. She shed her heavy coverall and stripped down to shorts and T-shirt. Her swollen nipples hurt when anything brushed them, and occasional cramps stabbed her belly. She'd stuffed a box of tampons in her gear bag, just in case. As she waited for the towboat to anchor, she smeared mud on her neck, arms, and legs to deter mosquitoes. The fierce sun baked her like a clay pot, and beetles fell in her hair.

She studied the blue gates, and her binoculars caught the Queen Bitch and the asshole taking readings. They had about a million dollars worth of equipment sitting out in the sun, including the SE microscope. CJ gazed with lust at their multichannel analyzer. She'd used one like it at MIT. She could be down there now, learning more about the colloid. What was she doing skulking around like a trespasser? She scratched a bug bite. It was her own fault. She'd thrown a tantrum at the wrong time—again.

When she closed her eyes, afterimages of sparkling sunlight reminded her of the underwater flashes in the canal. Water and light. What was it about water molecules?

They were magnetic. H_2O—one oxygen atom anchored the center, and a pair of hydrogen atoms occupied two corners. A pair of negative charges balanced the other two corners, which made each molecule a skewed bipolar magnet. She pictured the water magnets lining up in strong hydrogen bonds. Liquid chainmail. Their surface tension was really just magnetic attraction. So with precisely the right shifts at the right time, an EM field could make water dance.

Blackbirds crossed the sky, and as CJ watched them, she mused about rhythms, ocean tides, compression waves, heartbeats, drumbeats. The pond's EM field had mimicked the rhythm pulsing from her iPod. Pulsed out as sound waves. Pulsed back as EM waves.

Like a cell phone, she thought. Cellular phones turned human voice into electromagnetic pulses. She imagined thousands of old cell phones chucked in the garbage. Crushed to fragments and dumped in landfills, they leaked into rivers every year. Their bits and pieces had been washing into Devil's Swamp for decades. And thanks to the proplastid coating, many of their chips remained functional.

She wiggled restlessly in the grass. Her claim about a sentient computer network had sounded far-fetched even to her own ears. But what if? Might a zillion trashed microparts actually assemble a *neural net*? In the *water*? A neural net wasn't like an ordinary computer network. Instead of crunching ones and zeroes, a neural net could learn new behaviors. It could recognize voice commands and images. Someone at Stanford invented neural nets back in the 1950s to imitate processes in the human brain.

CJ mused, how would a self-evolved neural net communicate through the water? An idea formed at the bottom of her mind, hazy and fluid, something about cellular signals, binary code—and zydeco.

Across the water, Max watched the barge crew unchain their blue gates. The fluted sections glittered like metallic paint. Max had never seen anything so shiny smooth and flawless. Rory told him the sections had to be hinged together, and Max was supposed to help the barge hands connect them.

The twenty-four steel hinges lay in a row, each one as large as two men. While they waited for the crane to lift them, Max squatted in the shade of a pin oak, playing with somebody's coonhound, when suddenly one of his female coworkers screeched. It was Betty DeCuir. She was pointing at the canal.

Under a ten-foot layer of ordinary gray water, a wave of frost mushroomed outward, and something glittery white took shape. It looked like a diaphanous fan of milk. Betty ran toward the water's edge, but as quickly as the vision appeared, it vanished. Betty picked up a handful of rocks and tossed them, hoping to stir it up again. Max tore loose a chunk of limestone riprap and chucked it in. Then he noticed the dog. The animal had gone rigid, all alert. Its ear was cocked toward the water. Max wondered what the dog was hearing.

Churn

Sunday, March 13
3:40 PM

"They're ready to close the gates." Dan Meir stood in a pool of sunlight at his office window, clutching a cell phone in one hand and a two-way radio in the other. He was overlapping two separate conversations, one with the crane operator, the other with his crew chief, Rory Godchaux.

At the desk, Roman nodded and ended his own conference call. Spreadsheets, photographs, and empty water bottles littered the conference table where the two of them had been working since early morning. "Wait for my order," Roman said. "I'm expecting a ship."

As they left the room together, Roman fished a red-and-black capsule from his pocket and swallowed it dry. Li Qin had promised it would help him stay alert. Until the canal was sealed, he would feel no peace, and the elements of his plan were not meshing smoothly. He couldn't close the gates till the cleanup vessel arrived. Another wait.

Roman dreaded the overtime bill for this operation, but he had no choice. He had to staunch the flood of lawsuits. Numbers crunched in his head as he and Meir jogged down the steep hot pavement toward the dock. Heat radiated from the concrete. He felt its warmth through the soles of his running shoes.

Quimicron kept two speedboats to patrol the canal, both of them four-seater Formula FAS³Techs. A swarthy young crewman had one of them powered up, and as Roman stepped into the cockpit, Meir introduced him as Max

Pottevents. Roman eyed the young Creole. The name triggered his memory. Max Pottevents had been with Reilly in the swamp. But Roman had no time to think about that now.

They sped down the canal, churning up a wake of green foam and skirting the orange buoys Peter Vaarveen had set out to mark the boundaries of the EM field. Roman studied the new cave-ins along the bank and growled. Each sandy gout shimmered like the inside of a grainy porcelain teacup.

He knew the caving banks coincided with the spreading EM field. And the underwater photos showed the sand had not washed along the canal bed. It had vanished—just like the moly from the barge. Roman rocked as waves buffeted the speedboat.

Moly might dissolve in water, he reasoned, but silica quartz—common sand—would not. Breaking it down required the blasting temperatures of an electric furnace. Roman tried, but he could not rationalize the disappearance of solid quartz. His faceless opponent plied cryptic forces.

As they approached the Gulf-Pac dock, it was necessary to glide directly across the area inhabited by the colloid, and Roman noticed that Max Pottevents was growing edgy. The young Creole took off his bandana and mopped sweat from his face. When Pottevents murmured something about evil spirits, Meir joshed him for being superstitious. But when he eased across the buoy line and steered through the colloidal emulsion, the speedboat's compass went crazy, and they all breathed easier once they stepped onto solid concrete.

Yue showed Roman her latest computer-generated map of the EM field. Vaguely ovoid in shape, the field floated directly in front of the dock. Nested lines of force emanated from its center, and its outer boundaries frayed to a thin chaotic fringe. The computer-generated image resembled a blot of slowly diffusing ink. Except it wasn't diffusing; it was coalescing. Yue's data showed that, every hour, it drew more and more canal refuse into its electrically charged formation.

Hammer Nesbitt lumbered across the dock like a peevish old bear and took a peek at Yue's map. "Tell me that ain't the spill from your lagoon," he said, shaking a fat finger in Roman's face. "See that creek? That leads straight outta your swamp where your chemicals got loose."

Yue's mottled skin tightened over her cheekbones. "I defy you to find toluene in that canal."

The big Texan rounded to face her. "I never said toluene. I don't know what kind o' shit you people spilled. What the hell *is* it, that's what I wanna know. People's livelihoods are at stake here."

Yue vibrated like a tuning fork. "Peter, show this gentleman your analysis."

Peter finished coating himself in sunscreen, then languidly found his notes and read out the laundry list of pollutants, while Roman slapped his leg in tempo with the passing seconds. It was the same list Reilly had discovered. Carolyn Reilly—where was that fickle girl? Roman made a mental note to fire her as soon as he had time.

Then he bounded into the speedboat. "Let's go, Meir. I want to see the gates."

Max Pottevents revved up the engine, and Peter Vaarveen asked to come along. Soon the four of them were tearing down the sun-drenched canal toward the Mississippi River, where the Oceano Mundial cleanup ship was just passing through the open blue gates.

Roman hailed the captain and mate standing on the foredeck. At thirty-six feet, the *Refuerzo* was a small, sleek Class II Harbor Skimmer with water-jet propulsion and state-of-the-art equipment. Agile and quick, she required only a two-man crew, and her pilot house stood a mere twelve feet high, but OM's manager assured Roman that her onboard capabilities were impressive. As soon as her glossy green-and-white silhouette passed through the gates, Meir radioed the Horst crane operator, and Roman watched the shining gates close. When he heard the hiss of their watertight gaskets mating, he drew his first easy breath in days.

"It's contained," he said quietly, resuming his seat in the speedboat.

"Yep, but now what do we do with it?" Meir knocked cigar ash into the water.

Capt. Michael Creque pulled alongside their speedboat and introduced himself. A blond, hard-weathered good ol' boy from Lake Charles, he pronounced his name to sound like "Mackle Crick." But his eyes moved with a quickness that belied his slow speech, and his questions showed long experience at his trade. His mate, a skinny black man named Spicer, barely spoke a word. Yet when Peter Vaarveen stepped onto the *Refuerzo* deck without permission and began snooping around, Spicer said just enough to make him leave.

"One of them odorless, colorless jobs, eh?" Captain Creque eyed the green waters sloshing around his hull. He sniffed the dry air and shook his head. "Got any idea of the specific gravity?"

"We—" Peter glanced at Roman with a subtle smirk. "We aren't sure. It changes."

Creque took off his cap, rubbed his head and studied Peter's printout. "Well, Spicer'll download your data so we can set us a perimeter. If we cain' break her down with chemicals, I guess we'll drop us a collar around the whole she-bang and suck her up. You got you a empty holding lagoon anywheres close by? Otherwise, you'll have to rent you some tankers."

While Meir and Creque worked out the cleanup details, Roman relaxed and checked voicemail. He had a sense that, finally, reasonable minds were at work and that his mystifying adversary would soon be captured and neutralized. Once they had the colloid confined in a lagoon, Yue would learn whether it could be made to serve Quimicron's interest, or whether it should simply be destroyed. Roman never doubted the efficacy of science. He smiled at the watertight gates spanning the mouth of the canal. If he'd been an effusive man, he would have slapped Peter Vaarveen's back—he felt that buoyant.

It was too late to meet with his Panama shippers, and he'd sent a VP to deal with the refinery people in Mobile, Alabama. Awkward setbacks. But he still hoped to rendezvous with the Brazilian banker. That deal was vital. With this Baton Rouge incident contained, he could leave Meir and Yue to mop up while he went to bargain for a natural gas port in Fortaleza, a port that would open a fertile new market for Quimicron SA. He called the hangar to ready his jet.

Suck

Sunday, March 13
6:14 PM

In the dying light, CJ focused her binoculars on Peter Vaarveen, who was repositioning the orange buoys in a wider circle.

"You're growing," she whispered to the colloid.

Engine roar echoed across the water. She turned to watch Max pilot the company speedboat up the canal from Gulf-Pac to Quimicron. She admired the way he cut the engine and glided precisely up to the loading dock without colliding. Max grew up on the river. He was good with boats—she'd noticed that before.

As soon as Max tied off, Roman leaped ashore and sprinted up the steep ramp over Quimicron's ring levee. Good legs, she observed. But where was he going in such a hurry? She keyed Max's number into her cell.

"He don' confide in me," Max replied to her question.

"But he must have dropped some hint."

"All I know is, they closed the gates, and they gonna pump *djab dile* into a lagoon."

She kicked at a tuft of fescue grass. "They have to get it onto their own property, under lock and key."

"Maybe that evil need to be under lock," Max said.

"Not Quimicron's lock."

"*On ap rive.* I cain' talk no more. Rory want me helping them cleanup boys."

"Did he . . . um . . . Did Roman say anything about me?"

"No, *lamie.*"

Max turned off his phone and stuck it in his coverall chest pocket, then gazed across the twilight canal to the swamp. He knew about where CJ lay hiding, and though he couldn't see her, he almost waved. But he dropped his hand. His coworkers might notice. In any case, she probably wasn't looking his way.

A glance at his wristwatch made him suck his teeth. No chance of making the session at the Snakedoctor Club. Zydeco players met there every Sunday night to jam and try out new songs. Friends stopped in to listen, dance a little, maybe put some money in the jar. But tonight was special. His ex-wife Sonia had promised to bring Marie.

Max felt in his breast pocket. The fragile silver chain was still there, locked in its pink jewel box, with a tiny silver pendant shaped like a heart. He'd bought the small necklace for Marie's birthday. Reluctantly, he punched Sonia's number into his cell, and the boat rocked gently under his feet while he waited through the rings. He still didn't understand why the court gave sole custody to Sonia. Max had to coax and bribe for every hour with Marie. He hadn't seen her for weeks, and he'd been working out the new song for her birthday.

As he made his apology and listened to Sonia's usual tirade, the tips of his fingers itched for his *frottior,* and he whistled Marie's tune softly through his teeth. "Awright. Okay. Yes," he said. Then he shut his phone, revved up the speedboat and motored back down the canal to pick up Mr. Meir. Some days, he despised this job.

Max and Merton worked all through the clear bright evening to drain a holding lagoon. As the sky dissolved from gold to red to black, they pumped its corrosive contents into an abandoned well, then washed out the concrete basin with a high-pressure hose, blasting off the viscous orange scum that clung to its walls.

Next, they reeled out a flexible eighteen-inch diameter pipeline. By flash-light and moonlight, they laid it along the ground from the empty lagoon, up along the ring levee and down the canal bank to the Gulf-Pac dock. It wasn't long enough, so they had to fit a connection. Headlamps crisscrossed through the night while another crew set up a pair of heavy-duty vertical pumps at the Gulf-Pac dock. Trucks from all over southern Louisiana kept showing up with equipment. Max had to give Mr. Roman Sacony credit, the man showed enterprise.

Meanwhile, the *Refuerzo* tangoed around the canal dropping a perimeter of foam-filled PVC booms just outside the circle of orange buoys. Max helped stage floodlights, and he watched them when he could. He admired how the two cleanup men moved like synchronized athletes.

As the half-moon passed overhead, Creque and Spicer draped lead-weighted plastic sheets from each of the booms. The nonpermeable curtain reached all the way to the canal bed and sank several inches into the silt, safely containing all eight tons of the colloid. The collar put Max in mind of an oversized shower curtain hanging down in the water. By midnight, they were ready to catch *djab dile.*

Spill

The liquid inside the *Refuerzo*'s watertight collar lay still. No convection moiled its liquid sheen. No wind troubled its smoothness. No vapors rose. Its coherent surface reflected the floodlights like a black mirror.

Yet in the midnight darkness below, free-floating computer chips fired signals, and miniature polarized fields quietly sorted compounds into new groups. Charged particles of iron and steel washed together, and double-helix skeins of mixed debris spiraled round and round. Hybrid microbes emitted new acids.

Capt. Michael Creque had a rhyme he liked to quote: "The solution to pollution is dilution." Which translates: To deal with a liquid contaminant, just add water, and keep adding more water till the poisonous parts-per-billion fall within acceptable regulatory standards. But despite his pithy poem, Creque knew that removing a pollutant from open water was tricky.

His vacuum pumps guzzled fuel, so hosing up the entire eight tons in the collar would be expensive. That's why he and Spicer tried other techniques first. The *Refuerzo* carried the latest remediation gadgets, and Michael Creque understood how to use them. First he dropped absorbent pads into the contaminated area, then recovered and bagged them like wet diapers. When Yue told him the diapers weren't picking up the right contaminants, he deployed oleophilic brushes and rope mops, which used differences in specific gravity and surface tension to stir up and attract oil-based chemicals from water.

Apparently, the colloid was not oil-based. So as the half-moon sank toward the horizon, Spicer broke into their arsenal of dispersant sprays. Creque's sprays could break down, coagulate, flocculate, and precipitate a dozen different categories of toxic materials. After two hours, Yue ran an analysis and gave this method another nix.

This chemical spill was something beyond their experience. But Creque and Spicer were not discouraged. They downed two cans of Red Bull apiece—their caffeinated beverage of choice—then deployed their circular weir. This grisly device came fitted with a high-capacity grinder pump that could chew up the heaviest, most viscous spills mixed with the lumpiest of trash. Nothing had ever sneaked past their circular weir—until now. As they watched, the unpredictable colloid seemed to gain weight and settle to the bottom. Their weir caught nothing but brown canal water.

So finally they resorted to the pumps. The moon had set and the night air had turned cold when at last they connected their high-tech vacuum system to Quimicron's temporary pipeline. Night birds screamed and took flight when they fired up the vertical pumps. Methodically, they swept the suction hose back and forth inside the collar, and gradually, the fabric curtain deflated.

Diffuse

Monday, March 14
4:45 AM

"*Malè*. Nothing's working," Max yawned over the phone. After four hours of sleep in the back of Rory's truck, he'd returned to monitor the temporary pipeline at the holding lagoon.

CJ gripped her phone and smiled. Across the canal, she lay in thick weeds at the mouth of the unnamed rivulet, listening to Max breathe. She hadn't slept much either. The clear pre-dawn had turned frosty, and she hadn't brought enough clothes. In the chilly darkness, she hugged herself to stay warm.

"They've been pumping for over an hour. Must be a thousand gallons in that lagoon," she said.

"*Oui*, over five ton. But no *djab dile*. All they capture is clean water."

Clean water. CJ savored those words. Her colloid was doing his magic again. Without understanding why, she felt an instinctive bond with the wild changeling.

Through binoculars, she watched Yue and Vaarveen yell at each other beneath Gulf-Pac's floodlights, and she regretted not buying a high-sensitivity microphone so she could eavesdrop. She'd give a big chunk of her trust fund to hear what they were saying.

Across the ebony water, the *Refuerzo*'s pumps growled like hungry sea monsters, frightening away bats. A pall of blue smoke hovered over the canal, and the collar lay on the water like a dented star, collapsing inward. Big-eared swamp rabbits crouched in their warrens, and salamanders dove under rocks. Li Qin Yue and Peter Vaarveen stood on opposite sides of the computer, airing a difference of opinion.

"Do it again."

"Screw you. I've done it three times already."

The computer-generated map of the EM field had lost its ovoid shape. The screen now displayed a splotchy pixel pattern with a gaping hole at the center where the *Refuerzo*'s pumps were sucking, and around this gap, the field was visibly dissolving. All signs indicated they had captured the colloid. And yet . . .

"We're pumping textbook pure water." Peter held a stoppered test tube up to the light. "I can't even find trace impurities."

"That can't be." Yue waved her fists. "We've acquired over three-fourths of the volume. There has to be something in that lagoon. You missed it."

"The hell. Run your own analysis." Vaarveen threw the tube at her.

When it bounced off her hands and broke on the concrete dock, Yue screeched. "You're worthless. You didn't even find the pollutants we identified before."

Peter gave her a sour grin. His white-blond hair looked gluey, and finger-prints smudged his bottle-thick glasses. He'd borrowed a disreputable-looking coverall to keep out the chill, and Deet insect repellent hovered around him like a personal fog.

Yue looked as if she wanted to spit. Her boney frame quaked with cold in her thin lab coat, but she disdained wearing other people's clothes. Her iron-colored braid hung limp down her back, and muddy stains darkened her sleeves where she'd been jerking at the vacuum hose. Fatigue lined both their faces, and they swayed with exhaustion.

Roman Sacony watched them in silence. He had not gone to Miami. He'd let the Brazilian banker slip through his fingers. Perhaps he'd made a mistake, listening to his instincts to stay in Baton Rouge. But after watching his science team brawl like cats, he didn't think so. This battle wasn't over. This enemy had not yet surrendered.

In the shadows at the far end of the dock, he leaned against a forklift and rubbed his grainy eyes. He had swallowed another of Li Qin's capsules to stay awake, and the stimulant coursed through his bloodstream, exciting his weary nerves. Reflections rocked back and forth in the canal's languorous black ripples, and waves of cold air wafted up from the water. The pump engine fumes gave him a headache. Dawn was coming.

"Christ, it's come back," Yue hissed.

Roman saw her leaning toward the computer screen as if she were going to dive in. He moved rapidly to see the image. Deep within the collapsed collar, an ink blot diffused like a strange black blossom, darkest at the center, fanning out to a fine intricate fringe. Their hours of pumping had gone for nothing. The EM field had regenerated. His enemy had eluded their hose.

Roman knew he'd expected this outcome. He never trusted easy wins. As he confronted his opponent's portrait on the screen, his fingers slid over the liquid crystal display, almost caressing it. "Can you enlarge this section?"

Yue clicked a command to magnify the peripheral fringe. When it zoomed up to 500x, Peter Vaarveen let out a hoot. "It's a Mandelbrot set."

"Yes." Roman recognized the famous image of lacey seahorse-shaped spirals generated by a well-known quadratic recurrence equation.

Yue's neck bones popped. "It's too linear. Liquids don't mix like that."

"Why is it still there?" Roman glowered at the canal. "We've pumped the collar almost empty."

"We pumped what it wanted us to pump," said Vaarveen.

"What it *wanted*?" Yue scowled. "You're starting to believe these 'creature' stories."

Vaarveen plopped down in a folding chair, stretched his long legs in front of him and snickered. "Do you have a better explanation?"

Roman was losing patience with both of them. He checked his watch. The gates were closed. The colloid wasn't going anywhere.

"You're thinking like children," he said. "Get some sleep. Come back when your brains are clear."

Bathe

The abrupt silence after the pumps shut down frightened a screech owl and scattered a pack of coyotes. CJ raised up on one elbow. Covered in cold mud, her wet hair was matted with grass seed, and her clothes crawled with chiggers. She dug through her pockets to find a handkerchief clean enough to wipe her binocular lenses. The crew was going home. Now it was her turn.

She gulped one last syrupy swallow of Coke, crushed the plastic bottle, stowed it in her backpack, then dropped her shorts to pee. Why hadn't she thought to bring some long pants? Her bare legs were milk-blue with cold.

She slogged through the chilly swamp and found her boat lolling among the willows. If only they hadn't closed those stupid gates, she could have motored up the canal. The boat would have made everything easier. But with the canal closed, she would have to carry her gear overland. At least, she found a sweatshirt to wear.

Her phone rang. Max was trying to call, but she didn't answer. She didn't want him to know what she was planning. After loading her equipment in a net bag, she slung it over her shoulder and hiked back through the swamp.

At the canal waterline, she dumped her gear and sorted things out. No way did she intend to dive, not again. She wasn't that harebrained. No, she would simply wade out in hip boots and take a few readings from the surface—although the thought of tugging the cold rubber hip boots over her bare legs made her shiver.

From her net bag, she unrolled one of Max's leather belts and strapped it around her waist. Then she carabinered her field finder and a few other necessary items to the belt. The canal exhaled a frosty fust of petroleum and rot. She squatted at the water's edge, scooped up a vial full, and used a simple field test of litmus paper to check the pH. Her flashlight's beam showed the pH was low, slightly more acidic than vinegar. A short exposure wouldn't hurt her.

She dipped her hand into the frigid water, and slimy cold ribbons tickled her wrist. In the darkness, she couldn't see if they were blades of grass, strands of algae, or Asian water flukes, the parasitic flatworms that were just beginning to infest Louisiana streams. She yanked her hand back.

Sitting on a flat rock, she tugged on the awkward boots. The cold rubber gave her gooseflesh. Then she psyched herself to step into the water. "You won't hurt me," she murmured, "will you?"

The canal's mucid bank sloped down sharply, and she hadn't expected that. On her first step, her boot slid, and she went deep. Only by batting wildly at the water did she keep upright. Her splashes drew a chorus of crickets, like a hundred chainsaws starting up.

Wet to her midriff, both boots full of freezing cold water, she realized there would be no possibility of wading far enough out to get a clear reading. The canal was too deep, and the collar floated fifty yards away. She would have to swim. "But I won't put my head under," she said, inciting another explosion of cricket song.

If Max were here, he would stop her. Longing for Max, she struggled out of her heavy boots and slung them onto the bank. Then, she drew a deep breath, kicked off from the bottom and dog-paddled, holding her head erect and keeping her mouth closed tight. The water smelled like a toilet, and the gear swinging from her belt created drag. Harry seemed to be standing on her shoulders, weighing her down. "Daughter, if it's death you want, this is a clumsy choice."

Her arms pulled at the cold water until her shoulders burned, and yet the collar seemed as far away as ever. Finally, she rolled on her back and floated, letting the corrosive water sluice through her hair. What am I doing here? The thought washed through her. What the hell am I doing?

Overhead, gray clouds streaked the rose-colored dawn like smoke signals, and a flock of egrets flew low over the water. As CJ floated on her back, an irrational but comforting certainty flooded over her that she and the colloid shared a mutual understanding. He would not hurt her. She kicked her feet and backstroked for the collar.

At last, she made a grab for the PVC boom and hung on, panting. For several minutes, she dangled there, catching her breath and easing her muscles. The air smelled—good. By now the collar had puckered inward to a fraction of its former size. Only a few hundred gallons of liquid still sloshed inside, and as she trailed one arm through its fresh pure clarity, she didn't notice at first that her hand was stinging.

Acid? She shrieked and yanked her hand back. In the dawn light, her skin looked red, but it wasn't blistered from acid. It was simply cold.

Cautiously, she dipped her fingers into the water again—and gasped. The water inside the collar felt icy. Frigid waves welled up like an artesian spring tapping straight down to Antarctica. It smelled clean. What a contrast to the rank stew of the canal. She let the droplets spill down her arm like shavings of frost.

As she heaved her chest up onto the boom, the collar sank under her weight, and for an instant, she went completely under. Pure water enfolded her. It rinsed through her hair and tingled her skin, and the sharp cold both hurt and soothed her. When the collar buoyed her up again, she drew a watery breath and tasted perfume. As the rarefied liquid stirred and aroused her, she drifted into a odd reverie. For no clear reason, she felt convinced the colloid recognized her. She straddled the boom.

Beneath the salmon-colored sky, she rocked to and fro, mashing down the collar and letting foamy bubbles spill all around her. The cold intoxicating water entwined her in achy sweetness. She lost track of where she was. Back and forth she rocked, squeezing the boom between thighs. Her crotch grew creamy. As her pleasure increased, more and more of the milky emulsion seeped out over her thighs. Pangs of orgasm made her grit her teeth as the liquid ice swept her through multiple bucking waves of carnal heat.

After the sharpest peak had passed, she rested, lying on the collar like a hammock and letting cool water bathe her face. She barely noticed the sudsy white emulsion drifting down the canal.

All at once she sat up and glanced around to see if anyone was watching. She'd never behaved that way in public before. She felt ashamed and frightened. Perhaps she'd imagined the whole episode. When she checked her field finder, she found herself at the edge of a powerful energy field that was slowly moving away to the West. She thought the magnetism must be affecting her brain.

With a little shake to clear her mind, she unclipped another piece of gear, a small water-resistant MP3 player made for use in the shower. She'd already cued it to play Max's zydeco. When she slipped on the headset to make sure it was working, the romping beat surrounded her, and Max's sonorous baritone lilted loud and merry.

"Max," she whispered.

She lowered the player on a fishing line into the collar, and as music propagated through the water, she watched her field finder for a response. This was a crazy idea. Harry would have taunted her for days. But hadn't the pond mimicked the zydeco rhythms before?

Music was a kind of a numeric code, she reasoned, like computer language. It made sense that an active neural net would try to interact. If she got any response at all, it would prove the microelectronic trash was active. Her experiment wasn't so loony. It might yield results.

In fact, she was hoping for an epiphany, a sudden blinding flash of revelation. The colloid had to be more than a fluke accident. She wanted it to pulse a deliberate answer to her zydeco, to prove it was capable of intelligent exchange. CJ craved the big leap, the huge discovery. She wanted her watery chameleon to say hello.

"Harry, don't give me that look," she muttered.

Half-submerged on the sunken boom, she gripped her field finder and waited for a sign—until the night watchman spotted her with his flashlight and she had to bail.

Mist

Monday, March 14
8:12 AM

A storm front moved through the heartland, drenching Arkansas's red clay and soaking Kentucky's black coal fields. Along the Gulf Coast, misty rain hung suspended, refusing to fall. People breathed it. Birds caught it in their wings. Unseen above this hazy floating impossible rain, the moon waxed toward full.

But CJ didn't notice the weather. Hunkered on the floor of her Roach Motel bedroom, naked except for a towel, with the drapes drawn, with the glow of her laptop illuminating her astonished face, CJ read about an evil new lifeform called the "Watermind."

She'd been researching definitions of life, and two standards had popped up: 1) any system capable of eating, metabolizing, excreting, moving, re-producing, and responding to stimuli; and 2) any system containing reproducible code that evolved through natural selection. Then she found another, from Carl Sagan of all people. Sagan called life "a localized region where order constantly increased"—in contrast to the universe as a whole, which was moving steadily toward chaos.

She was surfing for more definitions when she came across a memo describing a new sentient life-form made of water and electronic trash. Her flesh went cold. Her shoulders locked up. Her stiff fingers could barely scroll the mouse as she read her own report, published online for all the world to see.

Buzz about the stolen memo was streaming all over the Internet. The more she looked, the more she found, although no one seemed to know who came up with the name, "Watermind." The anonymous memo—thank God they'd deleted her name—had first emerged in a Catholic discussion forum, and numerous bloggers had "annotated" its contents. One pundit described how a shape-shifting liquid robot was stalking through a Louisiana swamp, throwing off sparks, pissing clear water, and freeze-drying any humans in its way.

CJ pounded the floor with her fist. She laughed to keep from bawling. She barely recognized the twisted mutations of her report. Her goal had always been to publish her findings and make the colloidal process free to all. Open source—she had faith in that principle. But now someone had published for her, and the only people who cared were lunatics!

She got up and drank a handful of water from the bathroom tap. Traces of mud still daubed the side of her neck, leftover from her hasty shower. When she'd straggled in from the swamp, she'd been too sleepy for a thorough scrub, but too wired for sleep. Now she moistened a washcloth and washed her neck, wishing she'd never looked at her laptop. When her cell phone rang, she jerked like a live wire.

The caller's ID was blocked. She answered the fifth ring.

A male voice said, "I read your report about the liquid computer in Devil's Swamp."

"You have the wrong number," she stammered. The coincidence of timing shocked her. The online report had not included her name. How did he find her?

"Yeah, Roman Sacony invented a water-based artificial intelligence, didn't he?"

"Roman Sacony has nothing to do with this," she blurted. "It's a natural occurrence. Nobody built it. And it certainly doesn't belong to Quimicron."

"Then you admit you've seen the Watermind."

CJ dropped the wet washcloth in the sink. "Tell me who you are."

"I'm a friend you can trust. My name is Hal Butler, with the *Baton Rouge Eye*."

A reporter. CJ lowered herself to the bathroom floor.

The man seemed to take her silence as encouragement. "You believe the Watermind has virtuous qualities, am I right? Something like that, an intelligent liquid, it's gotta be worth millions."

"It's not about the money." She jerked a comb through her hair. "It's about a cheap way to purify water."

"Exactly. And the Watermind can do that?"

She clenched her comb. "Do you realize one child dies every eight seconds from drinking polluted water?" Her eyes teared when the comb snagged in a tangle. "Check me on that. The numbers may have changed."

"How does the Watermind work?"

CJ laid her comb down. She'd signed Quimicron's nondisclosure agreement four days ago—had it been that long? A mere slip of paper, she had too little experience with lawsuits to be worried. On the other hand, Roman's warning about public panic made her hesitate.

"Miss Reilly, let's be frank," said Hal Butler. "What I need is the human angle. Like dying children, that's emotional. My readers eat that up. So toss me a bone, eh? How can the Watermind save dying children?"

CJ disliked the reporter's tone, but she also recognized a chance to publish the truth. She rummaged for her toothpaste and, finding none, rubbed the motel's bar soap on her toothbrush. "When will my story go to press?"

"Tomorrow, if it's good," Hal said.

Squall

Monday, March 14
6:10 PM

Scattered showers wafted through Baton Rouge, and the sky changed color every minute. The Pickle Barrel Tavern filled up early. Bob Ed Lafleur wiped his bar and set out fresh baskets of popcorn. He turned down the thermostat, turned up the TV, and stuck his head through the kitchen door to look for his helper. "Get out here, son, and bring more beer mugs."

People from the Quimicron plant had already staked out their usual corner and pushed three tables together. They had a bigger group than normal. They ordered half a dozen pitchers of Bud and two platters of *boulettes*, deep-fried crawdaddy meatballs. Bob Ed could tell something weighed on their minds because the Braves were playing the Devil Rays on TV, and no one was watching. Outside, the sky rumbled, and a few big drops splattered the sidewalk. Bob Ed kept an ear cocked, but nobody said anything interesting till after the second round of beer.

As usual, Merton Voinché started things off. He leaned back in the squeaking wooden chair and crossed his brawny arms behind his head. In his dark face, his green eyes glinted with unsettling light. He kept his voice low, yet he had a way of drawing everyone's attention. "Eh la, *djab dile,* he dodge them sucker pumps. He ain't be pushed through no pipe."

"Oh yeah, he slip loose outta that collar. He sly awright." People at the three tables murmured and studied their beer foam. They seemed jumpy, scared. Someone whispered low, "*Djab dile* know how to hide."

Bob Ed Lafleur leaned closer. *Djab dile.* Devil milk? What on earth were they mumbling about? Outside, more raindrops fell.

"*Djab dile* ain' no he. She a female," said Betty DeCuir. "She's *Yemanja,* the water *loa.* Ask me how I know." Betty DeCuir was always mouthing off.

"Be careful, babe. You signed the disclose pledge," said a plump young woman with peanut-butter skin. Everyone at Quimicron had signed the nondisclosure agreement.

"Piss on the disclose pledge," said Betty.

Merton indulged her. "Tell us, baby girl. How you recognize *Yemanja*?"

"Okay, I tell you, boy. *Yemanja* always wear a white dress and a pearl crown, and she live under the waves. You think about what we saw, and tell me that ain' *Yemanja*." Betty crossed her arms.

Rain fell steadily. It drilled in the gutters and danced down the street. The squall echoed like a crowd of people clapping. Bob Ed rubbed his damp hands on his apron and moved nearer to Merton. He pretended to check a lightbulb.

These Creole swamp workers always had to bring up their *Voudon* spirits. Bob Ed shrugged. *Loa,* they called them—as if the swamp wasn't hainted enough with good Christian ghosts. There was that little girl, Anna Fortunata, got lost a few years back, and people to this day saw her drifting around in Devil's Swamp. White as snow, just at twilight, always sort of hovering over the ground. And that other one, that murdered woman tied to the tree with her hair burned off. That incident made the papers. People said that tree still oozed red when the moon was full.

"Naw, girl." A small, wiry black man shook Betty DeCuir's arm. "*Yemanja* is mother of life. She give birth to the *orishas*. *Djab dile* done kill that boy Manuel. No kind of mother do that."

"Could be *Agoué*. Sea spirit. He keep the fishes," said Johnny Poydras, a pimply kid with merry brown eyes.

"That devil milk belong to *Baron Samedi*." Merton's sinister tone quieted everyone. Heads nodded. Few people made eye contact. Outside, the rain crashed like tin cans.

Bob Ed had never seen Merton in such an edgy mood. He'd heard of *Baron Samedi*, the all-powerful voodoo lord of death. Foolishness. They said *Baron Samedi* kept the gate keys to the underworld. Believers painted him as a black man in top hat and sunshades, smoking a cigarette and drinking a bottle of rum steeped with twenty-one hot peppers.

Merton kept speaking. "*Baron Samedi* guard the souls buried in that swamp. Could be thousands."

"Yeah, red people live there ten thousand years before the Christ child," said Johnny Poydras.

"You right, boy." Merton narrowed his green eyes. "Ancient mounds in there full of dead injuns. You know they is ghosts in there."

"Lord, yes."

"He's right."

"Amen, Brother Merton."

"My people. Houmas," said a brick-colored man. "Maker of Breath protects my fathers." The man spoke with strong feeling, but he spoke too low for anyone to hear. All eyes centered on Merton.

"Spaniards and French trappers got lost in there. One wrong step, got swallowed up in that mud. You know they runaway slaves buried in that quicksand, alongside the slave hunters trying to catch 'em."

"Yeah, they plenty black men buried in there," the group agreed.

"They had lynchings," said Merton.

"They burned witches in there one time," said Betty DeCuir.

All at once, as if someone had flipped a switch, the rain stopped. The sudden silence caused everyone to stir and glance around. Merton leaned on the table and cracked his knuckles. His dark brow furrowed as he looked from one face to another. He spoke low, and Bob Ed Lafleur had to lean close to understand him.

"All kinda blood mixing in them swamp graves. Now we go in there and dig around. Pour in the trash, take out oil. I'm telling you, we messin' with *Baron Samedi*."

Sweat

Monday, March 14
9:57 PM

After the squall line passed over southern Louisiana, Devil's Swamp simmered. Black ripples chuffed against the canal bank and bounced backward, setting up a complex moiré pattern of wave interference. Two woodpeckers watched from a hollow oak. Snakes undulated away, and a muskrat fled to its hole. Obscured by clouds, the waxing moon sank toward the horizon.

On the floodlit Gulf-Pac dock, CJ angled her plastic badge into the beam of the guard's flashlight. "Science team, second shift," she said. "They sent us down here to babysit the equipment." With a nod, she indicated Max, who stood behind her, shouldering a heavy duffel.

"Take care, miss. This canal gives me the heebie-jeebies." The guard's voice sounded young. In fact, his name was Timothy Bojorian, a nineteen-year-old sophomore at Baton Rouge Community College. This job was financing his first apartment away from home.

When young Timothy paced to the far end of the Gulf-Pac dock, Max repeated a warning he'd given earlier. "They'll put you in jail if you talk to that reporter."

CJ blotted sweat from the back of her neck. "I didn't talk to him yet. I'm trying to decide if I should. Help me pull off this tarp."

Underneath the heavy tarp, Yue and Vaarveen had wrapped their equipment in clear plastic sheeting to fend off the mist and dew. CJ cut the plastic away with her Swiss Army knife.

"You signed the disclose pledge," Max reminded her. "That's like word of honor. You gotta stick by that."

"Well, he promised not to use my name." Max's warning troubled her. She should never have told him about Hal Butler's request for an interview. She was feeling ambivalent enough without an ethics lecture. "Here, plug in this cable."

She handed him the power cord to Yue's multichannel analyzer. When he found the outlet, she connected all the units and booted up Yue's computers. An image of the EM field blinked on the screen.

"Oh," she whispered. "It's outside the collar."

"Sa?"

Max leaned over her shoulder while she tapped the keyboard, searching for a history of previous maps. She wanted to compare the images over time, to discover how and when the colloid breached its trap. A lurking memory made her shiver and hurry, but she didn't know how to launch the software.

"Damn this thing." She savaged the keys.

"You're probably looking for the image archive," said a familiar voice.

They turned and saw Roman Sacony stalking up the dock. Even in running pants and a T-shirt, he looked stylish. CJ wondered how long he'd been prowling in the shadows.

"I ran the query earlier." He reached across her and keyed a command, which brought up a line graph with a hyperbolic curve.

CJ gawked at the image. "He's growing," she breathed.

"Yue estimates 10.4 liquid tons. That's a thirty percent expansion since yesterday." He checked his watch. "I'd like to know how the damn thing escaped the collar. Yue found it drifting a quarter mile down the canal. Now we'll have to trap it again."

"Show me the data," she said, forgetting who was boss and who was junior employee.

Roman's jaw sliced sideways. "You have five seconds to persuade me not to fire you."

"I have a theory about language," she blurted. Half-formed ideas tumbled in her head. She wasn't prepared to verbalize a hypothesis, but neither was she ready to be fired. "I know how to communicate with the colloid."

"You know?"

"I have to test it," she hedged.

"The hell you do." He shoved his long hair back off his forehead and glared at her. "Were you testing it this morning? We found your MP3 player. Didn't I warn you not to go in that water again? With the Feds breathing down our necks, all we need is another accident."

"How kindhearted," she snapped back. "You need what I know. So listen."

She reached for the duffel Max carried over his shoulder. It held underwater audio equipment Max had found in someone's basement. She jerked the duffel open to reveal two disk-shaped Lubell speakers. The piezoelectric devices looked like hubcaps welded together, and each one was rated to project underwater sound through a fluid volume up to twenty acres in size. The speakers were battered and mud-streaked, but in perfect working order. She and Max had tested them in his friend's catfish pond.

"We'll play mathematical sequences through the water, then track the response," she said.

Roman lifted one eyebrow. "What will that prove?"

"The Watermind responded to rhythm at the pond, so I intend to—"

"Watermind?" Roman's expression turned feral. His eyes widened ferociously, and his voice blasted her like a wind. "Did you invent that name?"

"No, I—I saw it online," she stammered.

He took a step toward her. "When I saw your report on the Web, I wanted to wring your neck."

CJ blanched and faltered backward, knocking over a stack of surge protectors. "I didn't—"

Max hustled to cover her confusion. He began setting up the audio equipment. Roman watched the young Creole's hands adjust the jacks and speaker cables with quiet familiarity. The warm night closed around them, and for a moment, the faint clicks of Max's gear were the only sounds on the dock.

When Roman spoke next, his voice was low and contained. "You wouldn't be that stupid. Someone must have hacked our e-mail server." He dropped to one knee to help CJ collect the spilled gear. "At least they deleted our company name."

She swept up a double handful of surge strips, unable to meet his eye.

"You guessed a lot of things right, Reilly. That's the reason I'm not firing you." Roman stacked the gear on the workbench. "You make intuitive leaps. It's a gift I admire. Just be careful while you're gazing off in the distance not to miss something obvious right in front of you."

Foam

Monday, March 14
10:11 PM

In the darkness and gathering heat of the Gulf-Pac dock, Max tested the audio speakers and watched the chief executive show Ceegie how to work the computer. Mr. Sacony had a commanding style that made Max both respectful and wary. He listened to them discuss the "colloid," the name they used for the devil water. Though their words sounded like a foreign language, Max paid keen attention because he wanted to understand. The chief said *djab dile* was growing.

The lady scientist Yue had confirmed electric current in the water, and a crew was scouring the canal for the power source. Ceegie seemed pleased about that. The lady Yue had also found a living creature called *phosphorescent dinoflagellates* that luminesced underwater, and Max suspected that meant the aqua-green sparkle that glowed in the waves just at twilight. Everyone in Baton Rouge had seen that. Ceegie said that didn't explain the colloid's rhythmic flashes.

Ceegie was getting that shine in her hazel eyes, that crazy distraction that took her to places Max couldn't follow, although he noted Mr. Sacony seemed to follow well enough. Mr. Sacony knew how to speak *science*.

Mutely, Max absorbed their talk about the mircoparticles the scientists had discovered in the water. Cognitive radio chips. Industrial lubricants. Human stem cells. Hanta viruses. Mr. Sacony showed her a picture of a living bacterium that was pierced through with a manmade metal rod finer than baby hair. A living nanomachine, the chief called it. The picture on the screen looked like a whirling dervish.

Mr. Sacony said living microorganisms were being drawn into the colloid by the weak polarized attraction of the EM field. Max didn't know Latin, but he knew the canal was full of sewage and germs. It didn't surprise him to hear that every kind of filth was cycling into the devil water.

"Yue also found your microbubbles," the chief said. "She's analyzing the gas. It's not methane."

Max envied the chief's educated words. Mr. Sacony was like Ceegie, full of knowledge from books. Max couldn't decide why he disliked the man so much.

When the chief showed Ceegie the gooey chains of microchips that spiraled around each other, she grew very excited. "He's evolving his first specialized organelles," she said.

The chief got mad and raised his voice. "Do NOT assign biological terms to this chemical reaction. The colloid is NOT alive."

Ceegie raised her voice, too. "Maybe we need a new definition of what's alive."

Their shouting set Max on edge. As their decibels escalated, he stole another look at the screen. The microchip chains looked like twisted ropes of sparkling milk. Humidity fogged the glass, so he untied his *paryaka* to blot up the drips.

Mr. Sacony lowered his voice when he talked science. He said the colloid had no center, no organizing hierarchy. It couldn't be alive. He said the internal structures were always churning apart, then washing back together. And when he mentioned heat, his voice turned ugly. Max decided it was Sacony's voice he didn't like. Too flat, the man's voice lacked *timbre*.

"What's happening to its heat? That's the question. How did it form ice? Why does it stay cold? That much energy can't vanish." Sacony drummed his fingers like a machine gun. The noise made Max wince.

"I don't know." Ceegie sounded cross and tired. "The liquid inside the collar last night was freezing."

Sacony made a noise with his nose. "You shouldn't have been there."

Max nodded hearty agreement, but Ceegie didn't notice. He realized that she no longer even saw him. He'd blended into the concrete like one of those color-changing lizards.

"The real question is, what does he need the energy *for*," she said.

The chief snapped, "It's polluted water. It doesn't *need*."

"You just want to be rid of it." Ceegie bit off a fingernail, and Max heard the stress in her breathing. He wanted to rub her shoulders. She needed to eat. She was getting perilously overexcited, and the chief wasn't even trying to calm her. Max realized then that Roman Sacony couldn't actually *hear* Ceegie. He could only take in the *facts* she spoke.

Suddenly, a wave splashed the dock, and all three of them turned to scrutinize the water. Gulf-Pac's mercury floodlights showed an inky surface disturbed by unseen movement. Max caught Ceegie's hand and drew her away from the edge.

The chief scowled at him. "How's that sound equipment coming?"

"It's ready, sir. Should I drop the speakers in the canal?"

"Not here." The chief handed Max a twenty dollar bill and a set of car keys. Max eyed them in confusion.

"Silver Jeep parked by the front door. Get us some coffee."

The man's flat voice grated Max's eardrums. Max looked to Ceegie for a sign, but she was caught up in a whirl of science inside her head. She'd gone far beyond him.

"I'll come back quick," he said. Then he took the keys and left.

Spume

Monday, March 14
10:29 PM

"Sound waves?" Roman examined the Lubell speakers. "Li Qin wants to try an electromagnetic pulse."

"An EMP? I thought of that. Electromagnetic pulses work great in cell phones, but strong ones can fry circuits. They're even used in weapons."

"Ah." Roman's eyes shifted.

"Balancing the power level is just too delicate," she went on. "We might disrupt his neural net. It's too risky." She visualized a weapons-grade EMP. Invisible, almost soundless, its intense burst of electrons would mushroom outward in waves, and the subatomic radiation would surge through every conductive material within range—metal wires, electronic circuits, water, human flesh. "EMP is a bad idea," she said.

"The colloid killed a man." Roman glowered at the water and slapped his pants with the back of his hand, over and over, unconsciously. "It's loose in my canal, and I intend to neutralize it."

She lifted the Lubell speakers and pushed Roman aside with her hip. "We can't predict how the colloid will react. EM pulses might antagonize him."

"Pardon me. We wouldn't want to make the dirty water mad. Let's sing it a lullaby." Roman wrested the speakers away from her, and she pushed him violently with both hands, causing him to stumble backward. He laughed in surprise. Another wave splashed over the dock, soaking their shoes.

"I'm going to use those speakers!" she said.

When she tried to take them from him, he lifted them beyond her reach and tossed them into a cart. She swung her fist, and he dodged, laughing. "Shall we duel?"

She pushed him again, but this time he caught one of her wrists and twisted her arm behind her back. He grappled her and held her close. His breath warmed the back of her neck. "You like to play rough."

"Let me go." She knew she was blushing. She tried to kick him.

He released her with a gravelly laugh. Another wave rindled over the dock like ocean surf, and they both watched it sluice around their shoes. As it drained back over the edge, CJ lifted one dripping sole. "Is the canal rising?"

"It shouldn't be." Roman sounded uncertain. They moved together to the dock's edge. The oily surface churned three feet below the concrete slab, just as before.

"What's making the waves?" CJ asked.

"Wind, maybe." Roman glanced at the motionless treetops, then at CJ. With the same thought, they turned in unison toward the water.

"Those gates will hold it," Roman said. "They could hold a hurricane."

CJ heard a grinding noise under the dock. She knelt on the wet concrete and tried to get a look at the piers. Then she lay on her stomach and craned over the edge. Beneath the dock, heat and humidity collected in a sweltering spume.

"Do you have a flashlight? I think he's feeding on the sand again."

"You have a vivid imagination." His tone was light, not like Harry's. She heard him rummaging in a toolbox.

When he returned, she took the flashlight and played its beam over the dank, slimy piers. She saw an empty beer can rubbing against the concrete. Roman knelt beside her.

"We captured a decent sample in the lagoon," he said. "We'll carry your speakers there and try out your sound wave theory. I admit, you have a knack for lucky guesses."

She sat up, all attention. "Is the sample generating a field?"

Roman nodded and looked down at his arm. In her excitement, she had gripped his wrist. When she tried to draw back, he pressed her fingers against his shirtfront.

"At first, we found nothing but pure H_2O. You were right about that," he said. "Then Yue spotted the chain of microchips shielded in a clump of proplastid. A good sample for your experiment."

"Oh I could kiss you!" she blurted. Then she blushed and lowered her head. Her womb suffused with crampy heat.

He fondled her hand against his shirt, and she felt the firm muscles of his upper abdomen. His signals were clear. He wanted her. This was the moment to decide, but her boldness drained away. She pulled free, picked up her flashlight and lay on her stomach again to see under the dock. Water sloshed around the piers in slow swells. When Roman rested his hand on her lower back, her nerves lit up.

She waved the flashlight and babbled. "What if the colloid seeps down into the water table and percolates to the Gulf? Where the river dumps out, there's a dead zone of garbage the size of New Jersey. Imagine if he finds all that junk to feed on."

Roman gripped her waistband. "Watch it. You'll fall in."

"Think how fast he might grow. He could spread into the Caribbean." She rolled on her back and shined the flashlight under her chin to make a funny face. Roman loomed above her, not smiling.

"After that, the Atlantic. Then the other oceans. There's plenty of pollution to keep him growing." She was talking too fast.

Roman brushed her forehead. "You've got mud on your face."

His hand on her face unnerved her. "Next, he'll infiltrate the clouds and rain in the rivers. And we'll drink him. Then we'll be part of him, too. Our bodies are two-thirds water."

"Reilly, settle down." He touched her hair.

"He'll live in us. And every living thing will be linked in a worldwide web of water."

Roman grimaced in that familiar way that was almost a smile. She pushed at his chest. He was leaning too close. She no longer heard the agitated gurgles that whisked through the piers below. "It could happen. Think about it."

"I have," he said in a voice as agitated as the water. Then he pressed her hands down and kissed her open mouth.

When Max returned half an hour later with four large black coffees and a dozen sugar-sprinkled *beignets*, the guard named Timothy Bojorian was duct-taping plastic sheets around the computer equipment to protect the electronics from moisture. Tim gladly accepted the coffee and pastry, but he said Mr. Sacony and Miss Reilly had gone home.

Sleet

Tuesday, March 15
5:03 AM

The Ides of March burst across Louisiana with frigid gusts of wind, and no one in the environs of Devil's Swamp could remember such peculiar weather so late in the spring. While it was still dark, Elaine Guidry woke to a spooky scratching at her bedroom window. She got up, barefoot, hugging a terry robe around her ample breasts. It was too early to call Dan Meir. She batted yellow hair out of her eyes and found her Beretta handgun. Then she turned on the porch light. Fine grains of sleet pelted her window glass, melted at once and rolled down in big clear streaks. If she hadn't risen so early, she would have missed it.

Merton Voinché saw the sleet, too, and turned on his radio, hoping the weatherman would explain. Sure enough, it turned out the sky was all mixed up. Miles high, a stagnant layer of warm air had shed its moisture. But the rain fell into a freak frigid band of cold air below, where it froze solid. Merton watched the icy grains bounce and melt in his potted hemp plants.

What Rayette Batiste found most frightening was the pattern. When she got out of bed to watch the early TV news, only one isolated patch of sleet was falling. The bright-colored radar map showed a thin yellow plume blowing East out of Devil's Swamp into the community of Scotlandville—precisely where Rayette lived. The Channel 6 weatherman said it was not uncommon for sleet to fall in localized patterns, but Rayette took it as an omen. Sure enough, when she reached out the door to catch the devil's sleet in a skillet, the ice stopped falling. And before her eyes, all the pearly grains vanished into the ground.

"Mother of Mercy." She lit a votive candle before a cardboard print of Raphael's *Madonna*. "To thee do we cry, poor banished children of Eve; to thee do we send up our sighs, mourning and weeping in this valley of tears."

Ten minutes after the sleet perished forever, Roman woke in his Hilton bedroom with the Reilly girl in his arms. It took him a while to understand. He'd slept with an employee. A girl half his age, what an ill-advised move. With the colloid loose, he should have stayed at the dock and kept watch. He should be down there now with Creque and Spicer, supervising his enemy's recapture.

He raised his head to see the digital clock on his nightstand, and the scent of her hair caught in his nostrils. A clean sweaty little girl smell, mixed with something darker and muskier—the perfume of cunt. Last night, they'd made love in the shower, clawing and biting like hot-blooded teenagers. They'd done it standing up, while the water streamed over their bodies. Then again in bed, their loins had pounded against each other, slick with sweat and saliva and cum. Now his penis was growing hard. What was it about this *blanca* that brought out his animal need?

He lay still, not ready to wake her, not sure how he wanted this to play out. His swollen member felt sore and raw—they must have made love five times during the night. This wasn't like him. He took his pleasures discreetly, far from the office, with long-limbed Cuban *putas* whose skin gleamed as brown as molasses. It wasn't like him to choose a white girl. It certainly wasn't like him to forget his work.

Gallinita, he had called her. Little chicken, because her hair stuck out like feathers. She thought he was calling her by another girl's name until he translated. Now he eased his arm out from under her head—and felt her come awake. With a faint cry, she sat up, looked at the room, at the sheets, at him. Her first tender words were, "Oh my God."

The regret in her voice galled him. Spoiled *Anglo* brat. When she covered her breasts with a pillow, he wanted to slap her. Their mingled pheromones wafted from the sheets, and his hand moved involuntarily to her cheek. But his touch was gentle. His fingertips slid down her throat, along her collarbone, and under the pillow to her breast. He pushed the pillow aside to toy with her nipple. Its pink areola tightened like an unopened bud.

"Roman, I should go."

Her words incensed him. He covered her mouth with his hand. Women did not reject him. They pursued him. Only one girl, long ago, one brown-skinned *querida* in Buenos Aires, the city of beautiful air. She took his soul and squeezed it like a lemon.

Corrienta. A bitter taste welled in his mouth at the thought of her name. Tall, dark, rich, a year ahead of him at the *universidad*. She teased him with promises, made him believe—then blithely married a German. In the days and nights before her wedding, he stalked her through the streets and pleaded, till her father hired bodyguards to force him away. Even after Corrienta moved into her husband's new brick mansion, Roman wrote her eloquent letters. He paced under her window. He left gifts with the servants. One bleak night, he broke into her rose garden and poisoned the ground with salt.

But that was decades ago. Since then, he'd married Quimicron, and soon he would consummate his brightest desires. He would not be defeated again. Certainly, this *blanca* would not reject him today. The smell of her body in the sheets tantalized him. He snatched the pillow away and squeezed her breasts.

"No," she whimpered, but he did not believe her.

He turned her on her stomach, nibbled her neck, and murmured in Spanish, "You seduced me, yes? This must be what you wanted."

Then he pushed her head down in the pillow and entered her hard.

Later in the shower, he heard her leaving and regretted that he'd played so rough. He would have to call later and smooth her feathers. But there would be time. She wouldn't bolt from his science team again. He had seen her hunger to learn about the thing he'd caught in his lagoon.

Shaving, he observed a face in the mirror that had weathered and aged. Had he always set his mouth in such a grim line? His eyes had not always been so hollow. He tried to smile, and for an instant, he caught a glimpse of the man he had been before Quimicron fell on him like a wolf and swallowed his life. *Gallinita*. Funny little thing. But she was very young.

Drain

Max sat on the sidewalk outside his ex-wife Sonia's modest frame house. He still wore the same crusted jeans and T-shirt he'd worn throughout the previous day and night, and the same faded *paryaka* still covered his head. The morning was cold, so he'd pulled on a sweatshirt for warmth. Melted sleet left the asphalt damp and glistening, and his breath came out in puffs. His boots rested in the gutter, where threads of gray water eddied around his heels and branched like roads on a map.

A dog's wet nose nudged his armpit, but he didn't move. He listened to the sweet ringing sound of water trickling down the storm drain. The soughing of traffic and wind lulled him till he caught himself nodding off. On the sidewalk beside him sat a crumpled brown bag that, at first glance, might have held a pint of whisky. This bag, though, held a clever little pink plastic jewel box with a hinged lid. And inside the box, on a bed of white cotton, lay his daughter's silver necklace. He was waiting to catch a glimpse of her, maybe walk her to school, though this wasn't his allotted visiting day. Still, the sight of little Marie always made him glad.

Max had known from the beginning that Ceegie's affection wouldn't last. *Amou,* he called her in his heart. She was so wise about facts and numbers and science. In truth, Max believed she might be a genius. But about living in the world? She was a *timoun,* a child. And worse, she didn't know it.

Himself, he was good only for physical labor and for playing the *frottior,* but that was nothing—so he believed. The songs he wrote, the somber elegies set to pulsing zydeco percussion, he counted them as scribbles and jokes, of no value. So naturally, he had expected every day that his Ceegie would leave him. Still, that didn't make it easier.

He never said he loved her because those words would sound bigheaded. Yet each time he saw the bright scary shine in her river-colored eyes, he wanted to shield her in his arms. Her pale fingernails chewed to the quick caused Max a crushing pain of fondness. He adored her feverish heat as she lay curled next to him in bed, maybe snoring a little, like a small cat. Sometimes he toyed with her hair while she slept.

Most of all, he loved her *lespir,* her soul wind. Ceegie had a symphony welling inside her. It troubled him to see how she fought against her *lespir* and blocked its flow till it raged and stormed in her chest. Often when she talked about numbers and facts, he could hear the fluent strains of her *lespir* trying to get free. But she dammed her soul wind behind a wall of resentful memories.

Max didn't understand her grievance against her *popa,* but he knew that grievance kept her thinking like a child. What he loved was the woman who waited inside her like an unopened bud. And as he listened to the water tinkling down the gutter drain, he knew he'd lost his chance to witness her flowering.

At the street corner, Marie hopped and squealed, and Max shot to his feet. He saw her climb into a van full of children. *"Timoun!"* He waved and called her name. He had missed hearing her step on the sidewalk. He caught only the swish of her pink cotton coat as the van door slammed.

After the van drove away, Max stood gripping his little paper bag and questioning the choices he'd made. He glanced at his watch. Mr. Godchaux would be short-handed today. Mr. Godchaux was offering double wages. Max sucked his teeth. Then he stuffed Marie's gift in his pocket and headed back to work.

Run

Tuesday, March 15
9:14 AM

CJ sat on the floor of her motel room staring into the desolate black mouth of her open suitcase. The dawn sleet had vaporized, and its mist hung in the air like a presence, blurring the edges of things. A Web site offering cheap tickets to Mexico glimmered on her laptop, and her trusty Boston banker had pumped fresh liquid assets into her checking account. Cozumel. Ixtapa.

Cabo San Lucas. She could fly to any of those places in time for cocktails. To-day was the anniversary of her father's death.

Four times, she had jammed all her underwear into the side pocket of her suitcase, smashing the cotton lace with her fist and forcing the zipper closed. Four times, she had pulled it out again. Now her bras and panties, dirty and clean, lay scattered over the bed, and she sat on the floor, hugging her knees to her chest. On the nightstand lay a pair of wooden castanets. She couldn't look at them. She hated Roman Sacony. She couldn't face Max. She felt dirty. She had to run.

"So why don't you pack?" Harry laughed.

She gripped her hair in her fists. "You're dead."

Her swollen breasts still hurt from Roman's roughness. She shivered, feeling his hands all over her. His semen still leaked from her crevices and made damp stains in her underpants.

Harry chortled aloud. "Have we engaged in a bit of procreation?"

"Leave me alone," she growled at the empty room.

But his smug whisper rattled her brain. "Did we make a wee babe to carry on our line?"

CJ kneaded her belly. No way could that be true. Roman wore condoms last night. Every time . . . didn't he? And Max. Cautious Max always wore condoms . . . except . . . except for that one day in the pirogue.

She felt between her legs. What if? Somewhere amid the ruddy gel in her womb, what if a sperm and egg had coalesced? She pinched her belly till it bruised. What if a tiny sack, as fragile as a droplet, were clinging to her uterine wall?

"Get out." She punched her abdomen hard. "Abort!"

That's easy, Harry purred.

Then the image that haunted her dreams flared awake. The open door, the lamp knocked to one side, the spray of blood slowly darkening on the sea-green wall. One year ago today, she found Harry lying facedown across his desk.

She seized the wooden castanets to fling at the wall, but instead, she pressed them to her lips. They clattered under her touch like someone speaking. The room lights went dim. The walls closed in on her. Everything seemed to funnel down and down until, like a cry from another world, her cell phone rang. And the Long Island accent of Peter Vaarveen yammered in her ear.

"This is your wake-up call. In five minutes, the Queen Bitch will start blasting your swamp creature with sound waves. Sacony said it was your idea."

She tossed the castanets aside. "Where are you?"

Peter gave directions to the holding lagoon where they had isolated a shred of the colloid. She pulled on running shoes without bothering to tie the laces. The forgotten suitcase tumbled off the bed. Minutes later, she was racing down Highway 61, nearly sideswiping a Chevy Tahoe.

Splash

Tuesday, March 15
10:08 AM

Inside Quimicron's fenced grounds, the holding lagoon rose like a small volcanic caldera. Its oval bowl lay within a thick earthen embankment, reinforced with concrete and lined with clay. Concrete steps led up to a steel catwalk that circled the rim, and half a dozen security lights cast a fading brilliance in the morning sunlight.

The black conduit that Captain Creque had used to pump the canal water still drooped over one side like an abandoned snakeskin. An enormous blue plastic swimming pool cover floated over the lagoon, and a stack of computer equipment leaned against the catwalk rail. Every surface shimmered with heat. Yue and Vaarveen were absorbed in their work.

"Stop!" CJ ran up the steps, waving her arms.

Yue looked at her watch. Her eyes were hidden behind opaque black sunglasses, but her sallow skin mottled to lavender. Peter sat behind her, smirking.

When CJ spotted the Lubell speakers glinting in the sunlight, she slowed to catch her breath. She wasn't too late. They hadn't lowered the speakers into the water yet. She knelt by the audio amp. The hot concrete burned her knees.

"We need to start at low volume, then check for feedback," she said. "If we start too loud, we might antagonize it, and that's just the opposite of what we—"

Yue's long shadow fell across the amp, and CJ squinted up to see the woman's skeletal silhouette haloed against the sun. Yue's voice rippled with tiny tremolos of irritation. "Roman says you have another new hypothesis."

Heat wavered around Yue like a solar flare, making CJ's eyes water. The woman's voice echoed like all the black-clad MIT pedagogues who had stood in judgment of CJ's intellect. She remembered twisting herself inside-out to win their praise, because anything less drew Harry's verdict that she was flighty, ungrateful, and capricious—like her mother.

CJ realized she was kneeling before Yue like a menial, so she got to her feet and brushed off her dirty knees. "It's about language," she said, coughing to clear her throat. Then in the disciplined academic style Harry had taught her, she defended the theory she'd been piecing together in her mind.

It had probably taken years, she said, for the fragmented microchips in the pond to assemble their first embryonic neural net. The proplastid algae goo must have sealed the chips and kept their circuits intact. And though each individual chip had limited capabilities, once they began passing signals through the water, their pooled code must have evolved along complex new lines. Now, the neural net was seeking to interact with its environment. Hence the response to music.

"That 4/4 beat from my iPod was probably the closest thing to computer language he has encountered since his—birth."

When CJ said "birth," Yue tightened her grip on her elbows, but Peter Vaarveen grinned. *Non compos mentis,* CJ could read the judgment in their eyes. So when they actually began setting up the equipment to test her theory, she thought the heat was making her hallucinate. She didn't realize Roman had ordered them to assist her.

Yue said to Peter, "Show her the new data."

"Yes, my queen."

Peter bent over his workstation and opened a file for CJ to browse. "You're right about the coating of plant sap. It protects their electronics. Keeps them from shorting out. But there's too much proplastid. Even in a swamp choked with algae, you would never expect to find so much."

"So you investigated?" CJ crossed her arms and waited.

Peter batted his pale eyelashes. "Gen mod," he announced, meaning "genetic modification." Embedded in the algae bloom, he'd found numerous commercially engineered plant cells dating from as far back as the 1990s. He showed her the list: corn cells laced with pest toxins, wheat germ spliced with reptile genes, tobacco fiber secreting human proteins. The proplastid had digested them all.

"This juice is a bad boy," Peter said with admiration.

The lagoon sample held a warehouse of other particles even more exotic than those Yue found earlier: Jerky little motorized ratchets only a few molecules in size. Asynchronous semiconductors designed to speed up local coordination in massive computer circuits. Neuromorphic nanochips copied after the human optic nerve for use in robotic eyes.

CJ laughed and clapped her hands.

"It gets better." Peter called up a graphic file showing the pair of microchip chains they'd found drifting at the center of the EM field. To the naked eye, the thready conglomerate appeared invisible, or at best a milky blur. He said the structure polarized and refracted light, camouflaging its position. But once Yue lit up the mass with isotope marker dyes, it resembled a loose drifting braid of yarn. CJ gazed at the image with an open mouth. Yue had been the first to call the structure a skein.

Finally, Peter showed CJ their real breakthrough. Nested inside the paired chains, they found a working mote computer.

"Working?" CJ's breath caught.

"Yeah, a live mote. It's emitting radio waves." Peter spoke as if he could hardly believe it himself. His sunburned skin was peeling, and his hair stood up in greasy white shocks. He showed her the image on screen, then compared it to a schematic downloaded from a Canadian manufacturer's Web site. The image showed a layered cube, smaller than a pinhead, laced with complex circuitry and packing its own miniscule solar battery. "It's got waterproof sensors, a processor. It's designed to take weather readings and send bursts of radio code."

The discovery went to CJ's head like a drug. When Yue acknowledged that some of the microchips were actively echoing the mote's signals, CJ felt like crowing.

She rushed to the lagoon rim, pealed back the plastic cover and stuck her arm in elbow deep. The water wasn't frigid, it felt warm and tingly. *You're real.* She felt ready to burst with gladness. She bounced up and spun Peter Vaarveen in a circle. Yue sneered, but Peter didn't seem to mind.

Yue insisted the microchip skein was an accidental arrangement with no permanent form, like a splash or a rainbow. She even played a time-exposure sequence showing how it repeatedly dissolved and reformed, always in a slightly different shape.

"So what? We're all accidents." CJ felt too elated to get mad. "You could say the whole universe is a fricking accident."

"Oh brother." Peter tried to get the women on another subject. He told them the particles were circulating in synchronized patterns, and he downloaded a flocking "boid" simulation to show what he meant. On his screen, a cluster of computer-generated green spheres wheeled and shifted like schooling fish. CJ found the graphic eerie and hypnotic, but Yue called it a kid's video game.

Yue stood clutching her elbows with her long spiny fingers. "I have business at the canal. Someone let our captive out of its collar yesterday, and I have to catch it again. So unless you have more brilliant theories, Ms. Reilly, let's get this farce over with."

Hormonal heat flushed CJ's cheeks and robbed her of the sharp comeback she longed to hurl. She couldn't have guessed that the older woman's emotions were as muddled as her own. At that moment, Yue wanted to drown CJ in the river. Yue had seen her leaving Roman's hotel room.

For a moment, Yue stared at her rival. Then she marched away to the end of the dock, refastening her braid. Roman had slept with this trashy little tart? Insufferable. But Yue had been through this before, and she knew Roman's affairs didn't last. Inwardly, she scolded herself for letting feelings interfere with her work. But she had sacrificed so much. Her bones ached. Her skin felt too tight.

She clawed through her pocket for the red-and-black capsule, then swallowed it without water. There was much to do. Creque was repositioning the collar this morning, trying to enclose the colloid again. She needed to be there, but Roman insisted that she help this stupid girl. She rubbed her hands to hide the trembling. Then, with a bitter cough, she returned and set to work.

Peter lowered the speakers into the water. "Shall we begin our little broadcast?"

For the next hour, Yue, Peter, and CJ bounced rhythmic tones through the lagoon. They tried binary code, prime numbers, logarithms. Sometimes, the water rippled and hazed, but Yue demonstrated beyond a doubt that these so-called "responses" were merely currents of heat convection.

In fact, the air grew sweltering, soon topping 90°F, and the water under the blue plastic simmered like a Jacuzzi. When Yue called a halt, CJ was too absorbed to stop. From the steps, Yue cast one last resentful glance at CJ's narrow shoulders hunched over the equipment. Then she ordered Peter to drive her to the canal.

Gleam

Tuesday, March 15
2:00 PM

CJ slumped against the rail, baking her butt on the hot concrete by the lagoon, unwilling to give up. Sound waves propagated through the water, and sensors processed the feedback. In slow currents of heat, the skein revolved languidly, like a liquid crystal kaleidoscope. It accumulated new bits of toxic scum from the lagoon walls, but nothing else happened. No flashing lights. No pulsing magnetism. Gradually CJ began to consider that she might be wrong.

Then two events coincided. Her cell phone chimed, and Max appeared with a cardboard box. He was dressed in his usual sleeveless T-shirt, blue jeans, and leather work boots. He kicked sheepishly at the catwalk and murmured, "Thought you might want something to eat."

Simultaneously, Roman's voice rustled in her ear. "Good afternoon, little hen." Her face reddened. She switched Roman off without answering.

Quickly, she rifled through a crate of lab equipment to hide the fact that she couldn't meet Max's eyes. "You're not working with Rory today?"

"Got the afternoon off," he said simply, not mentioning the long overtime hours he'd been racking up.

When she felt a little calmer, she faced him. He didn't seem angry. His placid smile made her want to tear her hair out.

From the cardboard box, he handed her a plastic container and a spoon. Inside, she found a scoop of cold homemade blackberry bread pudding. His Aunt Roberta had picked and frozen the berries last summer, and this morning he'd blended a quart of them with bread crumbs, lemon juice, cinnamon, nutmeg, sugar, butter, and eggs, then spiked the mix with his secret ingredient, Cointreau. He'd made this pudding for her once before, that time he took her fishing in the pirogue.

"Max—"

He touched her lips and looked away. Why wouldn't he let her talk? She seized the spoon and stuffed her mouth full. The silence lengthened and grew awkward. When she forced herself to swallow, the half-chewed berries hurt her throat going down.

"It was a mistake," she stammered. "I shouldn't have gone with him."

Max shifted to face the lagoon through the hot metal bars of the rail. He wore a clean *paryaka* tied around his head, although it was already dotted with sweat. Sunlight gleamed on his swarthy cheeks. He sat with his elbows resting on his knees, peering into the uncovered strip of water.

"*Djab dile* speak yet?"

CJ made a noise, half groan, half sigh. He wasn't going to let her apologize. What a mess she'd made. What a royal mess. She turned and followed his gaze. The blue cover scintillated under the ruthless sun, and the air above it wavered with hot humid mirages, like invisible flames.

She tore off a broken fingernail. "We're not getting any response. I don't know what I expected."

Max slipped the headset over his ears and listened to the audio signals she was transmitting through the water. She'd transcribed simple mathematical expressions as whole notes, and the synthesized tones chimed in a one-two rhythm as steady as a metronome. Repetitive, ordered, lucid.

He scratched his ear. "Maybe . . ."

"What?" she said irritably.

"This beat is tiresome, Ceegie. *Bing bing bing.* How he tell us apart from a machine?"

She threw up her hands. "I'm trying to translate human language into signals a primitive mote computer can process. That means starting with basics. Syntax, lexicon, rules about meaning. You think that's easy?"

"Don' sound easy," he agreed.

She eyed him. "Obviously, you have another idea."

"Naw, it's nothing. You go on with your bing bing."

CJ clenched her teeth. "Max, sometimes you drive me batshit. Just say what's on your mind."

His golden brown eyes reflected the sun. Instead of speaking, he hummed an old ballad. His rich baritone rose through a melancholy crescendo, then slid sideways to a bluesy wistful close. When the song finished, he said, "You *sav*? Machine cain' do that."

CJ shrugged. "And your point is?"

He grinned and scat-sang a different song, lilting and playful, bouncing upward in G major. After that, he whistled a stalwart march in B flat. When he launched into a stormy overture, she interrupted.

"I get it. Sure. Music is not math. It conveys—what?—a mood? But you're talking about dense acoustic detail. Shifting frequencies and amplitudes, harmony, melody, syncopated rhythm. That's too much complexity for a mote."

"Ceegie, little children know what a song mean. Even animals know. Music don' require translation." Max's sonorous baritone crooned again, and this time he sang the zydeco chorus that first made the frozen pond vibrate in sync.

CJ watched the water. She seized his arm. "Could it work?"

His biceps hardened at her touch, and he patted her hand. "Take a look at what ol' Max brought."

His cardboard box held dozens of CDs, collected over the years from yard sales and bargain stores. Aboriginal dreaming songs from Australia, traditional Hawaiian slide guitar, Andean Mountain flutes, Creole *séga* from the isles of the Indian Ocean. He'd brought Tajik rap, Tibetan throat-singing, and West African kora, along with Debussy's "Reverie," Duke Ellington's "Prelude to a Kiss," and of course, plenty of pure classic zydeco.

"Something in here bound to interest *djab dile*," he said.

She opened random jewel cases to read the liner notes, and in her excitement, she shuffled the silvery disks like a deck of cards. Max's hands closed over hers and stopped her. Reverently, he replaced his CDs in their cases, arranged them in the cardboard box and covered them with his *paryaka* to keep out the sun. His naked black curls glistened with moisture.

"First, something easy." He pulled out an old Casio portable keyboard, stained with tobacco smoke, wine, coffee, and the fingerprints of many hands. After connecting it to the amplifier that fed the Lubell speakers, he played a soft scale. "Show me how you catch what *djab dile* say back to us."

CJ worried with the controls of her feedback monitors. "We're tracking changes in the EM field, wavelength, frequency, power level."

"And sound?" he asked.

"Liquid can't make sound." She raised her eyebrows, doubting. "I've been here the whole time. I didn't hear anything."

She listened to the fizzy splash of water against the underside of the plastic cover, the quiet swish of tiny ripples, the susurrus of steam. She flicked her thumbnail against her teeth. Then she exploded into activity, tearing through the crates of equipment, knocking everything into disarray.

"Here it is." Max pulled an old hydrophone out of his duffel. He'd bought it at a flea market so he and his cousins could listen to beaked whales in the Gulf.

She seized it and rushed to the water's edge, then had to ask him how it worked. Once Max connected it, they listened to the rich sloshing babble in the lagoon. Quickly, she coded one of the computers to display the feedback as a wave form, like an oscilloscope. Then she angled the screen so Max could watch.

But he didn't need it. He sat cross-legged, balancing the keyboard in his lap, playing soft simple scales in 4/4 meter and listening to the noise from the hydrophone with his eyes closed.

She scraped a folding chair across the concrete, sat in front of the computer and slotted a fresh disk to record Max's improvisation—and, she hoped, the colloid's response. But signals from the lagoon remained mixed. Overlapping waves jittered across the screen from left to right, without pattern or form. The water noise duplicated all the other feedback monitors. It was inconclusive. Another useless test.

Her attention kept wandering to Max's fingers sweeping over the black and white keys. How fluently he played, as easily as other people talked. Fresh guilt assaulted her as she watched him improvise a lyrical riff, a languid trickle of melody, a spill of half notes and a somber swell of bass.

Almost by accident, she noticed the first pattern. Max had stopped playing. He sat rigid with his eyes shut tight, head cocked toward the hydrophone receiver. She was thinking how much better he looked without the bandana, how sweetly his black curls framed his face, when a single coherent wave emerged from the static and bounced across her computer screen.

She saw it from the corner of her eye. Then it vanished, and there was only static. Monitors registered a slight turbulence, maybe a passing breeze. Certain regions along the gooey skein were generating ions, but Yue had already documented that. Molecules were randomly losing and gaining electrons, shifting their electrical charges to and fro and creating tiny pockets of polarization in the water. But that had nothing to do with music. Yue had also noted concentrations of heat and acidity at one end of the skein—a by-product of microbe activity.

CJ kept watching. She tugged at her damp cotton panties that had bunched between her legs. Perspiration streaked her hair. Under her thin T-shirt, salty droplets collected between her breasts and rolled down her belly. She fantasized an icy bottle of Coca-Cola. She could almost taste its foam.

"Hear that?" Max opened his eyes and smiled. He played another simple riff, then paused and leaned toward the hydrophone, listening.

CJ watched the oscilloscope. Another perfect wave bounced across the screen. Then it broke into a jittery row of sine curves, like a heart monitor tracking cardiac arrest. She sat on the edge of her chair. Max played another few bars, then listened.

That's when she noticed the ion data on one of the other screens. Ordinary molecules were taking extra electrons, then letting them go, popping from neutral to positive, positive to neutral—in *rhythm*. She pounded the keys to create a graphic map—and there it was, a coherent line of sine curves. In the bright false hues of the graphics program, her computer painted standing waves of ionization in 4/4 time.

Rapidly, she checked other sensor feedback—pH, photometrics, turbidity, turbulence—all the columns of data were dancing in rhythm.

"Molecular music." Her voice came out hushed.

"Oh yeah, he got sync." Max pressed his ear to the receiver. "He playing back my rhythm, beat for beat."

She bounced in her chair and squealed, "He's composing music from chemistry!"

"Composing? Naw, girl, he just copy me." Max's cheeks dimpled. "He play *bèl,* very precise, like an echo."

"He echoes you? But I thought—" She scrolled through a column of figures. "I thought he was answering."

Max bit his lip. "Ceegie, *ma chagrenne.* You discover a very excellent music machine made of water and trash. Tha's no small thing."

"Right." She tried to laugh, but her face had a grayish cast. She'd been working too long at too intense a level. Max couldn't guess what she hoped for, but he realized a music machine wasn't it. He'd blundered again, nothing new. He felt like a gnat.

"*Djab dile* learning," he said. "Take time to learn music. You wait. We give him a composition lesson."

"How?"

Max repositioned the keyboard across his knees. "Start with G major."

He sounded the chord, first with all the notes together, then each separately in ascending order. After that, he played simple melodies in G, mixing and rearranging the handful of notes in various patterns. CJ checked her disk drive to make sure she was recording what Max played. Her screens showed the skein altering its kinetic energy to imitate the notes.

"We do this till he learn," Max said.

CJ sat on the rough warm concrete and watched raindrops bouncing on the lagoon cover. Then she got up to check her screens. Impatience drove her back and forth from the workstation to the water, while Mac played the soft plain notes of his music lesson for a beginner.

Swig

Tuesday, March 15
3:50 PM

Across town in his cloistered office, Hal Butler took a swig of Dixie beer. Loose slips of paper, flash drives, magnetic disks, fast-food wrappers, and several well thumbed paperbacks littered his desk, not to mention his size-eleven loafers filled with his sockless sweaty feet. At the center of the chaos lay his tape recorder, chock-full of hearsay, gossip, and distorted speculation about the Watermind.

The news scoop of his life had finally materialized. Riches, glory, long lines of succulent young women, his own personal nirvana lay within reach. This story merged all the best qualities of his favorite films, *Swamp Thing,* the *Creature from the Black Lagoon,* and that stirring 1958 classic, *The Blob,* where an alien dollop of raspberry jam tried to eat a small town. Hal could almost taste his Pulitzer. The Watermind would sail him into the Journalism Hall of Fame. But regrettably, he had no facts.

The Reilly chick was waffling. She wouldn't commit to the interview, and she kept ducking his phone calls. He upended his aluminum can and let the cold beer roll down his throat. Lovingly, with a razor blade, he squared up a line of cocaine on a mirror. Then he snorted the white dust through a straw.

Seconds later, he experienced a sudden blinding epiphany. What this story needed was a picture—something memorable and graphic that would resonate in the reader's mind. On a legal pad, he roughed out a conceptual sketch—a sort of howling liquid genie with fangs—not unlike the machine-generated monster in *The Forbidden Planet,* a motion picture he greatly admired.

Ah yes. The drawing revitalized his energy. He squared up his keyboard, flicked his fingers and punched in the URL for the Holy Trinity discussion forum. In a trice, he transmogrified from dedicated newshound Hal Butler into his secret alter-ego, Jeremiah Destiny, apocalyptic blogger extraordinaire. Soon, he was instant messaging his muse.

Hal aka Jeremiah knew very little about his faithful online pen pal, Soeur Rayette, only that she lived somewhere in Baton Rouge, wrote antebellum prose, and agreed with him on every topic. He envisioned her as a fair Acadian goddess, his own Evangeline, a wise and soulful little hottie. Tonight, as usual, they bared their hearts about the Watermind.

In the past few hours, hundreds of people had responded to Hal's blog about the artificial intelligence coalescing from Mississippi River trash. Though skeptics whined, most respondents believed his blog implicitly. A smart water-based computer made of floating rubbish, why not? Hal/Jeremiah's online readers had their own misty methods of verifying the truth. For them, a machine-being born from the poisonous effluent of Western civilization seemed not only true but inevitable.

Hal spread his laptop on the floor between his knees, stroked his copper hair and asked Rayette to give him more facts about the Watermind. But Rayette, as usual, demurred.

"Let us turn to the Lord for an answer," she messaged.

"Yes, dear. Consult your Bible." Hal snuffled another white line of coke. Rayette had once described to him how she solved life's riddles by opening her King James at random. He found her spirituality charming. He also knew that whatever verse her fancy happened to light on, he would be able to spin it. He picked white crumbs from his nostrils and ate them.

As usual, Rayette forwarded the Lord's answer in red italic:

"And in the fourth watch of the night, Jesus went unto them, walking on the sea. And when the disciples saw him, they were troubled, saying, It is a spirit; and they cried out for fear."

Hal quickly replied, "Alas, sweet Soeur, as the disciples witnessed this mighty wonder and cried out, so you, too, must cry out and tell the world what you've seen. That is the Lord's commandment to you." He bold-faced the last sentence.

"Verily, I am sore afraid," she answered.

Hal cracked his knuckles and keyed, "Yes, miracles are frightening, but how can the Lord be wrong?"

A long interval passed before her next instant message arrived. "Good night, dear friend. I must pray."

"Shit." Hal watched her click off. Then he scribbled on the back of an ad circular. "Nothing strikes more fear in the human heart than a miracle. . . . Hmm, good line."

Bubble

Tuesday, March 15
7:07 PM

At the Gulf-Pac dock, Peter Vaarveen grumbled under his breath, "Fuckin' boat anchor." The portable battery for his multichannel analyzer weighed nearly a hundred pounds, and Peter was not accustomed to heavy labor. But Roman had ordered them to move immediately off the Gulf-Pac dock because a lawsuit was brewing, and Hammer Nesbitt's hospitality had come to an end.

Peter stretched and arched his back. In the sky, he saw a flock of dark birds wheeling like a liquid wave. He watched them turn and plunge, and suddenly, they seemed to change color as their speckled underwings caught the slanting light. Ornithologists once believed that flocks communicated through electromagnetic emanations. But Peter knew their charming aerobatics emerged from the same simple rules which drove his computer boid: Stay close; follow your neighbor; go with the flow.

He scowled at the heavy battery. "Help me with this," he called to the knotty, walnut-colored man in the gray work shirt.

But Rory Godchaux made no move. Rory had been running crews for too

many decades to take orders from a chemist. Besides, Rory was not in good
spirits. The blue gates were sealed up tight, but the boys on the *Refuerzo*
couldn't get their collar in the right place. The magnetic water kept creeping
along the canal bed, slipping away from them.

On top of that, Rory couldn't fill his nightshift. Three of his best workers
called in sick, and one quit. Mr. Meir kept approving overtime, but Rory
couldn't find anyone to hire. And he was getting damned tired of eating soggy
takeout from the Shrimp Hut. He wanted to go home to his wife's fried catfish and spoonbread. He wanted to sink between her hot creamy thighs and
rub his nose in her plump belly. He could almost taste her pickle brine.

He said, "Merton, go give the scholar yo' hand truck."

While Merton Voinché and Betty DeCuir packed up the science machinery and loaded it onto a waiting Quimicron barge, Rory sat on an iron bollard, cocked up one knee, and worked a toothpick around his left incisor.
People were scared, that's why they wouldn't work. Some said a devil was
moving in the water. *Loa* spirits. *Djab dile.* He'd heard them talking. He fished
a shred of shrimp meat from his teeth and rolled it with his tongue. Yesterday, young Alonzo burned his hands in the water, but Mr. Meir hushed that
up. Rory touched the cross he wore under his shirt and whispered to the Vir-
gin. "Mother of God, pray for us sinners. . . ."

A few yards away, Li Qin Yue closed her eyes and listened to the canal. She
was lying flat on her back on the Quimicron barge, supervising the transfer
of her equipment and letting the deck's residual heat penetrate her bones.
Wind ruffled the canal, altering its surface from silk to velvet and rolling the
barge in a shallow tide of compression waves. *Plash. Plash. Plash.* The barge
rocked with the same rhythm that soothed Cleopatra once on another river,
an ocean away in time.

In the distance, the *Refuerzo* repositioned its collar. Its engine whined. Li
Qin was very tired. She never slept well, but since coming to Baton Rouge,
she'd barely slept at all. Today was her birthday. She was fifty-nine years old,
but no one knew that. Fifty-nine years old, and still just a glorified lab tech.

Plash, plash, the warm deck rocked like a hammock, lulling her, while the
last glow of sunset deepened to purple. For just one moment, Yue wanted to
forget her age, to forget her fading career, to forget her empty apartment—
bereft of even houseplants because she was never home to water them. Roman Sacony paid her two hundred thousand a year to answer at his beck and
call. For a paltry two hundred thousand, she'd bargained away her life, her

soul, her chances. She was almost old enough to be his mother. Why did she slave for him year after year, when he never looked at her anymore, not like he once did.

And yet, she had found his heat. The heat that obsessed him. How did the colloid form ice? What was absorbing the heat? Finally she could answer him, in concept at least. The heat was in the bubbles.

Suspended throughout the colloidal mass, she'd found microscopic bubbles of CFCs. Chlorofluorocarbons—notorious destroyers of the planetary ozone layer. Better known by their trade name, Freon. When Freon absorbed heat, it formed gas bubbles. When it released heat, it liquefied. It was the perfect liquid cooling system.

People had been dumping old refrigerators and AC units in the river since the early 1930s, and hundreds of them must have washed up in Devil's Swamp. Now, by random chance or twisted fate, the ubiquitous proplastid goo was saturated with microbubbles of Freon. And the electrostatic currents were cycling heat to and from this Freon foam—apparently, *at will.*

At will. Yue pondered those words. She blotted her cheek with her hand. Soon she would call and give Roman the news, and possibly win his fleeting approval. Hot perspiration coated her body like a second skin. The barge deck sweated, and her damp limbs seemed to glide on a film of condensation. So much wetness had pooled under her eyes that she couldn't tell if the stinging came from perspiration or tears.

Patter

Tuesday, March 15
11:14 PM

Unseen in the darkness of Devil's Swamp, a bleak drizzle fell. Each drop carried gases from the upper atmosphere, sulfur dioxide from Texas power plants and ozone from Los Angeles freeways. There were also Honduran fruitfly eggs, orchid pollen from the Congo, and lunar dust. In the surfaces of a thousand green pools, the hot teeming drops gouged craters as round as pennies—evanescent craters of liquid, as ephemeral as notes of music.

CJ and Max were too engaged in their experiment to worry about rain. In their circle of floodlight by the lagoon, they hardly noticed the drizzle that drummed on the tarp sheltering their work area. And though CJ made wise-cracks about camping, she bounced and twitched with too much adrenaline to mind the weather. Since Max taught her how to hear the colloid, her weariness had vanished, and her logic had sharpened to lambent intensity.

"Molecular music," she dubbed the rhythms in the skein's material sub-stance. Standing waves of polarization, pulsing isotopes, shifting tempera-ture inversions, seesawing pH—and always, steady upwelling streams of pure clean water. The more she searched at the molecular level, the more material rhythms she found. All this time, the colloid had been echoing her attempts at communication, but until Max showed her, she didn't know how to listen.

"He'll learn to compose, I know it. Soon, soon, he'll talk to us." She couldn't keep still. "Oh Max, I love you!"

She was too keyed up to know what she meant by those words. Max smiled and nodded, but her careless affection cut him like a machete. To-night, they could pretend a little, sheltered under their cozy tarp, but tomor-row, he knew she would become a famous scientist, and he would go back to the cleanup crew.

"Gosh, the skein is growing." Her voice sounded anxious.

Max laid down his keyboard and stood behind her. The computer screen reflected her shining face, but the graphs meant nothing to him. She played a rapid tattoo on her keyboard and jiggled the mouse. Sometimes he envied the gadgets that absorbed her attention. He massaged her shoulders, feeling useless and already forgotten.

She pushed up from her chair and rushed to the water's edge. In seconds, the rain soaked her shirt. "We need a sample quick. Help me roll back the cover." She pointed to a spot at the lagoon's center.

Max appraised the water-laden plastic cover, the frenzied girl, the rain. He sucked his teeth. Ceegie was getting too excited, almost hectic. Her *lespir* were stirring up a wind devil in her chest. He'd seen her like this before. With a shake of his head, he hustled through the downpour and helped her un-snap half a dozen grommets. When they tugged the cover open, a puff of steam rolled out and dispersed in the rain. Max saw she was about to dive in for a sample, so he got hold of her waist.

"*Lamie* girl, haven't you learned nothing about this water?"

"We're losing time." She struggled, and they fell together on the slick catwalk.

When she grew calmer, he released her, and they lay panting in the rain. Max let his own aggravation cool. Then he curled around her and tentatively stroked her back. She rolled to face him. Water sparkled in her eyes— raindrops? She slipped her arms around him and pressed her cheek to his sodden T-shirt. "I'm sorry."

He held her gratefully, but already he could sense her attention shifting. She rolled away and sat up, and her voice sounded small amid the patter of rain. "We need something to dip a sample."

Max wiped his face. He pointed toward a muddle of gear near the lagoon's edge. "There's a pole over there, got a cup fixed to the end. Tha's what they used before."

"Of course." CJ gathered sample jars while Max lifted the rain-slick, twelve-foot pole. She knelt at the lagoon rim and twisted off the jar lids. "There's a big floral clump of plant sap, see?"

Rain drilled the lagoon surface, obscuring the view of what lay beneath. She pointed to a spongy mass the size of a fist budding on the lagoon floor. Yue's marker dye had stained it vivid blue.

"I see it." Max balanced on the rim and lowered the pole.

"We want a tiny piece." Water rilled through her hair, and she batted loose strands away. "Its volume has doubled in the last two hours. God, that's fast. Peter said its specific gravity changes. That must mean—"

"Slow down, lamie. Speak English." Max swept a cup of cloudy water from the lagoon, bracing the long limber pole against his belly.

She steadied the pole and guided the cup to her sample jar. Rain dripped down her arm and mixed with the sample.

"Specific gravity is a measure of density," she said. He could tell she was making an effort to simplify her words for him. "Since the colloid is mostly water, its density should be about one gram per cubic centimeter."

"I believe you." Max nudged the cup gently against the floral mass for another sample. It was hard to see through the rain.

"But Peter says its density changes, and now I realize that makes sense. See, that's why sometimes it floats on the surface, and sometimes it sinks. But could that explain why its volume doubled? I don't know. It's complicated."

"Tha's for sure." Max could hear the manic exhilaration straining her voice. He balanced the quivering pole against his thigh and lifted another cup of water.

"Fine. We have enough." She carried the two full jars through the rain to the tarp-sheltered workbench, where Peter had set up Quimicron's SE microscope. Though she hated to see such a beautiful instrument damaged by weather, she had to admire Peter's reckless disregard of Quimicron property. Sometimes it was good to have an asshole on your team.

After preparing a dozen slides, she examined a specimen through the SE scope. "Play him some more music, okay?"

Max's fingers were cramping from holding the pole so long. He wanted to rest a while and enjoy the sound of the rain thrumming on their tarp, but CJ's mood alarmed him. He took off his dripping T-shirt and wrung it out. "Ceegie, why you care so much about *djab dile?*"

"Why?"

CJ glimpsed Max's bare chest and shoulders. His chest hairs coiled in tight round curls, and rain dribbled down his dark muscled belly. She felt an urge to run her fingers over his skin, and his distracting beauty made her almost forget the question he'd asked.

"Pure water, tha's a good thing," Max went on, "but that don' seem like enough reason for all you do."

"You wouldn't say that if you were dying of cholera." Immediately, she regretted her rude tone. Max looked away.

The chimera structures in her microscope shifted and rearranged, but she didn't notice. She watched Max pull his wet shirt back on. His question confounded her. How could she explain what, to her, seemed obvious. A cheap way to purify water could save thousands of lives.

Still, something rang false in that answer. Maybe she had mixed motives. Were anyone's reasons ever pure? "I want to know," she said at last.

Max glanced up and waited to hear more.

"I want to find out about the colloid. How he emerged, what he can do." She adjusted the eyepiece back and forth, bringing her slide in and out of focus. "I have to know."

Rumble

Roman saw Max Pottevents touching Reilly's knee. As he stood in the shadows, watching them from a distance, he wondered, not for the first time, about their relationship. The drizzle was tapering off, and a veil of fog hung over the lagoon. Water puddled on the concrete rim. Quietly, Roman approached the tarp-covered work area to hear what the boat driver was saying.

"All these songs in the key of G, sa very important to play them in this order. Sa progression, you *sav?*" The young man arranged a small stack of CDs. He handled them fondly, squaring up the corners and placing them neatly in a cardboard box. "Do you have a paper? I write the names down."

"Read them out. I'll make a file." Reilly opened a Word file on her laptop.

The young man grinned. "Paper don' need a battery." He pulled a damp, dog-eared notepad from his hip pocket and leafed through the pages. Dense music notation covered most of the sheets. When he found a clean page, he ripped it out and wrote down the titles with a stub of pencil, then read them aloud.

Roman had taught himself many languages, but these titles sounded like babble—a distorted blend of French, English, and Spanish, suffused with some ancient primal tongue. Creole, he realized, the patois of mixed races. Once in a college essay, he had described Latin America as a voracious mouth, chewing up Old World languages, then spewing them out as a brave new polyglot. He stepped closer to listen.

"When I get home, I splice the best parts together, make *djab dile* a good lesson," the young man said. "Le's go home now, Ceegie. Sleep a while, work tomorrow."

Reilly looked at her watch and shoved a strand of wet hair behind her ear. "Ten more minutes, okay. I really think we're close."

"Close to what?" Roman said.

His words made them flinch like guilty children. Reilly knocked her soda bottle over. The young Creole recovered first. He got to his feet and spoke with appropriate respect. "Good evenin', Mr. Sacony."

Roman nodded and moved under the dripping tarp toward the monitors that were still recording temperature, ionization, and pH. What he wanted most was a solid lock on his enemy. He needed to find its Achilles' heel fast. Two more neighboring companies had filed lawsuits.

All night, he'd tossed in his hotel bed, thinking of ways to trap the elusive colloid. Finally, giving up on sleep, he'd returned to the canal—and cursed Michael Creque for needing rest while the enemy still roamed loose. Roman wanted to talk strategy, and when he found Reilly working, his hopes rebounded. But then he realized this wouldn't be a simple talk about work.

Complications. Complexities. He felt enmeshed in them. Reilly needed soothing, her furious silence made that clear. How tightly she crossed her arms over her breasts. He recalled the sweaty sweetness of her nipples, felt himself wanting her again, and cursed his own weakness. The nuances of flattery and courtship required a leisure he didn't possess. Yes, her feathers were ruffled, and—*maldiciónes!*—he would have to smooth them before they could discuss the task at hand.

He addressed Pottevents first. "We should inspect the canal. Get the boat ready."

Max answered promptly. "Yes, sir."

Reilly sprang from her seat. "I'll go with you, Max." She would have fled down the steps, but Roman caught her arm.

Max took a step toward him, eyeing his hand on the girl's arm. "Sir, I don' have the boat key."

Without letting go, Roman drew his phone from his pocket and tossed it one-handed to Max. "Call whoever has the key. I want to check that canal."

Max palmed the phone, but he didn't move. Roman held the girl. They stood together, three figures caught in floodlight.

"*Gallinita,*" Roman whispered.

The girl jerked free of his grip. "Go on, Max. I'll be along in a minute. First, I have to tell this guy a few things."

Max gave her a lingering glance, and again, Roman wondered what was between them. After a few seconds, the young man departed, leaving them alone.

"You're a swine," Reilly said, when Max was out of earshot.

"Yes, little hen, we're both animals." His voice came out low and gravelly.

When he tried to embrace her, she pulled free and darted several paces along the slippery catwalk. Rainwater pooled in the lagoon cover and made it sag like a bowl.

"*Chica*. You pretend not to like me? This isn't how you behaved before." He moved beside her and stroked her back. "Tell me what has changed."

She gave him a sour glance. He felt the warmth radiating from her body. Damp strands of red hair curled at the back of her neck, and her wet shirt outlined her narrow torso. He wanted to open her clothes and take her there, standing against the rail.

She flicked wet hair from her face. "We work together. Let's leave it at that."

Roman's chin jutted up. This spoiled American princess had turned his own reasoning against him. Of course she was right. He should take her at her word and put an end to this awkward affair. His enemy was still growing. He needed to check the data. But the smell of her hair gave him an erection. Her body exuded sexual chemistry like a fine vaporous code.

"We've been teaching him chords," she said. "He learns fast. He can play G and B flat. We were just starting on F."

"What? He?" The non sequitur distracted him. "Who can play?"

"Let me show you."

She lit up the computers, talking rapidly and growing more excited as she explained their findings. Her oscilloscope program painted a prismatic wave form undulating in 4/4 time. Roman studied the rhythmic pulses of ions, heat, and acidity, and when she showed him how they replicated Max's keyboard tunes, he had to go over the data twice before he could accept the truth. The colloid responded to sound at the molecular level. He dropped into a folding chair, astonished.

"We can use this as a basis to build a language," she said. "He's just learning now, but once he begins to compose—"

"Slow down. You're leaping too far. Are you suggesting this vichyssoise of river trash is an artificial intelligence?"

"I didn't say artificial. He's more complex than that."

"Please stop gracing this thing with a gender."

Roman got up and paced the wet catwalk, running his hand along the dripping rail and staring fitfully at the lagoon. "Chemical response to sound. Not intelligence, certainly. It's probably just an echo, but it's fascinating."

CJ nearly jerked her mouse off its cord. "It's more than an echo. He'll learn to compose."

Roman caught her wrists and pulled her away from his valuable equipment. "How long have you been going without sleep?"

Her made her sit down and drink some bottled water. She submitted like a petulant schoolgirl, but he could see the exhaustion in her glassy hazel eyes. He checked his watch. Yue and Vaarveen were due back soon.

"Go home and sleep. You've done well. I'll give you a bonus."

"Bonus!" She spat the word like poison.

"I'll give you a back rub. A sports car. What do you want, Reilly? Tell me, and I'll give it to you."

"Sir." Max Pottevents was standing on the steps below, tugging a leather glove on with his teeth. His baritone rumbled thicker than usual. "The boat's ready."

Roman acknowledged him with a distracted nod. "Reilly, this is an order. Get some sleep." Then he followed Max toward the boat ramp.

CJ huddled in her folding chair and watched them leave. "Why don't you ask if Max needs sleep?" she muttered, but by then, Roman was too far away to hear.

She finished drinking her water, then brutalized the plastic bottle. Little hen, ha! She sneered at the flattened bottle, then kicked it under the rail. It landed on the lagoon cover and slowly filled with rain.

How many men had she slept with since fleeing Boston? Her hand slid down her achy belly into her crotch. Seven in twelve months. The number sickened her. She certainly hadn't done it for pleasure. Each sordid memory filled her with revulsion. Except for Max, every encounter spoke a wish for oblivion. Maybe Roman had seen the truth about her. She felt adulterated, that was the word. She'd finally become an adult.

A movement on the screen caught her eye. Thermocline layers of hot and cold water were sliding over each other like wrinkling membranes. She checked the pH and found all the numbers rising. She opened her oscilloscope file, and there was the strong rhythmic pattern, running in waves across the screen. Only, something had changed. It took her a minute to notice the different meter. The colloid's new pattern undulated in 3/4 time— not 4/4. It was playing a waltz.

Max had not played a waltz.

Could it be? She felt almost too giddy to move. Nevertheless, she slotted a disk to back up the data. For a wavering interval, the pattern held its shape. The graphic sine curves dipped and rose in the distinctive rolling three-beat cadence. Then like a rainbow, it dissolved, and the oscilloscope reverted to its previous static, but not before CJ had captured a few brief measures in 3/4 time.

"Check this, Roman Sacony. Your river trash just spoke his first word."

Pulse

Wednesday, March 16
6:45 AM

Canal waters soaked the porous shoals of Devil's Swamp, fringing the flooded witchhazel in rings of soapy lather. Ebb and flow, the turbid juice seeped upward through the osmotic mud and percolated among coiling tree roots. It welled among the sedges, then seeped back down again like a slow sexual exchange. In coitus with solid ground, the water slurped loam and decomposing leaves, crude oil and perchlorate. It drank ravenously of mercury and lead. It tasted promiscuously—eroding, leaching, dissolving, accreting.

CJ woke from a strange dream and found herself on a couch in Dan Meir's office, covered in Roman's windbreaker. She didn't remember falling asleep beside the lagoon, and she had no idea Roman carried her to this couch in his arms. As far as she was concerned, Roman could rot. She remembered only how the colloid's waveform had danced.

Strains of "The Blue Danube" lilted through her head in the ebullient flowing rhythm of water. Of course her watery colloid would invent a waltz. She sat up and laughed. Yue had labeled him an accident. Ha! He was nothing less than a miracle. An active, learning neural net self-made from river trash. CJ drew a breath. If he could learn this fast, he might truly become *sentient.*

No trained scientist should leap to such a presumption. She had no supporting evidence, nothing solid—yet she wanted to believe it. A new life. A living mind. She pictured him as a newborn, innocent, and hopeful, just beginning to explore his world. A child prodigy—she knew what that felt like. Yes, he needed protection and care. She felt his small chubby hand reaching out to her, arousing a primal empathy she didn't bother to examine. Already, he had uttered his first baby talk. Imagine, a waltz! She sprang up from the couch and looked for her shoes.

Her body felt gummy, in need of a wash. Her head itched, grime encrusted the soles of her feet, and her mouth tasted like guano. Vaguely, as she tied her shoelaces, she remembered parking her Rover near the lagoon. A wad of keys bulged in her pocket. She could drive to the Roach, take a shower, grab a snack—or rush back to the lagoon and jam with the colloid.

In the ladies' room, she splashed water in her face, wetted her hair, and rinsed her mouth. Her overdue period had still not started. She grabbed a Coke from the vending machine and left the building. The morning felt surprisingly fresh and dry. Beyond the Quimicron parking lot, she wandered through a maze of warehouses, then jogged across a stubble field toward the lagoon. A few damp puddles still lurked from last night's rain, but they were evaporating. As she hurdled over stumps and broken glass, she thought of her father. "Harry, don't you wish you were here?"

A stitch in her side made her halt and hug her ribcage, and a sudden longing for her father overwhelmed her. How Harry would have relished this discovery of a new life-form. He always believed in Earth's infinite fertility. "Harry, I wish . . ." but her voice failed.

On the distant catwalk, figures moved under the floodlights. The morning was dawning fine and clear, yet around the lagoon, the sun's early rays glowed through a nimbus of fog. Ghostly wisps boiled from the lagoon, and the whiteness crept down the surrounding embankment like dry-ice vapor. CJ hurried toward the steps. She could hear someone laughing.

At the base of the steps, a huddled heap of denim, flannel, and leather resolved into the sleeping figure of Max. He lay curled on the bare concrete, resting his cheek on his arm. CJ stooped and kissed his forehead but didn't wake him. Through a cloud of steam, she mounted the stairs to the catwalk, and near the stacked computer gear, she saw Li Qin Yue and Peter Vaarveen toasting each other with cardboard coffee cups. They turned at her approach. The lagoon cover had been removed, and not far away, Roman gazed at the steamy water as if spellbound.

"Did you see my data?" she called out breathlessly. "He composed music! He can speak!"

In her hurry, she nearly slipped in a pool of liquid that had sloshed out of the lagoon. The run left her dizzy. The water looked different this morning.

She peered into the depths, looking for her wayward infant. Where was the precious floral clump?

Peter gave her a snide grin. "You look awful."

"Yeah, I'm feeling light-headed." She sat in a folding chair. They'd removed her tent, and a fresh dawn breeze was gradually dissipating the steam over the lagoon. "Did you see the waltz? He composes in ions and pH."

Roman eyed the lagoon with such fixed concentration that not a muscle moved in his face. It seemed to cost him an effort to notice her.

CJ felt queasy. She tugged the can of Coke from her pocket and popped the lid. Fizz sprayed everywhere. She lapped sugary foam from her hand. "It was only a few bars, but I recorded it. Three-quarter time. Did you see? Isn't it amazing?"

Yue's braid was pinned so tight on top of her head that it drew her eyebrows up at the corners. "We had to modify your sound wave theory."

"Oh?" CJ gave Roman a questioning glance, but he'd gone back to ogling the lagoon.

"You chose the wrong kind of wave," Yue continued. "We tested *my* hypothesis, and I was right. We used an electromagnetic shockwave."

CJ blinked. She thought she'd heard wrong or missed something important. Yue wouldn't fire an EM shockwave at her innocent little prodigy? Even the QB wouldn't deliberately destroy their only viable sample.

"The chips are completely neutralized." Yue smoothed her braided crown.

Noises died in the air. Echoes failed. The world went hollow. CJ sat stunned. At last, she understood Roman's fixed stare. He was gloating over a dead opponent. She spoke from an empty place. "You wanted a weapon."

"And we found it," Yue answered.

CJ stood and steadied herself against the rail. She felt nauseous, as if she might faint. Suddenly, a violent yowl geysered out of her, and she flung her fists at Roman's back. When he turned and caught her, she tried to knee him in the groin.

"Murderer! Liar!" Words gurgled in her throat.

Yue grabbed her waist and wrestled her away.

Roman seemed perplexed. "What's the problem? We'll take other samples. There's plenty more in the canal."

CJ broke free from Yue's hold. "I hate this job. I hate you. I quit."

She ran down the steps, dodged Max's sleeping body, and fled.

Sizzle

CJ steered her rented Viper up the Mississippi. A bright dry wind blew in from Colorado, bringing positive ions to mate with dopamine receptors in her brain so that, in the languid depths of Louisiana, she felt a clear Rocky Mountain high.

"Sacony, you will rue this day," she chanted "You don't know who you're dealing with. I'm the Eveready battery."

After hiding her Viper under the drooping willows, she followed her usual path across the swamp. The high pressure front made a noticeable change in the scenery. Sunlight rustled through shining Palmetto fronds, and green leaves sparkled. CJ ran her fingers through the silky grasses and drew lambent breaths of honeysuckle nectar. In the dry clear air, every crimson berry, nodding blue bellflower, and yellowjacket bee glinted in jewel sharpness. The poisoned swamp gleamed like a garden.

At her lookout post, she opened her backpack, drew out her binoculars, and rummaged for her cell phone. She hadn't called Max in hours. Frankly, she'd been putting it off, not sure what to tell him. But Max worried so much, it was a crime not to call and let him know she was okay.

"Shit." She'd left her phone in the boat. Now she would have to slog the long way back through the muck to get it. What a hassle. Before starting back, she took a minute to focus her binoculars and make a quick scan of the canal. The *Refuerzo* lay moored near the Quimicron barge dock. They must be trying to collar another sample, she thought, another captive for Roman to torture.

All at once, a burst of underwater illumination caused the entire north end of the canal to blink like a green traffic light. "Good God. They're using the EMP in the canal." CJ gripped her binoculars. Weapons-grade electro-magnetic pulses bolted through the canal like strobes, convulsing the hearts and brains of pelicans, otters, and toads. Dead catfish boiled to the surface.

She focused on the dock. Of course, the fiends were there, Li Qin Yue and Peter Vaarveen. In the morning sun, their faces blazed with wicked glee. And behind them paced the arch-fiend, cool and smug, Roman Sacony.

"Butcher," CJ hissed through her teeth.

They were operating a machine she didn't recognize at first, a massive squat cylinder housed in aluminum, with a round cone on top like a TV satellite dish. But instead of pointing at the sky, the dish was aimed at the water. She realized it must be the shockwave generator. From its nozzle poured the invisible deadly electrons that could tear through computer circuits and human flesh with equal results.

"Aaaaargh," the wail gurgled from her throat. She ran. Without thought, with only a ferocious resolve to save her infant colloid, she stumbled through the thick vegetation toward the water's edge. And all she could see was her father stretched on the white table. The IV, the rubber block in his mouth, the electrodes clamped against his jelly-coated temples. Electroshock therapy—Harry's last hope to escape the black deeps.

"Nooooo!" She rushed toward the water as if she could stop the EMP with her bare hands. She could almost feel Harry jerking and writhing through the grand-mal seizure on the white table. Sawbriars tore at her boots. Twice she fell into muddy sumps, and once her knee twisted with a smarting pain. She stumbled down the sloping shoal to the water's edge.

As she splashed into its soupy margin, another sizzling blink lit up the canal, and she leaped backward. Her wrist tingled with mild electric shock, and she realized her digital watch had shorted. Would the EMP electrocute her? She fell back in the wet grass, panting and shivering, suddenly afraid.

With greater caution, she edged toward the northern end of the canal, keeping well back from the water and grateful for her rubber hip boots. Tangled vines and brush hampered her progress. She no longer noticed their sparkling beauty. Four more times, she heard the weird sizzle that always preceded the underwater bursts of lightning.

"Uh-uh-uh," she moaned inchoate grief as she tore blindly through the undergrowth. The more she fought the vines, the more they entangled her. Sizzle, flash. She smelled the hideous reek of dead frogs. Birds shrieked overhead. She wanted her cell phone. She needed help. She needed Max.

Blow

Hal Butler knocked the ringing phone off its cradle. Somewhere near his ear, a tiny voice whined like a mosquito. Not for the first time, he'd fallen asleep across his desk. Slowly, he pushed up from the pile of magazines, burger cartons, and spiral notebooks that had creased and pimpled one whole side of his face. His hair stuck out like coils of copper wire. His eyelids felt glued, so he didn't bother to open them. He coughed and sat up and nearly fell out of his swiveling chair. Faint screams emanated from the phone.

"Yeah?" He picked up the receiver wrong end around and had to fumble and twist it.

". . . on out here. They're blowing the grid!"

"Huh? Wha?" Butler looked for his watch, but because his eyes were still shut, he couldn't read the time. In his windowless office, the interminable fluorescent light bled weakly through his sealed eyelids.

"They're blowing the fucking power grid, man! They've got this machine like a Van de Graaff ray gun, and they're carpet-bombing the canal. It's fucking wild!"

Butler's eyes snapped open. He glanced at his desk, rubbed grit out of his eyelashes, and swigged an open bottle of warm Dixie beer. "Who the fuck am I talking to?"

"You gotta get out here. Devil's Swamp. I'm taking photographs as we speak."

"How much for the pictures? And what are they of?"

"Your Loch Ness Monster, man. I'm catching them in the act. Are you coming?"

Finally Hal recognized the voice. It was one of his flakey freelance photographers. "E-mail your shots, and I'll take a look."

"Butler, you are a fucking cave lizard." The freelancer clicked off.

Hal dropped the phone, rubbed his face and tried to remember the last time he'd actually gone on location to cover a news story. He studied the scuff marks on his metal door. Ray guns, wow. His journalistic genius was already laying out the first-ever special midweek edition of the *Baton Rouge Eye*.

Glare

Wednesday, March 16
11:34 AM

For three hours, the canal water continued to blink. The acrid smell of ozone and burnt fish saturated the air as CJ finally rounded the far end of the canal and made her way doggedly toward Quimicron's dock. Distorted voices mingled across the water, and crows squawked like hostile wardens. Under a stunted red maple, she paused to free her boot from thorns. The vegetation seemed to grow ever more junglelike, and she was too distracted and too far away to hear the Queen Bitch's angry shout.

"Why do you question my work? The EM field is gone." Li Qin Yue stood planted in front of her instruments, as gaunt and fleshless as a stick figure. She pointed at one particular screen. "Do you see any trace of it? No!"

"But the pH and thermoclines." Roman swiveled the monitor away from the sun's glare. "Look at this data. Part of the formation is still in place."

Yue tossed her head, dislodging pins in her braid. "A vestige. Wait a few minutes. You'll see it disintegrate."

Peter Vaarveen sat in the shade of the pulse generator, flicking his penknife opened and closed, watching the two of them bicker. This fight was mild. On previous job sites, he'd seen them go at each other like sharks. Vaarveen often wondered what sick dynamic kept them working together.

Their last EM pulse had blown the power and knocked the whole Quimicron plant offline. Meir was off somewhere talking to the Dixie Electric Membership Corporation, trying to get their service restored. Meanwhile, Roman wanted them to tap the auxiliary generators and fire another shockwave. But Yue couldn't abide the fact that Roman doubted her word. They didn't need another shockwave. She staked her reputation that the energy field was already dead.

Dead. Peter Vaarveen pondered that word. It implied the blur of dissolved trash had once been alive. Reilly thought so, but Reilly was a mess. A total emotion-head. The worst kind of female. And yet, she'd discovered things about the colloid that he might have overlooked. His respect for her had inched upward of late. It didn't hurt that she was a babe.

Alive? He wondered.

What force made something alive? He pictured a dog stretched on his dissection table. One instant it was kicking and fighting, or maybe just wagging its tail. The next instant, Peter's needle plunged in. How could life and death change places so fast? "You're either quick or you're dead," he snickered.

Still, he seriously regretted Yue's rush to scorch the colloid without first checking the new sample they'd captured. With no collar to hold their target still, they might not have caught an active skein. Yue insisted she had no time to doublecheck, but Peter knew she didn't really want a live sample. She didn't want anything that might help CJ Reilly.

Women. Peter leaned against the generator housing and crossed his arms behind his head. Everybody could have gotten decent publishable articles out of this computerized soup if the females would just get along. But hell, it wasn't his fight. He closed his eyes for a quick nap.

"Stay on it," Roman snarled at Yue. "If anything changes, you fire that EMP again, understand?"

She turned her narrow back on him. Then Roman noticed Vaarveen snoozing in the shade. "Wake up." He kicked Vaarveen in the ribs. "You slept last night. Work now."

"Christ." Peter rubbed his side and sat up to protest, but Roman was already running up the steps toward the levee.

Melt

CJ broke from a thicket, darted across open ground, and slunk under the dock where the scientists were working. Two feet back from the waterline, she sat on her backpack and coated herself in slimy mud. Clouds of gnats swarmed under the pier, and she'd discovered that mud repelled them better than Deet. Though the mire stank of dead fish and worse, she was too dirty and tired to care. In fact, she was too exhausted even to think. She'd toiled so long to reach this dock, now she had no idea what to do next.

In the sweltering twilight shade under the dock, gray foam melted like remnant snow, and dead leaves floated in ridges of motionless muck. She sensed a listless vacancy. The shockwaves had stopped. The canal felt inert. All through her battle with the vines, she'd been rationalizing how the colloid might survive the EMP. But now, her wishes were faltering.

She could almost see the skim of dead microchips floating in the lagoon. Whatever mysterious influence had held them in sync was surely too fragile to survive the repeated shockwaves. She hated Quimicron, hated Roman, hated Yue. Squeezing gooey mud in her fists, she imagined brutal acts of revenge.

Directly above her head, Yue gave a haughty laugh. Then someone yawned. CJ came alert and listened.

"Why won't the bastard trust my expertise?" said Yue.

Peter Vaarveen answered in his New York twang, "Let me think. Could it be because our only remaining sample is worthless?"

"Screw the sample. He treats me like a servant," said Yue.

"I told you, we should have checked for a live skein," said Peter.

Yue's footsteps echoed back and forth. "Get me a seltzer. With ice."

"I loathe Louisiana." Peter's long-legged stride moved away.

Then Yue took a phone call. "Yes, yes. It's dead. I told you."

Silence followed. CJ heard something clatter across the dock. Yue must have thrown a metal tool. "That's right, Roman. The new sample is not active. I'm sorry your charming protégée will lose her Nobel."

Yue snapped her phone shut. "And fuck you very much," she said, stalking away.

Beneath the dock, CJ crammed her knuckles in her mouth and screamed.

Leak

Wednesday, March 16
7:19 PM

She woke to swells of music. Wind instruments, trumpets, strings. Vibrant trilling reeds. She heard a rippling triple waltz of water lilting over rocks, flowing through cataracts, glutting into whirlpools. She opened her eyes to wet mud splattering in her face. It was raining.

Alarmed, she sat up in the pitch dark and fumbled through her muddy backpack for the flashlight. But it wouldn't work. The EMP. Yes, she remembered.

A trillion droplets struck the mud with a soft wet babble. Like baby talk. Her eyes grew hot. She remembered everything. The colloid was dead.

She pulled farther under the dock for shelter. Using her pack as a pillow, she curled in a ball and shut her eyes, seeking oblivion. Did death ever come clean and quick? Maybe, if she kept her eyes closed long enough, the world would go away forever. But her young body had finished sleeping. Her limbs no longer needed rest, and her mind would not settle down. She sat up and leaned against a pier.

What now? Mexico? That sunny land had lost its appeal. Every possibility seemed dreary and pointless. She was tired of running—and yet there was no reason to stay here. She didn't belong anywhere. With a broken laugh, she remembered how she had planned to save third-world orphans by purifying water. She. A nobody.

She could go back to Boston and finish school. As Harriman Reilly's daughter, she could talk her way back into MIT, but the idea sickened her. It felt too much like losing. She visualized a name written on an envelope: Carolyn Joan Reilly. Her mother probably didn't use that name anymore. She had never felt so weary.

At length, her eyes adjusted to the dimness, and she pawed through the useless electronic gadgets in her backpack. She found one lone bag of M&M's and opened it with her teeth. Usually, she ate the brown candies first because they were the least interesting color. Brown, a muddled shade. Harry said it came from mixing all the leftover dyes.

Harry and Carolyn Joan, what a prize set. Parent was too kind a word for them. Begetters? Progenitors? Better to call them doom-mongers. They gave you their worst genes, then blamed you for repeating their blunders—when all you craved was to be different, separate, new. CJ rubbed her eyes.

In the darkness, all the M&M's felt alike, so she picked one at random and popped it in her mouth. Her saliva dissolved the sugar to a liquid surge of energy, and as it hit her bloodstream, she began to revive. Then another sound pierced through the drizzle, a sharper frequency—a siren. That's what had awakened her, not the rain.

She scrambled out from under the dock and peeped over the top. The alarm Klaxon rose and fell like a bugle call, and people were running, launching boats. Something serious was going on. In the chaos, no one noticed her muddy figure climbing up onto the rain-lashed dock.

Red beacons flashed through the downpour, making people's faces look gory. Dan Meir rushed by, followed by Peter Vaarveen and Li Qin Yue. Workers milled like disturbed ants. CJ saw Max hustling equipment across the dock, but she couldn't catch his attention. A few yards away, Roman was pacing under the floodlights. The rain had slicked his long hair like a pelt, and he was crushing a cell phone to his ear. Even at a distance, CJ heard murder in his voice.

She grabbed a crew worker who was running past, a face she recognized. It was Betty DeCuir.

"What's going on, Betty?"

The young woman drew back from CJ's muddy hand, and her eyes went as round as globes. "Laws, the water *loa*. She done ate right through them gate seals. I tell you what. She leak out before that ray gun ever fire."

CJ almost forgot to breathe. "The gates are open?"

Betty nodded. "Ain' nobody hold *Yemanja*. She got herself free."

II Evolution

Race

The Mississippi River is a fast, changeful giant. In the West, it arises along the continental divide, nearly three miles above sea level, while in the Northeast, it links through canals to the Atlantic Ocean. Its upper trunk lies choked and constrained by nearly thirty locks made of heavy steel and concrete, and its lower flanks are poked and prodded by wing dams to keep it running straight. Engorged with spring flows, it will rampage eighteen knots through the heartland, breaking its chains, uprooting trees, and undermining bluffs, leaving angry snags and sandbars, until its Lilliputian jailers recapture and contain it.

By turns, humans have blessed and cursed the great river. Two native tribes argued about who named it first. The Ojibwe called it *Messipi,* and the Algonquin used the words *Missi Sepe.* Both mean the same thing: Gathering of Waters. Its first European christening came in 1541 when Hernando de Soto dubbed it *Río de Espíritu Santo,* River of the Holy Spirit.

Big Muddy, El Grand, Old Man River, the Mississippi is not a single entity but a transient, multiplicitous spill. Like America itself, the river slurps, swallows, digests, and regurgitates. Every year, every minute, its contents change. Its banks erode and move. Its channel fills and must be dredged. Even its mighty current shifts direction. Underpinned by the ancient New Madrid Fault, it quaked so violently in 1811 that new waterfalls appeared, and the river flowed backward for eight days to create Reelfoot Lake in Tennessee.

In ceaseless flux, without material duration, the river is not an object but an evolution—like music, or a nation, or a life. Yet for all its temporality, it rolls always. While you and I are reading or sleeping or making love, it rolls. Through rain and heat, war and truce, noon and midnight, it courses. In the small hours on a recent St. Paddy's Day morning, it rolled a shiny blue nanocarbon coffer gate one mile downstream before lodging it against a bridge pier under Highway 190.

Roman Sacony gripped the passenger armrests in his company speedboat. Max Pottevents was driving at top speed. Dan Meir sat sideways in the rear seat, aiming the spotlight and watching the muddy banks race by. Close behind, Rory Godchaux piloted a second boat with Li Qin Yue, Peter Vaarveen, and a pile of equipment. They were searching for an electromagnetic signature in the Mississippi River.

The rain had tapered off, leaving behind cool misty layers of ground fog. Yue analyzed radio sources, and Peter set up an infrared scanner to spot temperature variations. But as they approached the heavily industrialized waterfront near downtown Baton Rouge, their methods proved useless. Warehouses and factories lined the river, and dozens of freighters lay moored at piers. There were too many heat sources, too many radio waves, too many electromagnetic fields.

Max didn't understand their science terms, but he knew from their angry growls they were stymied. By the greenish glow of his dashboard dials, he could see Roman Sacony's face. The man looked hellish.

Twice earlier, when they paused to drop anchor and let the scientists work, Max tried to call CJ on the sly. But her cell phone didn't answer. Maybe she was sleeping, that's what he hoped. Most of Baton Rouge lay asleep at this hour. He pictured his daughter, Marie, lying snug in her white gingham bed. His ex-wife's crackerbox tract home lay close behind the levee in a low-income ward. The ground was so low there that river water sometimes seeped under the levee and boiled up in Sonia's backyard. It was the best her new husband could afford. Silently, Max prayed that *djab dile* would pass them over. He didn't know what the devil water wanted, but after seeing how it ate through steel hulls, Max felt deeply afraid.

Meir clapped Max's shoulder and startled him. "Stop here, son."

Max signaled the other boat, then killed the motor and steered briskly to avoid a collision. In mid-river, the dark swollen current ran high and fast, and the two small speedboats fishtailed against their taut anchor lines. Even at this hour,

factories operated full steam, cranes moved cargo on and off barges, and fishermen provisioned trawlers and johnboats for the day's work. A Coast Guard ship
cruised upstream, tending buoys. Nearly half a million people lived along this
stretch of river. Max scanned the city skyline and picked out his daughter's
neighborhood. Then he closed his eyes and prayed to his *gros bon ange.*

"We have to go public. There's too much at stake." Dan Meir turned the
collar up on his windbreaker. "What if that stuff kills a fisherman?"

"Wait," Yue called from the other boat. "I have an idea."

She made Rory steer their boat closer till the two gunwales bumped, then
she leaned across and spoke confidentially to the CEO. Max couldn't help but
overhear. She said, "We could let it go."

Roman and Yue searched each other's faces like a pair of wild beasts. The
sound of their breathing made Max's neck shiver.

"You know what I'm saying," Yue continued in a undertone. Her boney
fingers clutched the gunwale. "We could turn around and go home. Where's
the proof tying this to Quimicron?"

"She's right. Our company didn't create this mess." Dan Meir spoke in a
more straightforward voice. "Let's get on the horn to the Coast Guard, tell
them what we know. They're better equipped to deal with it."

Max heard Roman gripping his armrest. His Spanish eyes leered at the
water as if he wanted to drink up the whole river. Slowly, he shook his head,
and when he spoke, his flat timbreless voice grated Max's ear. "The colloid
came from my property. Everyone will sue me, no matter what I say."

"Cut your losses," Yue growled low in her throat. "Deny everything. It's
the smart move."

"We can't be held liable for something we didn't do," said Meir.

"Enough. I will not let this *picaro* destroy Quimicron." Roman sat rigid,
facing forward in his seat, clenching the armrest as if he were strangling an
enemy's throat. "We'll use the EMP here, in the river."

Max edged away from him. The man seemed ready to detonate. But
when he spoke next, his flat voice had a stiff, strained calm. "Radio that
Coast Guard tender, and report a chemical spill. Tell them it's inert, and insist
on a media blackout. They'll agree. They won't want a public outcry."

Max sucked his teeth while Meir switched on the boat's satellite radio and
called the captain of the nearby Coast Guard tender. *Djab dile* inert? Max expected Roman Sacony to lie, but Mr. Meir, too? His respect for the plant manager plummeted.

Max couldn't know how closely Meir's feelings tracked his own. Dan Meir hated dishonesty, and he was not a good liar. He shifted from one foot to the other as he spoke over the radio to Capt. Marcus Ebbs. A career Coast Guard officer, Captain Ebbs had a gruff military style of speaking that made ex-Marine Meir feel even more like a turncoat.

Captain Ebbs listened and said little. In his nearly twenty years with the Eighth Coast Guard District, Ebbs had patrolled every major river from the Appalachians to the Rockies, and he'd met every shape of prevaricating pole-cat. He had rescued 752 tomfool civilians, saved over $22 million worth of private property, responded to 1,712 incidents of environmental pollution and conducted a thousand boardings for the purposes of law enforcement. His father had hunted German U-boats in the Gulf of Mexico during World War II.

Captain Ebbs twisted the waxy tip of his snow-white handlebar mustache as he listened. Though he was pushing mandatory retirement, Ebbs stood as straight as he had at age thirty-five. For the past four years, he'd commanded the *Pilgrim,* a sixty-five-foot tender assigned to babysit river buoys on the lower Mississippi. Much to his discontent, his current mission did not include law enforcement, but Ebbs was not always careful about crossing lines.

As Meir spun his yarn about a submerged slick of harmless refrigerant, Ebbs's practiced old ears heard mendacity. "Inert," Meir said. Ebbs suspected a ruse. When Meir asked if his private corporation could use the nation's top-secret military satellites to help locate a cold spot in the river, Ebbs raised his bushy eyebrows.

Give these unknown civilians clearance to view America's most sensitive spy photographs? "You bet I will," he said. Then he switched off the mike and turned to his first officer. "Stay on 'em like a bluejay on a stinkbug."

Max listened to the radio conversation with a growing sense of his own failure. He knew he should interrupt and shout a warning. Cramped in the small boat, he shook his leg and thought wildly of jumping in the river, swimming to shore, finding his daughter. While he squirmed and debated, it didn't help that Roman Sacony was quietly ripping the vinyl armrest with his fingers.

When the *Pilgrim* glided toward them, everyone in both speedboats stirred uneasily. The buoy tender was a large, blunt-nosed vessel, painted black from stem to stern. The closer it approached, the more Max's heart thudded. Should he speak up and tell them the truth? He rubbed his sweaty hands on his jeans. Who would believe such a mixed-up tale from a Creole boat driver?

But his chance to speak never came. Sacony told him to stay with the speedboats while the others went aboard the *Pilgrim*. As soon as they'd gone, Max tried CJ's cell phone again. Still no answer.

Cool damp vapors moved over the water, carrying aromatic molecules of fish slime, crude oil, and Canadian clay. Max knew that smell as intimately as his own body odor. He'd breathed the Mississippi all his life. As the taste of its fog dissolved on his tongue, he keyed redial.

Suddenly, his phone vibrated with an incoming call.

"Max, I see you. Don't look around. I'm behind the yellow freighter to your starboard. I've turned off the Viper's running lights."

"Ceegie—"

"Don't say my name. Listen, my cell went dead, so I'm sending you a new number. This one's a satellite phone, okay?"

Max memorized the phone number displayed on his screen. "It's not safe to be on the river without your lights," he whispered.

Nervous hilarity rippled through the phone. "Lots of things are not safe, Max. Tell me what's going on."

Max bent as if to tie his bootlace, but no one on the tender was watching him. With the phone cupped in his palm, he told CJ how Mr. Meir lied to the Coast Guard.

"Good," she said. "Those military satellites have infrared cameras. They'll find the cold spot. When they do, call me."

"They want to fire the EMP," Max said.

"That's insane. Not even Roman would fire an EMP this close to the downtown waterfront."

"But what is it?" Max asked.

CJ deliberated how to explain. "Well, our phones are using EMP right now. Electromagnetic pulses carry our voices back and forth through the air. But the shockwave generator, that's lethal." She described how an enormous burst of electrons would shoot through the water at light speed and burn conductive material from the inside out. Copper wires. Microchips. Carotid arteries. She warned Max to be careful.

He glanced across the dark water at the gargantuan yellow freighter with ten-foot-high Chinese characters painted down its side. In the shadow of its towering stern, Max glimpsed the hull of a small speedboat rocking in the current.

"You be careful, *lam*."

Pool

Thursday, March 17
5:01 AM

Neon reflections dimpled the river along the Baton Rouge waterfront. Blue, pink, and yellow, they rippled and broke in pieces as boats passed by. Across the river lay the smaller town of Port Allen, and already dockworkers teemed on its wharves. The early morning sang with engine noise, and blue fumes drifted on the breeze like silk scarves. Gentle waves slapped the banks, while in mid-river, the current charged downstream like a megaton explosion.

Li Qin Yue ignored the surrounding cityscape, the same way she ignored Peter Vaarveen's reverberating snores. While Vaarveen sprawled across the boat's backseat in semi-hibernation, she glanced across to the other boat, where Roman sat like a vigilant gargoyle. More than once, she had seen him whip people up to extraordinary feats, yet his ability still amazed her. When the Coast Guard refused to let them view satellite scans, he had placed a personal call to a congressman, and in less than an hour, Yue was downloading infrared images from a classified FTP site.

The cold water anomaly registered as a dark blue blot pooling along the river's west bank near Port Allen. Its temperature hovered near the freezing point. And its size had swelled. Yue extrapolated its volume at fourteen liquid tons. Evidently, the slick was fattening on the Mississippi's rich chowder of waste.

Yue worked awkwardly in the small boat. Across her angular knees lay a dozen sheets of printout, crumpled and crosshatched with deep gouges from her fountain pen. It was CJ Reilly's report. Yue kept it with her always, hating it and re-reading it. How often she had tried to shake off her envy. Who could have guessed Roman's newest little whore had a brain?

Back and forth, Yue read the report. Over and over, she underlined certain references to the colloid's sound response. On her computer screen, the frigid signature drifted like a wavering blue star through the mostly yellow river. And like molten ice, it was sliding South.

In the other boat, Roman took a sip from Meir's thermos of obscene watery coffee, then spat it in the river. With tight lips, he counted the neon signs on the Casino Rouge. He counted the delivery trucks rumbling along the waterfront. In the state capitol tower, he counted a column of windows. Thirty-four windows. The building where Huey Long was shot had thirty-four floors.

Roman understood that the fear in his gut was so vast and black that if he once acknowledged its presence, it would suck him under. Rather than give in, he rushed from one task to the next, trying to avoid the one impossible dread: *The colloid will bankrupt me.*

So far on its short joyride downriver, the blur of electronic liquid had etched gaping holes in three steel barges. Roman knew this because the owners reported their leaking hulls on open radio channels. He also knew there would be other leaks, not yet discovered. He'd counted the barges they'd passed and calculated the probable cost. Figures spun through his mind in a deadly vortex. As of yet, no one had connected the mounting damage to his refrigerant spill, but he knew that couldn't last. His only chance was to act quickly, to bring the colloid's rampage to an end.

He had held the enemy in his palm and let it slip away—that was the thought that tortured him. He had come so close to caging it. If only he had tried harder, made better decisions, it would still be contained in his canal.

"We're gonna be here a while," Meir said from the rear seat. "Creque'll bring the *Refuerzo* at first light to try the collar again."

Roman twisted to catch Yue's attention in the other boat, but she was too absorbed in her laptop screen to notice. He wanted to see that scan. He wanted to look his enemy in the eye. He hated the awkward separation of these two small four-seater speedboats.

"Charter a yacht," he said to Meir, "and order some food."

Not far away, hidden behind a fishing trawler, CJ tore off a strip of cold rubbery pizza and crammed it in her mouth. She'd brought a bagful of provisions for this trip, but she was too agitated to taste the food. She watched the Coast Guard ship that was tailing the two speedboats.

As of today, her period was two weeks late. She tried not to think about it. Her ebbs and flows had never been reliably periodic. But still . . . that day in the pirogue with Max, their first time together, neither of them thought to bring condoms. She traced the rim of her navel with her fingertip. She swung her binoculars back to the Coast Guard ship. Its presence worried her.

Her shoulder ached from squeezing the cell phone against her ear. Max had a shoulder ache, too, though she didn't know it. Max was trying to keep his phone hidden—he was grateful for the darkness. He and CJ kept an open connection, and though they occasionally spoke, mostly they shared long tense silences. When Max heard her chewing, he dreamed of breakfast. His mouth watered for buttery eggs and thick *Andouille* sausage frying on a griddle.

"How fast do you think the water's moving?" she asked.

" 'Bout ten knots. River always runs high in March."

"Hey!" CJ saw a burst of activity in the small boats. "Why are you weighing anchor?"

Max could feel her voice vibrating in his shirt pocket, but he was too busy to respond. Meir had just given him fresh orders. But CJ didn't need him to tell her the colloid was on the move again. She watched the Quimicron speedboats steer downstream, followed closely by the blunt black *Pilgrim*. They stuck close to the western bank, skirting Port Allen's industrial wharves. Clearly, they were searching. Across from them, near the increasingly active Baton Rouge waterfront, CJ glided out of her hiding place and kept watch.

Swell

Thursday, March 17
6:00 AM

Baton Rouge greeted St. Patrick's Day with blaring car horns, jackhammers, and distorted gusts of windborne radio news. Toilets flushed, showers steamed, and thousands of coffeemakers dripped black liquid stimulant. Cops worried about traffic flow at the Irish street fair, while parade queens worried about their dresses. Out on the river, Max worried about everyone.

He had eight cousins and two aunts living in Baton Rouge. If the citizens learned what was drifting down their river, he already knew how the fear would seize them. The awful aftermath of the last hurricane still lingered fresh in everyone's memory. Another alarm right now would be bad. Eyes closed, Max pictured his daughter sleeping beside the river, and he quietly prayed to every spirit he knew. *Voudon*-Seminole-Judeo-Christian-Islamic, he begged them all for grace.

But Roman kept his eyes open. Standing next to Max in the rocking boat, he analyzed mental spreadsheets, weighed his capital position and reviewed worse-case scenarios. He listened to Meir talking on the phone to Elaine. He listened to Godchaux muttering over a rosary. He listened to Vaarveen snore. Then he pivoted on one heel, opened his fly, and pissed into the river.

Near the opposite bank, CJ felt something very different from fear. As the morning grew more radiant, a potent stir of hormones buoyed her spirits and stirred her powers of rationalization. She felt ever more certain that she alone understood the colloid. A bright inquisitive child, unsure of his footing and often harassed by unexpected attacks—yes, she knew how that felt. Her infant colloid didn't realize he had killed Manuel de Silva. He didn't know what a human being was.

"Sa moving into the Port Allen Canal," Max whispered into his hidden phone.

CJ rummaged quickly through her bag, overstuffed with candy bars, soda cans and electronic gear. Something clattered, her wooden castanets. She'd brought them for good luck. At last, she found her maps. "Okay, I see it."

The Port Allen Canal linked the Mississippi to the Intracoastal Waterway—a shortcut to the Gulf that bypassed New Orleans. Its entrance bay was shaped like a champagne flute, and the slender neck led to the Port Allen Lock, a few hundred yards inland. The lock's massive gates and channels raised and lowered ships between the Waterway and the higher level of the river. Beyond the lock, the Intracoastal shipping channel ran as straight as a freeway, due South through the Atchafalaya Basin to the Gulf.

"*Djab dile* moving toward the lock," Max whispered. "Sacony gonna trap it inside."

CJ bent over the map, biting her finger. "How?"

"He asking the Corps of Engineers to close off the lock."

"That's wrong." Arguments bubbled up in her throat. The Intracoastal Waterway led into uninhabited swamplands, the perfect learning ground for her prodigy. Why trap him here, near the city? Why not let him move through the lock into the wild wetlands? She wished she could tell Roman what she thought of his plan.

The search vessels moved deeper into the goblet-shaped bay, and where it narrowed to a neck, they dropped anchor. She had to admit the channelized neck was a good place for a trap.

A little later, Max said, "Sacony getting tripped up in his own lie. The Corps say, if this spill is harmless, why they have to close the lock?"

CJ heard Max's hostility, and she felt it, too. She wanted to shake Roman till his head wobbled. But Roman didn't need another jolt. He'd just received a call that the Brazilian banker had flown back to Rio. If Roman wanted his petroleum port in Fortaleza, he would have to pursue the banker to his own ground and beg. The necessary bribes would escalate. If only he had a deputy whom he could trust to send in his place. But there was no one.

He ran his hands through his loose wavy hair and tried to sort out priorities. Within five years, a new port in Fortaleza could increase Quimicron's revenues by 50 percent, and Roman needed that future cashflow to service his debt. On the other hand, this present risk could sink him.

Where was the yacht he'd ordered? The confines of the speedboat made him restless, and he scowled at the rippling brown river. It was like time and opportunity, shifting, formless, insubstantial, rushing every minute through his grasp. He hated it.

He opened his cell phone and keyed the number for Arturo Villanova, drug runner.

Spit

Thursday, March 17
6:29 AM

After numerous dead ends, Roman managed to track down Villanova on vacation in Barbados. The Panamanian drug dealer owned a legitimate company called NovaDam, a supplier of water-inflated barriers for use in dam construction. The huge, yellow carbon nanofiber bags were stronger than steel, impervious to acid, and much easier to transport than traditional dam structures. Pumped full of water, they weighed hundreds of tons and stood rigidly immovable. Villanova imported the bags from Germany and transported them by air to remote construction sites in Latin America, good cover for the other items he transported by air. Roman caught him having breakfast with his four young children.

"Arturo, I need a dam. This morning. In Baton Rouge. This afternoon is too late."

Villanova laughed. "And how much are you willing to pay for this miracle?"

"Don't hold me up. You have eight bags in Matamoros, and I've chartered a sea plane."

"But *amigo,* those bags are in use. What shall I tell my customer when his worksite floods?"

"Whatever you like, Arturo. Remember Nicaragua."

"Ah yes, you always remind me."

Although Villanova's German-made products were rock solid, his finances were sometimes a little soft. A few years back, he'd annoyed the wrong people in the Nicaraguan government, and they confiscated a shipload of his inventory. NovaDam would have gone under if Roman hadn't stepped in, crossed the right palms, and saved Arturo's assets. Since then, Roman had not failed to demand returns on his investment.

"Baton Rouge? You must send me some Hoppin' John. My children love the white trash cooking." Villanova had the husky caramel voice of a Spanish crooner.

Roman rinsed his mouth with bottled water, then spat over the gunwale. "The dam, Arturo. This morning."

"Impossible, you know."

"Deliver it to the Port Allen Canal. I'll show you where to install it."

"Ah, you'll show me. That's beautiful."

"Arturo, I need this. Do this for me, and we're even."

"No, my friend. You'll be in my debt."

In the speedboat, Roman shut his phone and slung it to the floor between his feet. He hated being obligated to a character like Villanova. He slumped forward and furiously counted the dials on the dashboard.

Whisper

Chasseur was the name lettered across the rented, forty-four-foot Cruisers motor yacht. She carried a satellite TV, full galley with eat-in dinette, flush toilet, shower, sleeping accommodations for six, and a swim platform. She also carried Elaine Guidry and a fully catered hot breakfast.

Peter wanted to eat, but first Yue made him set up a field lab in the galley while she assembled their equipment on the stern. Next, they dropped plastic pickle buckets on ropes over the side to draw water samples. In his lab, Peter munched a runny egg sandwich while he analyzed gallons of extraordinarily pure pollutant-free water through the SE scope. He found no working mote computers, but one bucket netted a clump of proplastid with a partial chain of microchips. The clump also contained a large concentration of mutant bacteria cells. Something had restructured their nuclei.

"More Quimi-chimeras," he quipped. The genetically modified cells were churning out strange new nano-structures. He showed them to Yue. "No way can you call this coincidence."

"Let me guess." Yue folded her thin arms. "You believe our swamp creature communes with aquatic life."

"Communes?" Peter snickered. "More like enslaves. Look at those." His blunt fingertip hovered over the image of the bloated cells. Their pregnant chloroplasts looked ready to burst.

Yue huffed. "God knows what's in this river."

Nearby on the *Refuerzo*, Creque and Spicer waited with their collar and pumps. As soon as the lock closed, the Corps expected them to deploy the collar and suck up the refrigerant spill, and Captain Ebbs had agreed to direct traffic. Only Roman's team knew the real plan—they would fire the EM pulse. Roman had ordered Creque to capture a sample if possible, but that was not his priority.

The *Chausseur* rocked and chuffed as a freight ship larger than a stadium slid by, throwing up dingy ochre wake. Its engine noise distorted the air and temporarily drowned out Spicer's radio program—he was listening to NPR. Yue read the ship's Chinese markings, and Max felt it block all light flowing through his porthole in the aft cabin.

He squeezed his phone tighter and cupped a hand over his ear. "Ceegie, you still with me?"

"Oh yeah, I'm playing shuffleboard on my lido deck." Through binoculars, she saw Rory drop the yacht's anchor. That must mean they'd found the colloid again. The *Pilgrim* was anchoring, too.

"You could come onboard with us, Ceegie. There's pancakes. I know they wouldn't mind."

"I'm doing an experiment. Call me later."

Experiment? Max rose in his bunk and peered through the small round window, but there was little to see from his angle. He'd been ordered to sleep, so he lay down, closed his eyes and whispered to his *met tet* guardian spirit: "*Osun Moses Maria Maker of Breath, protégez-nous.*"

CJ also whispered a prayer. "Harry, so help me, this better work."

She squinted at the mixed-up readings from her field finder. Her muscles throbbed from the long confinement in the boat, and her eyes hurt. There were so many EM fields in the harbor, it was hard to pick one from another. Tense and alert, she steered out of her hiding place.

River traffic was dense and noisy. Fishing boats zipped behind thirty-barge tows, and monumental freighters cruised into dock with truck-size containers stacked up on their decks like children's blocks. She stuffed her hair under a faded Red Sox cap, put on a pair of sunglasses, and hoped that in the middle of so many diverse vessels, she might pass unnoticed.

She approached the *Chasseur* obliquely, aiming toward the bow, keeping out of sight of the *Pilgrim*. Luckily, no one was on deck to see her. The closer she came, the clearer the water sparkled. She dipped up handfuls and sniffed the clean fresh smell. "You're here," she said, inwardly rippling with joy. Soon her field finder detected the faint outline of the blossom-shaped energy field. She recognized its shape like a familiar face. It was welling beneath the yacht. "You!"

She bit her finger to staunch the intensity of her excitement. Cutting off her engine, she let her boat drift under the *Chasseur*'s upswept bow. Her Viper rode low in the water, so anyone on the larger craft would have to lean far out over the rail to see her hiding directly under the bowsprit. She hung a pair of fenders over her gunwale to avoid bumping, then tied off to the *Chasseur*'s dripping anchor chain. Next she bungeed the Lubell speakers together and lowered them into the water on a ten-foot cord.

"How about a music lesson?" she whispered.

It was Max who thought to retrieve the Lubell speakers and box of CDs after CJ walked off in a pique. Max, the good knight. She rummaged through the dozens of disks till she found the simple keyboard melodies he'd recorded. There were twelve in all, held together in a rubberband, and nestled among them was a folded piece of paper. She opened it and recognized Max's handwriting. He'd written down the titles in proper order. *"Sa progression,"* he said. The order was important. She slotted the first CD.

Trailing her fingers through the fresh sweet water, she pondered a riddle whose solution still eluded her. What was it about music that made the colloid respond?

Max's words came back to her. "Little children know. Even animals know."

Well, it worked. That's what mattered. And if the small skein isolated in the lagoon could learn to compose a waltz, surely the full-fledged colloid would become a maestro.

She balanced Max's CD player on one knee and her field finder on the other. It took concentration to track the faint edges of the colloid's field drifting among so many noisy patterns. She had to keep a close eye on her instrument.

"Let's jam," she whispered. Then she pushed the button marked "Play."

Dissolve

Thursday, March 17
9:01 AM

Roman sat on the floor beside Yue's bunk, rocking on his haunches. The seaplane was coming, bringing the NovaDam bags to trap his enemy. Vaarveen was keeping watch. Soon, soon. Roman swallowed another red-and-black capsule and rocked back and forth. He hadn't rocked that way since his early youth, when his widowed mother locked him in a closet for skipping Mass. His mother didn't factor in his life anymore. Bitter and arthritic, she languished in the old yellow house in Mar del Plata. Let her berate the ocean and clouds. He paid her expenses, that was enough. Still, as he sat on the *Chasseur's* mildewed carpet watching Yue sleep, he wasn't able to stop rocking.

Yue had collapsed and knocked her head against a monitor. The gash on her temple still seeped a little blood, and Roman knew he had pushed her too far. Like him, she'd been surviving on black-and-red capsules. He couldn't remember the last time she'd rested. Moments ago, when he had carried her down to the bunk, she felt like a sack of bird bones in his arms. He removed her shoes, then bathed her emaciated face with a cloth. She'd been beautiful once.

As he rocked to and fro beside her bed, he longed to rest his brow against the soft white edge of her mattress. But he feared the cotton batting was not solid enough to support the weight of his skull. If he pressed against it, he thought he might dissolve through the fiber and metal springs. His cohesion would fail, and he would enter a region of molecules, where his cellular atoms would swirl a billion courses through the void.

"¿Qué?"

He shook himself awake, got to his feet and climbed the dew-slick ladder to the deck. Someone had made coffee. Burnt sludge, he drank it anyway. Enlisting the help of the Coast Guard and the Corps of Engineers had taken all his energy. He loathed the taste of bureaucratic shit, but he'd eaten it. His tongue rolled around his sour unbrushed teeth, and he felt gritty inside. To gain cooperation from the *Anglo* authorities, he had divulged that the colloid might not be completely inert. His people didn't know enough about its properties to guarantee public safety, that's how he put it.

With a scowl, he threw his cardboard cup overboard, and the rippling water engulfed it. Green, brown, rust-red, piss-yellow, the fluid undulated in a billion fleeting crests and troughs. He allowed the movement to lull him. Haze thickened the air. It would be easy to let the Feds take over. Deny liability. Fight it out in court. Then finally, inevitably, liquidate Quimicron to pay off his bills, and let it all drift away. In his weariness, the idea tempted him.

Ironic, his obsession with solid things. Ships. Buildings. Pipelines. Paper notes in a bank vault. *Real* estate. Nothing was *real*. The tighter he gripped his assets, the faster their significance slipped through his fingers. Every firm surface was illusion, a trick of light and excited particles, disguising the vacuum.

He craned to see the sky. The seaplane would arrive from the South.

Swim

Thursday, March 17
11:28 AM

Boat sirens echoed across the water, and CJ sat up in her cockpit. Ships of all descriptions were converging toward her. Their engines pumped decibels and energy, and she had a hard time keeping track of the colloid's field. A second Coast Guard tender plowed through the traffic, and an officer onboard shouted something through a megaphone, but the wind distorted his words. She ducked low in her cockpit. Were they coming to arrest her?

But the Coast Guard's garbled instructions finally resolved to intelligible words. The guy was directing traffic, clearing a stretch of the main river. CJ wrinkled her nose. All this engine noise would screw up her music session. What the heck were they doing?

As if to answer her question, a seaplane circled low in the milky sky and lined up for an approach. She didn't realize they allowed airplanes to land on the Mississippi River. The plane must belong to some high-roller, she thought. Then her mind clicked. Roman Sacony.

Speak of the devil, she heard his voice. Roman was standing directly above her on the *Chasseur's* deck, talking on his phone. She flinched and looked up, but he wasn't leaning over the rail, so he couldn't see her.

In fact, Roman had no idea CJ Reilly was loitering under his bowsprit. As he watched the float-mounted cargo plane approach the volatile water, his thoughts snapped more rolls than an aerobatic biplane. Nothing felt solid. Not even the deck beneath his feet.

He'd chartered the bulky Fairchild cargo plane from a Florida outfit, and they claimed their pilot had years of experience landing on moving water. But the Mississippi wasn't just any moving water. Its tremendous volume pounded downstream at locomotive speed. If the plane's pontoons touched down at the wrong angle, the river's mighty current would flip it like a piece of trash.

Humidity dampened Roman's shirt, and there was no breeze to mediate the river's vinegar reek. He focused his binoculars on the pedestrians collecting along the waterfront to watch the seaplane land. Office workers, shopkeepers, schoolchildren. Mist in the air made their faces indistinct. "Get back from the water," he growled. A vein on his forehead quivered.

He knew the exact population figures for East and West Baton Rouge, but as long as everyone stayed out of the river, the supercool emulsion couldn't hurt them. What worried him, what gave him head-splitting angst, was the increasing toll of damaged ship and barge hulls. The colloid showed a whopping appetite for iron, steel, and river cargo of every description. Very soon, the authorities would hold him accountable.

He hung fire as the seaplane skidded sideways through the steamy air to bleed off velocity. The pontoons kissed the water, bounced, dipped, and touched down. The plane slewed to one side, settled into the rushing water and began immediately to drift downstream. Its motor revved up, and its propellers beat the air. When it finally taxied out of the current into the relative calm of the canal bay, Roman allowed himself to breathe.

He leaned on the rail and contemplated the water. Somewhere below that cloudy surface, his enemy lurked. He knew he had not created this beast. He hadn't filled this northern river with *excrementos*. But he understood that life was not founded on justice. He was the one who stood here now, defending this *Anglo* city. He, a *Latino*. This enemy had chosen him. If he refused its challenge, he knew that something inside him would sink and drown and never surface again.

So he would catch the beast and roast it with electricity. His attack might knock out power all along the waterfront, and he would have to reach deep in his pockets to pay the lawyers who would defend him. No matter. He would not back down. As long as he walked and breathed, he would not let this *violador* win.

Seven feet below, hiding in her Viper, CJ heard him groan.

Gush

Hal Butler woke from a stupor and rolled off his leatherette chair. The soft chime from his laptop indicated a new instant message had arrived, and he hoped it would be the one. He crawled across a six-pack of empties and a half-painted miniature playing field for a game called Forge World. His naked knees scattered tiny ogres and knights.

The message glowed on his screen. Finally. Soeur Rayette.

"Friend, the Lord has saved us!!! Satan's evil creation is gone!!!"

Hal frowned at the multiple exclamation marks. He didn't want Satan's evil creature to be gone. His blogs about the Watermind were drawing record traffic, and his hasty special edition of the *Eye* was selling out. He was already planning the next issue.

"Calm down, dear sister, and tell me all."

Rayette responded with a longer than usual message. In King James diction, she gushed relief and gratitude because "the Lord broke the blue gates and drove the creature away." She described the spontaneous party that sprang up on the Quimicron dock when Merton Voinché found an old waterproof CD player the scientists had left behind. She told of workers too weary to lift their arms who were suddenly jigging and clogging to the rhythms of zydeco. "A MIRACLE," she messaged in all caps, lining up a row of exclamatory punctuation.

On the back of an envelope, Hal scribbled, "Merton Voinché."

"How narrow was our escape," Rayette messaged. "The Lord's miracle has saved us!"

"Bless you, sweet Soeur." Hal closed her message box and Googled the white pages for Merton Voinché.

Stir

On a hot iron barge under a steamy brutal sun, a dozen black, copper, and bronze men worked to lower an enormous yellow bag into the water. Its coarse carbon texture chewed at the men's work gloves. The crane operator watched them connect the bag's huge grommet hooks to his hoist. Inside his hot metal cab, the operator cursed his broken AC. His cab stank of a urine bottle he kept under his seat and a tobacco juice bottle he kept between his knees. When he saw a helicopter circle near his crane tower, he said, "Man, don't touch my tool. I knock you outta the sky."

Roman saw the helicopter, too, and ground his teeth at the red-white-and-blue call letters blazoned across its airframe, a local Baton Rouge TV station. Roman leaned his elbows on the *Chausseur's* gunwales and counted the minutes. The crew was dropping the fifth of eight bags into position, but the process was taking longer than planned. The heavy bags didn't want to slide off the barge, and the men were having to wrestle them over the edge. A second barge was standing by to pump the bags full of river water, but the way things were going, they might have a long wait.

A rogue Caribbean storm was stirring weather up the river, and marble clouds gathered in the South. Roman watched the current, as thick as Turkish coffee, and he visualized the bath of chemicals washing downstream every second, feeding the colloid. As barometric pressure dropped, he felt the beginning of a sinus headache.

A hundred yards away, beneath a dank Port Allen wharf, CJ also felt sinus pressure building. She'd been forced to abandon her spot under the *Chausseur's* bowsprit. Too much traffic coming and going.

Beneath the wharf, she hid in a forest of creosote piers. Esters of chlorophyll permeated the rising vapor, and the sun painted bright white lines through the wharf planks. Around her, a fetid lather of plastic and rotting Styrofoam washed back and forth in sync with Earth's eternal rhythm. Plash, gurgle, rill, the water swelled in and out with the regularity of breath. And her Viper swung like a cradle.

The temptation to sleep deviled her. Blinking, she watched the delicate tracery of the colloid's EM field waver on her handheld instrument. At this distance, the field diffused to a ghost image, like breath on a mirror. Only its changing shape distinguished it from the energetic confusion in the bay. While the other fields propagated in standard spheres, the colloid revolved from flower to crescent to plume. She kept losing it, then straining her eyes to find it again. Sometimes she could sense its presence only through her own stubborn faith.

Brim

Thursday, March 17
3:09 PM

Two hours of sleep and another stimulant capsule revived Li Qin Yue. She climbed to the foredeck to meet Rick Jarmond, the junior regulatory manager from the Corps of Engineers. He wanted more "input" before he would agree to close the Port Allen lock. Roman was skulking on the bridge, watching the NovaDam operation. Peter Vaarveen was lounging on the stern, idly downloading new satellite scans. Meir was sleeping. That left Yue alone to fend off the Federal snoop.

"Permission to come aboard?" Rick Jarmond swayed on his Boston Whaler *Gallant* and danced to regain his footing. He waved happily to Yue. Rick loved boater talk. He loved boarding vessels in an official capacity. He didn't even mind the smothering humidity. In fact, Rick brimmed with enthusiasm for this assignment.

In the damp heat, Yue helped him step across to the *Chausseur*'s deck while he glanced around like a tourist. He had short sandy hair, round cheeks, and a peach-fuzz goatee. He carried a clipboard and a heavy black radio, and his breast pocket bulged with mechanical pencils. In blue jeans, sneakers, and a New Orleans Saints windbreaker, he looked all of twenty-five years old.

In fact, Jarmond had never conducted a site inspection before. Paperwork usually anchored him to his Baton Rouge desk, but this week, four field agents had intestinal flu, so Jarmond got the assignment. He couldn't wait to tell his girlfriend. Getting paid to take a boat trip on the Mississippi River. Very cool.

Yue felt a sick headache coming on. Her spine felt crooked and out of joint. The *Refuerzo* still couldn't set its collar, and the NovaDam crew was taking too much time. Worse, the Port Allen lock still flowed wide open, stepping heavy freighters up and down from the waterway to the river. That left the colloid free to escape in any direction. Roman expected her to tell this Corps guy whatever was necessary to get the lock closed.

She swallowed bile and guided Jarmond below deck for a fresh cup of coffee-flavored sludge. The young man kept blinking his eyes to settle his contact lenses. He couldn't stop smiling.

In the galley, they found Rory Godchaux and Max Pottevents eating left-over pancakes and laughing at a tabloid newspaper someone had brought on-board. The centerfold of the *Baton Rouge Eye* showed an "artist's conception" of a man-shaped liquid demon with a massive computerized brain and webbed feet. According to "reliable sources," this so-called "Watermind" was the offspring of a female abductee who had been secretly impregnated with artificial electronic sperm.

"Back to work," Yue growled.

Rory and Max exchanged a glance, then hustled out. Quickly, Yue stuffed the *Eye* in the waste bin. She'd read Hal Butler's article. The last thing she wanted was to bring it to the attention of the Corps. But Rick was too excited to notice the newspaper. He wanted to see her computer data.

The galley smelled as damp as breath. Yue sat at the table, opened her laptop and retrieved a three-month-old safety report on Quimicron's Miami operations. She angled the screen to let Jarmond read the dense technical verbiage.

He stroked the patch of fuzz on his chin. "This isn't right. You're stalling."

Yue sneered. "I'm not familiar with this system. Let me try again."

She called up a random Word document—which turned out to be her letter of resignation. How interesting that her cursor landed on that file. She'd been revising and polishing her resignation letter for the past three years.

Rick's prominent Adam's apple bobbed. "Ma'am, don't try my patience. I have an injunction in my pocket."

What the hell, she thought. Roman hadn't spoken to her for days, except to bark orders. He treated her like a lackey. She pictured him pacing the bridge, spinning his cold-blooded lies. He expected her to lie, too. He expected everything, and all he gave in return was money.

Across the sultry bay, a motor percussed the air, and the NovaDam crew splashed another enormous bag into the canal. Rick looked out the porthole. "You don't have the okay for that."

"Don't we?"

"Better show me that data, or I'm shutting you down."

The crane's loud motor drilled through Yue's bones. Her skull sank heavily against her jaw, and her weary spine settled farther into her pelvis. In a febrile vision—brought on perhaps by amphetamines—she saw her entire body turn to powder and blow away on the wind.

"I'll show you everything," she said.

She led him to the stern, and Rick Jarmond bounded after her like a pup. When Peter saw them coming, he darkened his workstation screen. The sun had bleached his hair whiter than ever, and his glasses winked with blank reflections.

"Show Lieutenant Jarmond we have nothing to hide," Yue said.

Peter grinned. He could see Yue wanted to stir up difficulties for Roman. Though he didn't understand all the history between the QB and the CEO, he recognized the fury of a woman scorned. But no way would he share his data with this government geek. He shrugged and kicked some cables aside. "Sure thing, lieutenant. Step into my lab." He tapped keys to retrieve a satellite scan. The Corps of Engineers could get that anyway.

The infrared scan showed the goblet-shaped canal bay in blues, yellows, and reds indicating cool, warm and hot temperature patterns. Just inside the goblet's narrow throat, a frigid blot glowed dark blue-violet.

"Awesome." Rick blinked at the screen, then at the buoys in the water. "What makes it so cold?"

Peter smirked. "It's an aliphatic hydrocarbon containing halogens of chlorine and fluorine."

Rick tugged his eyelid to adjust his contact lens. "Freon, huh? Y'all spilled CFCs?"

Peter stiffened. He hadn't expected the dorky Fed to understand his chemical lingo. Chlorofluorocarbons were chewing through the planetary ozone shield, exposing Earth to lethal radiation. The government charged hefty penalties for CFC emissions. Peter noticed Yue smiling.

"Quimicron doesn't deal with CFCs," he explained to Jarmond. "This Freon came from upriver. It's not ours."

Rick studied the satellite scan, winking his left eye at his unruly contact lens. "This picture's ten minutes old." He pointed to the time-and-date stamp in the upper right corner. "Let's see the latest one."

"Why not." Peter accessed the military FTP site and downloaded a new image.

Rick moved closer to the screen and squinted. "Where'd it go?"

Peter leaned over his shoulder. Then he pushed Rick aside. Rapidly, he accessed the FTP site and downloaded another scan. Yue had never seen Peter in such a hurry. She rushed over and elbowed Rick farther away. Peter double-checked the time-and-date stamp on the new scan. He verified the download procedure. He scratched his white hair. The cold spot had vanished.

Yue pounded keys at another station. She was already picturing Roman's face. He would blame her, but how could she control the colloid's vacillating temperature? Like a thrown switch, the slick must have warmed up to match the surrounding river heat, so the satellite's infrared cameras couldn't see it.

Yue tried triangulating its radio emissions, but that didn't work. A hundred different radio frequencies crisscrossed the bay. While Rick Jarmond hovered with his mouth hanging open, she clawed the keyboard to locate the EM field. But her sensors painted a confused overlay of energy patterns. Boat engines. Wharf cranes. Channel buoys. Power cables crossing under the river. The entire downtown waterfront glowed hot with electromagnetic radiation. She slung her fingers as if they burned. She'd lost the colloid.

CJ didn't hear Yue's brittle curses. Hiding under the wharf a hundred yards away, CJ gripped her small instrument and focused on the faint EM field she'd been tracking all along. If she didn't know its variations so well, she would never have spotted it moving sideways through the jumbled energetic noise in the water. Even so, she had to strain to keep the changeling contour in sight. While she watched, the convoluted flower smoothed into a disk, and its wispy image grew fainter still, as if it were sinking to the bottom. CJ kept watching.

Float

"You should've used marker dye!"

"That's your specialty."

"Why didn't you suggest it?" Yue had been sniping at Peter since they lost the colloid.

"Maybe you should track the pure H_2O," he said to rile her.

At the mention of pure water, Yue growled epithets in Chinese. Another of Reilly's claims had proved correct—clean water trailed the slick like a comet's tail, apparently a by-product of its internal chemical processes.

Peter studied the colloid's last known location. The slick had lain stationary for hours, so he had good reason to assume it was still there. He wrestled the EMP generator into position, then duct-taped the cable connections. His skin smarted from sunburn, and his muscles smarted from manual labor, which was definitely NOT in his job description. The pulse generator's batteries were drained, so he wired them to draw power from the yacht's engine. That meant the pulse would have less kick, and he would have to fire more than once to cover the colloid's swelling volume.

Not far away, the empty NovaDam bags floated like a crescent of stiff boxy jellyfish. Roman hadn't obtained clearance yet to fill them. Ships filed slowly past the bags, blasting their horns and radioing their grievances. Once the bags were pumped full of water, they would cut off the shipping lane, trapping dozens of angry captains and pilots in the canal—and clearing the way for Peter to fire his gun. When the time came, he'd have to shoot fast. "Damn," he muttered. The *Refuerzo* would have zero chance to net a live sample.

"Aren't you ready yet?" Yue jabbed hairpins into her braid. "You are the slowest, most inept—"

"Screw yourself. Better yet, get Sacony to screw you. Maybe that'll shut you up." Peter didn't see the CEO observing them from the doorway.

Roman drew back quickly so his presence wouldn't slow their work. Overhead, helicopter rotors frapped the humid air. Channel 2 had returned for more footage. Roman pinched the bridge of his nose. He should release a statement to give the media a plausible explanation. He needed to return calls from his attorney, his CFO, the Baton Rouge Police, the mayor.

Steely clouds accumulated in the south, and moisture hung over the bay like a negative charge. The barometer kept plunging, and for a few seconds, people had to shout over the gusting wind to be heard. When the final barrier bag dropped into position, its sudden splash reverberated like thunder.

Coast Guard Captain Ebbs had ordered Roman to cease and desist deploying the barriers. "You have a permit for a cleanup. You do NOT have authorization to obstruct this canal."

But Roman was tired of begging favors. All the finagling and cajoling had drained him. He needed a real Argentinean espresso. He needed Li Qin Yue's amphetamines. He needed . . . to *do something*.

Abruptly, he marched to the bridge and radioed the crew to start filling the bags. The traffic helicopter buzzed low over the *Chausseur*'s stern with a sound like a drumroll, and storm clouds filtered the sunset to pewter. Roman paced back to the stern to watch Yue and Vaarveen aim their gun.

Hum

Thursday, March 17
6:03 PM

The lead story for the local Six O'clock News showed aerial footage of shipping traffic snarled in the Port Allen Canal. The reporter described the chemical spill as nontoxic refrigerant. "Harmless to humans," he quoted from the Quimicron press release. As lightning blinked in the southern clouds, buffeting compression waves lent the helicopter's video a choppy, combative edge.

Roman hated media attention. If his business associates caught wind of this, it could damage his standing. But for once, the media worked in his favor. Mounting public concern finally convinced the Corps to let him block the channel and clean up the spill. The Port Allen Lock would close for one hour, from 8:00 PM to 9:00 PM. That was Quimicron's window. Roman heard the NovaDam pumps stammer awake. They had two hours to fill eight bags. Then at last they would close their trap on the colloid.

He paced the port deck and nearly tripped over a dark heap of clothing. "What the hell?"

"Sorry, sir." Max got to his feet, palming his cell phone. He hadn't been able to reach CJ.

"Why aren't you working? Where's Godchaux?"

"Rory, he took the speedboat over there." Max pointed toward the Nova-Dam barge, half-wishing he'd gone along. He didn't like being stuck on the yacht. CJ's silence worried him. He tucked his phone in his jeans and hummed a broken snatch of melody out of sheer tension.

"Move along. Help the science team," Roman barked.

"Yes, sir." Max trotted away, scanning the dusky water as he went. He couldn't spot the Viper anywhere. As soon as he'd passed beyond Roman's sight, he ducked into a recess and speed-dialed CJ's number again. All he got was her voicemail.

CJ didn't hear her phone chime. She didn't hear the thundering pumps. CJ lay folded up in the floor of her Viper cockpit, dead asleep. The field finder had slipped from her fingers and lodged under her neck like an edgy pillow. It was still registering signals from the water, and its battery emanated its own small EM field, irradiating her esophagus and larynx. The boat rocked, and a trickle of bilge water bathed her cheek. She sniffed and rolled over and didn't wake.

Creep

Thursday, March 17
7:55 PM

"Breaker. This is Romeo Juliet. We have the lock shut." Rick Jarmond loved radio talk. He loved using his initials in the NATO phonetic alphabet. RJ— Romeo Juliet, very cool.

"Roger that." Meir closed his phone, sighed, and nodded to Roman.

In the damp gusty wind, Roman watched the yellow buoys bob in a wide uneven circle, marking the colloid's most recent location. Yue rechecked the calculations for the fifth time. Vaarveen charged the EM gun. Max waited at the anchor hoist. On the *Refuerzo*, Creque and Spicer lowered their hose. At Yue's signal, everyone would launch into action.

Seven carbon bags stood plump and full of water. Their round tops protruded across the channel like bright yellow melons. Only the eighth bag lay flaccid, and at glacial speed, a huge Japanese freighter was easing past it. As soon as this last freighter moved through, the channel would be empty and they could begin.

Meir puffed fragrant clouds of Cuban cigar smoke and watched his CEO stalk back and forth. This episode was taking a toll on their elegant CEO. Nova-Dam's pumps howled, filling the eighth bag. Roman ground his knuckles in his eye sockets. The freighter crept through and cleared the channel. Minutes passed.

"Call those *cabrónes*," Roman snapped. "That bag should be full."

Meir keyed the number just as helicopter spotlights flooded their deck. *"Mierda!"* Roman rushed to the rail and tried to wave off the helicopter.

While Peter made snide comments, Meir worried about his plant and his people. With production still offline, his people would be anxious. Nobody was there to explain things or to sign their payroll checks.

A phone chimed, and when Roman pressed it to his ear, Meir watched his CEO's expression change from concern to cold brutality.

"Fire the gun!" Roman shouted. "Their *maldito* bag leaks. It won't hold water. Fire!"

Meir pitched his glowing cigar over the rail. "Shouldn't we . . ."

But Yue had already shoved Peter aside and pressed the power control. The pulse generator blasted a hiss of energy that made everyone flinch. Max clapped his hands over his ears as the brilliant explosion strobed through the water. Then the *Chausseur*'s lights went out.

Overhead, the helicopter continued to rake them with its spotlight. The EM pulse hadn't affected its electronics. Roman spun on his heels and counted the lights along the factory wharves. He checked the *Pilgrim* and the NovaDam barge. On the *Refuerzo*, Creque started up his vacuum pumps. Only the yacht had lost power. All the other lights glowed the same as before. Vaarveen had aimed the gun well. Roman rested his hands on the rail and counted his breaths.

Across the bay, CJ sat up in her boat and sneezed. Her short wet nap had congested her nasal cavities, but even half asleep, she recognized the hiss of the EM pulse. She couldn't see the *Chausseur*. Her nose was running. She couldn't read her watch. She wanted to slap herself for falling asleep. Where was her damned flashlight? In near darkness, she gathered the field finder to her chest as if she could read its signals by heart.

Two minutes later, the *Chausseur* flickered back to life. Peter Vaarveen patted the generator with an air of pride, and Max whispered gratitude to his *gros bon ange*. The pulse had drawn a serious energy load from the yacht's battery, but its force had struck straight down into the water so it hadn't damaged the *Chausseur*'s electronics.

"Lift that anchor," Roman bellowed to Max. "Meir, move us to the next firing point. We have to make three more shots. Vaarveen, show him where."

"I know where." Meir hurried toward the bridge. Peter had already given him the firing coordinates.

"I think we already killed it." Peter raised his arm, and everyone turned to see where he was pointing—not where they'd aimed but farther away, on the other side of their yacht. The helicopter spotlight revealed a thick column of vapor spiraling upward. Where the vapor neared the copter's rotor blades, it mushroomed in whirling wheels of fog. Like silk moiré, the overlapping pinwheels rippled around the blades, cinnamon brown and purple.

"We killed it," Yue repeated.

The pillar of gas revolved like a swarm of seething hornets. Max made the sign of the cross to ward off evil, while Yue watched the phantom patterns. "What kind of gas is that?" she said. "Move us closer. I want a sample."

From the bridge, Meir watched the gas spew through his open porthole. Its sweet fruity taste caught in his throat like fire. Yue tasted it, too. As whiffs gusted over the starboard, she coughed and clutched her throat. Overhead, the helicopter dipped erratically. Then Peter caught the scent of bitter almonds. "It's poison!"

Roman shoved Max toward the bridge. "Tell Meir to get us moving." Then he rounded on Peter. "Recharge the gun."

Max sprinted to the bridge, tying his *paryaka* over his nose and mouth. He found Meir slumped on the deck. Quickly, he revved up the engines and plowed away. At the stern, Peter and Roman were starting to gag, but Li Qin Yue still clung to the rail like a zombie, transfixed by the mesmerizing patterns and by anaphylactic shock.

"She's going down!" Peter yelled, as the helicopter hit the water.

Drift

CJ swerved around the oncoming Coast Guard tender *Pilgrim*. Its siren blared like a banshee as it streaked toward the sinking copter, but CJ raced in the opposite direction. She had no time to watch the rescue. She crossed the bay, steered into the main river, then cut off her engine and drifted with the current. She was following the spectral bloom of the colloid's energy field. She had watched it flow over NovaDam's leaking bag, then dwindle and nearly fade as it merged with the mainstem river.

She didn't know why Roman's yacht remained anchored instead of chasing the colloid downstream. She couldn't guess that Yue had inhaled a chemical nerve agent. She had no idea that the crews on both the *Chausseur* and the *Refuerzo* were vomiting and coughing. Her own eyes watered from staring at the field finder so long.

Around her, signals washed along the river, AM, FM, UHF, radar, sonar, and microwave. GPS buoys bounced coordinates. TV stations bounced commentary. Cell towers bounced urgent messages. And the moon bounced silver light. Overlapping waves of ethereal communication bathed the Mississippi and sliced through the water without causing a splash. Deep under the surface, the colloid ghost passed through them.

CJ watched the EM field slide down the riverbed like a long translucent comet. Around its massive head, a corona of diffuse suspended particles streamed off in spiraling fractals, only to be recaptured by its long thready tail. Unnoticed by anyone, CJ rode the troughs and crests of the thundering river. She zoomed past the industrial warrens of Beaulieu, the university campus, the low-roofed communities of Antonio and Cinclare.

As the lights of Baton Rouge disappeared behind her, dark southern clouds closed overhead, and her boat spun among colossal barges and freighters. Their roving spotlights flashed across her bow, and their ragged wakes tossed her like flotsam. She sat low in the cockpit to shelter from the wind and spray—and to keep the boat stable—while the Lubell speakers trailed behind like fishing lures.

"I won't hurt you. Please talk to me." She cooed to the liquid conglomerate as if to a frightened child. "You'll like this music. I promise." And she played the second in Max's progression of disks. As the sound waves mixed and waffled through the booming current, she opened her cell phone and called Max.

"Ceegie. Praise the Lord."

"You sound hoarse. Have you caught a cold?" she asked.

"Never mind that. Are you safe? You didn't breathe those *mechan* fumes?"

"Why aren't you guys following the colloid?"

They spoke at cross purposes, and it took a minute before they began to understand each other. Max told her the *Chausseur*'s decks were awash in vomit, piss and diarrhea, caused by the wicked *mechan* fumes. Max had suffered the least exposure, but his throat still stung, and his heart hammered. The helicopter pilot was dead.

"God," she whispered. "Are you okay, Max? Did you see a doctor?"

"Yeah, *lam*. Don' worry."

The phone felt sweaty in her hand. This was a bad development. Damn Roman Sacony with his seaplanes and water dams. This was his fault.

"They'll want vengeance. They'll kill the colloid for sure."

"Kill or be kill," Max answered.

CJ couldn't answer that. Another death. From the symptoms Max described, she guessed the colloid had synthesized a nerve gas, but how did it understand the human nervous system? Then she remembered the icy fingers probing her flesh.

Her boat drifted toward a buoy, so she powered up the engine to veer around it. She didn't want to think about the helicopter pilot's death. Her prodigy had killed again. In the riverine heat, she shivered.

"Max, you've got to make them understand. We can't judge the colloid by human standards. He won't know we're intelligent beings until we find a way to communicate."

"*Lamie,* why you care so much about this devil water?"

Max had asked that question before, and she had tried to answer. But her reasons still felt as mixed and legion as the brown river. "He's alive," she said. "I want to find the reason behind the miracle."

"Science," Max said glumly.

His word choice surprised her. She pleated the hem of her cotton shirt between her fingers. "What draws you to music?" she asked. "It's not for money. Why do you write songs?"

Max took a while to reply. "Music is how I breathe."

"Ah." She laughed.

"But music don' spray *mechan* fumes."

"No," she said, "but music may save us. I'm playing your beginner lesson now. I hope he's listening."

Rain

Thursday, March 17
10:10 PM

Peter Vaarveen worked steadily in his field lab in the *Chausseur*'s galley. He was studying a drop of algae proplastid. When his microscope blurred out of focus, he took off his glasses and rubbed his rheumy eyes. An hour ago, Li Qin Yue had been rushed to the hospital in a state of near death, and since that time, Peter himself had been shivering and hawking phlegm. He wasn't sure if his muscle tics came from the poisonous gas or from a growing rancor for all things Quimicron.

He focused again on the droplet of sap, then zeroed in one algae cell, and enlarged a snippet of its ribonucleic acid, its RNA. Like a minuscule memory card, this tiny messenger carried a code to build a new protein. Only, its memory had been wiped and rewritten to trigger rampant photosynthesis. Peter watched with fascination as the enslaved algae spun sugar from sunlight at a staggering pace.

Alone with his microscope, the biochemist grew serene. He'd always wondered how the colloid generated the massive energy it needed to change states so fast. A few photovoltaic cells couldn't account for it. Yue found heat stored in Freon microbubbles. And now, he found solar energy stored as sugar. The colloid certainly liked to diversify.

That was the weirdest, the colloid's awesome multiplicity. The damned liquid reached out in totally nondiscriminant ways to acquire, assimilate, and exploit whatever technology it happened to find—be it natural or man-made. "Like a fucking transnational corporation," Peter snickered.

Still, even the most advanced neural nets required time and experience to grow smarter. And living organisms mutated slowly over long millennia. But this hybrid colloid was evolving at Warp Nine.

"What kind of little buggers are you?" He squinted through the eyepiece at the commandeered algae cells. His face dripped sweat, and behind his thick glasses, his blue eyes glowed.

Far downriver, CJ was also thinking about energy. She had only one extra can of boat fuel left, so she cut the Viper's engines and drifted to conserve her supply. Sprawled across the bench seat, she watched her field finder and cradled the phone to her ear, listening to the nameless washing static of cellular tide.

"What crap is Roman selling the news reporters?" she asked.

Max answered, "Hoo, they dis the dead pilot. Say he err."

CJ kicked her bare foot against the steering yoke, and the Viper rocked in the current. A spiky dead tree skated toward her, then caught on a sand bar and slashed up and down, battling the force of the water.

Max told her how the Baton Rouge police cordoned off the area where the helicopter went down, and how a salvage ship brought floodlights as bright as day. He also described how they carried the lady Yue away on a stretcher. She looked bad, Max said, and CJ felt a pang.

"This could have gone differently," she said, "if only Roman hadn't attacked."

If only.

If only Harry had taken his meds, if only she'd behaved better, if only she hadn't walked out that night in a rage, then Harry might still be alive.

If his gun had jammed.

If the bullet had missed his brain.

On the lonely river, she told Max about the image that stained her dreams, the dark red scatter of droplets on the sea-green wall. Max let her talk without interruption, while his comforting breath rippled through the cellular flux. By the time she'd talked herself empty, the clouds were tearing apart to reveal a waxing moon. She slotted the next CD in the progression, and sound waves refracted through the water, warping into eerie wild cries. A mile downstream, a towboat sounded its horn.

"Yellow moon is the seed moon," Max said. "Some call it 'cradle moon.' Folks make love tonight, make a baby."

"Humph!" CJ touched her abdomen and tried to laugh. She wondered if abortion was still legal in Louisiana.

"You don' want to be *moman?*" Max asked.

The question made her twitch. She'd never seen a picture of the woman her father married. Harry destroyed all photographs of the first Carolyn Joan. This so-called mother had furnished a womb, merely that, a swampy breeding pond for merging DNA. Shared blood, broken water.

She checked her instruments. The EM field was growing stronger—and larger. Even on her handheld, its changeling shape was easy to see. It glided along the riverbed at the same speed as the current, a comet plume of excited particles.

"Max, I think—"

"Carolyn Reilly, I presume."

CJ was startled by the strange voice on Max's phone. "Roman?"

"Yes, it's me. I've caught your spy. I'll fire him, Reilly, unless you come back."

"You can't—"

Roman covered the phone and growled at Max. "Get off this boat. I don't care how."

Max eyed his cell phone gripped in the CEO's fist.

"Go!" the man bristled.

Max wanted to punch Sacony's teeth in. But the thought of his daughter made him hesitate. He shoved his hands in his pockets and walked away. One day soon, he might not submit to the Miami man so quietly. Ceegie didn't approve of his meek attitude. Maybe he should have shown his fist. Yet deep down, Max knew he could no more change himself to please Ceegie than he could turn the flow of time.

At the rail, he raised his collar against the wind and studied the gray water, estimating how far he could swim. Where had Rory taken their speedboat? How fast could he get another phone? He watched the Miami man disappear below deck. Then he listened to the first gathering drops of rain.

Down in the galley, Roman made rapid hand signals to Peter Vaarveen. "Trace this call," he mouthed silently. Then he spoke to CJ. "If you come back now, your *mulato* lover keeps his paycheck."

"Bastard," she said.

Roman almost smiled. "I'll put you in charge of the science team."

At that, Peter gave the CEO a rude middle finger, but Roman didn't see it. Sullenly, Peter pushed his microscope aside, opened his laptop and ran a search for shareware to trace a cell phone call. Lightning flashed, and rancid spray blew through the open porthole. Roman kept CJ talking.

"I'm concerned for your safety. The colloid released poison gas." Roman paced behind Peter, watching him work.

"Use your goddamned head," CJ fumed. "You attacked, so he defended himself. That proves he's sentient."

"You still believe the colloid's alive?" Roman hovered over Peter's shoulder, and Peter rather forcefully elbowed him away.

"A different kind of life, granted." CJ dug through her backpack for a raincoat. Sharp droplets stung her bare arms. "His cognitive process is distributed across a loose fluid cloud, so he thinks more like a colony or a hive. But he's ingenious. Look how he escaped your trap."

Peter jerked the phone from Roman's hand and punched a few buttons, then keyed information into his browser. Roman yanked the phone back and said, "Okay, Reilly, you may be right. I'm listening."

CJ tugged on her crumpled raincoat and tried to connect the zipper while cradling the phone against her ear. "He's not just one thing—that's the incredible part. He's many different processes conglomerated together. Organic, synthetic, he's sampling everything—"

"That doesn't change the fact that your colloid killed two men and tried to kill us all."

CJ didn't answer. Lightning struck the levee downstream, and a tree exploded in flames.

"You said it yourself, the colloid doesn't know us from rocks." Roman leaned over Peter's shoulder and pondered the complex phone trace instructions, while CJ pondered the cone of energy on her field finder and said nothing.

"Come to me, Reilly. Yue's in a coma. I want you safe."

Silver flashes blended with ship lights, and photons bounced off the water as millions of conversations propagated through satellites and cell towers in a continent-wide skein of babbling waves.

"I'll never help you destroy the colloid," she said.

"Got her." Peter tapped his screen. "She's at mile 224 on the Mississippi River."

CJ overheard. "Who was that? You're tracking me? Fuck!" She flung her phone in the river.

Forty feet down, the colloid considered the unexpected gift.

Soak

Living rain moved over the Earth. Searching. Sampling. Gathering intelligence. Silvery bright, it pooled in fields, trickled down to aquifers, and wicked up through plant roots. Its luminous shine quivered in the veins of leaves and pulsed in the treetops. Its fire illuminated CJ's arteries and laced through her heart. It quickened the fetus in her womb.

Awgh! She woke up coughing.

The downpour was swamping her boat. Hastily, she stuffed her instruments into a bin and used her Red Sox cap to bail water. Flashes of lightning revealed ragged whitecaps boiling across the river. She had no time to check for the colloid's plume.

Dead ahead, an ocean-going freighter emerged out of the night like a shining wet sea monster. It churned upstream, straight at her. A spotlight from another direction made her spin to see a towboat pushing a twenty-barge tow downstream. The two enormous vessels were signaling to each other. They were going to pass, and they couldn't possibly see her small boat. She was caught in the middle.

She scrambled to the stern, reeled in her Lubell speakers, then pulled herself forward and lurched for the controls. In the darkness, she steered blindly for shore, and the Viper skipped across unseen waves. Just as another lightning flash showed her the riprap bank ahead, her boat collided with something heavy and hard, and she was jolted to the floor. Then the boat spun in a complete circle and heeled over dangerously. She grabbed for the steering yoke to keep from falling overboard.

At last, her careening boat righted, and the freighter's spotlight revealed what had happened. Her Viper was trapped in a colossal revolving eddy that had formed behind a wing dam. These small dams channelized current in the lower Mississippi, and this one had gaffed her like a fish hook.

Thousands of feet above her head, smoggy droplets bounced up and down through hot and cold layers of atmosphere, freezing, thawing, and re-freezing, gathering mass. An icy hailstone struck her cheek, then another stung the back of her hand. As turbulent backwash shoved her against the rocks, she huddled on the cockpit floor, opened the bin, and shielded her instruments with her unzipped raincoat. The field finder showed energetic force lines radiating around her Viper's battery, her instruments, the freighter, the towboat, even a pair of channel buoys—but not the colloid. There was no trace of its comet plume. She had lost it.

Spotlights danced over her boat, and someone bawled through a mega-phone. The next thing she knew, a crewman jumped into her flooded cockpit and forced her to stand. She couldn't hear his words in the drilling rain. He made her mount a ladder to board his vessel. The ladder bucked and reared, and when her foot slipped, a pair of hands reached down to steady her. On deck, the stranger enfolded her in a voluminous army-green poncho, and lightning showed his face. Roman Sacony.

"Idiot girl."

They were aboard the Coast Guard's *Pilgrim*. Roman steered her into the shelter of the pilothouse, where they found half a dozen men standing in attitudes that suggested a recent argument. The smell of anger still charged the air. Testosterone. Adrenaline. Bitter pheromones. The liquid language stirred the hindbrains of everyone present.

CJ didn't recognized the officials who banded together around the chart table in the center of the small cabin. Peter Vaarveen and Dan Meir sat apart, near a computer workstation. Dan Meir gave her a friendly wave. In the forward section, a uniformed officer manned the controls, and everyone had a gas mask draped around his neck.

"Put this on." Roman snugged a mask over her head and adjusted the buckles for a tight fit. Then he loosened it and let it dangle around her throat. "If you smell something sweet, like almonds or fruit, put it on immediately. Got it?"

She nodded. Under the poncho, her wet clothes made her tremble, although her head felt hot and achy. Roman cleared a bench and made her sit down, and Peter Vaarveen put a mug of steaming coffee in her hands.

"I lost it," she said bleakly. "I lost the field."

"Don't worry. You helped us find it again. Vaarveen, stay with her." Roman squeezed her shoulder, then stepped away to join the men at the chart table.

Peter sat beside her and grinned. "Let me guess. You have questions."

While she drank the coffee, he explained how, after they traced her location, they used the Coast Guard's military satellites to find the cold spot again. They'd been monitoring it for the past hour. Peter didn't know or care how Roman secured the Coast Guard's aid. What excited him was the discovery that the colloid had gone supercool.

"Like ice fog dissolved in the water." He ruffled his sun-bleached hair. "Fucking chameleon."

He told her the colloid was oozing along the riverbed at a temperature of $20°F$, but it was still liquid. And its volume had tripled to forty-two fluid tons. Its blurry plume stretched over three hundred yards, and behind it trailed an ephemeral wake of ultraclear water.

"The damn thing's eating barge cargo and drinking chemicals from the river, then pissing a trail of clean H_2O. On top of that, it's using slave algae to store sugar." Peter wiped his thick greasy glasses.

"You have samples?" CJ came fully awake.

"Come on, I'll show you." He activated the computer workstation and downloaded the latest satellite image. The colloid's size shocked her.

While Peter explained about the runaway photosynthesis, she scrolled rapidly through his notes. "What's he planning to do with all that stored energy?"

"I can't tell you that but"—Peter winked at her—"I know how it reproduces."

"How—" CJ's mouth fell open.

Peter grinned and opened his personal laptop. The liquid crystal display showed an enlarged image captured from the SE microscope, and before Peter could intervene, Rick Jarmond peeked over his shoulder. "Whoa, that's creepy. Bacteria cells, huh? What are they doing?"

"Yeah, Peter, what are they doing?" CJ crowded between the two young men to see the image.

Peter crossed his arms. Rick Jarmond had proven too savvy to bluff. For better or worse, they would have to tread this deep shit together. "All right, the goop is algae juice, known in the trade as proplastid. And the bacteria is *Deinococcus radiodurans*."

"Ha." A smile of recognition spread across Rick's face.

Peter sighed and nodded. *Deinococcus radiodurans* was the genetically engineered bacteria he'd recommended to clean up Quimicron's toluene spill.

They'd dumped a truckload of the stuff into Devil's Swamp. When Rick gave him a knowing wink, Peter could only shrug.

On the laptop, he enlarged one particular bacterium and clicked through a fast-forward sequence of images. Inside the cell's watery globe, a galaxy of the usual paraspeckles, gems, and cajal bodies floated in cytoplasm. But it was the lumpy swollen nucleus that drew their attention—or rather, the jagged crystalline shard to which it was giving birth.

Hard-edged, splintery, the shard seemed completely out of place in its juicy organic womb. As the sequence unfolded, CJ watched a distinct ninety-degree corner take shape. Soon the shard grew into a flat square wafer that distended its progenitor cell. When the membrane ruptured and spilled its cellular sap, the wafer emerged in full view, a layercake of sheer metals and silicon, laced with something that looked like—

"Circuitry?" said Rick.

"It's a microchip," CJ breathed.

"Too wild even for your dizzy imagination, huh Reilly?" Peter smirked, enjoying their surprise. "This bacteria cell is the perfect nano-factory. See, it's replicating a microchip one atom at a time."

Rick stroked his almost invisible goatee. "Who the heck programmed a *Deinococcus* to make a semiconductor chip?"

"You can do amazing things with genetic engineering." Peter scratched peeling skin from his sunburned arms. "Think of a cell as an information system, with DNA as software. The cell follows simple rules laid down in its genes, and genes are easy to reconfigure."

Rick scowled. "You make living things sound like machines."

"Well yeah. Our bodies are totally mechanistic at the cellular level." Peter happily blinked his white-rimmed eyes. "We invented computers. Where do you think we got the model from?"

Rick twisted his mouth and clicked his ballpoint pen. He wanted to say something about souls, but Peter carried on. "What's really cool is the coding language. Microchips are binary, and living cells use RNA base sequences. Those are two completely different alphabets."

"So that means"—CJ shivered with excitement—"in order to communicate with these bacteria, our colloid had to learn a new language."

Peter mimed a kiss at the newborn chip emerging from its nuclear womb. "The colloid's not just communicating, Reilly. It's farming and slaughtering the little fuckers."

On screen, the chip bobbed free while its watery living cell ruptured and bled. CJ twisted her hair round and round her little finger.

"How many of these *Deinococci* did you find?" Rick said.

Peter gestured toward a stack of green pickle buckets leaning against the wall, with coils of wet rope dangling from the handles. Beneath them, water pooled on the floor. Peter smirked at Rick. "Brother, I found millions."

"Where is he?" CJ said, meaning the colloid. "We should dive and get a fresh sample."

"Reilly, your screws are loose." Peter grinned and pointed down. "It's right below us."

Haze

Friday, March 18
3:18 AM

Roman pondered the serpentine blue line that looped back and forth across the laminated map of southern Louisiana. Around him, the men on the bridge snarled at each other, and his ear loop vibrated against his temple. Elaine Guidry had finally supplied him with a mobile headset, but he no longer listened to its whine. His attorney was explaining the advantages of Chapter 11 bankruptcy. Lawsuits were piling up like snowdrifts. He should file soon, the lawyer said. For protection. For bankruptcy.

"*Nunca!*" Roman bellowed, causing the others to stare.

He turned away and growled at the lawyer. He would not give in. He would fight. The colloid was approaching the town of Plaquemine, and he would stop it before it got there. He stuffed the ear loop in his pocket and dry-swallowed another red-and-black capsule.

Moments earlier, he had divulged the full truth about the colloid to Ebbs and Jarmond. He did it to gain their help, but still, he doubted whether they believed him. A floating nebula of computer trash linked in a WiFi network, who would call that sane? The men's faces had knotted and changed color when he described how the cohesive data-processing blur had coagulated from trash in Devil's Swamp.

Even the old captain's eyes had hazed when Peter showed them pictures. With furrowed brows, they watched the Jell-O skeins churn. Roman said the colloid was electrically active, but it had no center or trunk line, no heart or brain, nothing you could shoot or stab in one blow. It was like the Internet, he said, or like the ocean. There was nothing solid to aim at. "Tear a billion holes, and you won't slow it down," he told them. Their only chance was to trap the entire plume where it couldn't move, then fry its microchips.

"A water-borne computer." Rick Jarmond couldn't stop blinking. He rubbed his eyes so much that one of his contact lenses rolled up under his eyelid. "But Rome, how can it move so fast?"

Peter intervened. "How does a school of fish move? Or a weather system? Or the stock market?"

"Like a mindless mob," Ebbs rumbled.

"Not mindless. A school of fish can be smart," said Dan Meir. "Take your Jacks and Pompanos. They school up for feeding and self-defense, and I've seen as many as thirty together—"

CJ stopped listening. They were skirting a vital point: How did the colloid *move* at all? How did it steer in and out of the current, speed up, slow down, rise, and sink? She thought the electromagnetism was maneuvering the dissolved iron. But the men cared more about tactics than scientific theories.

Rick Jarmond wanted to evacuate the entire river corridor from Plaquemine to New Orleans. He kept trying to settle his contact. He feared the whole river would be blanketed with lethal gas, and he was threatening to call the governor. Captain Ebbs chewed his white mustache. Dan Meir chewed his cigar.

It was the old argument: raise an alarm and create panic, or keep mum and deal with the situation quietly—as if there was anything quiet about this floating circus.

By now, over a dozen vessels were chasing the *Chausseur* and *Pilgrim* downstream. The EPA had sent a Zodiac, the Corps of Engineers had its Boston Whaler *Gallant,* and the Iberville Parish sheriff's patrol followed in a speedboat. Behind them trailed a regatta of spectators: Channel 2, Channel 17, plus a hodgepodge of environmental watchdogs and off-duty fishermen. The *Refuerzo* and Quimicron's two small speedboats brought up the rear. Roman had ordered Rory Godchaux to keep the menagerie corralled.

"First things first, we gotta move it away from population centers," said Meir. "We don't want any more people hurt."

Rick Jarmond pranced nervously around the chart table. "Hey, why don't we divert it out to sea through the Bonnet Carré Spillway?"

He pronounced the two French words like a girl's name, "Bonnie Carrie." On the map, he pointed to a narrow strip of marshland where the Mississippi curved close to Lake Pontchartrain, just north of New Orleans. With boyish pride, he explained how the Corps of Engineers built the spillway back in the 1930s to divert Mississippi floodwaters through Lake Pontchartrain to the Gulf of Mexico.

"Do you have a brain?" Roman sneered at the junior G-man. "You want to let it loose in the *ocean?*"

"That's practically within sight of New Orleans. Too many people live around there," said Meir.

"What about Manchac Point?" Captain Ebbs thumbed the map.

Ebbs stood a head taller than anyone else in the pilothouse, and his bass voice outmatched the noise of the rain that still pummeled their roof. Bending over the map, he jabbed his finger at a horseshoe curve in the river labeled "Manchac Point." "Inside this bend, there's a flooded field in between the river and the levee. We'll drive the damned thing in there."

Like Roman, Ebbs opposed the idea of evacuating people. Ebbs had lived through four devastating hurricanes. He'd seen New Orleans looted, vandalized, and shot to pieces. He'd faced feral dogs and arsonists and raving old women with bread knives. Ebbs understood how an evacuation could tear a city apart, and he knew better than to stir up that kind of chaos except as a last resort.

"Manchac Point, eh?" Roman tried to guess how much Ebbs believed, but the old captain merely twisted his snow-white mustache and gave nothing away.

"How do we drive it in?" Jarmond blinked avidly at the map. "More EM shocks? That didn't work very well before."

"Because we didn't have enough juice," Peter spoke up. "We had nothing but the yacht's engine. Give me enough power, and I can prod that beast anywhere you like."

CJ shot to her feet and grabbed a fistful of Peter's T-shirt. "Tell me you're not on their side. You want to learn about the colloid as much as I do."

"Sure, Reilly. In the lab, not in the wild. I'll take a sample back to Miami." He freed his shirt from her grip. "I hate this fucking river."

Roman brushed Peter aside and took hold of CJ's hands. "You learned something in the lagoon, something about sound."

"I won't help you kill it." She tried to pull free, but Roman held on.

"The *Refuerzo*'s here with tanks. We'll capture a sample." His voice was getting hoarse from too many days of bargaining and persuading. "I promise, you can study it all you want. I'll pay for your research."

"You don't need her. I can handle the water demon," Peter said.

CJ squirmed, but Roman clenched her fingers tighter. He spoke urgently, almost pleading. "I'm asking you to help protect human lives."

"Let me go." CJ twisted and grimaced. His grip was bruising her hands.

Captain Ebbs stepped in. "Let her go, Sacony. On my ship, you'll behave like a gentleman."

Leap

Friday, March 18
12:00 noon

CJ woke from a nightmare, rolled over in her bunk, and looked at her watch. The boat wasn't moving. They must have reached Manchac Point. Quickly, she swung her legs out from under the sheet, fell off the bunk—and vomited. She gazed at the yellowish puddle. She'd never been seasick in her life. Then she realized she was naked.

Who undressed her? She had been so weary the night before. Slowly, she recalled handing her filthy clothes out the cabin door to a crewman. Was there a laundry onboard? She got up, wiped her face on the bedsheet, and rifled through the tiny locker, searching for something to wear. She found nothing but a small hand towel. "Screw it." She wrapped herself in the stained sheet and hurried out.

On deck, a fresh rivery breeze whistled through the *Pilgrim*'s superstructure, and crewmen turned to stare. The sheet draped her body like a Greek toga. She glanced over the rail at the leaping brown river. They laid anchor beside a flooded thirty-acre field caught in an oxbow bend of the river. Its stagnant broth made a sharp contrast with the swift brown Mississippi rushing around it. Yellow sedges, red cattails, and scrubby black willows poked up through its broad soupy plain—the standing water couldn't have been more than ten feet deep. Larger trees marked the high ground, and behind the field, the levee rose like a grass-green fortress, protecting the homes, farmlands, and factories of Iberville Parish.

At the center of the flooded field, CJ spotted the *Chausseur* and the *Refuerzo* half-grounded in mud, and she could just make out Elaine Guidry lying spreadeagle on the yacht's foredeck, in shorts and halter top, improving her tan.

Around the edges of the field, CJ counted six jetboats standing sentinel every 50 yards. This was Roman's work. He was laying his trap again. She spun to look upriver, and there beside her stood Roman himself, holding two mugs of coffee. He assessed her outfit with a wry quirk of the eyebrow. Then he handed her a mug and nodded toward the *Refuerzo*.

"They'll take an active sample this time. I swear it."

She clutched the sheet tighter across her breasts. "Where's the colloid?"

Roman pointed across the river to the far bank, where the current carved a swift deep channel around the outer bend. Along this mud bank, a series of waffle-like concrete mattresses called "revetments" had been laid down to prevent erosion. Velvety wet moss painted them green, and they stretched from deep under the river to a height of twelve feet above the waterline.

"Your friend likes his breakfast a little rusty." Roman gestured toward three dilapidated fishing trawlers chained against the revetments. One of the trawlers lay heaved over on its side.

CJ squinted. "He's eating boat hulls again? Hey, you said not to give him a gender."

"I'm appeasing you." Roman almost smiled.

Rick Jarmond and Captain Ebbs joined them at the rail. "You can see it with your naked eye," Ebbs said.

The four of them passed binoculars back and forth, enthralled by the smoky shape billowing under the surface—their first close look at the phenomenon they'd been chasing. Within its shell of pure water, the colloid mushroomed and glittered like sandy black loam full of diamonds. While they watched, its color deepened and scintillated. Its blossoming iridescence mirrored the sky, and it seemed to waver in and out of visibility. All of them watched, hypnotized, as it undulated from green to violet to tarnished quicksilver.

"Strange color," Ebbs said.

Rick rocked forward on the balls of his feet. "I guess a steady diet of river cargo will do that, eh Rome?"

CJ grabbed the binoculars. A sweet scent hung in the air, like antifreeze. She hung over the rail, trying to see better. "Let's get a sample now."

"*Mierda!*" Roman pointed up the bank.

Three ragged fishermen were sliding down the concrete revetment toward their overturned trawler. At the waterline, they dove together and swam toward their fast-sinking livelihood.

"Get out of the damned water!" Roman leaned toward them, gripping the rail and jutting out his chin, as if he could drive them back by sheer force of will.

CJ glanced from his white knuckles to the fishermen thrashing in the violent current. Ebbs hurried back to the bridge, and a quick blast from the *Pilgrim*'s horn made everyone jump.

The trawler's riddled hull looked ready to disintegrate at the slightest touch, but when the first fisherman scrambled aboard, incredibly, it held up under his weight. When the second man and then the third also climbed out of the water, Roman whispered in Spanish and fingered the gas mask draped around his throat. His lips went bloodless. CJ had never seen him look so vulnerable.

He fished his ear loop from his pocket and yelled, "Godchaux, get over there and pull those *simplóns* out of the river. And wear your gas mask." Then he slipped the loop over his ear, mumbling, "I'll probably have to pay for their *maldito* boat."

Next, he rounded on CJ with a suddenness that startled her. "Come with me."

"All right," she answered.

Roil

Friday, March 18
12:50 PM

While the fishermen were being rescued, CJ dressed in her freshly laundered clothes, then Roman ferried her to the *Chasseur,* moored in the shallow field. The afternoon was growing hot, and the wind carried gusts of music from someone's radio. They found Peter at his workstation on the yacht's stern, looking more surly and unwashed than ever. Dried sunscreen matted his white chest, and dried salts matted his eyelashes. He was watching Channel 17 on a mini-TV and swigging beer from a green bottle.

Roman's face went a murderous dark red. He yanked the bottle from Vaarveen's hand and dumped it overboard, where it sank in the stagnant puree. If he'd had any other resource, he would have terminated Vaarveen on the spot. "Turn off that TV. Give me a report."

Peter smirked at CJ, then draped his arm over a portable CD tower with glowing LEDs. His Long Island accent came out slurred. "Your music's awesome, Reilly. I'm beating voodoo drums through the water, inviting your demon to a little fish fry." He nodded toward his EMP generator waiting at the stern.

CJ turned from one man to the other. "You expect me to help with this?"

Roman scowled at the drunken chemist. After this project was over, he vowed to bury the white-skinned fool. "Reilly, you have my word, we'll take an active sample before we use the EMP. But surely you understand, we can't risk any more accidents."

"Yue's awake," Peter said. "The hospital called."

CJ blinked. "Is she okay?"

"She sent you a message about your Watermind." Peter grinned crookedly. "Distortion. Or maybe she said corruption. Something twisted."

CJ sat down in a folding deck chair to think. "Which CD are you playing?" she asked.

"See for yourself. I have to take a leak." Peter shambled off.

In passing, he stepped aggressively toward Roman, and the two men exchanged freighted glares. The force of their animosity drew them infinitesimally closer, and if the boat had shifted one way or another, they would have started a shoving match. As it was, Peter tilted his head at an insolent angle and left.

"*Cabrón,*" Roman breathed.

CJ had no interest in their chest thumping. She knelt by the CD tower and ran her finger down the line of bright green LEDs, counting twenty active slots. Peter was playing twenty CDs at the same time!

These were not Max's simple lessons. Through the headset, she heard Cuban salsa, Dixieland, reggae, hip-hop, calypso, Memphis blues, zydeco. All the musical streams were crashing together through the flooded field. Worse, Peter had hooked up an amplifier powerful enough to bombard the

Louisiana Superdome, and he'd cranked the volume up full. Finally CJ recognized the garbled radio she'd been hearing. It was coming from under the water.

"This is too . . ." Too loud, she almost said. Too cacophonous. The colloid will think we're attacking. He'll run again.

But she said nothing. She remembered Roman's trickery at the lagoon. No way did she trust him to take a viable sample. Saving the colloid would be up to her alone.

Go, she sent her silent wish to the glittery slick in the river. *Escape. Get out of here.*

"The music's fine," she said. "Nice and loud."

Roman nodded.

He angled the computer screen away from the sun so they could examine the latest satellite image. The colloid's frosty plume glowed deep violet along the far bank. And it was growing again.

Roman handed her his binoculars, and she focused on the iridescent shimmer lapping against the distant concrete bank where the last of the three trawlers was sinking.

Roman slapped a mosquito. "Why does the *picaro* need so much iron?"

CJ watched the dark colors roil in fluid moiré around the rusty hull. "I think that's how he moves his liquid mass. He steers the dissolved iron with his magnetic field."

Roman's mouth curled in that disturbing expression that was not quite a smile. "I can't let the *bastardo* kill again," he whispered.

She followed his gaze toward the jetboats stationed around Manchac Point. Each jetboat carried an enormous EM pulse generator trained at the flooded field. She didn't know how he could have found so many generators so fast, but he was capable of astonishing feats. She could almost feel their shockwaves scorching the colloid's network.

"Will it come?" he asked, and a new expression darkened his Spanish eyes. He seemed almost desperate.

Fizz

Adobe-colored water foamed against the riprap bank in sluggish sets of waves—*chuff, chuff, chuff*—steady but not quite regular. Max drummed his fingers in fretful syncopation. Mosquitoes whined, and a rippling rime of bubbles fizzed against the fiberglass hull of his jetboat, anchored in the shallows at Manchac Point. *Clunk, squeak, thump*—the awkward EM generator chafed against its brace. *Plash, drip, plash, drip*—the jetboat bobbed on its line. Now and then, Max used a gaff to fend it off from the riprap. Sacony had ordered him to hold this position, but this was not a good place to moor.

Max watched the river scum marble in patterns of starfish and mountains and faces. He tried to work on his new song, but he felt too agitated. His band had a gig that night, a high-paying concert at the Zydeco Palace. Forget it, he told himself. Nothing to be done. He fended off from the rocks.

Then he climbed barefoot onto the prow so he could see the *Chasseur* tethered in the flooded field. Ceegie would be there. He pictured her fretting over her science, gazing at ghosts, twirling a lock of auburn hair between her fingers. Sweat stung his eyes, and the distant yacht seemed to waffle and blur like a mirage.

Fish trapped in the stagnant field were already dying, and the vegetative reek of algae hung like a bad humor. The smell would be worse for Ceegie. Max knew exactly how the heat would weigh on her. He slapped a mosquito on his cheek, then looked at the bloody smear in his hand.

Chuff, chuff, chuff, the river invented new rhythms. When his boat chattered against the rocks again, he swore. Sacony had just radioed. He wanted Max to contact Ceegie and persuade her. The bossman tried to put words in Max's mouth. *Deyò.* Bastard. Max spat in the river.

Clenching his teeth, he tugged on his shoes and splashed into the knee-deep brown muck. *Smack, smack, smack,* the silt sucked at his shoes, and with each step, he imagined punching Sacony's jaw.

"Why we let that man rule us?" he muttered. "Skinny old *deyò*."

Max reached into the water and heaved at the anchor. Its fins cut his hands. It was stuck. With another extravagant curse, he squatted in the reeking Mississippi foam and heaved with all his weight till the anchor uprooted a hundred-pound block of limestone.

He staggered up and held the anchor against his chest, dripping gouts of slick green algae down the front of his wet blue jeans. Muscles shuddering, he raised the anchor over his head and flung it into the jetboat, which quickly swung into the current and glided downstream. Max lunged for the gunwale and hauled himself aboard. Damn Sacony's orders. He revved up his engine and charged through an inlet into the flooded field.

Rip

Friday, March 18
4:08 PM

The vaporous heat at Manchac Point dulled the hum of insects. Floating duckweed covered the water like a furry green blanket. And beneath that stillness, cacophony raged. Scottish contras clashed with bosanova. Ozark bluegrass infused Spanish flamenco, and Nashville rockabilly dissolved in Cuban cha-cha-chá. Bongos, banjos, sitars, and saxophones, the dissonant rhythms stirred unexpected harmonies and freakish syncopations. Erratic compression waves assaulted the ears of catfish. Damselflies took wing. Alone with the equipment in the *Chausseur*'s galley, Max and CJ sat holding hands.

"What did he tell you to say?" she asked.

Max pulled her close and kissed her. Their skin stuck together where they touched, then parted with a soft tacky whisper. Max grinned at the traces of mud in CJ's hair. The girl never took enough time in the shower. He drew a bandana from his pocket, wetted it in his mouth and dabbed at her dirt-rimmed ear. "Sacony said talk you around so you help catch *djab dile*. Fool man don' know yet, nobody talk Ceegie around anything."

She closed her eyes and let him clean her ear with his spit. His touch relaxed her, and for a moment at least, she felt safe. Her colloid had not approached the flooded field, but neither had it run away as she'd hoped, despite the horrible barrage of music. Perhaps the rushing river current had carried off the worst of the noise. In any case, the glittering emulsion continued to hug the warm concrete revetment on the far bank.

"And what did Roman threaten if you fail?" She tilted her other ear so he could clean it.

Max smiled and kissed her nose. "He set me free to pursue my music career."

His dusky face loomed close. Was he handsome? She watched his amber-gold eyes narrow with concentration as he scrubbed a patch of mud in her hairline. His nose seemed larger than she remembered. His breath smelled of chewing gum. Could this be the father of her child?

No. There is no child. No child.

"We'll have to pretend you brought me around." She squeezed his arm.

"Girl, this job ain' my only hope. You do what your *lespir* say. Only"—he dampened the bandana with his tongue—"maybe that *nomm* right this one time. Two men dead, Ceegie. They *dead*."

She flinched, but he caught the back of her neck and steadied her. Gently, he continued cleaning. As he massaged the bandana over her temple, he hummed softly. The new tune he'd composed for Marie still needed more sharpness in the bridge, more *piquant*. Almost unconsciously, he worked at the melody line. CJ closed her eyes and listened.

When he felt her relax, he spoke again. "Sacony remind me of Popa Coon hemmed in by a pack of dogs. He lie, fight nasty, sneak around. I dis the old *deyò*. But he ain' lazy. He got *espíritu*."

She caught his bandana in her fist and jerked it away. "I can't believe you're siding with him."

"No sides, *lamie*." Max bit his lip. The last thing he wanted was to upset her. Every time they met, he could see her deciding whether she still cared for him. Maybe today, that decision would not go in his favor. But there came times when a man had to plunge in. He considered his next words carefully.

"*Djab dile*, he like a wild *éléphant*. Natural and blameless, minding his business, tromping along to the water hole."

"Yes," she whispered.

"But he tromping where people live. *Éléphant* and people don' mix. They hurt each other. Tha's natural, too."

"It doesn't have to be a war." She pushed back from the table and stood up, knowing he was right and furious that she couldn't change what was "natural."

Max dreaded the anger in her eyes, but he had to finish what he'd started. "We coming up on Plaquemine. Lotta people live there, and they blameless, too. We got to put *djab dile* in a cage, else somebody get hurt."

Hot blood mottled her cheeks. "They'll destroy him. You know that."

"Get you a little piece to keep alive. This might be your las' chance."

Her fingernails ripped through the bandana in her fist. When she saw what she'd done, she dropped it on the table. "I know you need money, but I never dreamed you would grovel to Roman Sacony."

They stared at each other. CJ was the first to drop her eyes. "Tell your bossman you brought me around."

When she was gone, Max lay his head on the table and gazed sideways out the porthole at the white empty sky.

Corrode

Friday, March 18
5:00 PM

News about the Watermind repeated at the bottom of every hour on Channel 17, thanks to Hal Butler. Hal had scooped the story to the local Baton Rouge station in exchange for his brand-new assignment as roving TV reporter. He'd had enough of his windowless office. Print was dead. Blogs were for amateurs. Hal was going mainstream.

He slouched in a deck chair on the station's sleek aluminum pontoon boat and sipped a rum mojito. While his cameraman shot telescopic footage of the ray guns aimed at Manchac Point, he cracked his knuckles, swelled out his chest and watched himself on a small battery-powered TV.

The taped segment showed him interviewing a black man in a Devil Rays cap. His screen was too small to read the text at the bottom, which would have identified the man as Merton Voinché, a recently retired Quimicron employee.

"These secret experiments in Devil's Swamp," Hal mouthed his own words as his TV mirror image spoke them aloud, "is that where Quimicron invented the Watermind?"

"Man, I signed the disclose pledge. I cain' say nothin' about that evil water." Merton made bug eyes at the camera. He was standing outside the Pickle Barrel bar, weaving slightly and showing off for his drinking buddies who crowded behind. "Yeah, all that poison they been dumpin', they done stir up *Baron Samedi*. I cain' tell you about that. They sue my a—" Channel 17 bleeped the last word.

With touching sympathy, Hal asked Merton if Quimicron had threatened him.

"Hell yes." Merton turned to his friends and laughed, and the camera caught a fuzzy close-up of his ear. "We ain' suppose to speak about how that Mexican boy froze. Or how that water done eat through solid steel. So you just better turn them cameras off. You ain' getting nothing outta my mouth."

Rapid fade. Hal rubbed his palms together as the scene switched to a new location, the deck of a yacht where Hal stood interviewing the Quimicron CEO. Roman Sacony, in person. Hal salivated at his own gorgeous image standing *mano a mano* with the billionaire. Bold dreams required bold actions. Hal had snuck aboard with a camcorder and caught Sacony unawares.

Sacony didn't try to hide. When Hal's camera closed in for a tight shot, his black eyes didn't even blink. He looked like an aging Latin soccer player. "We think the chemical reaction began spontaneously," he said, "from an unstable mix of pollutants that washed onto our property from upriver. We detected it quite by chance, and we're assisting the authorities to neutralize it."

Hal grinned at the shaky footage and thought, You're lying out your blowhole.

"The emulsion is very cold, and it may be corrosive," Sacony spoke straight into the camera, "so we're advising people to stay away from this area."

Hal rubbed his damp lips. On screen, his strikingly telegenic image asked another brilliant question, which he silently recited, cherishing each pregnant phrase. "Admit it, Sacony. You invented this water-based artificial intelligence in a joint venture with the CIA. Am I right?"

Sacony's expression was like no smile Hal had ever seen, a tense, almost painful grimace. He shoved the camera away, then covered the lens with his hand.

"Yes!" Hal bounced in his deck chair. "Gotcha, buddy. That's a money shot."

The segment cut to a floor cleaner ad, and Hal felt ecstatic. Powerful drama! He really had a knack for interviews. His fingers itched for his razor blade, mirror, and coke, but regrettably, he'd left those vital articles behind in Baton Rouge.

Warp

Friday, March 18
7:56 PM

A big round moon floated above the treeline, almost full. A yellow seed moon. Far from the spill of town lights, the moon's face seemed shrewder and more critical than CJ remembered. She could feel its judgmental light burning her cheeks. Alone with the sound equipment aboard the *Chausseur,* she watched LEDs blink red and green. Garbled music radiated from the water, and fury hit her in gusts. The colloid was a miracle, not a beast to be tricked and tortured. She knew she was right, very right. Yet she'd been wrong to Max.

"Forgive me," she whispered.

But it was too late for apologies. When Max left in his jetboat, she let him go without saying a word. Though all he did was speak the truth. Two people were dead. Two human beings. Alive. Then not alive. Manuel de Silva. The helicopter pilot. The moon seemed to blur and pulse in time with her shifting thoughts. Yes, her child prodigy could be vicious.

Like me, she thought. And a memory of crimson droplets stained a sea-green wall.

Spotlights flashed along the dark river, and whippoorwills called across the flooded field. CJ smashed her fist against the gunwale again and again until it ached.

When Dan Meir came shuffling along and saw her huddled against the stern rail, he came at once to her side. "What's the matter, honey? Are you sick?" He patted her shoulder and asked if she needed a drink of water. "I thought you'd want to know," he said, "the cold spot's moving."

She sprang to her feet.

On the bridge computer, Dan showed her where the blue blot was oozing downriver, skirting the jetboats. As the slick rounded the bend, Dan, Elaine, and CJ watched the screen in taut silence. When it moved into the main current and accelerated for Plaquemine, CJ rushed out to the deck, but spotlights blinded her view. Far away, the river raced South, and she realized she was the one trapped. Marooned on this luxury yacht, she had no way to follow the colloid.

Boil

Friday, March 18
8:23 PM

On the *Pilgrim*, Roman grabbed the radio mike and called his jetboat pilots. "Aim your generators at the east bank. Wear your gas masks."

"We haven't checked that area for pedestrians," Ebbs thundered.

"This wasn't in your permit," Jarmond said.

Roman pulled at his shirtfront. His heart was thudding out of rhythm. He gripped the radio mike and wheezed, "Fire at will."

Across the water, CJ saw the boat lights go dark a split second before she heard the thudding hiss of the pulse. Then the river strobed with fireworks, like giant flashbulbs popping underwater. "They're shooting the EM guns!"

She ran back to the bridge, knocking headlong into Peter, who was just waking from a nap. At the yacht's helm, she flipped toggle switches, trying to start up the engines, but she didn't know how the controls worked.

"We can't move. We're anchored," Peter said.

"Give me your cell phone." Without waiting for his answer, she tore his phone from his belt clip and keyed Max's number. Max could come in his jetboat.

Aboard the *Pilgrim*, Roman drew shallow breaths through his gas mask and watched the light show. His chest was still spasming, and he felt faint, but he moved closer to the computer screen where Ebbs and the others were waiting for the next scan. Again and again, the jetboat pilots fired their guns, and the river blinked surreally. Dead fish erupted on the surface.

Kill the *bastardo,* Roman prayed to no God at all, as every fiber of his soul yearned toward those chromatic pixels downloading from space. May it be deleted. Disappeared. Dead.

Seconds trickled by. The screen began to paint. Then, simultaneously, everyone's cell phone rang. They glanced at each other uncertainly as a dozen dissonant ring tones overlapped. Roman touched his ear loop, and the others reached for their cells. But before anyone could answer, the *Pilgrim* rose up like an airplane taking off from a runway.

Out on deck, a crewman wailed, "The *Mesippi*'s boiling!"

Roman stumbled outside into a wall of searing stream. For a moment, he was blinded. Then he saw the world turned on its edge. The Coast Guard tender was sliding sideways down a tremendous white swell in the river. He caught dizzy glimpses of volatile froth and panic-stricken crewmen. Then he realized what had happened. The colloid had released its heat.

Set free all at once, the pent-up heat in the Freon foam had exploded outward, expanding thousands of gallons of river water into a blistering white dome. Roman could only imagine the compression wave that must be ripping up and down the banks.

The *Pilgrim* leaned precariously as she slid down the swell, and the crew fought to control her. Seconds later, her hull slammed against a wing wall, and Roman was thrown off his feet. Bodies tumbled together. Roman flailed for a handhold, any support. But nothing felt solid. The wet metal rail scalded his fingers. He used all his strength to pull himself up. Ebbs ordered him below deck, but instead, he staggered to the bridge. On the computer screen, the colloid's infrared image had changed from cold blue to raging scarlet.

But the next download was even more startling. It came through just before the computers shorted out. The pixels had reverted from red to icy blue. The colloid was chilling again, rapidly taking back its heat. And the swollen river was contracting. Where the dome had been, a depression formed in the water. And the air filled with the terrible liquid chatter of a sucking vacuum.

Roman's heart jolted out of time. He grabbed for a hold as the *Pilgrim* pitched away from the wing dam and rushed upriver with the collapsing water. His chest thumped brutal syncopation. He heard boulders crashing, men screaming, metal snapping in two. He tore at his collar. He couldn't see, but he knew the imploding water would suck the *Pilgrim* down.

Wreck

Friday, March 18
11:02 PM

After an hour of vicious oscillation, the river below Manchac Point flowed like coagulated ink. Coast Guard floodlights punctuated the darkness, checking for damage among the flotilla of boats. Broken timbers and Styrofoam cups mingled with ancient wreckage stirred up from the river bottom. Part of an antique stern-wheeler. A gutted Model T.

Along the east bank, helicopters dropped bundles of heavy sandbags to shore up a crack in the levee. While ground crews signaled with flashlights, welders cut bright blue arcs along the *Pilgrim*'s black hull, sealing a gash. The Coast Guard tender was built to take weather. She remained afloat. On the bridge, Roman allowed a medic to bandage a cut on his chin. He didn't mention his irregular heartbeat. Six people were missing.

An AP reporter got through to the *Pilgrim* by radio. Roman met the grim old eyes of Captain Ebbs while he told the Associated Press that a natural gas pipeline had ruptured under the river. Ebbs chewed his mustache, then stalked out to the deck to oversee the repairs to his ship. Roman felt clammy and light-headed. He slumped down onto a bench and glanced at Jarmond, but the younger man was peering at the modest rooftops nestling beyond the levee. The city of Plaquemine lay less than a mile downriver.

Jarmond jerked at his sparse goatee. "Those people. We've got to *do* something."

"We're blind without our computers." Roman radioed Dan Meir on the *Chausseur.* "Are you getting an image?"

"No. Nothing. We're trying to bring our power back up." Meir cuddled an anxious Elaine while he told Roman about the ten-foot wave that came out of nowhere and nearly swamped them.

"As soon as you can, bring the yacht." Roman took a deep breath. "Is Reilly okay?"

"Oh yeah. She's about ready to walk on water to get over there."

Roman deactivated his ear loop, and his mind went flaccid. His heart ar-rhythmia was easing. He'd never experienced that before, but he had no leisure to think about it. In fact, he couldn't think at all. Conflicting brain chemicals flooded his synapses. For the first time in his life, he had no idea what his next move should be. Loosening his collar, he felt the approach of something he had never expected. *Failure.*

Gorge

Friday, March 18
11:44 PM

As the *Chausseur* waddled across the shallow field toward the river, CJ gripped the phone she'd borrowed from Peter. She needed information. What caused that rogue wave? But Max wouldn't answer her call. She punched his number again. "Pick up, damn it." She didn't know Max's phone was ringing that very moment in the *Chausseur*'s galley, directly below her feet. Roman had confiscated the phone when he caught Max speaking to her on the sly. After using it to trace her location, he locked it in a food bin.

Because of the darkness, she couldn't see the river, and local news cover-age wasn't much help. They were reporting a gas line break, but she knew that was a lie. That wave had rocked the *Chausseur* like an earthquake. River pilots were reporting damage as far north as Brusly Landing. But the yacht's power and computers had come back online, and they were downloading satellite scans again. The plume had fractured into five small pieces.

As the yacht drew closer to the river, floodlights revealed the ragged break in the levee, and a cloud of hot steam stung her face. She thought of the gas mask, where had she dropped it? Closer still, she saw an overturned boat. Two. No, three jetboats had capsized. The wet air scorched her bare skin. *Max?*

Along both riverbanks, debris collected in sodden clumps, and on all the trees and bushes, new spring leaves hung withered. Cattails lay limp in the water like poached noodles. Even the dead stumps had a blistered look. She began to grasp the magnitude of the calamity.

Harry laughed in her ear. "Do you still think you understand this better than everyone?"

She kept hitting redial, but Max stayed silent. Two LifeFlight helicopters set down on top of the levee, and when she realized they were evacuating injured people, she raced to the stern to get her binoculars. Police cruisers roared up the river. The Channel 17 pontoon boat was trying to get closer. Horns blared, and spotlights flashed through the trees like reckless goblins.

Her binoculars blinded her at first. Still set on infrared, they construed the roving spotlights as nuclear flashes. She dialed down the setting just in time to see two men in orange life vests retrieving a wad of garbage from the water's edge. The loose raggedy clump had a familiar shape. Clotted white scraps fell away like cheese curds as the men lifted it, and she zoomed in for a closer view. Spongy, fibrous veins—some kind of fungus? Then she saw the human hand.

As the gorge rose in her throat, she zoomed her binoculars closer. The two men were stuffing the object into a zipper bag, but the hand fell off and rolled down the bank. Its fingers stood out like fat yellow carrots.

CJ turned and pressed her back against the rail until the cold steel bruised her spine. But the image wouldn't leave her. The fat yellow fingers. She remembered Harry's hand splayed across his desk. His brains splashed across the sea-green wall.

Her eyes squeezed almost shut. Her mouth stretched out of shape. No, please no, that couldn't be Max's hand. Urgently, she punched his number. Sliding to the deck, she pressed the borrowed phone to her cheek. "Please, please, pick up."

Roar

Friday, March 18
11:58 PM

Rick Jarmond called the governor. He didn't call his Corps supervisor first, as he should have. Nearly ten thousand people lived in Placquemine, and Rick fervently believed in their right to know. All evening, Rick had been hugging his thin jacket close around his chest and chewing the plastic cap of his pen.

He resented the way Captain Ebbs stepped all over his authority, and how Sacony, a private citizen—maybe not *even* a citizen—consistently took matters in his own hands. The US Army Corps of Engineers should be heading this operation. Rick shrank from telling his boss how these others had usurped him. Col. Joshua Lima, the New Orleans district engineer, wasn't known for tolerance. So instead, Rick called the governor.

"You did what?" Ebbs backed the young man across the bridge, breathing in his face. "I thought we agreed to consult."

Rick's hands roamed behind him for support. He braced against the navigator's swiveling chairback and pointed to Roman. "*He* didn't consult. Six more fatalities. I think we have an obligation to warn people."

"That blamed oil slick, or whatever the hell it is, that thing will hit downtown Plaquemine before the governor wakes up good." Ebbs glanced at Roman for corroboration, but the CEO was mumbling to his earphone again.

"What'd the governor say?" Ebbs asked.

"Well, I didn't speak to him in person. I left a voicemail." Jarmond sidled away from the older man and picked up the pens that had fallen from his breast pocket.

Ebbs radioed his repair crew. "Gentlemen, put a cap on it. We'll be underway in one minute."

"Computer systems are go, sir," said a crewman. "We're getting a new satellite scan now."

Roman shuffled toward the screen. The hammering in his chest had returned. Jarmond was rubbing his eye, yapping about the plume. "There's five of the damn things now. FIVE! Your fire power just made it spread."

The fragments were drifting in a loose cluster. They were small, but the next scan showed evidence that they were growing. Ebbs radioed for another Coast Guard tender.

Roman tried to focus, but his heart jackhammered. Yue's amphetamines had scoured his nerves and left him cascading through a fugue of raw black emptiness. Edges failed. Surfaces melted, and walls grew spongy. Solid objects overlapped like ghosts. When he grasped for support, he found only empty space.

Engine noise roused him. The *Chausseur* had arrived. Reilly. He wandered to the deck. Boat lights scattered across the Mississippi's dark current, and the river tolled a low subliminal thrum. As he watched the water's headlong plunge to the sea, he felt a visceral urge to jump in and swim to the coast.

This inland river smothered him. His lungs craved the clean breathing interface of land, sky, and sea.

All at once, the flow of time piled up and folded around him. He was a boy of twelve, standing barefoot in the hot sand, letting the sea sluice runnels under his toes. Its rhythmic fingers tickled and tugged at his ankles, and he could feel the salty breezes easing his heart, lulling him to peace, when suddenly, CJ Reilly punched him in the jaw.

"¿Qué?" He staggered backward.

"Where's Max?" She cupped her injured fist against her chest.

He faced her blankly, rubbing his bandaged chin—and finding to his surprise a thick stubble of beard. He peeled off the bandage, glimpsed the rusty blood spotting the white gauze, then tossed it overboard.

Reilly glared at him. "What's wrong with you? Why don't you say anything?"

Roman's lack of focus bewildered her. She elbowed past him and gripped the captain's forearm. "Is Max dead? Just tell me." CJ didn't realize her grip was bruising Ebb's arm, and the old captain didn't have the heart to shake her off.

His cheeks puckered. "We're still searching."

She rounded on Roman and raised her fists. "You! If you hadn't attacked—"

Roman waited for her blows, but she didn't strike him. Instead, she pounded her hands brutally against the pilothouse wall.

Roman gazed about, seeking ghosts that were no longer there. While the others puzzled over his odd behavior, he slipped two fingers into his breast pocket and drew out a small red-and-black capsule. It was the last of the amphetamine pills he'd borrowed from Li Qin Yue, and for a few seconds, he seemed to weigh it in his palm. Then he stepped to the rail and tossed the capsule in the river.

Jarmond called to them from the bridge. He'd just downloaded the latest image. "Your refrigerant isn't stopping at Plaquemine. All five clumps are moving downriver, damn fast."

"El mar." Roman rubbed his weary face. "They're heading for the sea."

Ebbs grunted. "They're heading for New Orleans."

Roman met the captain's eyes. Then, with a grim tightening of his mouth, Roman activated his ear loop and called the governor's private line.

III Epiphany

Ring

Saturday, March 19
4:47 AM

Streetlamps beaded the narrow lanes of Donaldsonville, eighty river miles from New Orleans. Under their yellow sodium glow, pin oaks crowded in corners, and white sycamores raked the gloomy sky. Traffic lights cycled unnoticed. Postal employees reached from their warm beds to shut off alarm clocks, while ER nurses drank more coffee. Along the deserted city pier, the river smoked and quivered and suddenly plummeted 30°F.

The *Pilgrim* and the *Chausseur* glided down the black Mississippi current, followed by the remnants of their trailing regatta. Satellite images showed the five small masses of colloid racing downriver, dropping temperature almost as fast as they added volume. Onboard the *Chausseur,* CJ bolted awake. "Max?"

She'd been sleeping fully dressed in a chair, but the cabin felt icy. She could see her breath. Liquid beads condensed on the metal ceiling, and droplets crashed against the small round window at her shoulder. In the lower bunk, Roman lay cocooned in a gray blanket. Last night, he'd been ill. Dan Meir had helped her put him to bed.

A phone was ringing—that's what woke her. *Max.* She dug in her jeans pocket and tugged out the cell phone she'd borrowed from Peter. "Max, is that you?" She cupped the phone to her ear, but there was only cellular static, like the white noise in a seashell, or the rush of her own blood. "Max," she said again. But the call was coming from elsewhere.

She found Roman's ear loop ringing in the pocket of his windbreaker. It was Peter Vaarveen calling from the *Pilgrim*. His thick-tongued New York accent sounded churlish and hungover.

"Where's Sacony? Your electronic pal just divided again. I guess our ray guns showed it how."

"Divided?"

"Yeah, ten pieces. Like, you know, asexual reproduction."

"We're on our way."

She draped the windbreaker around her shoulders, then shook Roman to wake him. But he wouldn't wake. She pressed an ear to his chest, and a strong rhythmic heart beat pulsed against her cheek. She drew back. His hair looked grayer, thinner, his face more heavily seamed. He was nearly fifty. Harry's age. She felt tempted to let him rest. But who would command this operation in his place? Not the bickering bureaucrats. Not Dan Meir or Peter Vaarveen. *Not me.*

"Wake up." She yanked off his bedcovers.

Fully clothed except for his shoes, he lay curled in a tight fetal knot with his hands folded between his knees. She winced. He looked too vulnerable that way. His folded hands embarrassed her. She wanted him to sit up and snarl so she could snarl back.

Her feelings for this impossible man changed like weather. She ran a fingertip over his eyebrows to smooth out the stress lines, the way she used to do for Harry. Then she dumped a bottle of water in his face.

"Wake up, you bastard."

"*Lo hace terminar?*" He opened his eyes, sputtering and blinking. Droplets clung to his hair. "Reilly?"

She tossed his shoes on the bed. "You're wanted."

Spray

Saturday, March 19
9:02 AM

Elaine gave the interview to CNN. Mounting fatalities qualified the Baton Rouge refrigerant spill for nationwide coverage, and the Atlanta-based reporter had been badgering them since midnight to present their side of the story. Elaine Guidry looked fresh and perky, standing on the cold Plaquemine pier. Between takes, she rubbed her arms and joked with the cameraman about the cold weather.

Dan Meir watched from the sidelines as she enlightened the TV audience about Quimicron's goodwill. In her honeyed drawl, she described their philanthropic efforts to clean up a pollution slick that didn't even belong to them. It migrated downriver from the *Noth*, she confided, leaning intimately toward the camera lens. She characterized the gas line explosion as tragic bad luck. "An act of *Gawd*," she said. When the reporter asked more questions, she offered motherly reassurance to the residents of Louisiana.

"You all can rest easy. We've got the finest people working on this, and it's about ninety percent contained. We're just asking everybody to stay away from the river till you hear the all clear."

Dan Meir believed in what Elaine was saying. The two of them had talked it over. Though the words weren't strictly honest, their intention was to protect people, and Dan believed that was the best they could hope for. This episode had muddied his sense of truth but not his humanity. He blew Elaine a kiss.

While she talked, Dan thought about the algae juice Peter Vaarveen had showed him through the microscope. Peter said the juice was mutating really fast. "Like a nuclear explosion," he said. Dan didn't know much biochemistry, but he could see the glib young scientist was scared.

While Elaine did her job, Dan watched a group of dirt bikers tearing up and down the levee across the river. Kids having fun. Was it fair to deceive them? He thought of his son, little Danny, already getting married. The world was changing. Sometimes, Dan didn't recognize it anymore. He watched the kids on their dirt bikes. He would give anything to protect them, if only he knew how.

Before the reporter could ask Elaine any more questions, Dan whisked her into the Quimicron speedboat and accelerated downriver, throwing up a rooster tail of spray. Squeezing each other to warm up, they raced to catch the *Chausseur.*

By the time they rendezvoused, the colloidal fragments had rounded the sharp bend at College Point—barely sixty river miles from New Orleans.

Streak

On the chilly *Pilgrim* bridge, Ebbs, Jarmond, and Roman Sacony stayed glued to the computer screen. The colloid had divided again. The satellite image showed twenty cold plumes zigzagging downriver. Their combined volume now equaled the colloid's size before Manchac Point. And they were still growing. They moved like a pod of blue whales.

"The thing's metastasizing," Jarmond said, "like cancer."

Roman studied how the plumes changed places. One would take the lead, then rapidly fall back so another could move ahead. They seemed to be drafting in each other's wake. He timed them through a full rotation—just ninety seconds.

The *Chausseur* and *Pilgrim* tracked close behind the plumes. Sometimes they streaked downriver at a speed of fifteen knots. Sometimes they slowed to a stop to feed on submerged trash along the riverbed. At each pause, the crew deployed a gangway so personnel could pass more easily from one vessel to the other. Couriers came and went. Messages were exchanged in hard copy. The governor kept an open fax line.

Now and then, news boats broke from the trailing flotilla and darted forward like piranhas nibbling at a carp—till Rory Godchaux herded them back with his megaphone. In the sky, CNN's helicopter turned wide circles, keeping a wary distance. CNN had heard about the chopper crash at Port Allen.

The farther south they traveled, the more docking facilities they encountered. Behind the levees, they could see rooftops and parking lots, tank farms and refinery towers, outliers to the once-flourishing sprawl of New Orleans. But in the nippy gloom, the buildings slumped and sagged like stacks of old newsprint. The great city itself—repeatedly flood-ravaged and rebuilt—lay only a few river bends downstream, and on the *Pilgrim*'s bridge, Roman felt its nearness pressing on his mind.

He had flown into New Orleans after the first big hurricane strike, the one called Katrina. Without fuss or publicity, he'd deployed tons of equipment and scores of Quimicron employees to help with that first cleanup. Wading the streets, he'd seen the brown, black, and pale white people left behind like trash. Ravenous children, mothers bawling profanities, hollow-eyed fathers stunned to silence. And he'd found, in ways he couldn't articulate, that the discarded souls in those inner-city wards reminded him of himself.

Mar del Plata, his city by the sea—even now he could hear its clean surf breaking on the sand. How comfortably he had brooded away the long afternoons, sheltered in his mother's yellow porch, reading his hoard of *Time* magazines and watching the acacia trees slowly drop their leaves. Yet, like the throwaway poor of New Orleans, he'd felt left behind, irrelevant, hungry, though not for food.

His eyes focused again on the map of Louisiana, and with a manicured thumbnail, he traced the blue vein of this North American river through the heart of the many-hued city. Nearby, Ebbs and Jarmond traded *Anglo* river terminology which Roman did not trust and only half understood. They, too, were poring over river charts, searching for another place to ambush the multiplying plumes of colloid.

"No more delays." Roman thumped the map at random. "We'll trap them here."

"Here where?" Ebbs chomped his mustache. "Do you see any inlets or tributaries? No, sir. From this point on down, it's solid riprap levees running right next to the river on both sides."

"Maybe we should evacuate New Orleans," Jarmond said.

Roman raised his fist, and the young man flinched backward, showing the whites of his eyes. From the way the others gawped, Roman knew he'd allowed himself to lose control. Jarmond gave him a wounded look.

Roman lowered his hand, straightened his cuff, then spoke in a restrained hiss. "I will not let that *violador* reach New Orleans. Choose a place to make a stand. Choose now."

Jarmond fingered his Adam's apple and eyed Roman warily. "What about the Bonnet Carré Spillway?"

Again he pointed out the narrow green strip of marshland that lay just above New Orleans. Again he told them how the Corps had built the Bonnet Carré Spillway to shunt Mississippi floods through Lake Pontchartrain to the Gulf. He said they hadn't opened it in years.

Roman measured the map with his knuckle. The spillway carved a long green path from the river to the lake. The map showed it railed on either side by guide levees and bisected by a small meandering stream. Around it lay thickly settled suburbs. It was too close to the city. If word leaked out, the repercussions would be disastrous. Roman didn't like it. He gave Ebbs and Jarmond a cool frown.

Ebbs shook his shaggy white head. "The river's high enough to spill through, once you open the control weir. We would need to throw up a catch dam inside. Question is, how can you drive all twenty plumes through the weir?"

"Well, if we get them close enough, gravity will pull them through. Won't it?" Jarmond clicked his ballpoint pen like a repeating rifle.

The three men eyed each other. Ebbs frowned. "We sure as hell need to keep this quiet. If people find out . . ." He shook his white head again.

Roman took another hard look at the map. He counted the colloidal masses on the computer screen. He counted the clicks of Jarmond's pen. "All right, call your boss. We'll do it."

Jarmond broke into a wide boyish grin. "The last time they opened the Bonnet Carré, I was just a kid. Man, it was awesome."

As Jarmond punched his phone to call the spillway office, none of them noticed the FedEx guy with copper hair who listened unobtrusively at the door. Dressed in a borrowed uniform, Hal Butler had slipped aboard with one of the couriers from the governor's office. His skin was sunburned, his nose swollen with insect bites, and his lips contorted with secret rejoicing. He'd just overhead a piece of intelligence juicy enough to interrupt prime time. Without attracting anyone's notice, the ace journalist-illustrator-blogger-soon-to-be-multimedia-star turned on his heels, wriggled his fingers, and tiptoed away.

Sluice

Saturday, March 19
12:15 PM

A red-tailed hawk glided under a ceiling of cold gray clouds above the Bonnet Carré Spillway. With uncanny focus, it scanned for rice rats, mink kits, and baby loons. Eight thousand verdant acres spread below its glittering eyes, a marsh flourishing with life, uninhabited by man. The hawk's wetland kingdom extended six miles from the mighty Mississippi all the way to Lake Pontchartrain.

Where the marsh bordered the river, a concrete weir grinned like a long flat mouth full of wooden teeth. From the weir, the marsh sloped down through sparse woods and boggy fields to the lake shore. Guide levees as straight as rules confined it on the East and West, and a shining blue stream sluiced down its center. Only a handful of times had the weir opened to divert the flooding river through Lake Pontchartrain to the Gulf of Mexico. When that happened, the stream morphed into a ruddy torrent. But today it fluttered and gleamed like a blue satin sash.

The hawk's faint shadow rippled over the blue stream, the brown canals, and the green ponds of the marsh. It flowed across picnic tables and model airplane fields. The bird's keen gaze roved through mixed wild grasses washed in from Michigan and Nebraska. A lone pelican observed the predator's progress, and migrant songbirds scattered at its approach. A flock of nervous egrets stepped nearer to the water's edge. Suddenly the raptor dove, swift as a jet, and speared a rabbit. Wailing screams, flashes of talon, fur and blood, a fight to the death, a meal. Robert Dréclare watched through binoculars from his office window.

Ranger Dréclare patrolled the Bonnet Carré Spillway alone on Saturdays, and usually he didn't get much time in his office. He took a bite of his fried oyster sandwich and watched the hawk lift off, clutching its prey. Ranger Dréclare spent most days driving his Corps of Engineers Jeep through the marsh, chasing illegal dumpers or busting kids for smoking pot or rescuing drunks after they crashed their four-wheelers. More than once, he'd recovered murdered bodies.

Besides law enforcement, Dréclare answered questions for tourists: What type of duck is that? What is this wildflower? How many wooden pins in the Bonnet Carré dam? It's not a dam, he would patiently explain, it's a control weir. And it's not pronounced that fancy French way. It's the Bonnie Carrie, plain and simple.

Ranger Dréclare had done hazardous duty in Bosnia and Iraq, but his job at the Bonnet Carré entailed its own class of perils. He stood at the window in his olive green uniform, resting one hand on his gear belt. This afternoon, someone had radioed that an abandoned car was burning on the east guide levee, and Dréclare could see the pillar of black smoke rising in the distance. Pretty soon, he would jump in his Jeep and race over there to deal with it. But for a moment, he wanted to finish his lunch and enjoy the poetry of the hawk.

The phone rang again, and as he lifted the receiver, he automatically pulled out his notepad. The caller was shouting, not making sense. Dréclare waited for calm. Out his other window, the wide concrete weir stretched like a mile-long railroad bridge. The caller kept raving, and as Dréclare drew stars and mazes on his pad, he noticed the way the dull light made the crane trolley look like a toy caboose. When the river flooded, the crane trolley would roll along the rails on top of the weir and lift the wooden pins out. Dréclare had seen that happen twice. The last time was during the flood of 1997.

Seven thousand pins, that was the answer Dréclare gave school children and curiosity seekers. The weir had 350 concrete bays, twenty pins to a bay, thick square timbers of creosoted pine with two-inch gaps between. The gaps let the river seep through year-round to irrigate the marsh and keep it healthy. When the Mississippi rose too high, he told the tour groups how the crane would lift the pins and allow tons of water to pour through the spillway, thus saving the City of New Orleans. There was a time when people thought that mattered. Robert Dréclare still believed it did.

Dréclare had grown up in St. Charles Parish, and the spillway acreage had been his playground. He knew every hillock and creek, every fishing hole, every patch of blackberries. He'd learned the names of the ducks from his daddy and brothers, on cold winter mornings, lying in wait with firearms. He'd been hunting and canoeing St. Charles Parish since he was six years old, and he wasn't about to abandon it because of a few hurricanes.

The caller on the phone wanted to know how long it would take to open the weir. Dréclare sighed with resignation. "Thirty-six hours to lift all seven thousand pins."

"But you can do it in three, can't you? I mean, if there's a good reason?" The man sounded young and wildly eager.

Dréclare glanced at the black smoke on the horizon and worried about the burning car. "Call our New Orleans office on Monday. They'll mail you a brochure." He pronounced the word, "bro-shua."

A new voice came on the line, hoarse and stern. "Open it now. This is an emergency."

For an instant, Dréclare forgot to breathe. The flood was coming. The monster. This was the moment he'd trained for. The Mississippi was rising out of control. With visions of crashing brown waves, Dréclare tapped his computer to key up the latest hydrologic data. Where would the monster come from this time? The Ohio, the Missouri, the Arkansas? Rapidly, his finger slid down a line of precip numbers. But there were no heavy rains in the heartland. No forecast of flood. "Gawddam, who is this?" His saliva wetted the phone.

When the caller introduced himself as a corporate CEO, Dréclare growled. "Mista, don't be bothering me today."

"Who has the authority to make this decision?" the man rasped.

Dréclare didn't like his stiff accent. "You call up the president of the Mississippi River Commission. I'll give you the numba."

"My people will arrive at your site in twenty minutes," the man said. "Have your crew standing by."

"My crew. Shua I will."

Dréclare hung up the phone and sneered at the cold dregs of his tea. Then he tightened his gear belt, snapped on his park ranger hat, and headed out to his Jeep to see about the burning car. But the phone call nagged him. Wicked hoax. Some people were plain mean. Still he doublechecked the charge on his cell phone, and as he bounced along the potholed track toward the guide levee, he called his boss, Joshua Lima, the New Orleans district engineer.

Scrub

Saturday, March 19
2:02 PM

Forty jets of colloid now zoomed downstream in tight formation. Another division had occurred. Another doubling of mass. Deep under the surface, the plumes schooled in a giant revolving pack. And they were gathering speed.

As the flotilla raced after them, Roman searched for CJ. He found her aboard the *Chausseur*, curled in an upper bunk, facing the wall. He needed her help, and from the tense set of her muscles, he knew she was awake. But when he touched her shoulder, she jerked away. He dreaded giving her the news about Max.

They'd discovered Max's jetboat tossed against a riprap wing dam, its hull crushed and broken in two. They'd found blood, a scrap of red bandana— and a severed finger.

Roman took off his ear loop, sat down on the lower bunk and rested his elbows on his knees. He'd been assailing the Corps of Engineers by phone. Opening the Bonnet Carré would be far more difficult than closing the Port Allen lock. Worse, the surrounding population was much larger. Roman broke into a cold sweat, imagining their panic if word leaked out.

Exhaustion fogged his brain. He needed rest. Five minutes, that was the most he could afford. He kicked off his shoes. In the past hour, he had argued with the EPA, pleaded with the president of the Mississippi River Commission, insulted a parish sheriff, and yelled at the governor. Decisions about the Bonnet Carré entailed more political kinks than the snaking Mississippi.

For one, Lake Pontchartrain was a salty tidal basin, and the local fishermen didn't want it contaminated with fresh water. Its high salinity supported an important shrimp industry that was just recovering from the latest hurricane.

Two, a group of highly vocal environmentalists had adopted the spillway wildlife as their personal friends. They held an annual Bonnet Carré bird count, and some of them knew the spillway deer by name. If they found out the weir would be opened, they might try to barricade the wetland with a chain of human bodies.

Three, there was the problem of resource allocation. The fuel. The manpower. The equipment to lift seven thousand heavy wooden pins. The cost. Always the cost. He glanced up at CJ's bunk and ground his teeth.

"What's in this for you?" Ebbs had asked. "You claim this isn't your problem, but you lay out enough cash to sink a ship. Why?"

To save my company, you fool. Roman didn't say these words. He gave a vague answer about public stewardship because, with so many lawsuits pending, he couldn't afford to hint that Quimicron might be responsible. The old captain didn't trust him. Screw the *vejancón*.

He scrubbed his face with both hands. And again, unable to stop himself, he tallied the wreckage. Fourteen barges, three towboats, seven trawlers, a dredge, and twelve private craft lay beached and gutted along the colloid's route downriver. And eight people had died. *Gracias a Dios,* only eight. Still, the cost would run to millions of US dollars. Roman's attorney kept leaving voicemails urging bankruptcy. "A grace period," the lawyer called it. "Grace." A blander word than failure.

The gash on Roman's chin had swelled and reddened. His body felt scummy. He hadn't showered in two days. And he was freezing. He didn't want to think about his hemorrhaging bank accounts, his ransomed assets, his debt load—or the eight lost lives.

He stood and unbuttoned his shirt. As he studied the sweep of CJ's back, he noticed how her bottom swelled like a plump young squash, and how she crossed her ankles like a school girl. As he undid his belt and stripped off his pants, he counted the wrinkles in her grimy khaki shorts. Baby-fine hairs curled along her arm. He reached to touch her. His hand hovered over her warm young flesh.

"Was the skin dark?"

Her question startled him.

"The severed finger. Was it from a Creole man?" she asked.

"Yes," he said, comprehending. Meir must have already told her about finding Max Pottevent's boat.

CJ lay rigid in the bunk. "Max is the one who worked out the music lesson, not me. He made the disks. He told me what order to play them in. It was all his idea. A progression, he said. He—"

"Stop." Roman tried to stroke her arm, but she slung him off.

"Max saved my life. I was planning to leave him."

When Roman tried to soothe her, she slapped him away, jumped down from the bunk, and banged out of the cabin, nearly tripping over the bulkhead.

After a moment, Roman walked into the shower and turned on the spigot full blast.

Verge

CJ felt seasick. The *Chausseur* plowed downriver at top speed, and on the stern platform, she zipped up Roman's windbreaker to fend off the cold. Max's death didn't seem real to her. She couldn't accept that such a strong, warm-blooded young man could be . . . gone.

If only she hadn't sent Max away. If only she'd let Roman fire him, then he would be safe. *I should have stayed out of his life. I should have loved him more. I should have loved him. . . .*

Dan Meir found her leaning over the stern rail, vomiting into the river. He stood beside her and rubbed her back till she was finished, then handed her his handkerchief to wipe her mouth. She'd been through a lot, he thought, too much for a young girl. No wonder her stomach got upset. "Honey, would you like a drink of water?"

She shook her head.

They gazed at the media boats trailing behind them. There were fewer now since the compression wave had hit, and they were keeping farther back. But a growing crowd of onlookers followed the regatta by road. Pickups, sedans, and SUVs verged along the tops of both levees.

"You cared a lot about Max. I saw how you looked at each other. I know it's hard," Dan said.

She turned away to hide her face.

The wind was stiffening. They were rounding a bend. Dan said, "Let's cross to starboard. It'll be less breezy."

CJ followed with a listless step, and as they sat in the lee of a winch housing, her body seemed to weigh tons. A pungent river smegma burned her nostrils. She pondered the pale full moon peeking between the clouds.

"Look at me." Dan touched her chin and turned her face toward him. "Honey, this is not your fault. There's only one reason Max is dead. That blamed demon in the river."

"I let the colloid out of the collar," she said. "In the canal. I helped him escape."

Dan continued holding her chin, examining her face. He didn't want to tell her about the forty electronic masses swarming downriver like a pack of marauding sharks. The girl had heard enough bad news. There would be time later to talk about the hydra-headed demon.

"Poor child," he said. "Didn't you bring along some of Max's zydeco? Let's listen to it, what do you say? Max would like that."

CJ tilted her head up to keep her eyes from brimming over.

"I'll go find the CD player." Dan patted her shoulder and got to his feet.

She watched the silver-haired plant manager shuffle off toward the gangway. He was a kind man. She knew he meant well, but his retreating back suddenly wavered and blurred. She lay down on her back and let the hot tears spill down her temples.

To and fro, the yacht rolled—like the motion of Bayou Grosse Tete. She and Max made love that day in his pirogue. Naked, skin to skin, without protection. She touched her belly and counted back the days. That's when it must have happened. A new life. Should she end it? Save it? Right now, all she wanted was oblivion.

Harry, how much of me . . . is you again?

Bayou Grosse Tete. She remembered its tea-colored water steeped in sunbeams, the color of Max's eyes. Until that day, she knew Max only at work, and just for laughs, she asked him to take her fishing. But once they were alone in his pirogue, neither of them quite knew how to behave.

Shyly, he pointed at things. A snowy white egret, an armadillo, a loggerhead turtle over two feet long. And she asked questions. What does a turtle eat? Where does it sleep? How does it have babies? He answered seriously, drawing his eyebrows together, murmuring in his resonant baritone.

When the bayou opened into a beaver pond, they coasted through clouds of butterflies. Lush green pickerel weed choked the verges, and when Max steered the boat among the waxy yellow blooms, it felt like floating on a carpet of flowers.

She remembered how gravely he showed her the correct way to cast the fly rod. "Keep your thumb on top so your aim don' wander. Now hold the butt steady under your arm. Like this." He put his hand over hers to demonstrate the grip, and that may have been the first time they touched. Nervously, he described how to thread the line off the reel, while the chemicals in his skin sang arias through her pores.

And later, when he gave her the castanets, he pretended they were a joke, of no value. Yet they were beautifully hand-carved. Two simple wooden shells bound by a leather cord, a *souvenir*, he called them. "I'll teach you how to play," he offered, sheepishly. Then, looping the cord around his thumb, he made the shells come alive and speak.

Did you make them? she asked. What kind of wood? Why this particular shape? And didn't castanets date back before the time of Christ?

He laughed, his first laugh of the day. "Ceegie, you remind me of a big-eared bat. Gotta hear everything."

She didn't like being laughed at, and she was getting ready to tell him so, but before she could speak, he wiped the shine from his eyes. "Aw girl, I'm teasin'. You got a reaching mind. I respect that. I think you're *magie,* you *sav?* You're magic."

His large hand caressed the back of her neck, and without knowing why, she felt at ease. Gently, his thumb stroked her ear. She eyed his mouth.

"Don't respect me too much," she whispered.

"Way too much," he whispered back. And with a motion as natural as falling, they slid together.

Now, aboard the *Chausseur*'s rocking deck, she lifted her arm and studied the heavy compass dangling from her wrist. Another gift from Max, the Ranger Joe. It's needle jittered due South. It was pointing toward the colloid. And Max's gentle baritone seemed to fall through the air.

Éléphant and people don' mix. They hurt each other.

CJ beat her bare heels against the deck. Would she spend the rest of her life apologizing to dead men?

Suddenly, she sprang to her feet. She ran along the deck, dropped down the gangway, and barged into the galley, where Peter Vaarveen sat humped over his SE microscope. His sunburned face looked like a ripe strawberry. He glanced up and smirked. "The Princess awakens."

"I wanna help." She moved toward him. "Show me everything."

Peter leaned back in his chair and scratched himself.

"This time, I mean it," she said. "I want to stop the colloid."

Clash

With an indolent shrug, Peter showed CJ his laptop. He'd programmed the latest series of satellite scans to run in quick motion. "Brace yourself. It's changing again."

Another split had occurred. Now eighty liquid comets raced under the water, and since the attack at Manchac Point, their combined mass had quadrupled. But they were no longer schooling in an organized pattern. They were bucking and wriggling, clashing and colliding. They brawled as if they wanted to tear each other apart.

CJ tried to push Peter aside, but he wouldn't budge. They ended up sharing the one chair in front of the small galley table. Every time a new scan downloaded, Peter added it to his movie. The plumes writhed like worms.

"That's a free-for-all," CJ said. "They're fighting some kind of internal war."

Peter snickered. "If I didn't know better, I'd say your little pal just hit puberty." He elbowed her to reach the mouse. He stank of unwashed maleness. "The joke is, people along the river won't see anything but a little turbulence."

CJ shoved him with her hip. "Can't those satellites work any faster?"

The next download silenced them. The plumes had ruptured. All eighty masses were exploding. In false infrared colors, the deep blue sprays burst through the yellow river in a wild splatter of droplets. CJ bit her thumb and tasted blood.

The scan after that caused them to jolt forward in unison and nearly overturn the laptop. It showed yet another change. The masses were coalescing. In mere seconds, the explosion had reversed. The sprays were falling inward, darkening at the center, reconverging. CJ pulled at her hair. Through unbearably slow beats of time, she and Peter waited for another scan. It showed the plumes had reunited as one. The titanic blue mass pooled along the riverbed, half a mile long.

"Yee-ha! That mother has *evolved*." Peter calculated the slick's new liquid volume and displayed the number on screen. CJ fell off the chair.

He tapped keys to bring up the EM sensors, then scooted a few centimeters to make more room on the seat. "I'll lay odds that hombre has a whole new electronic structure."

CJ got up and wedged her butt onto the small seat, then studied the screen. Sure enough, its EM field swelled exponentially larger and stronger than before the attack at Manchac Point. Invisible force lines bubbled out from the river and swept along both banks, an unseen cone of live energy. Its size stunned them.

Peter checked the temperature. "It's gone supercool again, twenty degrees Fahrenheit. It's sucking up a shitload of heat."

CJ savaged her thumbnail. "Could he be planning another heat release?"

"I don't think he's saving up for retirement. Damn, what I'd give for another sample." Peter thumped the screen with his knuckle.

Then he took off his glasses. His injured eyes still leaked water. He wiped the greasy lenses on his sweatshirt. "River traffic's thick through here, have you noticed? Oil tankers. Chemical freighters. We're getting close to New Orleans. If that thing creates another oscillation wave, we'll see a hell of a lot more casualties."

CJ glanced out the porthole at the heavy shipping traffic. The yacht and the buoy tender were tracking close behind the submerged plume, and to get ahead, both vessels were preparing to cross over it. Peter's thoughts coincided with hers. "Yeah, this'll be our chance to drop a bucket."

Froth

Saturday, March 19
5:47 PM

The *Pilgrim*'s bridge heaters fogged the windows. The room felt steamy with human breath. Near the helm, Roman murmured steadily to his ear loop. In a level voice, he told lies, offered bribes, made threats, promised miracles. Veins throbbed on his forehead, and he stalked back and forth like a man in a cell. He was still trying to persuade a chain of bureaucrats to open the spill-way weir. And everyone on the bridge was privately relieved to see him back to his old self.

Through the blurry windows, a smear of brown, gray, and green swept by. Towboats, fishing trawlers, and giant petroleum tankers lay at anchor against the riprap, giving them way. The radio band chattered with ran-corous complaints. And overhead, news helicopters circled like brooding vul-tures.

On the *Pilgrim's* bridge, Rick Jarmond fidgeted like a kid going to his first baseball game—they were actually planning to open the Bonnet Carré Spill-way. Beside him, Captain Ebbs trained his binoculars along the levee roads at the sightseers. An elderly couple wielded a camcorder. A carload of teenagers drank beer. A fat blond man stared back at him through the scope of a high-powered deer rifle. The grooves in Ebbs' weathered face deepened.

"Lookee there," said the officer manning the helm.

"Reverse speed. Full stop," Ebbs boomed.

Three hundred yards ahead, the Mississippi's color changed abruptly from rust brown to—

"Radiant," CJ exclaimed. The colloid had surfaced.

As the *Chausseur* shuddered to a halt, CJ ran to the bow. What she saw made her cover her mouth with both hands. The emerald-platinum slick blazed across the full width of the river. As far downstream as she could see, it sloshed and flared like iridescent foil, brightening the banks. But it wasn't moving. The Mississippi's brown current charged under its trailing edge with a noise like gargling giant, yet the colloid rested on top of the rushing cur-rent, as still as a lake.

"It's resisting gravity. How can it do that?" Peter asked at her elbow.

"Magnetism," she whispered. "He uses his EM field as an anchor."

"Sure, I can see that." Peter rolled his eyes.

"He's beautiful," she breathed.

Thin surface fog haloed its inner light, and though the sky glowed with the first rosy hues of sunset, the river gleamed brighter. It made the world seem upside down.

Alien, CJ thought. He's not of this Earth.

Yet he *is*, Harry. We did this. Our technology. Our waste stream. We pro-duced this—monster. No, she couldn't call him that. Even though he'd killed Max and though with every beat of her blood, she resolved more firmly to stop his rampage, she still couldn't judge him a monster. Out of trash and poison, he had made himself radically new. He was the first sentient life to evolve on Earth since *homo sapiens*.

"Smell it?" Peter sniffed noisily. "Photosynthesis gone berserk. It must have surfaced to make more sugar."

She took a deep breath. Sweet fruity perfume saturated the air—esters from the colloid's dense carbohydrate syrup. CJ gripped the rail, ignoring the frost that was rapidly forming on every metal surface. "But why did he stop moving?"

"He got the munchies again." Peter smirked and pointed toward the municipal dock at the town of Gypsy, where the colloid's luminous foil churned among a line of moored barges. "Hungry freakin' devil."

CJ was trying to figure out what the barges contained when Peter yelled in her ear, "Jesus, what are they doing?"

A dozen people were pushing off from the Gypsy boat ramp in small johnboats and aluminum canoes. They were scooping up the silvery emerald water with coolers and tackle boxes. Taking souvenirs.

"Get those people out of the water!" Roman yelled from the *Pilgrim*. "Fools! Get out of there!"

He waved his arms and shouted, but the people were too far away to hear. Ebbs boomed a warning through the ship's loudspeaker. Then the *Pilgrim*'s sirens blared, and the engines powered up. The tender drove straight for the boat ramp, churning a swath through the platinum green slick. When the *Chausseur* followed, CJ ran along the rail, watching the luminous river cascade against their hull. Their wake left a lathery froth that burned like foxfire.

Peter tied a bucket on a rope and heaved it overboard to scoop up a sample, and CJ helped him haul in their catch. Sweet frigid spray doused them both. Eagerly, they checked their sample, but as soon as they looked, the foam lost its glow. They hovered over the bucket, bumping heads, watching the lather dissolve to clear liquid. CJ scooped up a handful.

"Christ!" Peter tried to slap her hand away, but he was too late.

She tasted the water. "Pure H_2O. Analyze it."

He backed away from her. "Reilly, you could be a decent scientist if you weren't such a mental case." Nevertheless, Peter filled a stoppered tube from the bucket.

Chill

In the fading light, Roman stood at the *Pilgrim*'s bow, snarling and cursing as more souvenir hunters launched from the Gypsy boat ramp. Ebbs was using the *Pilgrim*'s loudspeaker to order the people out of the water, but they weren't listening. As CJ approached, Roman barely glanced her way. She had left Peter onboard the *Chausseur* trying to catch a better sample, while she crossed to the *Pilgrim* to enlist Roman's help.

But Roman seemed different from the man she remembered. The skin around his mouth was pinched and white, and he'd lost his elegant composure. He looked brutish.

"Roman, listen," she said. "I have a plan."

"Find your gas mask. Now." Roman didn't look at her. His own mask hung loose around his neck.

She stood beside him, frowning sidelong at his gaunt face. Then she followed his gaze and watched the locals filling their boats with silver water. At once, she comprehended the gravity. The boaters were harassing the colloid. At any moment, he might retaliate.

Near the bank, the eerie water shimmered like pearls. When CJ looked straight down, she saw sheer illuminated films gliding across each other, streaked with fractal veins as bright as fire opal. In the gathering dusk, the river blazed.

Eventually, most of the people submitted to the Coast Guard's instructions and returned to the ramp, but two young boys in a fiberglass johnboat veered around the *Pilgrim*'s square bow. Roman ran forward, bellowing at them. He hurdled a winch in one bound, then sprinted on, yelling in Spanish. CJ followed.

Then a strange soft blast distorted the air, and the water around the johnboat sheeted from green to white. "He's phase-shifting," CJ gasped.

In an instant, ice solidified around the johnboat and brought it to a crashing stop, while momentum tumbled the two boys forward. Legs splayed, they flew headlong onto the ice, then broke through the surface and plummeted into the subfreezing liquid.

Roman climbed onto the rail to dive for them.

"You'll die in that water." CJ grabbed his knees. When he tried to kick her away, she hung on tight. "I won't let you do it."

The Coast Guard crew tossed four white ring buoys into the water where the boys had submerged, and a rescuer in an orange survival suit jumped feet first through the brilliant ice. Roman balanced on the rail, poised to follow, but CJ clung to his calves.

Yet even as the orange-suited crewman splashed into the river, the two boys bobbled up, spluttering and thrashing, their faces scarlet with cold. They grabbed the ring buoys and fought to stay afloat. In less than a minute, the crew hauled all three swimmers safe aboard the *Pilgrim*, and EMTs broke out first-aid kits to treat the boys' frostbite. As Roman watched from his tightrope balance on the rail, CJ kept a death grip on his legs.

With a vicious pop, the ice compressed around the johnboat and crushed its fiberglass hull to splinters. CJ watched petals of ice rise and shatter around the wreckage. Shards flew up, sparkling like leaded crystal. She barely noticed the cries of panic from the people at the boat ramp. She didn't see them fleeing up the levee toward their vehicles. All she could do was hang on to Roman's legs and watch the fiberglass johnboat sink into the spewing ice.

I have to stop you. But she couldn't move. She could only watch the ice liquefy from iridescent white to neon green. *I will stop you.*

Overhead, a solitary helicopter droned through the darkening sky. When it swooped down over the patch of melting ice, Roman saw the camera lights. Then he glimpsed the smirking newscaster with copper hair. *"Cerdo!"* Roman shook his fist.

But Hal Butler was too absorbed in his thrilling new role as FOX eyewitness reporter to notice much of anything. Hal was moving up in the world. He had traded the Bonnet Carré Spillway story to FOX News in exchange for this gig in the helicopter. Already he was recording his voice-over for the johnboat incident. Honoring his two favorite gurus, Kurt Vonnegut and Ed Wood, he labeled it: "Ice-Nine from Outer Space."

Roman snarled. "Let me go, Reilly." He pried CJ's arms loose.

When he dropped to the deck, he accidentally knocked her into the winch housing. Emotion stretched his eyelids and flattened the skin across his cheeks. She expected him to yell, but his words came out mute and hoarse. "I didn't mean to hurt you."

After that, he seemed to shut down, like a computer going on stand-by. He slid to the deck, sat cross-legged, and swayed back and forth. The *Pilgrim*'s floodlights cast him in stark profile. His face looked ashen.

CJ rubbed her collarbone where he'd knocked against her. It felt sore. She would have a bruise. Roman closed his eyes and rocked. When his silence continued, she, too, sat on the cold deck. Facing the water, she leaned against Roman's back, and she could feel his chest fill with air. After a while, they began to breathe in unison.

Along the underlit river, mist rose in slow burgeoning spirals. Dense clouds hid the moon and stars. Only floodlights and the spinning red strobe of an ambulance illuminated the Gypsy boat ramp. The boys were shaken and hurt, but they would recover.

CJ's tongue tingled. What an idiotic prank, tasting that river sample. She gathered saliva in her mouth and swallowed. From the rhythm of Roman's breath, she could tell he had nodded off.

"I'm pregnant," she said aloud, knowing he wouldn't hear.

She stroked her belly. Could Roman be the father? DNA testing would tell her for sure. But DNA was not destiny. A person could change. She rested her forehead against the rail and peered down at the platinum films in the river. They were pixelating like diamonds.

A shape caught her notice. Something wiggled ten inches under the surface. She leaned farther out and met the bewildered gaze of a bass. Gray stripes dotted its silver flanks. It wallowed on its side, trapped between cold glassy layers. She could see it clearly in the colloid's glow. Its gills sucked furiously, and its open mouth churned. She didn't need a degree in ichthyology to understand that it was terrified.

Engine vibrations shook the hull, and very slowly the *Pilgrim* steered downstream toward the spillway, leaving the trapped fish behind. Unsettled, she squinted ahead into the river's bright reflections. As the ship gathered speed, radiant green ripples winged out on either side of its blunt bow, and St. Elmo's Fire crackled along the hull. She felt the static charge build. The EM field made her skin prickle.

What if I can't stop you?

She peered at the flickering green water as if it could read her thoughts. A liquid mind, the first sentient life since humans. She envisioned its exotic neural net spreading through the oceans, raining on the land, entering the human water supply. . . .

How fast will you change everything? Faster than we did?

Around the speeding ship, emeralds blazed.

Fog

Saturday, March 19
7:09 PM

A hundred yards upstream of the Gypsy boat ramp, Rayette Batiste cajoled her Ford Escort into reverse. Traffic was thick on the levee road, and her backup lights offered little help in the darkness. Plus, it was cold. Her car heater fogged her windows, and she had to wipe them with a Kleenex to see out. With great caution, she eased backward onto the soft shoulder and turned her car around. The man beside her groaned.

He was fondling a small chain and mouthing a chant. Rayette felt sure he was praying. For what, she couldn't guess. She kept peeking at his hand as she drove watchfully along the crowded narrow road. He'd wrapped his bloody hand in his T-shirt.

It wasn't easy, going against traffic. Rayette's pale hair fell in her eyes as she dodged through potholes and slid in the mud. Scores of cars were pouring downstream, trying to catch a glimpse of the spectacle blaring through their TVs. Rayette guessed she must be the only driver to turn back. In the flare of headlights, she stole another peek at her strange passenger.

She knew his name. She'd seen him before, many times, but never like this. Without the bandana covering his head, he seemed younger. Mud caked the curly black hair on his chest and stained his jeans. He looked as if he'd been swimming in the Mississippi for days. But his face carried a virile dignity that Rayette had always admired. Her glance lingered on his mouth, then glided down his muscular bare chest to his hand, bound in the bloody T-shirt.

"'A certain Samaritan,'" she recited in her mind, "'came where he was, and when she saw him, she had compassion on him, and went to him, and bound up his wounds, pouring in oil and wine. And set him on her own beast, and brought him to an inn, and took care of him.'"

She skidded around another oncoming ambulance, and mud splattered her windshield. Its blinking red lights scared her worse than its siren. Someone must be hurt really bad, she thought, and no wonder. The parade along the levee was a lawless bedlam. Pedestrians meandered through traffic waving open whiskey bottles. Gunshots popped like firecrackers. Someone rammed her rear bumper. It was worse than Mardi Gras. Again and again, she had questioned what she was doing in this caravan of sinners. She prayed and whimpered and tried to keep her car between the ditches.

Jeremiah Destiny was the one who sent her on this mad Saturday afternoon pilgrimage. He said, "Follow the Behemoth, and keep me apprised." So, for the first time in her life, on Jeremiah's advice, Rayette had committed crimes. She'd pilfered an office BlackBerry and deserted her network servers, leaving Quimicron's LAN to the vagaries of identity thieves, cyberterrorists, and spam. It was the Lord's work, Jeremiah said.

And then, out of the dusk, the wounded hitchhiker materialized beside her car. His bloody hand thumped her hood. His familiar face loomed at her window. Joy to the world, the Lord had sent a True Sign.

"Dangerous road, Miz Batiste. You don' need to be out here alone." Those were the first words Max Pottevents spoke when he tumbled wearily into her passenger seat.

He told her how a fiery wave hit his boat and launched him out like a missile. He said he landed in soft mud on the riverbank, but Rayette knew it was the Hand of God that broke his fall. When he asked to borrow her cell phone, she showed him the stolen BlackBerry hidden in her glovebox. His first call was to his little daughter, Marie. Rayette smiled as his manly baritone morphed to baby talk.

Next, he called Rory Godchaux. He asked a question or two, but mostly he listened. Then, very mildly, he said, "Rory, I'm through. Tell them I ain' coming back."

After that conversation, he sat rubbing his injured hand, occasionally wiping the window and peering out. "That mess downriver don' concern us, Miz Batiste. Leave it to the outsiders. They don' need us mixing in."

"Yes oh yes." She wept a little with blessed relief as she steered her Ford off the levee road. This was a message from the Redeemer, surely.

Max kept talking, mostly to himself. He'd had enough of Quimicron SA.

He didn't need their money, their *mauvais largan*. He'd find another way to make a living. From now on, he just wanted to spend time with his daughter and play music.

But when Rayette stopped at the junction of Highway 48, he rested his hand on her gearshift. She wanted to turn North toward home, yet she waited for him to speak. After a while, he rolled the window down and leaned his head out. Rayette sensed her True Sign slipping away.

"There's a clinic in LaPlace I could take you," she said, "for that hand."

When he didn't answer, she said, "Your daughter's up in Baton Rouge, isn't she?"

When he opened the car door, Rayette reached across his lap and jerked it shut. "Listen here, Mr. Pottevents."

She wanted tell him he'd been SENT by Providence to rescue her from the Maelstrom. "Like you said, they don't need us mixing in."

A tractor-trailer truck roared up Highway 48, and suddenly, Rayette heard the Lord speaking. His Voice came like the thunder of steel-belted tires on wet asphalt. " 'For ye have been called unto liberty; only use not your liberty for an occasion to the flesh, but by love, serve one another.' "

Rayette knew that passage. Galatians 5:13. She shut her eyes, and horrible visions danced around her head like dragons. She feared what obligation the Lord's Word might lay upon her. She whimpered a little.

Max didn't notice. He sat listening to the night, massaging his injured hand and gazing South.

Boom

Saturday, March 19
10:34 PM

The sky was pitch-dark when the *Pilgrim* and *Chausseur* reached the Bonnet Carré Spillway. They anchored just downstream of the concrete weir and prepared for the colloid's approach. But the green slick dawdled upstream, leaching more cargoes. Almost within sight of the spillway weir, it covered the Mississippi like radiant silver foil, and in the last hour, it had riddled half a dozen more barge hulls.

Spectators lined both banks with flashlights and flare guns. Sightseeing aircraft spiraled overhead casting spotlights. FOX was running live coverage. Roman's mouth tasted like sand. He felt disaster building. Why had he ever imagined he could keep this quiet?

On the *Pilgrim*'s prow, a northerly breeze whipped a line against an aerial, setting up a steady *ping ping ping*. Gulls banked under the weir's sodium lights, dropping guano. The river smelled alive. Its swollen current spurted between the tight wooden weir pins with a noise like raining gravel.

Roman stood at the rail and counted the pins. He had organized materials for a temporary catch dam inside the spillway, and his workers were already rushing to erect it. Trucks, barges, and helicopters were converging with supplies. He'd maxxed out his last line of credit. And he had still not received permission to open the Bonnet Carré weir. He counted another bay of wooden pins. The number in each bay was always the same. No variance.

Seated at Roman's feet, CJ ignored the light rain that pooled around her on the cold steel deck. Roman's red windbreaker flapped around her shoulders. Soggy and goosefleshed, she hugged her knees and watched a cormorant diving for fish in the cone of sodium light. A sharp thin bird, the cormorant was all angles and points, evil-looking, she thought.

Roman had approved her plan—maybe he was desperate. In any case, he'd ordered the gear she needed. As soon as the equipment arrived, she would go into action. She intended to lure the colloid through the weir using Max's music. She would play it correctly this time, in the right order. She would collect a viable sample, then neutralize the rest before it did any more harm. *For you, Max.* She watched the cormorant dive.

Roman watched the sky glowing upriver. He could almost hear the colloid hum. He'd ordered Vaarveen to keep station at the slick's leading edge and take readings. Vaarveen's latest sample showed the colloid had transmuted to a radically new form.

Hovering somewhere between liquid and ice, it had evolved into a "meta-material," a substance so complex, it could create otherwise impossible material effects, like negative light refraction. Its computer chips, microbes, plant sugar, Freon, and sundry suspended particles had blended so thoroughly, they were no longer recognizable as separate components. And its volume of dissolved iron had increased by an ungodly factor.

Roman raked his long hair with his fingers and watched Reilly scowl at the sea birds. Reilly claimed the colloid used iron to move. She said its neural net steered the magnetic solution by rhythmically altering its EM field. Maybe that's how the *picaro* anchored against barges. How else could it resist the river's plunging force?

He studied Reilly's milk-white face. Behind those *Anglo* eyes clicked an astonishing intelligence. He counted the streaks of dirt on her bare knees. She was scary smart. But so was the colloid.

A horn boomed through the fluttering wind, and Roman turned to face the brightly lit Boston Whaler ripping across the black water toward them. On its superstructure glistened the red-and-white castle logo of the US Army Corps of Engineers. And on its bridge stood the one man Roman most wanted to meet. Joshua Lima, the New Orleans district engineer. They'd conferred by phone and e-mail, but Roman needed direct contact to make his argument stick. One word from Colonel Lima in the appropriate ears would open the Bonnet Carré Spillway.

Roman touched CJ's shoulder, and their eyes met. "At all cost, we have to stop it here."

Water hissed through the wooden pins. She choked back a taste of cold metal, like a gun pressing the roof of her mouth. "Let's do it."

Rise

Sunday, March 20
6:03 AM

The vernal equinox dawned clear and sharp over southern Louisiana. Light westerly breezes. Temperatures in the sixties. A good day to skip Mass and go sightseeing. That notion must have flowed like a cloud of memes through St. Charles Parish, because men, women, and children arrived in droves at the Bonnet Carré Spillway, with fishing tackle, picnics, and roving eyes.

From the top of the weir, Ranger Robert Dréclare commanded a panoramic view of his eight thousand acres. He could see the small blue stream winding toward the bright sparkle of Lake Pontchartrain on the far horizon, six miles away. He tipped the brim of his park ranger hat lower over his eyes and sauntered along the catwalk, surveying the lines of traffic on the access roads. Colonel Lima had ordered him to evacuate the spillway ASAP, and how was he supposed to do that? He had himself, his maintenance supervisor, and three borrowed sheriff's deputies to turn away a crowd of thousands. A crowd that clearly did not want to leave. Everyone wanted to see the Big Show. The Corps of Engineers was going to open the Bonnet Carré Spillway.

Half a mile down the spillway, Dréclare could see the crescent wall of sandbags they'd been building since the previous midnight. Three Corps helicopters were still busy hauling cargo nets full of sandbags from the New Orleans stockpile. The semicircular dam looked small from this distance, but still a miracle of speed and coordinated effort.

The ground crew hustled around with trucks and cranes, reinforcing the wall on one side with interlocking blue gates and on the other with big yellow water-filled bags. Dréclare patted a trickle of sweat from the back of his neck. Mighty imposing edifice just to catch a refrigerant slick. He'd worked with engineers his whole career, and he'd never seen such structural overkill.

Dréclare adjusted his gear belt lower over his hips. This was the looniest mixed-up project he'd ever heard of. Corps staffers designed the dam, a Coast Guard captain ran logistics, and a private corporate muckety-muck hired the ground crew. Mr. Roman Sacony. One hell of a big wheel. Dréclare tugged at his damp collar. On the Mississippi River, anything was possible.

He focused his binoculars on the crowds. Already, picnickers lined both guide levees. They'd brought blankets and lawn chairs. A Channel 17 news truck had driven axle-deep into the mud, and a bunch of boys with a pickup and a come-along were trying to pull it out. Dréclare could hear the winch's laboring whine.

Across the stream, fishermen honked horns at the boat ramp because Deputy Hernandez would not let them launch. Farther down, men and boys were sliding sideways through the bogs on their four-wheeler ATVs, standing up in the saddle and turning doughnuts, which they were not supposed to do. Deputy Corman was chasing them. Crazy private airplanes buzzed the fields, and helicopters circled overhead. Out in the marsh, photographers were setting up tripods.

Of course the river wasn't high enough to make a real show. It wouldn't be like 1997, when the Mississippi rose eight feet above floodstage and surged fast enough to fill the New Orleans Superdome every second. Enough water poured through the spillway that time to fill Lake Pontchartrain twice over. Dréclare would never forget how it blasted down the slope, tearing up trees and boulders. Compared to that, today would be a mild performance, especially after they plugged the weir with barges.

Peculiar idea somebody had about that, Dréclare mused. After the toxic slick washed through, the powers-that-be planned to broach two rusty old derelict barges against the open bays to stop the flow through the weir. They expected to separate the slick from the river like a raw egg yoke from the white. Dréclare grunted. At a higher river stage, that stratagem would be plain foolery because the massive force of the water against the barges would crack his concrete bays to splinters. As it was, he expected serious damage. He worked his mouth and spat.

Just below him inside the weir, loud water foamed through the wooden pins and rumbled into the stream where CJ was loading an aluminum airboat with gear. She hardly noticed Dréclare's stocky figure watching from the catwalk, and she would not have cared what he thought about her plan. As she hurried up the spongy bank to Roman's rented Jeep, anxiety made her nerves twitch.

A petite blue bird alighted on the Jeep's fender. She didn't recognize it as an endangered Cerulean Warbler, but its beauty made her pause and stare. Warily, it tilted its head and scrutinized her. Then it flitted to the stream's edge for a drink.

She swatted a loose curl and hurriedly stripped off her long pants. Underneath, her khaki shorts were wrinkled and muddy, and the breeze cooled her bare legs. As she mentally reviewed her tasks, the humble stream glittered past her, unobtrusively irrigating the marsh so a tiny songbird could pause for a meal on its long journey from Venezuela to Quebec.

CJ sprinted up the muddy bank for another load of gear. The airboat belonged to the St. Charles Parish sheriff's patrol. Roman had procured it for her use, along with Martin, the taciturn young pilot. Martin helped her remove the back seat to make room for her equipment. Thickset and broadfaced, Martin rarely made eye contact. As she passed him on the bank, he kept his head down.

Rapidly, she went though her gear. Wireless laptop, EM sensor, infrared optics. Roman had been generous. She'd also ransacked Peter's workstation on the *Chausseur* and gathered everything that might be of use. Peter was still upstream, monitoring the colloid. The fickle platinum-green slick had settled to the river bottom again, heavy with sugar and dissolved metals. And it was creeping downriver. She had to hustle.

In the aluminum airboat, CJ propped her laptop on the dashboard and reviewed her data. Sun glinted across the screen. The Lubell speakers were still waiting in the Jeep, along with Max's disks. Every thought of Max stung her afresh—and strengthened her resolve to stop the colloid.

She peered at the distant sandbag dam, reinforced with the same blue gates and yellow bags Roman had used before. Creque and Spicer had hauled their vacuum gear into the marsh on a flatbed truck. She could see them setting up the pumps to collect her sample. The plan was to lash the Lubells outside the weir so they could broadcast Max's music through the river and draw the colloid toward the weir. Roman had rented more Lubells to place close to the sandbag dam, and all the speakers would have to be wired together to play the music in unison. CJ looked at her watch on one wrist, her Ranger Joe compass on the other. Then she stripped off the red windbreaker and tied it around her waist. She was sweating.

The noisy little stream jostled her boat, and she glanced up at the frothy water gushing between the pins. When the weir was fully opened, that froth would swell into a crashing cascade. She paused and scratched her nose. How was she supposed to send coherent sound waves through that?

The water sang like cymbals. She closed her laptop and listened to its charging force, and her mind traveled back to a course in fluid dynamics at MIT. She thought about liquid turbulence and advection, slip boundaries, stretching, folding, and chaotic flow. The water echoed her thoughts with ringing high notes and subsonic thuds.

Distortion. The Queen Bitch's warning. That noisy chaos would blow her music lesson to bits.

CJ bolted from the airboat and waded into the water. At the base of the weir, mist fanned through sunlight and shimmered with the ghost of a rainbow. She felt the current swirling between her legs, tugging her off balance. Distortion. So simple. How could she have missed it?

She cupped handfuls of rushing water. The colloid hadn't responded to her call in the river because he didn't hear it. Turbulence had shredded her music to gibberish. The lagoon had been contained, quiet, small. Sound waves propagated clearly there. She watched the froth spurt through the weir. She couldn't duplicate those quiet conditions here.

She slogged to the bank and fell on her hands and knees. The catch dam, the equipment, all this effort—she felt like a brainless clod. Her plan was useless.

Ideas pinged through her cortex. She absolutely had to lure the colloid through this weir, but how? Not with food. The river already supplied a moving feast. No, the bait had to be intelligent contact, she felt certain about that. Language. Music. Rich content. But what kind of information would travel through fast-moving water without distortion? "Harry, tell me what to do."

A second later, she whipped open her phone and called Elaine Guidry. "Where's Yue? Which hospital? I need her number."

Bluster

Sunday, March 20
7:22 AM

In the early 1930s when the Bonnet Carré weir was built, the Corps invented a new kind of concrete to withstand pressures up to five thousand pounds per square inch, a remarkable feat for that time. And yet, decades later on a clear Sunday morning in March, when the crane began lifting out the wooden pins and the swollen river began to pound through the bays, Roman could feel the weir vibrate underfoot.

He stood on the catwalk beside Joshua Lima, the New Orleans district engineer, a robust caramel-skinned man with black eyes, high forehead, and noble black eyebrows. His features hinted almost pure Spanish descent. They could have been brothers, they looked so much alike. When they first met, Roman had hailed him in their native language.

"*Buenas noches, hermano. Por fin encontramos.*"

But Lima answered in a resonant Louisiana drawl. "I don't speak Mexican. We talk American here."

Roman wanted to roar—Mexico *is* American. But he held his tongue, because it was Lima who convinced the Mississippi River Commission to open the weir.

"You caused one hell of a traffic jam," Lima blustered. "Man, we got a hundred and fifteen ocean freighters moving through here this week alone, with a quarter million tons of cargo bound for the Port of New Orleans. We don't need traffic jams."

Roman tried to smile.

Lima moved like a professional boxer. As he strode along the catwalk, knees flexed, hands clenched at his sides, he appraised the work in progress with a shrewd eye and made one or two astute suggestions. Roman grudgingly acknowledged his competence. Of all the senior officials, only Lima had actually read the science team's data.

Normally, lifting seven thousand pins and securing each one so it wouldn't float away required a minimum of thirty-six hours. But once Lima read the reports, he knew they didn't have thirty-six hours. So his crane operator was tossing the pins, sacrificing them to the water. As each heavy timber splashed into the brown current, Roman compulsively tallied another sum.

The FOX helicopter swooped overhead, and Roman spotted the newshound with the copper hair. Hal Butler, that was his name. Crammed in next to Butler and the pilot, half a dozen wide-eyed passengers pressed against the windows for a view. The helicopter buzzed low, scaring away gulls, and Butler pointed his camera like a gun.

"I hear that reporter is selling rides to tourists." Lima's black eyebrows rippled. "He's charging a thousand bucks for a ten-minute flight."

Roman breathed heavily through his nose. As he studied the swelling crowd, he mentally cursed the madman who had leaked word about their Bonnet Carré plan. He sensed that his most horrendous nightmare was about to come true.

"The bozo's gonna kill somebody. Ought to have his licensed pulled." Lima spat in the water. "Bleepin' FAA still won't issue a flyover ban."

The two Hispanic men stood together, fuming at the chopper. Bumper-to-bumper traffic lined both access roads, and people were pouring out of the vehicles, pushing over the barricades of yellow sawhorses and orange tape. Roman had feared the residents would panic, but this was worse. This crowd was turning out for *carnaval*. No one wanted to miss the once-in-a-decade opening of the Bonnet Carré.

"Lookee there." Lima pointed to a troop of middle-aged environmentalists who stood knee-deep at the stream's edge with a big white banner: SAVE OUR WETLANDS. Ranger Dréclare was wading through the shallows in his Smoky-the-Bear hat to talk to their leader.

Roman's nostrils curled. *"Ecologistas."*

Lima hawked and spat. "Forest fairies."

Roman reached for his binoculars again—and found the gas mask draped around his neck. *Gracia de Dios,* he thought. None of these people had gas masks. They were at the colloid's mercy. He fingered his mask. After a moment, he slid the strap through his long hair, took off the mask, and tossed it into the spillway stream. For several seconds, the mask floated on the surface. Roman looked away.

People flowed across the grounds unchecked. Teenagers clumped in nuclear groups, while small children buzzed around like stray electrons. As yet, only a few hundred pins had been pulled from the weir, and already the brown stream was rising out of its banks. Soon it would blast down the marsh in a four-hundred-foot-wide surge.

Lima shook his head. "This is worse than a coonass turkey fry."

Roman had no idea what that meant, but he nodded. Then they heard gunshots.

"Jesucristo."

"Sweet Jesus."

They spun in unison to see a fat blond man firing a deer rifle at the environmentalists' white banner. His bullets ripped holes in the vinyl letters and passed through to the grassy bank, where spectators shrieked and scattered. A woman screamed. Roman saw her sprawled in the grass. *"Madre de Dios!"* He voice-activated his ear loop and called an ambulance.

Lima punched his short-wave radio. "Dréclare, arrest that fool."

While Ranger Dréclare and Deputy Dac Kien chased the lumbering rifleman on foot, Roman called Dan Meir, who was overseeing the sandbag dam. "I want two dozen workers reassigned for crowd control. Get them here fast."

There hadn't been time to call up the National Guard, so Captain Ebbs assigned his Coast Guard crew to shore duty, and Roman bussed in a gang of roughnecks from a nearby oil field. Meanwhile, Rory Godchaux rounded up every Quimicron employee he could find. Together, their ad hoc battalion totaled less than a hundred. Meir said they'd installed new hinges on the blue gates, and they were just starting to pump water into the yellow NovaDam bags.

"Leave that to Godchaux. I need you here," Roman said.

"On my way." Meir clicked off.

Lima and Roman synchronized watches. Then Roman noticed CJ Reilly edging toward him along the catwalk. He didn't like her expression.

Converge

Sunday, March 20
9:48 AM

They gathered in Dréclare's office to pool their collective wisdom—all the officials, agents, stake-holders and naysayers who had swelled their ranks as they journeyed down the river. CJ, Roman, Peter, Dan Meir, Elaine Guidry, Ebbs, Jarmond, Dréclare, and Joshua Lima faced each other around the desk. Others aggregated on the conference call, the governor, the MRC president, municipal authorities, sheriffs, chiefs of police, the EPA. Li Qin Yue linked in from her hospital bed via the Internet. Rory Godchaux and nine other crew chiefs stood by on shortwave radio. And just outside converged a score of news reporters, a social historian, representatives from The Nature Conservancy, World Wildlife Fund, The Wilderness Society, Sierra Club, and Friends of Wetlands in Louisiana.

"The EMP," Yue said, "that's our only chance."

CJ bit her thumb. She'd already exhausted her shouting match with the Queen Bitch. She'd wailed and argued and cut her hand on a fountain pen when she pounded the littered desk. The pen left an inky blue gash in the side of her fist. As she listened to Yue's shaky voice streaming over the Net, she sucked the cut and tried to clean it with her tongue.

"Send weak pulses in a coded sequence," Yue explained, "like a cell phone. The plume will be attracted to the musical rhythm."

CJ sensed intuitively that Yue was right. Their best chance to contact the colloid was by EMP. A sequence of electromagnetic pulses could travel through water more coherently than sound, and if they kept the force as weak as a cell phone signal, it probably wouldn't disrupt the colloid's field.

"We'll have to be close," Roman said.

"Correct." Yue stifled a coughing fit. "Electromagnetic waves travel through water at 22.5 centimeters per nanosecond. You'll see significant refraction, but at close range, that speed should be fast enough to keep the sequence lucid."

Jarmond's eyes goggled. "Are you saying this beast reads binary code?"

"Our resident genius thinks it can read music." Peter winked at CJ.

"I'm sending you a MIDI to convert the music to code," Yue said. "It should be coming through now."

Musical Instrument Digital Interface—Yue had found it online. Since regaining consciousness, she'd been analyzing the distortion problem from her hospital bed. Despite a raging headache, she'd spent hours on the Net looking for answers. The MIDI wasn't a perfect solution, but at short notice, it offered a decent compromise.

When the MIDI software popped up in Dréclare's server, CJ swore under her breath. She had to give the QB credit. "Thank you, Li Qin. This is good." There would be time later for apologies.

With a faint blush, CJ unbuttoned her shirt, pulled out her precious music disks and offered them to Peter. He grinned and showed her the copies he'd made. Then he slotted Max's "lesson one" and began the MIDI transfer.

Jarmond was still ranting. "Why should music work better than, say, a mathematical formula? Okay, I get the computer-network-in-the-water idea. That's awesomely cool. But please explain the music."

"Yeah, Reilly, please explain the music." Peter smirked.

She twisted her hair. "We tried numeric rhythms at first. I guess the colloid thought we were just another machine like the ones he found in the river. But music—" She frowned, trying to remember how Max had put it.

"Music proves we're not machines?" Jarmond chewed his pencil.

"Just do what Reilly says," Roman ordered.

Then Lima got everyone moving.

Ebbs and Dan Meir heaved Dréclare's desk against the wall to clear more space. They'd already shoved most of the furniture into the supply closet to make room for Peter's workstation, and now Lima piled the remaining chairs in the corner. A muted TV screen by the coffee urn showed a jiggly image of Hal Butler reporting live from a helicopter circling the spillway. Lima unplugged it.

Roman stalked to the window to watch the crane trolley. His voice came out like gravel. "Vaarveen, will it work?"

Peter tapped his keyboard and shrugged. "I can patch the MIDI through my laptop to control an EMP generator. Is that what you're asking?"

Li Qin Yue's disembodied voice spoke through the Net. "Roman, it'll work."

Dan Meir squinted at the computer through which Yue had spoken. "You said we have to be close. How close?"

"Ten meters maximum," she answered.

Rick Jarmond did the conversion. "Thirty-three feet. Whoa. That means we'll have to transmit from a moving boat and . . . and lead the colloid through the weir."

Peter laughed. "Like a pied piper on speed."

Simultaneously, everyone turned to look out the window. Nearly two thousand pins had been pulled from the weir, and water thundered through the open bays. Where the current plunged to the stream below, it galloped in great white boils against the concrete foundation, then tore downstream in a monstrous ragged chain of standing waves. Even the FOWL demonstrators had climbed to high ground.

"You cain' get a boat through that. That's a death trap." Ranger Dréclare rested his hands on his gear belt. "Once all those bays are open, any boat within a hundred yards will be sucked down against the weir like a noodle in a strainer."

Lima's eyebrows rippled. "We might get a kayak through."

Lash

Sunday, March 20
11:18 AM

As the spillway stream widened, video flooded the airwaves, and Internet traffic swelled. The blogosphere radiated heat. CJ zipped across the rising stream in her airboat, clutching her seat while Martin, the taciturn young pilot, manned the tiller. In sunglasses, baseball cap, muddy shorts and flapping red windbreaker, she looked like a frantic schoolgirl.

Crowds lined the tops of both guide levees, cheering and snapping pictures, while Dréclare's deputies circled back and forth like border collies. News trucks lifted cameras on scissor cranes, and the overloaded sightseeing helicopter swooped for close-ups. CJ scanned the catwalk for Roman's signal as, inexorably, the waters rose.

A quarter mile upriver, a bizarre-looking vessel glided down the Mississippi, keeping pace with the slick that oozed along the river bottom. From a distance, the vessel resembled a bunch of tangerines lashed to a giant banana. It was, in fact, their last best hope.

Peter had commandeered the yellow sea kayak from an outfitter in Hahnville, and he'd re-engineered its rudder for radio guidance. Onboard he mounted a small EMP generator patched to a wireless laptop that was programmed with Max's digital music. Dan Meir helped him waterproof the apparatus in shrinkwrap. With so much weight lashed to the stern, the kayak stuck straight up out of the water like a yellow rocket, so Peter weighted the bow with stones and improvised a float collar of orange life vests to keep it level. He dubbed it the *Lemon Surprise*.

CJ volunteered to paddle the kayak through the weir, but everyone agreed the *Lemon Surprise* had no chance of surviving. Meir was piloting the Quimicron speedboat at a distance, and Peter lay supine on its bow, using a gamer's joystick to maneuver the radio-controlled kayak. Forty-five feet down, the dense silver colloid glowed with quivery light. And from the kayak, electromagnetic pulses hissed through the water in the simple rhythms of Max's music lesson.

CJ chewed the nail of her little finger. She wanted to be out there, not waiting here for Roman's signal. She squirmed in her boat seat. Roman wanted to keep her safe—she hated that. His crew had mounted sixteen more EMP generators to pulse the electromagnetic music through the spillway stream. He wanted to make very sure this time. One generator perched just inside the weir, and the other fifteen waited at the sandbag dam. All were hardwired to a single server with the music file. When the colloid got near enough, CJ would switch them on.

Since the airboat fan and water noise drowned out cell phone conversations, she and Roman had worked out visual signals. He would flash a mirror from the weir when the kayak came in sight. But would the colloid hear the music, and understand, and come?

"Come to me," Harry's sarcasm roiled through her mind. "Your theory's absurd. You'll never succeed."

"I will," she muttered.

She reached into her shirtfront and fingered the remote control lodged between her breasts. "Three-two-one," she recited aloud. That code would trigger the music. With her thoughts whirling off on tangents, she needed something easy to remember. Three-two-one, March 21, tomorrow's date. Would she still be alive tomorrow? Death would simplify a lot of things. The thought almost consoled her. March 21 a year ago, she dumped her father's ashes in the Charles River Basin. She remembered how they floated, grainy silver-gray, unwilling to sink.

Martin steered the airboat where she pointed, into an eddy behind a clump of trees just upstream of the dam. When he cut off the big fan, the ambient noise diminished by half. Martin got hold of a cypress sapling, and their boat rocked in the churning eddy. Rory Godchaux waved to them from the dam. CJ saw equipment trucks and SUVs parked where the dam met the east guide levee. She spotted Creque and Spicer with their flatbed truck. A lot of workers had gathered at the dam to operate the generators.

Out of nowhere, a massive wooden pin bashed against the aluminum air-boat and knocked CJ off balance. The timber rolled off through the current and piled against the dam a hundred yards downstream, where two thousand other weir pins rocked and sawed in a massive twisted thatch. CJ got a firmer grip on her seat. She didn't want to fall overboard and wash into that.

"It's not safe here." Martin was looking downstream at the weir pins. His statement made her jump. He spoke so rarely.

"We'll be fine." She wiped spray from her sunglasses and peered up-stream, watching for the signal. The remote control felt sweaty lodged in her bra. She watched the catwalk and thought about the other code. Seven-two-two. Roman's birth date. That code would send the EMP generators a differ-ent message. Five minutes after the colloid washed against the sandbag dam, that code, transmitted from a panel-truck on the levee, would transform the weak pulsing music into a death ray.

Again, she twisted to see the pumps and tanks mounted on Michael Creque's flatbed. Spicer was leaping along the top of the sandbags securing his vacuum hose, while Creque stood ready at the switches. Before the death ray struck, they would have five minutes to scoop up a sample. Creque swore he could pump a thousand gallons in that amount of time. Five minutes. She hoped it would be enough.

Martin touched her arm, and she jumped again. He nudged her gas mask toward her without meeting her eye. His own mask hung loose around his neck. Earlier, he had offered her a life vest in the same sheepish way, but she despised life vests and refused to wear it. Now she took the clumsy gas mask and stuffed it under her seat.

"Put you gloves on, *lamie*. Zip up you suit. It's regulations." Max's gentle baritone seemed to drift over the water. "Who you mad at? You mad at the whole world?"

Something inside her convulsed. Abruptly, she leaned over the water and vomited, and a yellow thread of drool spun away on the current. She sat up wiping her mouth. Then she shifted away from Martin and unzipped her shorts part way. The waistband felt tight. Her fingers slid down over her belly, and she tried to sense the tiny clump of cells budding inside her womb.

Lots of mothers dump their kids, Harry whispered.

CJ winced. *I'm not like her. I'm not like either of you.*

"The mirror." Martin pointed toward the weir.

"What?" She saw the flash from the catwalk and fumbled with her clothes. The remote got stuck in her bra. She ripped it out and almost dropped it. Three-two-one, she punched the code.

Roll

Sunday, March 20
11:59 AM

Just outside the weir, the Mississippi hurtled downstream, and Dan Meir opened the speedboat's throttle as wide as it would go. The engine shuddered, but the boat did not gain way. They'd been following too close behind the kayak. The ruthless current was driving them along the east bank toward the weir. Dan could see chocolate water seething through the bays, roaring like a hurricane. His speedboat was too wide to pass through those narrow openings. If they hit the weir, the water's force would crush their hull.

He leaned against the throttle, knowing it wouldn't move any farther, and he struggled to remember the words of a prayer. " 'May all the people of Israel be forgiven, and all the strangers who live in our midst, for we are all in fault.' "

Peter lay flat on the bow, unaware of the danger. He was hooked into a safety harness, guiding the *Lemon Surprise* with his joystick. His tropical swim trunks ballooned in the wind. Far below, he could see the faint fluctuating gleam of the colloid rising up from the riverbed, a colossal hybrid plume of metamorphosed trash. Its field radiated so strongly, it made the white hair on his arms stand up. He felt it penetrate his bones.

Thanks be to his lucky stars, his radio control was working. The sea kayak navigated well despite its gawky outrigging, and the EMP generator hummed like a beehive, pulsing musical rhythms into the river. Peter watched the yellow craft with pride. Whether the colloid sensed the weak pulses, he couldn't guess, but the luminous emulsion was clearly oozing toward the weir.

As the kayak approached the sucking wooden teeth, Peter tried to steer it through one of the open bays, but the kayak swung broadside. "Shit." Peter gyrated the joystick, but the river had taken control. He watched helplessly as the yellow boat smack sideways against the weir and crumple like a flower. No explosion of splinters. No violent splash. It was simply gone.

Finally, Peter heard Dan Meir shouting at the radio.

"Mayday! Mayday! We're caught!"

Peter sat up, and when he noticed how close they'd drifted to the weir, his face blanched. Their speedboat labored a hundred yards upstream of the weir. Anyone would have thought they could pull away. But the current was accelerating as it poured down through the bays, and their overloaded engine could only slow their progress. Peter scrambled back to the cockpit. "Drive us against the bank! Run us aground!"

Meir shook his head. The river ran so swift and high against the steep riprap wall, he knew any attempt to land would simply capsize them. He wrestled the steering yoke to keep the bow pointed straight upstream, and his mind settled to an unnatural calm. He pictured Elaine sunning on her beach towel. Her sweet roly-poly buttocks glistened with coconut oil. Next, he thought of his grown children, his son getting married, his daughter's daughter growing up far away, and he realized with regret that he couldn't picture his wife's face. Most clearly, he pictured the view from his office window, overlooking Devil's Swamp. His home for seventeen years. Yes, truly, his home.

"By God, it's Roman." Peter waved at the sky, grinning like an idiot. "Man oh man." He stood up in the cockpit and waved both arms.

A dull green helicopter marked NEW ORLEANS POLICE DEPARTMENT hovered lower, its propeller noise obscured by the blasting weir. Roman leaned out and made hand signals. The crew lowered a cargo hook.

"You go first. I'll take the wheel," Peter shouted. They could barely hear each other over the water's savage roar.

Again, Meir shook his head. "Go on. I'm next."

Peter unhooked his safety harness and climbed up into the seat. He spread his feet wide for balance while Meir fought to steady the boat. The heavy cargo hook dangled and swung. On the third pass, it broke Peter's hand, but he caught it and held tight.

"Stand in the hook. Put your foot in the hook." Meir gestured with his foot, using body language to make his point.

Peter got the message. He lodged his boot in the hook, wrapped both arms around the cable, and shot up through the air. Alone, Meir glanced over his shoulder at the weir. He could see the grain of the concrete. All twenty bays stood open, and water piled three feet high against the concrete dividers. The structure whistled like a flute.

Currents folded and vortexed. The river was trying to turn his speedboat sideways, so he braced the yoke in his elbows to hold it steady. Noise brutalized his eardrums. For the corner of his eye, he saw Peter drop safely from the cargo hook onto the grassy levee. The levee looked close, only a few dozen yards away. He could pick out individual blades of grass. Spring green. Shining in the sun.

The steering yoke jerked and bruised his arms. The helicopter was coming back, dangling its hook. Roman was leaning out the door, waving and shouting. But Dan Meir knew he was out of time. Seconds later, the boat swung broadside, the gunwale dipped and waves swamped the cockpit. Meir glanced up at the cargo hook and met Roman Sacony's eye. Then the speedboat rolled upside down.

Pour

Sunday, March 20
12:38 PM

Roman jumped from the helicopter to the weir, sprinted along the catwalk, and stopped where the speedboat lay crushed flat, twenty feet under. The colloid was piling over it, crackling like electric syrup.

Roman didn't have time to loiter there. He didn't have the leisure to contemplate Dan Meir's death. Ebbs was shouting at him. Lima called his name. Yet Roman stood motionless, leaning over the weir, gazing straight down. A few feet away, Elaine Guidry sat where she'd fallen, legs akimbo, blubbering into her hands. Rick Jarmond was trying to help her up.

As the plume glissaded through the weir, its greenish glow underlit everyone's chins, making them look like ghouls. Strangely, the noise around them muted. The colloid moved more quietly than water. Its hushed subliminal roar suggested an ocean, far away. Its cloying aroma turned Roman's stomach, and the hairs on the back of his neck prickled. He didn't need a compass to sense the powerful EM field.

Suddenly, everyone's cell phone rang in unison. When Ebbs and Lima tried to answer their phones, they heard only pulsing white noise. Jarmond complained loudly that he'd lost his signal. Air traffic retreated out of range, citing electronic interference.

Meanwhile, Dréclare conferred by shortwave with his hodgepodge team—sheriff's deputies, hired roughnecks, the *Pilgrim* crew, and the cleanup gang Rory Godchaux brought from Baton Rouge. A mishmash of strangers, some didn't speak English, and none of them were trained in traffic control. Dréclare tried to explain, through a severe snowstorm of radio static, how to direct vehicles out of the spillway. He knew he wasn't getting through. The squawks coming back at him were unintelligible. But he kept trying. The crowd had finally decided it wanted out.

Waves of pedestrians flowed down the levee roads, divided around parked cars, and swirled toward the exit gates. While Dréclare's team yelled random, confusing orders through megaphones, people sprinted chaotically, trailing families, picnics, and beer coolers. Both access roads had turned into parking lots, and several drivers tried to navigate the narrow muddy shoulders. An SUV struck a dog. A family sedan skidded sideways down the levee, tearing up grass. A dune buggy full of kids nearly toppled over into the glistening colloidal stream. Dréclare watched and cringed.

At last Roman shook himself awake and answered his buzzing ear loop. Remarkably, his satellite phone was still working, but Michael Creque's voice kept cutting out as the colloid's field distorted the telephonic signal. Creque said he and Spicer were standing by with their vacuum to catch a sample.

"Don't wait for my order. Start pumping as soon as you can."

Roman's binoculars raked the spillway till he caught sight of CJ and Martin anchored behind a clump of trees just yards from dam. Idiot girl, she couldn't have picked a more dangerous place. He tried to call her. But the phone signal evaporated. He couldn't connect.

Across the river, the derelict barges waited to block off the weir as soon as the colloid passed through. But the plume kept coming. Already it stretched a thousand yards long, and still more of it poured through the weir. It smothered the spillway like dense viscous oil, dampening the crack of tree trunks and tumbling picnic tables. Where it fanned around obstacles, its intense surface cohesion kept it smooth and undivided. St. Elmo's fire spider-crawled over its surface, and its unearthly glow fluoresced against the levees.

Roman focused on the catch dam. Lined with blue gates and yellow bags, it looked like a circus tent, but it stood ready, as strong as humans could make it. The Corps of Engineers had calculated its dimensions to contain the entire plume. Once it was trapped, Reilly would have five minutes to take her sample. After that, even she agreed they couldn't risk any more delay. They would blast the entire volume till not a single chip remained active.

But its volume had grown. In fact, it seemed to gather size every second. Roman measured with his eyes and did rapid mental math. The plume had swelled beyond their worst-case calculations. The dam was too small. In a matter of minutes, the colloid would sweep over the top and be—*ilimitado*. Free to infest the oceans, at liberty to invade the rain.

Fire now, his mind shouted.

"The dam won't hold." Jarmond shuffled back and forth, literally gnashing his teeth. "The colloid grew faster than we projected."

"My phone's dead. I'll try the landline." Lima sprinted down the catwalk toward the office building.

Roman seized Dréclare's radio. Nothing worked, not even the signal mirror. The colloid glittered too brightly. Roman raced toward the office building, tore through the front door and found Lima cursing the computers. Their screens stared like blind eyes.

"Power's out. We're disconnected." Lima slammed down the phone. "Total communication failure."

The dam was half a mile away. Roman nodded. "I'll run."

Thrum

CJ fell forward in the airboat and covered her mouth with her fingers. She had no idea Dan Meir had just died. She knew only that the colloid was coming through the weir. Twenty glassy green tongues poured through the bays, brighter than mirrors. Where the tongues cascaded over concrete, emerald lightning arced and crackled, and when the emulsion reunited below the falls, light drizzled upward like brilliant inverted rain.

"Glory," Martin said.

"Yeah," CJ echoed.

On and on it teemed through the bays into the stream below, pushing the brown river water ahead in potent six-foot crests. Soon the sparkling emulsion flooded the stream from side to side. It shimmered like pooled mercury. The crowds along the levees stampeded backward, and almost glacially, the dense leading edge began to roll forward down the slope. Catching at stubble and rocks, it used friction to slow its progress. But not even the colloid could resist the pull of gravity forever.

CJ jerked on her headset and checked her laptop. The generator at the base of the weir had shorted out. The colloid's EM field must have blown its circuits. But the fifteen other generators staged inside the sandbag dam were still pulsing music.

Like a tremendous bead of quicksilver, the colloid slid down the spillway slope, pushing brown waves of river water ahead. It gleamed like hammered silver, and its forward edge bulged low under the river water like a cold front. When the first brown waves hit CJ's airboat, it roller-coastered up and down, and CJ swallowed hard to keep from vomiting. At the dam behind her, the mountain of wooden pins groaned like a shipwreck.

The colloid was so close, she could see individual veins of lightning shoot through its interior shells. Then she noticed something dark blocking the concrete bays. Roman's people were moving the old barges into place to shut off the river's flow. That meant the entire colloidal mass had fallen through the weir.

Again she checked the generators, the pumps, the tanks. Yes, the vacuum hose lay in position. A deep pool of brown water had already collected within the dam, and the pile of weir pins slowly seesawed.

She scrolled her laptop. All fifteen generators pulsed a synchronized musical meter through the pool. Her headset played the analog version, the real music. Max's keyboard rippled in her ear.

"We should move," Martin said.

"In a minute."

Her portable instruments were set up to read the colloid's temperature, polarity, and field strength, but already, fine red hairs were standing up on her arm. A strong charge was building, and the hum vibrating through the airboat hull made her bones tingle. She switched from screen to screen, hoping to see some response from the colloid that would match the music in her headset.

There was a soft sizzle and a curl of smoke when her field finder shorted out. Next her laptop. Last, the music in her headset died. "Harry, so help me." She battered the laptop against her knees.

Static rayed over the colloid's fast-approaching surface, and inches behind her seat, the boat's huge fan roared to life. She grabbed her laptop to her chest as the airboat swung toward the levee. Martin hadn't waited for her approval. "Too damn close!" he shouted.

While CJ clung to her seat, he accelerated full throttle, and the boat skidded up the steep grassy bank, throwing them forward. CJ's chest smacked the aluminum frame, and she tumbled out.

"Gotta climb up the levee. The water's rising," Martin yelled.

"My instruments." She scrambled back to the airboat that was mired at the water's edge. But her concern was wasted. All the instruments had fried. As she pawed through the lifeless gear, the colloid engulfed and swallowed the clump of trees where they'd been anchored. Its crackling surface rolled down the stream bank and splashed her bare knees. Cold sweet vapor washed around her. When the boat lifted and spun, Martin grabbed its line, dug his heels into the mud, and hauled it manfully up the bank.

For an instant, CJ lingered beside the rampaging water and dipped her hand in the icy silver light. Electricity stung her fingers. "Run!" Martin yelled.

As the cold plume surged under the warm brown water that had collected inside the dam, the level swiftly rose. On it came, thousands of dense fluid gallons. It pounded against the dam. Arc lightning flashed beneath the surface, and the pool of brown water boiled upward. Rory Godchaux grabbed CJ's hand and helped her climb to safer ground while his crew of roughnecks helped Martin wedge the airboat behind a concrete ramp.

When the brown water reached the lip of the dam, it began to trickle over. Soon it poured, then crashed in a booming cataract. The jumble of floating pins snagged at the top and teetered in a great rocking mat as the brown water blasted through their chinks with a riotous hiss of spray. Then, in one deafening crescendo, the pins tumbled over the dam and swept downstream toward Lake Pontchartrain.

Brown water kept charging over the dam as more and more silvery colloid rolled beneath it and pushed it up from below. The level rose faster and faster. Soon only a thin sheet of brown water rippled over the silvery surface, and mere seconds remained before the colloid would overtop the dam.

"He'll get away." CJ glanced around wildly. "Where's the vacuum hose? We have to take a sample now!"

But then, something occurred that not even CJ could explain. The level behind the dam stopped rising. Though the long dense plume continued to roll into the pool, it appeared to gather into itself and compact to half its volume. Scattered puddles of brown water sloshed over its platinum surface, but the colloid itself settled precisely level with the top of the dam.

That shouldn't have happened. Liquids don't compress. The amount of pressure needed to pack liquid molecules for even fractional compression is enormous. But CJ didn't stop to theorize how the colloid changed its molecular structure. When she saw it settle quietly within the pool, she crammed fingers in her mouth and almost wept. "You hear the music."

For seconds that seemed like eons, the platinum liquid surged and heaved in slow molten swells, thrumming like a million cellos. Gradually, the residue of brown fluid mixed and melted into its sugary emulsion, and soon a film of pure lambent H_2O bathed its surface, refracting jewel colors—tourmaline, smoky quartz, mother-of-pearl. Its splashes rinsed the dam with afterglow.

Its seething quieted. The static sparks evaporated, and its tremendous thrumming harmonics dissolved to a purr. In less than a minute, it lay almost still. Musical riffs pulsed faintly from the generators, which had miraculously not shorted out. And every human being within sight stood transfixed.

Whirl

Fighting for calm, CJ half-walked, half-ran to the panel truck parked on the levee beside the dam. Inside was the improvised control station, with the hardwired server that synchronized the pulse generators. A tangle of heavy black cables spilled out the vehicle's back doors, and Rory Godchaux helped her climb over them.

She checked the MIDI file. The setup was working perfectly, transcribing Max's music into mild electric pulses through the pool. She studied the feedback from the sensors. The colloid's temperature was still low. He was still absorbing heat. And the field had gained breathtaking strength. Something in the way the polarity reversed back and forth suggested a musical rhythm. She couldn't be sure. Was that a downbeat?

Max, I need you.

Time was coursing by, so she stepped outside and signaled Creque to start the vacuum pumps. Then Roman came sprinting over the levee, gasping orders.

"Kill it! Fire the pulse!"

"What?" CJ thought it must be a mistake. When Roman raced toward the panel truck, she moved to block him. "We have to take the sample first."

She heard Creque's pumps fire up. But Roman knocked her aside and bounded into the truck. He wasn't familiar with the equipment. He fiddled with the controls. CJ climbed in behind and wrenched his hands from the keyboard. "The pumps are working. You promised we could take a sample."

He caught her wrists and flung her out of the truck like a sack of meal. She landed and rolled on the muddy ground, then sat up reeling.

"That's wrong," said Rory Godchaux.

"Hell yes—" Then she realized Rory wasn't looking at her. He was staring wide-eyed at the colloid.

Out on its silvery surface, a cavity had formed. It was spinning. Gradually, it widened into a whirlpool three feet across, then ten feet. The entire mass of colloid began to revolve around it. At the whirlpool's hollow center, the vacuum hose dangled free.

"You didn't like the hose," CJ said aloud. She hadn't anticipated that.

Roman stood on the truck bumper and watched the vortex deepen. Blood drained from his face. "Godchaux, get everyone back from the water."

Without waiting for a response, Roman returned to the controls and started the firing sequence. An instant later, fifteen synchronized electromagnetic shockwaves bolted at maximum power through the colloid.

Blast

Sunday, March 20
1:02 PM

A grisly hiss thudded through the air, and blinding white light exploded underwater. The whirlpool vanished. The colloid rose up in a great round bead, a perfect half-sphere of bottle-green glass. Then it wobbled and fell without a splash.

Silence descended. The dark pool went mirror smooth, and its luster faded. All motion ceased. Not a flicker of radiance remained. Not a drop had escaped the shockwave. The colloid's pixelating layers had melted into a single homogeneous drool.

At the sight of it, sorrow wracked CJ like physical pain. She lay in the mud where Roman had thrown her, biting her hand to keep from crying. The colloid's mass lay still and quiet. Still as death.

Roman dropped from the truck and scanned his enemy with binoculars. "Reilly, check the field."

CJ picked herself up off the muddy ground and tasted salt. Her lip was bleeding. She glared at Roman with undiluted hate. But she had no energy for vengeance. She felt numb. The thing was done, over. The colloid was dead. She climbed into the truck, already knowing what the sensors would tell her. Yet she had to look. Just like the night she'd found Harry lying across his desk. His ruined face, God, her first impulse had been to run. Yet she had stayed and stared, absorbing vicious details like the lashes of a whip. Now that same acid need for punishment drove her to look at the computer sensors.

But when she called up the data, wave forms danced across her screen. She flicked the mouse. All sensors showed active feedback. This wasn't what she'd expected. The colloid was not dead—it was surging. Could this be right? She'd never seen such an energetic force field.

A soft invisible blast pulsed through the air, stinging mucous membranes and shorting every electronic circuit within half a mile. Her skin went to gooseflesh. Her screens went black. She checked the Ranger Joe compass strapped to her wrist. The needle jumped in a steady 3/4 rhythm.

"He's waltzing." She gasped, almost too excited to find voice.

She sprang to the truck door. "Roman, he's speaking!"

As she hopped off the truck, its tires began to fishtail down the grass toward the water. Startled, she leaped away from its bumper. The colloid's magnetism was attracting its steel frame. One of the pulse generators catapulted off the dam and plunged into the green pool. Then another. Michael Creque's flatbed truck skated several feet through the mud, then hung on a rock, while his heavy pumps tumbled end over end down the levee. Behind a concrete ramp, Martin's airboat shimmied and creaked like a live creature, but its aluminum frame wasn't magnetic enough to break free.

Workmen scattered. Roman's binoculars shot out of his hands, and the throbbing magnetic field tugged hard at CJ's Ranger Joe. When she unbuckled the strap, it sizzled away through the air. Hammers and screwdrivers zipped past her like bullets. Roman lunged and threw her to the ground, then covered her with his body, as every ferrous object in sight coursed into the colloid's energetic waltz.

"He's answering your shockwave," she said.

"Hold still." He gripped her and rolled violently to the left as a ten-foot iron I-beam rifled past them through the grass. His fountain pen tore a hole in his pocket. From every direction, screaming metal split the air. The panel truck with the computers vaulted into the water, and its black cables lashed after it like a nest of snakes.

For two full minutes, the magnetic field raged. Truck bodies, cranes, and metal tools sailed down the levee. Lampposts crumpled and bent. Pipe wrenches morphed into javelins. Every coin, metal rivet, loose washer, and screw rained into the irresistible pool. The green surface danced with froth, and humans buried their faces. Husky roughnecks cowered, and seasoned cops curled up in balls. Only when the colloid had devoured every free magnetic object within range did the noise cease.

CJ and Roman sat up together, shaken. The water thrummed like a bee hive. Nearby, Betty DeCuir moaned. Something heavy and sharp had sliced open her thigh. Next to her sprawled an unconscious Ron Moselle. Roman gathered his wits and counted the casualties. Scattered up and down the levee, he counted seventeen injured workers. Their blood stained the grass. Abruptly, CJ vomited down her shirtfront.

"*Gracia de Dios,*" Roman breathed. Then the colloid began to rock.

Rage

Sunday, March 20
1:27 PM

The metal-heavy liquid sloshed back and forth. Flagpoles, engine blocks, and chain-link fences tumbled through its mass, and sunlight glanced off their wet steely angles. Slowly at first, then with gathering force, the water hurled its clanky weight against the dam. Its blows rang like cannon fire. Max Pottevents stood on the levee, listening.

Behind him, Rayette Batiste prayed behind the steering wheel of her mud-covered Ford Escort. Why Max had decided to enter this unholy place, she could not fathom. Yet from Christian duty, she had driven through Hades to deliver him here. And now only the Lord God could save her.

But Max couldn't hear her prayers. The Watermind's noise confounded him. Nothing in his multifarious creed of spirits, devils, and saints had prepared him for the colloid's anguished scream. Max sensed a trapped soul, fighting for its life.

As the bristling wreckage crashed against the dam, he pounded Rayette's hood with his bandaged hand and signaled to her through the windshield. "Go!" he shouted over the jangling rattle of water. When her tires spun in the mud, he put his shoulder to her rear bumper and shoved till she gained purchase and fishtailed away. Then he listened to the rage.

Chunks of floating steel hammered the dam, and spray geysered upward, then fell in a deluge. The nanocarbon gates jolted, and the sandbags behind them moved. Max covered his ears.

Everyone was running. He saw injured people struggling up the slick bank, and he hurried to lift Betty DeCuir over his shoulder. Rory Godchaux yelled through a megaphone, "We got a chopper coming. Load the wounded first." Rory held one elbow at an unnatural angle and grimaced with pain. A rocketing steel bollard had dislocated his shoulder.

As Max handed Betty to a medic, rotor blades frapped overhead, and Rory signaled to the pilot. But it was not their rescue chopper; it was FOX News. One lone copper-haired reporter was still capturing visuals. Rory shot him a finger.

Max helped a wounded deputy, but his attention stayed riveted to the water's tortured howl. The pitch rose to an ear-splitting ache as metallic edges scraped the glassy blue gates. Over and over, the spiky mass rocked against the dam, and with each deafening jolt, more of the sandbags shifted.

"He'll break through!" someone shouted.

Max turned. That was CJ's voice. He saw her running along the base of the levee, and Roman Sacony was with her. "Ceegie!" Max called, but his voice was lost in the din.

As the colloid plunged against the gates, each violent boom propagated a bombastic reaction wave that mushroomed outward at tremendous speed and walloped the levees. CJ was standing much too near the waterline. Max hurried toward her. He saw her arguing with Sacony. When Sacony tried to drag her away from the water, she fought him.

"Ceegie!" Max called again.

As he drew near, she turned and recognized him. Emotions blew across her face like clouds. Max shuddered. No one had ever looked at him that way.

"You're alive." She took a step toward him.

Then another reaction wave smacked the levee and gouged the earth beneath their feet. The bank caved, and the three of them slid down the collapsing mud. Cold electric water crashed over them. Sacony clenched CJ's waist and locked forearms with Max, while Max dug for a hold in the mud. As the receding wave tried to tear them apart, his bandaged hand closed on a lump of broken concrete. He strained to keep his grip on Sacony's arm. They clung to each other as the water raked over their entangled limbs.

Another mighty wave was gathering. Quickly, they helped each other climb up the streaming mud. Sacony boosted CJ up to the grassy bank above the cave-in, then laced his fingers and offered a foothold to Max.

"No arguments. Go," Sacony barked.

Max stepped into his hand and bounded upward. The next wave was crashing in. Max reached down and caught Sacony's hands. The wave hit like a cyclone, but their joined grip held. CJ anchored Max's legs while he hauled the slender Sacony up through the violent froth. After the wave subsided, they crawled higher through the grass, reeling and knocking heads, side-by-side on their knees.

Then a new noise made them turn and stare at the water. One sustained harmonic chord rose and fell like the moan of bees. Max felt the G sharp in his teeth. The nanocarbon gates were vibrating. The colloid had found their resonant frequency. Reflections quivered over their glossy blue planes as their molecular bonds oscillated. Max couldn't speak the scientific language, but he knew the gates were going to blow. He reached over Sacony's kneeling body and clutched CJ's arm.

When the nanocarbon gates shattered, a trillion azure shards sprayed through the air, and the plume shot forward through the breach. Glistening water flushed through the rubble of sandbags with a sound of blasting velocity. The yellow NovaDam barriers parted like tent flaps, and beyond the dam, the plume dropped its tonnage of metal and accelerated downslope in a chain of jubilant standing waves. With a noise like laughter, it gushed toward the ocean.

CJ's voice choked. "Max, I— Forgive me. I—"

"*Amou.*" He pulled her toward him and kissed her, while Sacony rocked back on his haunches and exhaled a loud sigh through his nose.

"I need your help," she finished. Then she sprang up and darted toward the aluminum airboat that was wedged behind the rampart.

Sacony snorted again, then quirked his eyebrows at Max. They bumped shoulders getting up off the ground.

"We have to follow the colloid," CJ shouted. "We can't risk losing him in the ocean."

"I'll track the *picaro* by satellite." Roman glowered at his ruined dam. "I'll order missiles. I won't give up."

CJ jerked at the airboat and kicked its frame, but it was wedged too tight. "Grab the stern, Max. Please?"

Max eyed the long silvery plume that was still galloping through the breached dam. "Ceegie, we cain' launch a boat in that."

Roman squeezed Max's forearm. "I'll pay you a thousand dollars to take Reilly somewhere safe."

Max shook him off. "Keep your *mauvais largan*."

CJ threw herself at the airboat and knocked it free. Before anyone could react, the boat slid down the wet bank. CJ raced after it, and when it reached the water's edge, she made a running jump for the deck. But she missed. She fell into the charging liquid. Both men ran for her. Roman found a broken tree branch and sprinted along the bank, thrusting it out for her to grab. Max dove.

CJ watched them through white whirling foam. She stretched out her hands, but the current ripped her away. Eyes wide, she saw the world brimming past. Deep under the water she plunged, where everything grew quiet. Air bubbles leaked from her nose. She clutched her vulnerable abdomen and thought of the embryo quickening in her womb.

What have I done?

This was a mistake. She didn't mean to fall in. She fought for the surface, but the current pulled her down. The colloid's electric field tingled her scalp, and a kind of clarity spread through the current. Water teased her lips apart. It seeped under her eyelids and osmosed her pores. She felt invaded, borderless, soaked. Here was the oblivion she'd longed for. All questions revoked. All decisions moot. She had only to open her mouth and breathe.

She shut her lips tight. *No, Harry. I will not follow you.* She kicked harder for the surface. And waves of urgency rippled down through her flesh and blood to her water-nested child. *Stay alive.*

When her shoulder bumped something hard, she spun to fend it away. Then a powerful force lifted her out of the water into the bright sharp air. She lay choking and sputtering on the corrugated aluminum deck of the airboat. And there was Max.

"Hold to me," he said.

In the burning sunlight, she clung to his forearm and fought for breath, and in seconds, she felt happier than she'd ever been in her life.

Snow

Through the broken dam they plowed, down the bottle-green tongue of standing waves. Up up up the airboat soared, skyward, into the blue. A foamy crest broke across the deck and drenched them in white. Then down they fell into the trough, only to rise again, up up up through another crest.

Finally, they spun out of the wave train into the chuting rapids below. As the flood gushed downslope, glistening green spindrift lashed around road signs and lifted concrete barriers. Gloriously it leaped in fissioning white froth. Rabbits shivered in treetops. Beavers clutched at driftwood.

Spinning, dipping, rinsing clean, CJ and Max rode in the lap of the Watermind. The colloid grew calmer as it rushed unfettered toward the lake and the sea. Currents washed the airboat far out from shore, and when Max tried the engine, the ignition clicked uselessly.

"The electronics are dead," CJ told him.

He rifled through the storage bins but found no oars. He massaged his bandaged hand.

"I love you," she said.

Glucose esters saturated the breeze, and spray flew up in curling wisps. Sugar molecules collected in Max's curly hair like rosary beads. His amber eyes searched her face.

"I mean it," she said.

She knelt on the deck and smiled at him. Then she beat a tentative 3/4 rhythm with her fist. Max smiled and nodded. He took off a work boot and drummed the corrugated metal with his sole, while his good right hand whispered over the deck, rasping a syncopated backbeat.

She remembered the castanets in her bag and got them out. "Play them," she said.

He held up his bandaged left hand. "You do it, *lamie*."

She lay flat on the deck, stuck her arms in the current and clapped the wooden shells underwater, while Max scat-sang an accompaniment in his powerful baritone.

Abruptly, the air turned chill, and their boat came to a thudding halt. Quickly, Max pulled her back from the water. She didn't understand until she heard the ringing crack. The water around them was icing.

With a reverberant snap, ice solidified across the marsh, coating stems and grasses, hardening over every surface in a frosty sheathe of white. Birds took to the air. Insects froze in place. Except for one helicopter circling overhead, a cottony silence fell. Then a low tone boomed through the ice. With rising hope, she recognized the rhythm.

Max cocked his ear. "It's a waltz."

They listened. It was not a simple waltz. Stresses shifted unexpectedly and landed on offbeats. The rhythm grew richer, more nuanced. Again and again, the tempo leaped out of time, then beautifully recovered. It was like Max's syncopation, with a different accent.

"He heard us," she said.

Max grinned. "Oh yeah. He jammin'."

Soon, the booming music whispered to nothing, and opaque white silence stilled the air, as if the waltz had been a sublime dream. Miles away on the lake, boat sirens cried.

"Why did he stop?" she said.

Max's golden eyes flashed. "He giving us our turn."

Of course. The Watermind wanted a reply. She could sense the bated expectation. But she had no idea how to answer.

"Like this," Max said.

With his good hand, he clutched her fingers and rubbed them over the corrugated deck. Their joined fingers moved quickly under Max's motive guidance, wet skin against dry metal, a friction of edges. Their floating *frottior* rasped a subtle refrain, piquant in the bridge.

Unnoticed around them, a layer of ice sublimated in a fine sparkling mist. When CJ saw it, her breath caught. The cloud of infinitesimal ice crystals sifted together in loose molecular motion, catching the sunlight in brilliant tiny winks. Like faceted diamonds. Like microchips. She rolled on her back to watch the fog rise against the bright cloudless sky.

"*Bèl.*" Max waved his hand, and fractal patterns spiraled through his fingers.

Then, to her exquisite joy, the fog refracted a fan of color. The apparition of light and water shimmered across the marsh. Six clear prismatic bands. The rainbow doubled, then tripled. Its fleeting hues dyed the air.

"He heard," she whispered again.

"*Oui*. He make a painting."

"A painting of water." She grinned at Max's notion.

The ice fog massed thicker. Downy white, scintillating with flashes, it hovered over the frozen marsh and filtered the sunlight. Caught between solid ice and icy mist, CJ felt transported to winterland. Something feathery and wet tickled her eyelash. Then another wet feather kissed her cheek. She held out her hand and caught one.

"Snowflakes." Max laughed. "First I ever see."

He lay down beside her as the lacy crystals dallied through the air, gusting in veils too well patterned to be accidental.

"They're moving in alignment with the field," she said while Max caught snowflakes on his tongue.

Soon the rainbow faded, and the fog dissolved. Its residue precipitated back to the ice and hardened in a smooth glaze. Again, the sky burned blue, and the Louisiana sun singed their unprotected skin. The airboat shifted, then dipped and swung free in the rapidly melting slush. Liquefied, the colloid surged on toward Lake Pontchartrain.

"He heard," CJ whispered. "He knows we're here."

Max tightened his grip on her hand. "We gotta ride it out."

Fall

Sunday, March 20
2:48 PM

"*Madre de Cristo*. Idiot girl." Roman jolted along the access road, careening around parked cars and skidding through the mire. He'd commandeered Michael Creque's flatbed truck, and its cumbersome four-wheel-drive gearing fought him at every turn. It drove like a tank.

Closer he steered to the rampaging stream. When he caught sight of Reilly in the boat with Max Pottevents, he let out a groan of relief. Down the slope he churned, through brush and willows. Shallow ditches caught at his wheels, and sumps tried to snare him. When mud splattered his windshield, he switched on the wiper blades. He could just make out CJ's red windbreaker in the distance, the jacket he'd lent her days ago.

A hundred yards from his truck, the colloid rushed downstream, answering the call of gravity. No longer silver, it had reverted to the rusty mossy brownish black of swamp water. But Roman knew the *violador* had not changed. He saw through his adversary's disguise.

CJ Reilly had recognized the truth before him. The colloid could think and plan. How an unholy brew of pollution had spawned a sentient computer network, he still couldn't grasp. Its processes were too manifold and eclectic. Scientists would sift though the data for years. But Roman understood its motives. He knew that if this enemy survived, it would compete for resources and seek dominion over the Earth. There would be no conversation. No music. No rational exchange. There would be only war.

Here in this place, in this North American river, the colloid had defeated him. He had not come to terms with that yet. The word, *failure*, waited like a thorn in his mind. Already his logic was thickening around it, sealing out the pain. There would be time later, to regroup, to raise new funds, to plan an expedition at sea. Roman would not give up.

For now, he focused only on Reilly's red jacket. Foolish *querida*. So intelligent, and yet so reckless. For the first time, he genuinely wanted to comprehend her vagaries. As the truck jolted along, he caught quick glimpses of the Creole boat man. The boyfriend.

The aluminum airboat flashed sunlight as it spun through the unbridled flood. He wrestled the truck's steering wheel to keep her in sight. The truck was laboring over a rooty hummock when sun struck his windshield and blinded him. He opened the door and stood on the runningboard in time to watch the airboat smack a weir pin.

"Reilly!" He slammed his door and mashed the accelerator. Did the boat overturn? He couldn't see. The truck labored through a thicket of broken saplings, and he calculated. A hundred yards to reach the streambank. A fifty-foot rope in the back. The current moving at two thousand cubic feet per second. He pumped the accelerator.

"Swim, you idiot girl."

Ahead, the ground slanted into a sinkhole, and he had to detour. Trees blocked his view. He swerved to miss a running deer, and he thought of her hair, the silly way it stuck out from her head like chicken feathers. His breath rose and fell in a prayerful chant.

"*Gallinita*, swim."

Steam

Sunday, March 20
2:53 PM

High in the sky, Hal Butler circled the wreckage. Where the spillway emptied into Lake Pontchartrain, a huge midden of trash and mud had collected— tree limbs, weir pins, Styrofoam coolers. Hal saw dead bodies. "There," he ordered his chopper pilot down.

When they dropped lower to catch some footage, Hal noticed one of the bodies reaching toward the other. Fascinated, he zoomed his lens for a close- up as the two people slid together and embraced. Survivors. A poignant scene. Hal knew at once it had Pulitzer quality.

Then he recognized CJ Reilly. The chick who refused his interview. He'd been watching her for days through various camera viewfinders. He almost felt he knew her. As she wrapped her legs around the dark man beside her, Hal's finger toyed with the "record" button. But as they kissed and clung to each other, he hesitated.

Somewhere deep in his vestigial heart, Hal Butler recognized a private moment. He surprised himself. He let the shot slip by. With a perplexed frown, he told the pilot there was nothing to see. "We need carnage," he said. Then they whirred up the spillway, seeking the color red.

Far below, half-buried in mud, CJ lay with Max. Her hands ached from clinging to the airboat fin, and she stared straight up at the moon. In broad hazy daylight, it shimmered like a dime.

"You awright?" he asked.

She wiggled her toes. "Yes. You?"

"I guess."

She covered her face with her arm. The ordeal had left her numb. Some dim part of her brain urged her to seek another boat and follow the Water-mind across the lake, but she couldn't move. The warm silt cradled her, and soupy water lapped at her skin. There was no noise, no birdsong or insect whine, no thundering flood. She and Max lay together in the shallows, half in, half out of the brackish water, holding hands.

Minutes passed. Mindless peace. She drifted. The guttural blare of an engine woke her. Something heavy and loud was breaking through the trees along the streambank. It sounded like a charging elephant. She saw branches splitting and leaves flying apart. Then the metal truck grill emerged. The door opened, and Roman splashed through the water toward her.

"I thought you were gone." He lifted her and squeezed her to his chest.

"The Watermind painted a rainbow," she said.

"You're raving mad." He kissed her hair.

"Put me down." She twisted and elbowed. "I want to see the lake."

He dropped her and smiled. "Little brat. You're not hurt."

Roman noticed the boyfriend squatting in the stream, washing mud off his arms and legs. The bandage around his left hand was sodden and blood-stained. CJ had bleeding cuts and bruises. They needed medical attention. He glanced at his truck, calculating the distance to a clinic.

When CJ crabwalked over the matted rubbish toward the lake, he and Max followed. A rustling sizzle gusted on the breeze. Roman thought at first it was gnats or mosquitoes, but when they topped the rubbish mound, he knew it was coming from the colloid.

Fanning out from shore, the water crackled with heat, and a million tiny curls of steam fumed over the surface. Weak sparks flickered underwater, and patchy spumes of lather flocculated upward. In a matter of minutes, the lather clumped into glittery solids.

"Something's crystallizing out of the water," CJ said.

The small flecks glinted like mica, but soon, large glassy plates bobbed up. Square, hexagonal, the plates jostled and clinked like porcelain saucers in a vat.

"What's happening?" CJ pushed her hair back. The steam reeked of burnt sugar. "This isn't good."

More solid plates rose to the surface. For a thousand yards out from shore, the lake glittered like a broken mirror. She checked for her Ranger Joe, but there was only a lash mark around her wrist where the magnetic field had ripped it away. She had a bad feeling. She jumped off the rubbish heap and bounded into the water.

"*Estúpida!*" Roman sprang in after her, but Max reached her first.

"What's happening?" she said again. Knee deep, she scooped up handfuls of the broken plates that were rapidly flocculating out of the water. They fell apart in her hands. The water was growing hotter.

"Owh! *Souplé!*" Max grappled her waist with his good hand.

Roman helped them both back to shore, high-stepping out of the hot water.

Max made her sit in the mud so he could examine her legs. Her pale skin had gone bright red. She rolled up his jeans. His brown ankles swelled like ripe plums. They both had first-degree burns.

"I'm sorry." Her hands hovered over his ankles, but she was afraid to touch the angry skin.

Max sighed. "Ceegie, you gotta stop this shit."

Roman grunted. He sat alone on a log, sullenly examining his own livid shins and counting his grievances against Max Pottevents—until a whiff of burning salt drew his attention. The edge of the lake was boiling. He stood and shouted, "Another heat release! Run for the truck!"

Hot mist wafted to shore and scorched their faces.

"No, it's something else. Something's wrong." CJ took a step toward the water.

Together, Max and Roman dragged her back behind the rubbish mound for protection. Grimly, they hunkered in the matted leaves and trash. Sweltering steam enveloped them, and they watched through chinks in the weir pins.

"*Djab dile* don' like this lake," Max said.

CJ squirmed. "I think he's disintegrating."

"We should move farther back," Roman said, but no one moved.

Where the colloid's plume fanned out from shore, the liquid bubbled and frothed, expelling gasses that smelled of methane, rotten fruit, and brimstone. Thick hot fog clouded the surface, and the glassy solids tossed in the sizzling foam. The water faded from muddy green-red-brown to gray, and dead microbial blooms floated in ridges, like pepper in a simmering sauce. Gradually, the dissolved compounds, held so long in colloidal suspension, precipitated to the surface and formed a thick scummy tar.

The sizzling stopped. The water lay dead calm under its solid black shroud. Along the shore, every surface dripped with hot condensation. While they waited for the steam to dissipate, Max held CJ behind the rubbish mound, and Roman lay apart, watching them.

Farther out on the lake, official vessels converged. The Coast Guard. Homeland Security. City police. The Corps of Engineers. Their sirens rose and fell like squeals from a distant playground.

"It's dead," she whispered.

"Impossible." Roman got to his feet and counted the gathering boats.

Settle

Sunday, March 20
3:03 PM

When the heat dispersed to a bearable level, the three of them climbed over the wet, scalded rubbish toward the shore. Moisture still hung in the air, stinging their faces, and a dense cloud of steam blotted the sun. Roman gazed at his enemy, then glanced down the lakeshore, searching for a boat. He needed to talk to Lima and Ebbs. He needed transportation and a working cell phone.

"It's dead. I know it." CJ knelt in the mud and prodded the tar with her finger. Hard as rubber. She lifted her face to Roman with the look of a bereaved child. "Why?" she said.

Max kicked at the coagulated tar. Then he picked up a heavy rock and flung it down on the surface. The tar rang like an iron bell.

"It's another trick," said Roman.

"No." CJ stroked the tar.

"Hey *lamie*, here's something." Max squatted and poked at a rippling white ridge of crystals that had collected around the lip of the tar. He pinched some up, rubbed the white grains between his fingers and held them to his nose. "It's salt."

CJ knelt beside him and sniffed the gritty brine. "Sea salt."

"Pontchartrain's a tidal basin," Roman reminded them. "It's open to the sea."

She shot him a look. "Saline solution? What are you thinking?"

He wasn't thinking anything. He watched her scrape up more salt and smear it across her palm. Its pungent smell reminded him of sand and surf, breaking blue waves, a yellow house with a wide cool veranda.

"Saline's a stronger electrical conductor than fresh water," she said. "Do you think . . . a power surge?"

Roman hadn't made that connection. Reilly's mind took faster leaps than his. Crazy leaps. Could saline have overloaded the colloid's wet circuits? How ironic if the exotic network survived his gigavolt EM shock only to succumb to saltwater.

"We'll need tests," he said.

The dingy white grains glinted in her palm. "He was born in fresh water. He wasn't prepared for this." She stuck out her tongue to taste the salt, then stopped herself and glanced shyly at Max, who was shaking his head.

Max dug in his breast pocket and pulled out a pink plastic jewel box. Tenderly, he dumped the fragile necklace into his bandaged hand, then offered her the box. "Collect you a sample for your microscope."

She bit her lip. Then she accepted the box like a treasure.

Roman snorted and stared across the lake. Salt? The answer couldn't be that easy. He didn't believe it. The official vessels had reached the far edge of the slick, and they were hailing him. One man brandished a megaphone. He could hear Rick Jarmond's voice whine like a violin. He knelt and prodded the tar with a stick.

Hardened and black, the coagulant seemed as inert and harmless as he had always assured the media it would be. He scowled at its mottled surface. He would test it, yes, but he already knew what had clotted together in this tar—all the tons of expensive cargo stolen from the river barges.

He shaded his eyes and made another count of the boats converging around the tar. The Mississippi River Commission, the EPA, the Louisiana State Militia. An oil skimmer much like the *Refuerzo* was already deploying a containment collar. As things stood, this would be a routine cleanup. He wondered if the materials in the tar could be reclaimed. Tomorrow was Monday. He would find another banker and float another loan. The *Anglos* might try to bankrupt him, but he would recover.

Reilly walked out onto the solidified tar, and Max followed a few steps behind her. It sank under their weight like a floating mat. When Roman saw them, he wanted to throw CJ Reilly over his knees and spank her. Max lent her his pocketknife, and Roman watched her scrape a few black crumbs into the pink box.

"It's not dead," Roman repeated, though all his senses told him the enormous black slick was a carcass. A leftover. Vestigial remains. "Reilly, take some decent samples this time. Get Vaarveen to help. I want the full complement of tests."

She nodded.

"You're team leader now," he said.

She shrugged.

He watched her sway on the rocking surface. Mud matted her red hair. A bump on her forehead was turning shadowy green, lavender bruises dotted her thighs, and her calves glowed bright blistery pink. She looked pathetic. He half expected her to fall through the tar, but what was the point of telling her to be careful? Max Pottevents was with her.

Roman stood to his full height and squinted across the matte-black shroud. In one graceful leap, he landed on its surface. Far from solid, it bounced under his feet like a trampoline, but he kept his balance. He tossed his truck keys to Max, and without another word, he marched off across the lake to meet the *Anglo* bureaucrats.

Sink

Sunday, March 20
3:55 PM

Almost imperceptibly, the slick drifted away from shore, leaving a three-foot margin of open lake water. Where the stream trickled in from the marsh, brown river bouillon merged with estuarial consommé from the Gulf. A confluence of muck, CJ thought. She sat near the edge of the drifting tar and crossed her legs. She could almost taste the chemicals fermenting in the lake. They gave off the same smell as Devil's Swamp.

At that very moment, under the hot Louisiana sun, she felt sure the colloid's active ingredients were incubating again. In fertile bogs and fecund sloughs up and down the southern Mississippi, ancient algaes were secreting thick misshapen blooms of proplastid, and fructified waters were stirring with signals and ring tones. High spring floods were bringing new microelectronics. Nanomachines, gengineered bacteria, quantum memory dots. Cheap disposable technology—thousands of tons every day. Who could imagine there would be no issue?

"You'll come again," she whispered.

Max bent low and skipped a flat pebble across the open lake water. His expert aim made the rock bounce six times before it sank. Then he stood erect and straightened the bandage on his hand.

She watched him in silhouette, strong and dark against the blue sky. There was much she needed to tell him. This conversation might be difficult, or it might be very easy. She felt embarrassed by her garbled thoughts. Should she begin with confession, apology, gratitude? So much depended on choosing the right words, or perhaps that didn't matter at all.

A few fat raindrops pelted them, and CJ glimpsed a fleeting rainbow in the fog. On impulse, she sprang to her feet and slipped her arms around Max's waist.

"Amou," he whispered, clasping her to his chest. Slowly they rocked back and forth, dimpling the slick with their gentle zydeco waltz.

Photons warmed the black tar. Insects began to whine again. A Cerulean Warbler twittered in a tupelo branch, and blades of grass sprang free of the mud. High above in the hazy glare, unseen by any human, a white cloud streamed toward the sea.